Nailing It

Anna Jefferson is a fiction writer and playwright. She has written for stage and screen since 2005 and has toured her work throughout the UK. Born in Scunthorpe, Lincolnshire, her work draws on her abiding love of northern England. Anna lives in Brighton with her husband and two children.

@annajefferson
@annajeffersonauthor

Also by Anna Jefferson

Winging It

Nailing It

ANNA JEFFERSON

ORION

An Orion paperback

First published in Great Britain in 2021
by Orion
an imprint of The Orion Publishing Group Ltd,
Carmelite House, 50 Victoria Embankment
London EC4Y 0DZ

An Hachette UK company

1 3 5 7 9 10 8 6 4 2

A CIP catalogue record for this book
is available from the British Library.

ISBN (Mass Market Paperback) 978 1 4091 8601 4
ISBN (eBook) 978 1 4091 8602 1

Typeset by Input Data Services Ltd, Somerset

Printed and bound in Great Britain by Clays Ltd, Elcograf S.p.A.

www.orionbooks.co.uk

To friendship

Prologue

I can pinpoint the *exact* moment I fell in love with Nick. Not just liked him, but could see a future with him. A proper future, with a shared toothbrush holder and insurance on each other's shit cars. It wasn't a light bulb moment. We hadn't done anything momentous. We weren't having a life-altering conversation or clinging onto each other after sweaty knee-trembling sex.

It was fifteen years ago. We were both twenty-three and were watching TV in my shared place. It was a disgusting house, with black mould lurking ominously in damp corners of the bathroom or creeping up from behind the toilet cistern like octopus tentacles. The kitchen was circa 1970, but not in a kitsch 'hipster' way. The cooker was a stand-alone with gas hobs and a pull-out grill at head height. The gas wasn't connected properly, so we had to hold our breath when lighting it, as if that would protect us from the potentially fatal explosion that was a very real risk.

On the night in question, Nick had his arm lazily wrapped around me, my hand resting on his stomach under his T-shirt, our breathing slow and in synchrony. We were watching *Stars in Their Eyes*.

Matthew Kelly was interviewing Keith from Bolton, a construction worker with a burning ambition to make it as a semi-professional singer on the cabaret circuit.

'Thank you, Keith,' Matthew grinned. 'We will see you in a minute.'

And moments later, Keith emerged through the glitter curtains wearing a brown leather jacket and a Paul Weller-esque wig.

'Chris de Burgh!' I announced confidently. 'It's Chris de Burgh. I bet you a tenner.'

Keith took to the mic, and sure as shit, started singing 'Don't Pay the Ferryman'.

'Told you!' I beamed and put my hand out. 'Cough up, Nick!'

'Are you shitting me?' he teased.

'Nope. A bet's a bet!' I said.

He pulled me closer to him and whispered in my ear, 'It's Chris de Burgh night, Emily. They're all Chris de Burgh!'

'What?' I exclaimed.

'The last guy was singing "Lady in Red". And the one before him, "Spanish Train". They're all Chris de-fucking-Burgh.' He laughed unselfconsciously. Nick has the most infectious laugh and a face that only looks more handsome when he's happy.

I clutched my sides as I laughed with him, then he cupped my face. 'God, I love you, Emily,' he said, and pressed his lips to mine. And in that moment, as I kissed him back, I knew, without hesitation, that I 100 per cent loved him too.

Chapter One

'Can I get you anything else?' The waitress hovers over my laptop, hand on hip, looking accusingly at the empty cappuccino cup.

'No, I'm fine for now, thanks. I might get a sandwich in a bit,' I lie.

I've been in the café for two hours and have been getting the most out of the £3.40 coffee. Three pounds forty, though. For a coffee. It's an outrage. I deserve to use Mummies Rest's Wi-Fi for that price. And don't get me started on the spelling of the café's name. It should be Mummy's Rest, surely. That said, I can't imagine any 'mummy' in her right mind coming in here for a rest. The plastic-coated tablecloths are stained and sticky. The smell of fried food sits heavy in the air and soaks into all your clothes. The overpriced coffee is bitter, and most importantly, the aisles between the tables are so narrow that there is no way you could get a pram through. Which is exactly why I come here. One child at school, one at nursery, and limited chance of being disturbed by anyone else's children; it is, for a short while, like being a grown-up with my own identity again.

I take the last slurp of my coffee, forgetting it is stone cold, and get a mouth full of granules, which I discreetly dribble back into the mug. Checking my watch, I have forty minutes until pick-up time and an estimated two hours of copywriting to meet my deadline.

'Right,' I say aloud, and open Facebook for one last scroll before returning to my work. One of the mums from school has started a crafting business and is clogging up my feed with pictures of felted animals and miniature clothes for dolls. Who buys this stuff? The comments section is a name-check of most of the other mums in the class, congratulating her on how clever and creative she is.

'They're super cute. You are so clever and creative!' I type, feeling an overwhelming blanket of self-hatred envelop me.

I close down the window, and stare at the document I've been working on for most of the afternoon.

'Think,' I mutter. 'Just fucking think.'

An elderly lady on a neighbouring table looks up and tuts. Well, it's all right for her. She doesn't have to write 150 succinct words promoting the benefits of wooden floor polish before 2.45 p.m. What even is wooden floor polish? Surely you'd just give your floor a quick Hoover and if there were any stains, give them a once over with a wet wipe? Wouldn't polishing the floors just make them really slippery? Why would you want to buy a product that's going to intentionally make your house a death trap and have you walking around like Bambi? Come on, brain! Just write anything.

'My manager says you're going to have to buy something else if you want to sit here.'

I jump in surprise, a girlish scream escaping me. 'OK, sorry. Yes, I'll have a herbal tea,' I reply.

'What kind?'

'Peppermint.'

'That's two pounds,' the waitress puts out her hand.

Jesus. I'm good for the money. When have I ever not paid for a drink? Apart from that one time when I realised I was late picking up Sophie and Lucy, but that was only because I was in a rush, and I did return the next day to settle up.

'Two pounds for a herbal tea? It's just a bag and hot water, how can it be that much?' My cheeks burn with outrage and British embarrassment for complaining about it.

'But it's not, is it?' the waitress replies. 'It might be a drink, but you also sit here all day working and my boss says he pays for the heating, and the electricity.' She nods at the plug socket, which houses my phone and computer charger.

'OK. Fine.' I root around in my bag, retrieve my wallet and reluctantly hand over a two-pound coin.

'One peppermint tea coming up.' I can just imagine the smirk on her face as she walks away. I check my phone. Shit. Thirty minutes.

A WhatsApp message pings.

Helen: Can we get a wine club date in soon?
Tania: Yes. I'm free right now.
Helen: I was thinking next Friday?
Tania: Yes.
Helen: Emily?
Me: Count me in. PS: Know anything about floor polish?
Tania: Do your own work you lazy cow. Unless you want to teach my yoga class?
Me: See you next Friday. xx
Helen: Looking forward to it.
Tania: Namaste.

I became friends with Helen and Tania when Lucy, Polly and Falcon were weeks old. From the outside, the three of us don't look like a natural friendship fit. Our politics, relationships and choices on schooling couldn't be more different, but our love for each other is solid.

Tania used to be my pregnancy yoga teacher. She was

5

fiercely independent and has continuously made brave life choices. She also makes a mean kale salad and eats meat in secret as her partner, Spiral, has been a committed vegetarian for the last thirty years and had wrongly assumed that Tania was the same. She goes along with it for an easy life, and mainlines sausage rolls whenever we're together instead.

Helen takes care of everyone. She takes care of us. Just as Tania is the fire, Helen is the warmth. We met on my first trip out with Lucy when she was three weeks old at the baby cinema at the bottom of my road. She was my first 'mum friend' and I have held onto her tightly ever since. Solo-parenting her daughter while her husband works away might be some women's idea of hell or loneliness, but Helen has made a nest for her and Polly, who is her rainbow child. She holds onto her ferociously, as if she thinks that if she lets go, something might happen. She follows a strict routine, and through that she radiates love.

I start to scroll through early pictures of the three of us on my phone, clutching our babies and grinning at the screen through life-weary faces. We look both young and ancient in the same frame.

'Here's your tea.' The waitress clatters the cup down, spilling scalding water on the table and pulling me from my daydream. Balls. Ten minutes until I have to leave. How did that happen?

I open Google, do a quick search on floor polish and find an advert for an inferior brand to the one I'm promoting. I cut and paste the blurb into a word document, and start to doctor it, playing around with the sentences so they are different enough to not be plagiarism.

I do a final word count, change the font to a more mature Georgia, then email it over to the client. Not my best work, granted. Not even my own work, some might argue, but I've done it, and have seconds to spare before collecting Lucy from school and then racing to the nursery for Sophie. I give myself a mental pat on the back and close down my laptop for the day.

'Does Lucy *have* a PE kit, Mrs Jones?' The teacher asks, as Lucy comes racing through the classroom door and wraps her arms around my legs with a thud. I kiss her forehead and give her sandy-coloured hair a quick, unselfconscious sniff.

'Yes of course. When does she need it?'

'She needed it today,' Mrs Elwood replies drily.

'Oh, sorry. I didn't realise it had started.'

'The reception class all started PE at the beginning of the year. A note went out in all book bags as a prompt, as well as a footnote to the school newsletter. And then a reminder note a couple of weeks afterwards. But I thought I would raise it again, as she doesn't seem to have her PE kit this half term either.'

'OK. Sorry. I'll make sure she has it for next week,' I reply quietly.

'That would be appreciated,' she says and dismisses me, as she turns to the woman next to her.

'Evie. Your mother's here!' Mrs Elwood's voice fills with warmth. 'Hello, Angela. I'm so pleased to have seen you. I just wanted to say a heart-felt thank you from all the staff for your efforts at the family fair. The tombola alone raised over three hundred pounds! What a wonderful start to the school term.'

'It's a small gesture compared to all the hard work you all do at the school,' Angela replies shyly, as Evie strops out of the classroom and throws her book bag down at her mum's feet.

'Hello, sweetheart. Do you think you could pick that up

7

for me?' Her daughter kicks the bag and Angela lets out an embarrassed laugh. 'Ooh, you rascal,' she smiles awkwardly as she picks it up herself.

Angela is dressed head-to-toe in Joules' signature florals and is carrying what looks like a Mulberry handbag. I have been watching a very similar one on eBay for the last three days. It's beautiful. I look down at my Topshop circa 2009 handbag. The faux leather is cracked and split. It complements my over-worn skinny jeans that have lost their shape and my well-loved Breton T-shirt, my signature style since becoming a parent.

'Come *on*,' Lucy pulls at my arm. She wraps her hand around mine and tugs me out of the school ground with a force greater than her small body. I strain to have one final look at Angela. She's laughing at something Mrs Elwood is saying and squeezes her forearm with the familiarity of an old friend.

'Are you friends with Evie?' I ask her.

'No,' Lucy replies without hesitation.

'Why's that?' I probe.

'Her dad's something important at the school and she tells everyone she's the boss and will get us in trouble if we're not nice to her.'

'Does she now?' I reply thoughtfully, wondering what that could be. Headteacher maybe? 'Hang on. Where's your coat, Lucy?' I ask, as a gust of wind blows up her grey pinafore as we walk down the road towards the nursery to pick up Sophie.

'You didn't give it to me this morning, so I had to do indoor play at lunchtime.'

Bloody hell. What must the school think of us?

I am trying to walk quickly past the newsagent's with Lucy to avoid the daily request to buy sweets when my

8

phone buzzes in my back pocket. I answer it without checking the number.

'Hello, Emily speaking.' I use my 'potential business' voice.

'Em. I'm at the school and Mrs Elwood said Lucy is with you. I thought I was picking her up?' Nick is breathless.

'It's Monday, Nick. I always do Mondays.'

'Since when?' He's panting like he's been running.

'Since we organised this. It's in the shared calendar. Are you even checking the shared calendar? What's the point of having a shared calendar if you're not going to check it?'

'All right, all right. Stop saying "shared calendar". I got it wrong. I thought because I got them last Monday, that—'

'That's because I had a smear test, which is, by the way, also in the—'

'Shared calendar. Got it. OK. No, I don't have a snack with me, I'll get you one in a minute,' he mutters.

'Do you have Sophie with you?' I stop walking and pull Lucy to a standstill.

'Yes. Course I do, I thought I was picking them both up, didn't I?' His annoyance penetrating through his voice.

'But we always pick Lucy up from school and then get Sophie. That's the way to do it.'

'That's *your* way, Em. I might do things differently. Stop it, Sophie. Look Em, I've got to go. Sophie's trying to get things out of my coat pocket.'

'Right, shall I see you back at home?'

'Yes. Great. See you in ten minutes.' And he hangs up without saying goodbye, like they do in *EastEnders*.

The house is cold. I put the central heating on and flick the switch on the kettle. The cat mews loudly as she weaves between my ankles.

'Did we forget to feed you this morning?' I ask her. It was Nick's idea to get a cat, I've always been more of a dog person. Lucy named her Peanuts, which, on paper, seemed entirely acceptable, if not very feline, but in reality, when shouted from the backdoor at feeding time, sounds remarkably like 'Penis', which I'm not entirely thrilled about.

'In Egypt, when cats die they pull their brains out of their nose and wrap them in toilet paper,' Lucy tells me, matter-of-factly.

She's sitting at the kitchen table, having emptied the contents of her book bag out, and is systematically making neat piles of rice that have fallen out of the bag from God knows where.

'Are you hungry?' I ask.

'Yes,' she answers without looking up, engrossed in her activity.

'What would you like?' I enquire.

The doorbell chimes.

'Daddy!' Lucy squeals and runs towards the door, jumping up to pull the latch.

Sophie pushes past her, shouting, 'Why did you forget me, Mummy?' and marches into the sitting room, followed by her big sister, to play with their doll's house.

'Nick.' I nod.

'Sorry about that, Em. No harm done though, hey?' he smiles, feebly.

Something has changed. I can't put my finger on it. Is he wearing a new coat? No, that's not it. Haircut? Nope. No, it's the colour of his hair. It's darker. He's dyed his hair.

'You look different,' I remark and he self-consciously runs his hands through his hair.

'Oh, it's just something new I'm trying. It's an eight-wash thing, or something like that. Anyway, it's just, ummm, temporary.' His cheeks flush. 'So, how's work going?' he changes the subject.

'Fine. Thanks for asking,' I reply. 'Was there anything else?'

'No, no. That's it. I was just making conversation.' He's leaning against the doorframe with his arms folded. 'I bumped into Helen last week and she said your work was a bit slow, but she must have got her wires crossed.'

'No, all good here.' I need to brief Helen to not talk to Nick about me. She can still be friends with us both, I'm not that much of a dick to make her choose. I realise that plenty of people manage to maintain mutual friends after they split up. We don't have to divvy them up – one for me, one for Nick – of course we don't. However, things *have* changed now, massively so. I don't necessarily want Nick knowing everything about my life. It's not really any of his business any more.

Nick rests his head on the frame, and makes an irritating smacking noise with his mouth. He's never been good at reading a situation, like when it's time to leave. The lip-smacking becomes unbearable so I ask, 'And you? How's everything going with you?'

'Oh, just great.' He runs his hands through his hair again and I wonder if he'll actually wash it eight times this evening to return to his usual salt-and-pepper colouring. 'The pub down the road from Simon's does a mean biryani, so that was a find.'

'Eating out? That sounds nice,' I reply curtly.

'What?' Nick snaps defensively. 'Why would that be a problem?'

'Nothing. Forget it,' I say. Although it's not nothing, clearly, but I try to steer the conversation on to safer ground and ask, 'Is Simon still away, then?'

'Yep. Yessiree. Still jet-setting, living the life. Leaving good old Nick to house-sit. That's me. House-sitter extraordinaire.' Why is he talking like this and when did he start referring to himself in the third person? This is excruciating. 'And work's good. Yeah, everything's good.' He nods.

He exhales slowly and rubs his hands together as if cold. I know this move. It's what he does when he's run out of things to say to people he doesn't know well, while he lets his brain reboot and thinks of another line of conversation.

'So,' he finally offers up. 'Just checking, it's definitely me that's picking up tomorrow, isn't it?'

I close my eyes in despair. 'Nick. You've got to get on board with this, I can't organise everything. Just look at the fucking calendar, will you?'

'Yep, I thought it was tomorrow. Just checking.' He looks beyond me into the house. 'What happened to the Rothko poster?' He points at the empty space on the wall in the hallway.

I shrug. 'I fancied a change.'

'Shame, I liked that.'

'You can have it, Nick. It's just behind the sofa. I can get it now, if you want?'

'No. No, there's no storage at Simon's. He said make myself at home but I don't think that involves redecorating. I just liked it there. On that wall. Anyway, I'd better be off. Bye girls!' He shouts.

'Bye Daddy!' They chorus from the sitting room.

I show Nick to the door, as if he is a guest, which, I suppose, he is. As he walks up the path, I catch a whiff of his aftershave on the breeze. An unexpected wave of emotion chokes in my throat and I gulp it back down. He's changed his aftershave, the one I'd bought him for his twenty-sixth birthday and then every subsequent birthday since then.

The smell was so synonymous with Nick that if I smelt someone else wearing Cool Water as we walked through the town, it was like inhaling an imposter. Someone posing as Nick. He used to smell like home. But not any more.

I rub my eyes. Tell myself to get a grip. Then gently shut the door.

Chapter Two

'OK, so what are you thinking of having done today?' Helen opens her huge wheelie bag and starts unpacking the heated rollers, hairspray and roll-mat that holds various-sized scissors. 'Is it just a trim or are you looking for something a bit more radical this time, Mrs Tyler?'

'Ooh, you do tease me, Helen. Just a bit off the back and maybe you could put some of the layers back in?'

Helen billows out the apron. 'Arms through, Mrs Tyler. No, it's this way round, you wear it like a bib not a coat. That's it.'

'Can you give me one of those head massages you did last time as well, Helen?'

'Sure.' Helen digs her long fingernails into Mrs Tyler's wiry grey hair.

'Oh that really is lovely, it really is.'

Mrs Tyler is one of her least favourite customers. She's great for a bit of gossip about the other residents, and she tips – which is more than Helen can say for most of the pensioners – it's just that when Helen rubs her head, she makes sex noises, which sound entirely inappropriate for a woman who can't have done it for at least two decades.

'Oooh, Helen,' she groans, 'could you just do it a bit harder on the base of my neck. That really is lovely,'

'That's it, Mrs Tyler. I'm sorry, or I won't get a chance to get around to everyone else otherwise.'

'No, I understand. You're in demand here, as it should be.' Mrs Tyler smooths down the apron over her knees. 'I told my eldest daughter I was getting my hair done by you again. She told me I should let her take me to the precinct. That it would be cheaper to go there and they'd do a better job.'

'Did she now?' Helen runs the wire roll brush through her hair a bit too aggressively.

'But I said to her, I bet they don't do head massages in the precinct like you do. She said she didn't know, so *I* said I'm happy sticking with you for now. Even though you are more expensive and you might not be as good.'

'Well, that's very charitable of you, Mrs Tyler.' She clips up clumps of the older woman's hair that instantly fight their way out again, and sprays water on the section she's starting to trim.

'Did they offer you a drink when you came in?' asks Mrs Tyler.

The nursing home has a very distinctive smell. A powerful combination of fungal infections, talcum powder, bad breath and milky coffee that turns your stomach and makes you never want to drink or eat anything from their crockery in case it's covered in death.

'I've brought my own, thanks.'

'Oh, I see. In one of those reusable cups? I know all about those. They sell them on my programme.'

Helen is in Mrs Tyler's bedroom, but it could be anyone's room here. Every single one is identical. The hospital bed, the uncomfortable plastic-coated seat in the corner for guests, the cheap MDF bedside table with the Bible in the top drawer.

Mrs Tyler has a few personal items dotted about to make the place feel more like her own: a hand-knitted blanket on

15

the bed, framed photos of family on the windowsill and a carriage clock on the bedside table next to a stack of Ruth Rendell books. What's happened to all her other belongings, Helen wonders, all those things she's lovingly gathered and collected over a lifetime?

'Do you like crime fiction, Mrs Tyler?' she asks.

'No. I like raunchy books. I asked my daughter to bring me *Fifty Shades of Grey*, and she brought those mysteries. What am I meant to do with those? They'll give me nightmares. Are they any use to you?'

'No, I'm not much of a reader, myself. I prefer a good series to binge on the TV. Right, keep your head still while I just straighten up your fringe.'

'Who are you doing next?'

'Just don't talk for a couple of seconds until I've finished this.' She is nearly nose to nose with Mrs Tyler, who's clamped her lips shut but her stale breath still travels directly up Helen's nostrils. 'Right, I think that's you done then. You sit still and I'll get the mirror so you can see what it looks like around the back.' She tilts the mirror on the table and holds the hand mirror behind Mrs Tyler's head. 'There. Happy?'

'It doesn't look like you've taken anything off.'

'Well, I have, it's all on the floor.'

Mrs Tyler cranes her neck to look down. 'Ah yes, I see. Can you pass me my handbag?' Helen passes her the small mock-crocodile-skin bag and starts clearing all her things away, slotting the scissors into the correct compartments and pulling the grey hair out of the roll brush.

'How much it is again?'

'Ten pounds, Mrs Tyler. Same as last time.'

'My daughter says they only charge pensioners seven pounds in the precinct.' She rummages around in her purse.

'Here's ten pounds for the haircut, and fifty pence for you.' She hands over the money and snaps the clasp shut. 'So, who's next?' she enquires again.

Helen sweeps up the cut hair into a dustpan then unfolds the piece of paper that one of the care staff has given her with the itinerary handwritten on it. 'Let's see. You. Then Mrs Jacobs.'

'Oh, have you cut her hair before?'

'No, not yet.'

'She's new. Be warned. She does not stop going on about her son, that one. No one can get a word in edgeways. You'd think he invented the wheel, the way she goes on, but he only manages the Co-op in Woodingdean. Who else?'

'After Mrs Jacobs I've got Mr Hughes.'

'Well, that won't take you long, he's virtually bald. But he loves a chat about being a sailor. Just tell him you don't like the sea or you'll be there all day.'

'Thanks for the advice, Mrs Tyler. And then finally Mrs Owen.'

'Well, you'll be finishing early today then, Helen.'

'Why's that? Arms up. That's it, and that arm out, thanks.' She folds up the apron and slots it into the top of the wheelie bag.

'Mrs Owen died last night, so she won't be wanting her hair done.'

'Bloody hell,' Helen mutters under her breath. She'd only met Mrs Owen for the first time last week and she seemed fine. One moment, they're here, the next, the beds are stripped ready for the next resident. It all seems so functional somehow, like they never really existed. She can hear Chris's soft Liverpudlian voice in her head: *I don't know why you're doing it anyway love, it's not like we need the money*.

Her husband was right, but that was 100 per cent not the

point. Helen loves all the old dears here, even the ones with no social filter, which is most of them. They are such a refreshing change from the stuck-up parents she meets every day at Polly's private school. And where else would she find out the best way to get a grease stain out of fabric (iron it with a brown paper bag) or the secret ingredient to the perfect cauliflower cheese (a spoonful of wholegrain mustard and a pinch of sugar)?

On top of that, she has always been independent and being financially reliant on her husband doesn't sit comfortably with her. The money she makes as a mobile hairdresser is peanuts, but it gives her and Polly some pocket money to spend on an outing somewhere and she loves being around people. She is her own boss, works to her own hours and feels she's making a small, but not insignificant, positive change in people's lives. A good haircut is like a fabulous coat, it hides a multitude of sins.

'So, will you be back again in two weeks, Helen?'

'Yes. Same time good for you, Mrs Tyler?'

'Any time's good for me. It's not like I'm going anywhere, is it? Unless I die, of course, that's always a possibility.' She runs her hands through her hair and tuts. 'I'm sure you normally take more off, you know. It doesn't look any different.'

'Well, maybe next time we'll go for a complete makeover. What do you think?'

'Oh yes! Could you make me look like Joan Collins?'

'That's a deal. Bye, Mrs Tyler.' She pulls the suitcase out of the room and makes her way up the corridor to see her next client. If she keeps on schedule, and now she doesn't have to see Mrs Owen, she should be done by 2 p.m. and will have time to put a wash on before picking up Polly.

*

Helen holds the phone to her ear as she unlocks the car door, waiting for Chris's answerphone to kick in.

'Hey, Hels,' he responds after three rings.

'Hi!' she replies, delightedly. 'I didn't think you'd answer. I was going to leave you a message to let you know I missed you.'

'I'm just grabbing a late lunch before getting back to it. God, it's good to hear your voice. I've missed you too,' he sighs contentedly and Helen can imagine his gorgeous face smiling, his big blue eyes and unmanageable flop of blond hair that she's forever trying to trim.

'What's going on at your end?' he asks.

'Oh, just finished cutting the old folks' hair and now I'm off to pick up Polly,' Helen lowers herself into the car and puts the heating on to warm against the October chill.

'I can't wait to see you girls. It feels like it's been ages this time,' he replies.

'We can't wait to have you back. Polly is so excited. She's been making lists of what she wants to do with you. I'm not even sure if I'm invited, or whether these are secret plans for the two of you.'

'Oh, yeah? What are we doing?' he asks enthusiastically.

'Well, lots of the plans revolve around you taking her for pizza or buying her sweets.'

'Obviously!'

'But she'd also like to take you to the aquarium as they've got a new baby shark there—'

'Sounds good! And what do *you* have planned for me?' he asks playfully.

'And I,' she pauses, 'would like to take you to bed at the first available opportunity,' Helen purrs.

'Now *that* sounds like a plan I can get on board with immediately.' She imagines him grinning down the phone.

'There should be something arriving in the post for you over the next few days, so keep your eye out for it.'

'What is it?' Helen asks excitedly.

'You'll just have to wait and—'

'Sorry, Chris, hold on, there's someone else trying to get through,' Helen pulls the phone from her ear and sees 'Mum mob' illuminated on the screen and her heart sinks.

'I've got to answer this, Chris. Mum's trying to ring.'

'I wonder what *she* wants?' he asks grumpily, all the previous warmth draining from his voice.

'I've got to go, I love you.'

'I love you too,' he replies. 'And tell Polly—'

She cuts him off and answers the call waiting.

'Mum?' she asks, trying to mask the surprise in her voice, as it has been weeks since they've last spoken.

'Helen? It's Janet.' Her mum, for as long as Helen can remember, has referred to herself by her first name. She says it's because 'Mum' makes her feel old, but Helen has always persisted in the hope that one day she'll accept her birth-given title. She wanted Polly to call her Janet too, but Helen drew the line at that, adopting 'Nana' instead, which sounded the least stuffy of the grandparenting names.

'Why haven't you been answering your phone?' Janet asks sharply.

'I haven't had a missed call from you. Is everything OK?' Helen turns down Radio Two, which that sparked up as soon she put the key in the ignition.

'No. Oh course everything's not OK. Or I wouldn't be ringing, would I?' she snaps.

Helen tries to imagine herself surrounded by a circle of white light that her mum's sharp words can't penetrate, just as Tania had taught her. She hears crickets in the background and can picture her mum sitting on her second-floor balcony, overlooking the kidney-shaped swimming pool of her serviced apartment in Spain. She will be on one of the two cream mock-iron outdoor seats nestled around the table, her arm resting along the balcony rail. The sliding doors to the two-bed apartment will be wide open to let a cool breeze wrap around the flat, taking away the stale heat of the day. It's 2 p.m. in Brighton so at 3 p.m. in Costa Del Sol, Helen's mum will be thinking about having a light afternoon snack. She never eats much, just a bit of cured meat and bread, washed down with a bottle of Rioja. She hears her mum gulp and wonders how far into the bottle she is already. She cannot remember a time in her life when Janet wasn't angrily clutching a glass of something.

'What's the problem, Mum?' she asks.

'He's been in here again, Helen. That's the problem. This is my apartment; they shouldn't just be allowed to waltz in whenever they bloody feel like it.'

'Who's been in?'

'The man downstairs. What's his name? Geoff? Liam? Something like that. You know the one I mean. He has a scruffy beard like a homeless person,' she replies.

'And doing what, Mum?'

'What do you mean?' Janet snaps. She takes another noisy gulp. Helen has been in this situation, many times. Her mum's drunk and venting – she has run out of people to call over the years as she slowly alienated everyone – so always resorts to her daughter to let off steam. It's been a few weeks since her last vin-rouge-fuelled phone call.

'What's he *doing* in your apartment?' Helen gently probes.

'I don't know. Moving things. Leaving letters, that kind of thing.' Another loud gulp.

'The post? Is he bringing up the post, Mum?'

'Among other things, yes,' she barks.

21

Helen sighs. 'That's because you asked him to.'

'Why would I ask *anyone* to come into my apartment? This is my apartment, Helen. Mine. Is that clear?' She is now breathing quite heavily. Helen can imagine her face turning hard, with angry creases folding in around her puckered mouth.

'When we spoke last, you said you couldn't be expected to go down to the reception to collect your post every day and that someone should bring it up. Remember?' she speaks slowly and clearly. 'He's just bringing you your post like you asked him to. If you don't want him to do it, then you should ask him to stop.'

'But why's he coming in? Why does he need to come into the apartment, Helen? Answer me that. You can't, can you?' she vents.

'Because you asked them to, Mum. It's a serviced apartment. They have a key. And you don't have a bloody letterbox!' Helen rubs her forehead with her free hand.

'Well, there you go then!' Janet announces, as if she's been right all along.

A silence hangs between them. A twinge of anxiety prickles at the base of Helen's neck. Janet's drunkenness is nothing new, but her confusion is. She has always had a knack of bending the truth, but not completely forgetting it. How much is she actually drinking these days? Helen brushes off her unease and tries to lighten the conversation.

'What's the weather like?' she ventures.

'It's on the turn now. I have to wear my thick pashmina to sit out on the balcony in the early evening. But it's better than the rain, I suppose.' She takes another large gulp.

'Polly's enjoying school,' Helen offers. 'She's starting to make friends and she really likes her teacher.'

22

'Well, of course she's doing OK, Helen. She's your daughter. She's resilient.'

Helen allows herself a fleeting moment of pride. This is the closest she'll get to a compliment.

'I don't know why you send her to a private school though; it'll do her no good, not in the long run. She'll go through life thinking she's better than everyone else.' And just like that, she knocks Helen down again.

'Well, that was our choice, Mum. And as I said, she's happy.'

'That's something, I suppose. Although if you have money to burn on posh schools, you could at least fork out for an easyJet flight to come and see me once in a while. When was the last time you came over? Five years ago? Six? A lot has changed since then, Helen.'

'It was just over a year ago, Mum. Polly and I came out to see you for a week over Easter,' Helen replies, matter-of-factly.

'I'll have to take your word for it, Helen, but it feels a lot longer than that.' Janet takes another audible gulp.

'Well, how about you tell me when would be good, Mum. I have tried, but any date I suggest, you say you're busy, and now we're tied to school holidays, but tell me when's good and we'd love to come out and see you,' Helen replies.

'I'll have a look in my diary when I next have a spare moment,' Janet huffs, put out that she's been emotionally checkmated. 'I have to go now. You will have a chat with Liam about the post then, will you.

'Wouldn't it be easier for you to do it, seeing as he's only downstairs?'

'Can't you just do one thing for me, Helen? It's not like I ask a lot.'

'Yes,' Helen whispers, defeated. 'Of course I can, Janet.'

'Thank you,' her mum replies brusquely, before hanging up.

Helen turns the key in the ignition, vowing for the hundredth time to never speak to Polly the way Janet talks to her.

Chapter Three

'What's for dinner?' Spiral asks as he throws his canvas bag down with a thud and flings off his para boots, leaving them in a heap in the vicinity of the shoe rack. 'I'm absolutely famished.'

'Well, prepare to be dazzled. It was our cooking day today,' Tania replies. She offers him her cheek as Spiral greets her with a kiss.

'Lovely. I forgot.' He smiles weakly.

'Yep. We've both had a *lot* of fun,' Tania tries to muster up some enthusiasm, but her voice sounds flat and sarcastic. She watches Spiral open the fridge and retrieve a beer. He looks relaxed and calm, in contrast to Tania, who feels so wound up she's almost fizzing.

'Great! What did you both do?' He sits down and Tania notices how he simply morphs around the mess on the kitchen table instead of clearing it up. There's a layer of flour covering everything, including the piles of free newspapers that are stacked on the table, waiting to be taken out to the recycling. Tania had asked Spiral to move them this morning before he left for work, but he had, as usual, forgotten, so she'd left them there as a one-woman protest and cooked around them.

'Well, we went to the open market to look at all the different seasonal vegetables, and Falcon chose the ones he wanted to cook.'

'That sounds productive?' Spiral suggests.

'Yes. You'd think, wouldn't you?' Tania sighs. She un-screws the top off a half-drunk bottle of red wine on the sideboard, and pours herself a generous glass, taking a big gulp before continuing. 'We spoke to the greengrocer about where they came from, and he told us he "wasn't a fucking teacher, didn't have time to tell us where every single item in his shop came from, were we actually going to buy anything and why wasn't that boy at school as he looks about ten". Which was pleasant. So Falcon learnt a new phrase today: "Fucking teacher." And we have been trialling that one out in a number of situations, including at the old woman at the bus stop, the bus driver and the Amazon delivery guy as he dropped off a parcel for you. So all in all, it's been a mediocre day on the home-schooling front.'

Spiral looks poised to say something, then seems to think better of it. Tania opens the oven door and smoke billows out. She uses a tea towel to pull out a baking tray covered in what can only be described as charcoal.

'Do you know where the parcel is now?' he asks quietly.

'What parcel?' Tania replies, as she chucks the tray in the sink and throws open a window. How can three courgettes and an aubergine produce so much mess, she wonders, as she ineffectively flaps the tea towel around to dispel some of the smoke.

'The Amazon one you mentioned.'

'No. Last seen with Falcon so it might be in his room with him.'

'OK. Cool. Thanks. Do you think it was a high-vis jacket?'

'How the fuck should I know, Spiral? I might be a bloody superwoman but I can't see through envelopes,' Tania's tolerance levels are currently at an all-time low, and Spiral is unintentionally challenging the very last of her reserves.

'Sorry, I just thought . . .' he trails off.

'Anyway, why are you buying one of those? Don't they give you one at work? What kind of operation are they running, Spiral? It's a bit much to ask you to cough up for a high-vis, isn't it?'

'It's fine,' he reassures her. 'I'm sure they'll pay me back.'

'That's what they said on your last job with the steel-toe-capped boots and we never saw a penny of that, did we?' She raises an eyebrow.

'This is different,' Spiral mutters.

'Go on, then. Tell me about your first day,' Tania asks, her voice softening. It was, after all, her decision to do the majority of the homeschooling so that Spiral could take on some more work to bring in the cash. She had initially embraced the idea wholly and naively. The thought of being Falcon's spiritual and educational guide aligned strongly with her ethos: she assumed it would complement her yoga practice and her general all-round drive for enlightenment. She compared the role to that of a guru, guiding without leading, nurturing a young mind. Equipping Falcon with the emotional and practical skills to truly find his place in the world. She is also far more organised than Spiral, so she had assumed that she would naturally be better at it all round.

However, so far, it has mainly been a daily test in not losing her shit. It has only been six weeks, she reminds herself. With the October half term just out the way, she cannot categorially declare the idea an error at this stage, she needs to give it a year as they'd agreed and then assess the situation.

'I'm fucking knackered,' Spiral responds after a thoughtful pause. 'They've got us working like dogs up there. I'm completely done in.'

In reality, he'd been picked up at 8 a.m. by his mate

Andy. They'd driven over to the festival site where they were met by the other members of the production team and the site manager, Jimmy. They'd then sat and had a coffee and a pastry provided by the company, which was very pleasant. After a fag break, Jimmy had instructed Andy and Spiral and the other guys where the marquees were to be put up. They'd spent an hour or so doing this, then Jimmy returned with a banquet of Indian food for lunch, which they'd taken their time to enjoy. After that, they'd put up the small marquee, stage and backstage area, had a spliff and then driven home via a quick congratulatory first-day pint at The Gladstone. All in all, Spiral had had worse days.

Tania sits down heavily on the chair next to him with a sigh. 'Sorry about dinner, Spiral. There's some dahl in the freezer, I'll stick that in the microwave. Can you nip over to the shop and get some naan bread? That'll be OK, won't it? We haven't had curry for ages. Yeah, that'll be OK,' Tania mutters to herself, resting her head on his shoulder. He smells faintly of sweat and cigarette.

'Course. No problem.' Spiral finishes his beer, adds the bottle to the overflowing recycling box and pulls his boots back on.

'You haven't forgotten that it's your day with Falcon tomorrow, have you?' Tania squats down to locate the dahl from the back of the under-counter freezer.

'That's tomorrow is it?' his questioning tone immediately puts Tania's back up.

'Yes. Tomorrow, Spiral. It's Tuesday. You teach him every Tuesday, so I can run my classes. This isn't news, this is a reminder of something that happens every single week. You did let the foreman know when you took this job, didn't you?'

'Yes,' he replies defensively. 'Yes, of course. I wish you'd

28

give me some credit sometimes. I just forgot what day we were on.' He throws his coat on with a huff. 'Now, is there anything else you want from the shops?'

'Nope. No. Just naan.'

'Right, I'll be back in a minute.'

As Spiral slams the front door, Tania rests her head in her hands. She can feel the annoyance dissipating in his absence. He never used to wind her up so much. But then she never used to home-school a five-year-old, she thinks, as she drains the rest of the bottle into her glass.

She can hear Spiral on the phone as he walks up the path and knows he's calling Jimmy to see how the fuck he's going to get out of work tomorrow. She sighs heavily and decides that this is not a battle she wants to pick. Spiral can sort his own shit out this time.

Chapter Four

Sophie's head is tucked into my armpit, arm sleepily flopped over my stomach. She still has the chubby creases that give the impression of muscles on her upper arms, even though she's three. Her eyes are clamped shut and mouth wide open, breath whistling in and out. I must have fallen asleep as well while reading to the girls as it's now pitch black outside and all the street lights have turned on.

I gently push a stray hair from Sophie's forehead and remove her arm with the care and precision of a surgeon, one wrong move and she'll wake up, which would almost be worse than death on the operating theatre table. I ease myself out of the bottom bunk, and once both feet are safely on the ground, I pull her duvet up to under her chin and tuck her in with her favourite toy, Bunny. Her cheek is covered in light creases from where she's nodded off on my cardigan.

I check the top bunk. Lucy is also fast asleep. Her body looks so long in comparison to Sophie's short, solid frame. She has Nick's high cheekbones and pronounced philtrum. I rarely get to see the children this close up for any length of time and I take in her features, resisting the temptation to stroke her peach-soft skin. I watch her rapid eye movement and wonder what she is dreaming about, before gently kissing her cheek and heading downstairs.

I check the clock on the kitchen wall as I flick the switch on the kettle. It's just gone eight o'clock.

It's around this time I start to feel a little bit lonely. It creeps in slowly, undetected like carbon monoxide, and then suddenly, BAM! There it is. Whistling like tinnitus. Once noticed, it's hard to ignore. It's not a desperate loneliness. Not an *I can't get out of bed* loneliness. It's more of a light coating, which I try to shake off like a soggy woollen throw.

I turn on the TV and flick through the channels before scrolling through endless suggestions on Netflix. I have no one to argue with about the merit of a good Scandi-Noir series, or whether Ryan Gosling could be considered a 'serious' actor. I can watch what I want, for as long as I want. *Shipwrecked* – yes. *Naked Attraction* – why not? *The Bachelorette* – who wouldn't want to watch grown men weeping about not being given a rose by a woman who gives absolutely no shits about them?

If Lucy and Sophie sleep through the night, I might not speak to another soul for anything up to twelve hours, apart from the cat, who I think has taken a genuine dislike to me since Nick moved out.

I've never been particularly comfortable in my own company. I've always liked to think I am, in the same way I like to think I'm politically engaged and always recycle. But when presented with the facts, it turns out I have no idea who the Home Secretary is at the moment, and often put the milk cartons in the bin, as I can't face washing them out.

The truth is, I'm bad company for myself. I get restless. The chatter in my head takes over and I can't finish anything. I get halfway through a job and then remember something else I should be doing, only later to come back to a half-emptied dishwasher or piles of wet clothes on the floor ready to be hung out that I've completely forgotten about. I need structure. I need goals. I need deadlines. I need company.

It's the lack of noise that's so disquieting. Nick is a noisy person. A loud-eater. A fridge-slammer. A heavy-treader. Without his constant motion, the house comes to a standstill once the children are asleep.

I scroll through the emails on my phone. A sustainable fishing company in Cornwall has got in touch, asking me to quote for a marketing campaign. And there's one from the floor polishers. They like the copy but ask if I can make several small amendments. I look through the suggestions to pace, tone and content. They are basically asking me to rewrite the whole bloody thing by the end of tomorrow. Fabulous. Writing Groundhog Day.

I pull the crocheted blanket that Nick's nana knitted off the back of the sofa, draping it over my lap, and watch the shit hit the fan as *The Bachelorette* gives her reasoning for not selecting a bawling Tony from Toronto as her life partner, and allow myself a moment to consider what Nick's up to. I know I shouldn't. It really is none of my business now. As long as the girls are happy and we're communicating as well as can be expected, that should be enough.

But I can't help wondering if he's out tonight, and find myself starting to get wound up. Maybe he's at that new pub with the fabulous biryani? I imagine him on his second or third pint, sitting at the bar making small talk with the bar staff, mopping up the end of his curry with a chapati and eating noisily, his mouth open without anyone to tell him he has sauce speckled in his beard.

I don't want to be in the pub. I want to be here, at home with the girls, so I don't know why the prospect of *him* being there winds me up so much. Maybe it's the thought of him out spending money he owes to my parents on a night he can't afford, like he doesn't have a care in the world.

I pick up my mobile and scroll through to his number,

thinking up an excuse to ring him to see if there is the background hum of a night out, then think better of it and put it back on the arm of the sofa.

Communication is so transactional at the moment. I wonder if we will ever get to a place where we can speak with any kind of warmth to each other again. But I guess transactional is better than ripping strips off each other.

'Come on in, then,' I beckon to Peanuts. She pushes the door to, pads over to me nonchalantly and jumps up in my lap. Circling around and kneading the blanket with her sharp claws before curling up, tail twitching. She purrs contentedly as I stroke her sleek fur.

'We're all right, aren't we?' I ask her. She yawns, stretches out with a shudder and closes her eyes in response. Maybe as long as she's fed and occasionally petted, she doesn't care who's looking after her. Wily minx.

I wonder if Nick feels lonely. It can't be that easy being in someone else's flat, having a drawer and some wardrobe space in someone else's spare room. Simon has always been one of Nick's more easy-going friends, but that still doesn't detract from the fact that it's not Nick's place. He says he likes his own company, but does he like it *all* the time? Simon had kindly told Nick he could stay there rent-free until he gets himself back on his feet, whatever that means. When Simon's away with work, which is the majority of the time, he said the girls can also stay. They think it's brilliant, like camping. I think it's desperately sad, like a man who's lost his way.

This was only ever meant to be a temporary state. A four-month trial to see if our situation could improve. I never wanted to be a single parent, of course I didn't. Four months seemed a long enough period of time to see if there was any possibility of healing the rift, or if not, if we could move on with our lives constructively and positively. But it's already been three months since Nick moved out, and it doesn't feel like anything's changed at all.

Now, Nick can mix whatever colours he wants in the machine, leave the frying pan 'soaking' in the sink overnight. He can watch match after match on Sky Sports without interruption. Nick can live without compromise. As can I.

I look at the TV. Tony from Toronto has been asked to leave the villa; he's a really ugly crier. His leather-tanned face folds in on itself as he sobs his goodbyes to the other contestants, who all give him a patronising pat on the back.

I check my phone for the umpteenth time. No new messages. No new emails. No new notifications from any social media.

I mute the TV and scroll through to the number of my oldest friend, Rachel. We have known each other since primary school. She, unlike me, is a proper grown-up.

Having fallen pregnant at seventeen to an utter dickhead from school, she *had* to grow up fast. I left for university while she stayed at home, raising her son in a northern town that feeds on gossip and judgement.

I have to be careful not to lean on her too much. With her living four hours' drive up north it's easy for her to become my phone-a-friend in times of crisis.

Her son, Callum, is now twenty. He's a grown-up too, and towers over the pair of us. Rachel has always maintained she is his mum, not his friend, but they make a brilliant team.

Single motherhood created the most independent, incredible woman I know. While I was getting off my head at university in Brighton nightclubs, fucking anything with dreadlocks and going on marches for causes I was painfully ill-informed about, she was raising her son.

And now, at thirty-seven, the tables have turned. I am sat

at home with my sleeping babies upstairs and Rachel has her adult life back again.

She answers after two rings.

'I was just thinking of you!' she shouts down the phone over the thud of a loud bass.

'Where are you?' I ask.

'Sorry?'

'WHERE ARE YOU?' I shout.

'Hang on. Hang on. I'll just go outside. I can't hear a thing in here. 'Scuse me. 'Scuse me.' Right Said Fred's 'I'm Too Sexy' starts playing.

'What *are* you listening to?' I ask.

'Sorry, that's better.' The music is replaced by background beer garden chatter. 'What did you just say?'

'I just asked where you were. Was that Right Said Fred?'

'Yes,' Rachel laughs. She has the most joyful laugh. It's loud and guttural and full of happiness, and completely unselfconscious. 'It's Matt Robinson's fortieth. Do you remember him? He was in the upper sixth when we were in the fourth year?'

We still categorise everyone from home by what school year they were in, regardless of how old we all are now. That, and what trainers they wear.

An image of a boy in red jeans with floppy hair flickers into my mind and then dissipates like oil on water.

'Maybe. I'm not sure.'

'Well, anyway, he remembers you. We're upstairs in the Red Lion. He's hired possibly the worst disco in Lincolnshire, if not the world. The guy running it is about eighty and his musical selection ends in 1993. Bit like your music collection, Emmie.'

'Oi, fuck off!' I tease.

'Yep, I'll be in a minute,' Rachel responds to someone.

35

'Who was that?' I ask.

'Matt.' Even without seeing her face I can tell she's smiling.

'What's going on?' I quiz, tucking my legs under my bum on the sofa and turning the TV off completely so she has my full attention.

'Nothing!' she protests.

'Rach? I'm not having that. I know you too well for you to bullshit me.'

'OK, OK. Well, I don't really know to be honest. Oh thanks,' she says.

'For what?'

'Matt just brought me a drink out.'

'Matt just brought me a drink out!' I imitate and immediately regret it.

'Forget it, Emmie,' her tone has changed. I've embarrassed her.

'Sorry, sorry, sorry. I'm just jealous. I'm at home with no possibility of a social life and you're out there living the dream,' I apologise.

'I'd hardly call getting pissed up in the Red Lion to Kris Kross living the dream,' she scoffs.

'You know what I mean. Sorry. I didn't mean to be a knob,' I mutter.

'It's fine. I don't know what's happening, to be honest.' She takes a gulp of whatever Matt has given her. 'There's not a huge amount to say. We bumped into each other in Morrison's in Grimsby a while ago. He's moved back for a bit, as his mum's not very well. We got talking. He's nice,' she says.

'Well, good for you, Rach. You deserve some fun.'

'Don't I fucking just?' She has started to develop her signature three-pints-in slur. 'And I hadn't had sex in over two years, you know?' she adds. 'Two years? I'm surprised it hadn't sealed over.'

'Wait. You've shagged him? Rach, have you shagged him?' I squeal with all the excitement of a teenager. We could be sitting in our favourite café in Grimsby, smoking fags and dissecting our previous night at Scott Parry's house party when his mum was on holiday in Tenerife.

'I might have!' she teases.

'WHAT! This is huge news. Why didn't you tell me? When did this happen? Was he any good? Have you done it more than once?' The questions cascade from my mouth like a landslide. We know everything about each other's lives. Why do I not know this massive piece of information?

'Well, it started—'

The sitting room door creaks open. Sophie is standing in the doorway in her nightie, ruffled hair pointing in twenty different directions. 'I fell out of bed,' she whispers without opening her eyes.

'I've got to go. Sophie's up,' I whisper. I stand up and Peanuts leaps off my lap with a discontented mew.

'Never mind. Next time. I love you.' Her voice becomes louder as she rejoins the disco.

'You too.' I sign off and scoop Sophie up in one well-practised move. 'Toilet, then bed,' I tell her as she flops sleepily over my shoulder.

And just like that, I'm back to being Mum.

Chapter Five

'So has it arrived?' Chris asks excitedly.

'No, what am I looking out for?' Helen asks. Polly is asleep and she is running herself a bath. She's added a large dollop of Chanel N°5 bubble bath and inhales the decadent smell as the mirror steams up with the heat.

'Never mind. I just thought you could describe what you looked like in it before I came home.' His voice is thick with anticipation.

'Well, I'm getting naked now . . .' Helen leaves the suggestion hanging. She and Chris have always had a healthier-than-average sex life. It obviously took a battering after Polly was born, but they still fancy each other, and in the absence of seeing each other regularly in real life when Chris is offshore, they try to keep things alive over the phone. Although, for the most part, Helen's contribution is predominantly fictitious.

'OK,' he whispers. 'What are you doing?'

Helen sits on the toilet and starts to wee as the bath continues to fill up. 'Well, I am peeling off my silk knickers you bought me last time you were home,' she lies, looking down to see her discarded Marks & Spencer multibuy cotton briefs on the bathroom floor.

'You're so hot,' he replies breathlessly. 'Take off your bra,' he pleads. 'Is it the matching one?'

'Sure is,' she purrs, as she stands, remembering just in

time not to flush the loo, and unhooks her equally practical M&S nude-coloured bra. It looks good underneath a white top, but can give the impression you're nippleless, which, frankly, is no one's phone sex fantasy.

'What are you doing now?' he asks in a whisper.

'I am just lowering myself into a bubble bath.' She turns off the taps, and steps one foot in and then the other, careful to not drop the phone in the water.

'Describe what you're doing.' He is barely audible. These are the conversations that get her completely hot, absolutely turned on, to know that he is touching himself thinking of her. She loves the idea of him thinking of her when he's away. Chris has described how the other men sit around wanking over the posters of Angelina Jolie and Kim Kardashian they tape to their bunker walls. Not Chris; he's thinking about her.

'OK, I'm running my hands down my stomach,' she breathes deeply. 'It's wet and warm.'

'Yes,' he pants. 'What next . . .?'

Suddenly, she remembers the conversation she had with Janet after the nursing home the other day, and realises she hasn't told Chris about it. How weird she was, how confused she sounded.

'Tell me what you're doing now,' he pleads. His breath short and she knows he's about to come. 'What are you thinking about?' he gulps loudly.

'Umm about, just about – um—'

'What are you doing now?' he pleads, clearly on the edge.

'What are *you* doing?' she tries to sound seductive, but she's lost her train of thought. It's now more, 'just giving you a ring to remind you to pick up some blue-top milk', than 'I am covered in suds and on the verge of an orgasm.'

39

'Oh my God,' Chris groans deeply, swallowing hard. A moment later he asks, 'Did you come too?'

'Absolutely,' she sighs. Maybe now isn't the best time to bring up her mum.

Chapter Six

'Great session, people. I can see some real improvements. Some of you have clearly been taking time for your practise between classes. Remember to drink lots of water and I hope you all have a peaceful and fulfilling day. Namaste.' Tania bows deeply, hands pressed together in prayer pose, as she is met by a sea of mumbled 'namastes' in response.

As the class clears out, she lies back on her yoga mat, stretching deeply and taking a moment for herself. She has half an hour before she needs to be home to take over from Spiral before he heads out to work. The 6 a.m. sunrise yoga sessions are a new venture and have proved hugely popular, every one fully booked with a waiting list. She takes a deep breath, holds it for the count of five and releases slowly, attempting to fix an image of peace and fulfilment in her mind. But it's no use. She can already feel the weight of the day ahead starting to creep into those parts of her brain that she has spent the last hour trying to clear.

She silently lists her morning gratitude affirmations one by one.

Thank you for this day.
I'm filled with happiness and gratitude.
I'm grateful to feel the air in my lungs and the beating of my heart.
I'm thankful simply for being alive.

I'm grateful for who I am and what I have.

I am so grateful for the new day ahead and for the many opportunities coming my way.

She opens her eyes slowly and purposefully, hoping by some miracle that a higher force has shifted her mind, so she's now looking forward to a day of homeschooling with the curiosity of a cat and excitement of a newborn lamb.

But the bottom line is, teaching her son bores her. Spending time with him and him alone drives her up the wall. She's not interested in the things he's interested in. She loves him, that's a given, but the moment Falcon starts to offload whatever is in his brain her thoughts immediately drift to what she needs to buy from the Co-op. Or did she set up the standing order for her contact lenses. Or is Spiral's passport due to be renewed. She doesn't care which one Marshall is from *Paw Patrol*. She doesn't want to sit on the floor with him and pretend to be a dog while he barks at her and throws breadsticks for her to fetch. She finds interactions with young children testing and plain hard work. She would far rather be doing something else almost every single time.

Spiral, on the other hand, commits himself wholly to every conversation he has with Falcon. He asks questions around and about every thought. He gets behind what his son is saying and laughs at his jokes. Actually laughs, not pretend laughs. To start with, Tania just put it down to Spiral having a sense of humour so underdeveloped that it aligned with that of a very young child. But as the weeks have dragged on with homeschooling, she's noticed that the boys bowl in with smiles on their faces on their days together. They finish each other's sentences as they tumble through stories of the adventures they've had.

Tania always thought she was the one who connected

with people emotionally and spiritually, not Spiral. He was a good wingman. He'd get the guitar out around a campfire and take charge of the barbecue when needed. He can put a tent up in no time at all, but it was Tania who hugged deeply and nodded encouragingly when she listened. Not Spiral.

The thought that this might potentially not be the case is a most uncomfortable revelation. When she and Spiral first discussed the idea of homeschooling, Tania had embraced it fully.

She hadn't anticipated that it would mainly consist of bollocking a five-year-old to put his shoes on so they could sit in the library counting down the seconds until Spiral returned from work. They said they would trial homeschooling for a year. Just a year. It's not even a full year when you take into consideration Christmas and summer holidays. And then they can have a rethink. Then Spiral can give it a go. Or they could consider starting Falcon in mainstream education. But she will see this year out. Surely you can't fuck up a child's development that much in a year, she reassures herself.

As Tania starts rolling up the yoga mats and stacking them in the corner of the room, her phone beeps. Probably Spiral texting to ask her a question about Falcon's breakfast that he's more than equipped to answer himself. She both savours the fact that she is the conduit to the smooth running of their household, and finds it deeply irritating in equal measure.

She looks at the screen. Oh fuck, she'd completely forgotten about the arrangement she'd made for the following week.

Mum: Arabella! So looking forward to seeing you and my little cherub next Wednesday. I have a table booked at 1 p.m. at The Ivy, don't be late like last time. Kisses.

Tania takes another deep breath and repeats her gratitude affirmations once again, this time with a lot less conviction.

Chapter Seven

I stare at my naked self in the full-length mirror in my bedroom. Mum has been emailing me article upon blog upon feature about how to 'reconnect with yourself' after a break-up.

I don't know the last time I properly looked at myself in the buff, but my shape has changed. 'Thickened', as my nanny would say. My hips look broader and the stretch marks that score my lower stomach are faded and pucker my skin like a roast chicken. The dark bush of pubes spider down my upper thighs. I can't remember the last time I had a bikini wax. Probably around the same time that Nick and I last had sex. It had been almost a year without sex when he moved out, and that was three months ago. No wonder I've got a bush like David Bellamy.

The lack of intimacy crept up on us. One or the other would find an excuse when a hand ventured into the other side of the bed. It started with suggestions of just cuddles instead, blaming tiredness or stress or not being in the mood. I don't know who was the first to mention it, but a naked cuddle was the first step. Just spooning in bed with a heavy arm resting on your waist. Hot, sleepy breath on your neck.

And then we started to wear clothes in bed. Apart from when the children were babies and I was feeding during the night, we'd always slept naked. That might have been because we met while travelling in Thailand, where we slept under mosquito nets in stiflingly hot beach huts, the air sitting heavy and thick in the rooms even when the wooden shutters were thrown wide open. The first night we shared a bed in Asia, we both slipped silently under the thin cotton sheet unclothed, and remained so almost every night from then on, our bodies slotting together like a game of Tetris.

But some months back, without a word, Nick crept into bed in his boxers and a faded T-shirt of a half marathon he'd done years back, and I dug out my old jogging bottoms and a vest top that had been demoted from day wear, and we started sleeping like that. The cuddling was slowly and wordlessly phased out, until we would both climb into bed on our own sides, roll to the edge of the mattress, and an invisible but very real floor-to-ceiling barrier was erected between us.

The sex-shaped void in our lives was seamlessly filled by the boundless affection and love that we received from Sophie and Lucy. They would pile into our bed in the early hours, finding the space between us reassuring as one or both of them splayed out, enjoying the room. I would wake to find a rogue arm strewn across my face, or a pair of small feet unconsciously kneading my kidneys like a cat.

And then one day I woke up, the children were in their own room, and I rolled over and saw a stranger in my bed. I had once loved this man with such an all-encompassing, messy ferocity, but now I no longer knew him.

Of course, we can blame the cracks that began to appear on the lack of sex, but the real rift between us was down to Nick. How one 'mistake' had snowballed until Nick was incapable of knowing what the truth was any more. How he constructed a web of lies to keep himself and us safe, but it was those very lies that nearly lost us our home. I know I had my part to play in this, but it wasn't me who threatened everything we had created for the girls because of stupid pride.

I gather my tits up and hold them at what would have been their height when I was twenty-something, pushing them together to imagine what I would look like if I just had a bit of filler. Nothing dramatic, it would just be like reflating a party balloon that's been discovered behind a curtain a week after the celebrations.

I look at myself and try to find three things that I love about my body, as the article suggested, to say aloud. I clear my throat.

'You have nice teeth.' My voice sounds weak and hollow and not like my own. I am crippled by embarrassment, unnecessarily given that I am the only person in the house and no one can see me. Urgh, this is painful. I have a big piece of work that I need to be getting on with. I should just stick my clothes on and head out to Mummies Rest to crack on with it. My phone chimes, I check it – Mum Mobile.

'So?' she asks.

'So what?' I reply, feeling slightly silly all of a sudden.

'Have any of the articles been useful, darling? Several of them were forwarded onto me by Diane who does the shift after me in the library on Tuesdays. She said it was tremendously useful to reconnect with herself after she started the menopause.'

'Well, I'm currently completely naked looking at myself in the mirror, so yes. I am following the advice.'

'Oh well done, Emily. Is that the one where you give yourself compliments?' she asks enthusiastically.

'Yes. I'm struggling a bit, to be honest.'

'I quite enjoyed that one. How many have you got up to?' she asks.

'One. My teeth.'

'Oh Emily, that is poor. You're beautiful and clever and strong. You can certainly come up with something a bit better than that.'

'I'll give it a go,' I reply reluctantly.

'Seriously, Emily, self-care is extremely important. You can't look after the girls properly if you don't look after yourself.'

'OK. Look, Mum I'm going to go, I'm getting a bit chilly,' I look around for my grey sweatshirt, but can't see it.

'I mean it, Emily. You can't run on empty. It's not going to help anyone and you are holding a lot together right now, so you have to be in a good place.' The 'good place' line jars. Has she picked that up from *Woman's Own* or is it from another article Diane has suggested?

'Don't worry about me. I'm fine,' I try to sound breezy, to convince her how absolutely fine I am.

'But I do, Emily. That's my job. Please look after yourself. Now, think of two more wonderful things about my wonderful girl, then put your clothes on before you catch your death. Your father's calling from downstairs. We're going to go to Newark antiques fair in a moment and your father is making a meal of it. GIVE ME A MOMENT, RICHARD, I'M ON THE PHONE! Gosh, he is impatient. Love to the girls.'

'And to you and Dad,' I reply as she hangs up.

I take a deep breath and stare again at my body, trying to find two more things to say aloud to myself.

'You have strong shaped eyebrows,' I announce. I do. I really do. The hairdresser told me so. I could probably have done this whole exercise dressed, looking in the bathroom cabinet mirror at this rate, seeing as everything so far has been a comment from the neck upwards.

47

I slouch down onto the edge of the bed and rest my head in my hands. I don't think it's positive body reinforcement I need at the moment, it's a break from my own brain.

A small sob escapes, and I draw in a long quivering breath. Come on, Emily, get it together, I tell myself.

I stand to find my clothes as my phone chimes again, so answer it at arm's length as I retrieve my sweater from under the bed.

'Hello?' I shout.

'Hi, Em, sorry to bother you but – Em, are you naked?'

I turn around sharply to face the screen. Nick's face stares back at me. Oh my God. He hasn't rung. He's FaceTimed.

'Shit, Nick!' I accuse. But this is my fault. I should have checked before I'd answered.

I grab the top and cover my chest, turning the phone away from me. 'Jesus, Nick. Why did you – shit. What do you want?'

'Sorry, sorry. I was just – erm,' he dithers. 'Erm, so I should . . . I'll ring back on the main, the, you know, land-line for mobiles. Fuck – you know.'

'Yep.' I press 'end call,' and sink back down onto the bed. Moments later the phone chimes again. This time I check before answering.

'Hi,' Nick says sheepishly. 'Everything . . . OK?'

'Yes,' I reply curtly as I pull on my knickers and jeans. 'Let's not talk of that again. Now, what was it you wanted?'

'Right. Yes. Have you had a call from the nursery this morning?'

'No. No, why, have you? Is everything OK with Sophie?'

'Yes. Yes she's fine,' he replies, hesitating. 'Well, she's physically fine but—'

'What does that mean, Nick?' I suppress the rising panic. 'And why have they started ringing you instead of me? I'm the primary contact, Nick. They should have rung me.'

'Yes, I know. They said they'd tried you first, but it had gone straight to voicemail, but anyway. So—'

'And what do you mean, "physically fine"? What's happened?' Nick has never been any good at getting to the point.

'OK, so. Sorry. She's fine mentally as well, obviously, it's just that—'

'NICK!' I snap. 'Spit it out.'

'Right, yep. So the nursery has asked if we could both go down for a meeting with them ASAP as there has been an incident they would like to discuss with us. Involving Sophie.'

'What kind of an incident, Nick? Seriously, stop talking in riddles. Is she OK?'

'Well,' and he clears his throat self-consciously. 'It appears Sophie has been showing her vagina. To other children. She's been pulling down her underwear and – how did Betsy put it? – "exposing herself" to some of the other children,' he coughs again. The irony of the FaceTime 'incident' moments ago is not completely lost on us.

I lower myself slowly back onto the bed. '"Exposing herself"?' I mock. 'Is she joking? She's three years old, Nick. She's only just out of nappies. She's not a pervert! And Betsy is about a hundred. She's probably scared of her *own* vagina. What did you say to her?'

'I said we'd go down. Together. This afternoon,' he responds calmly.

I take a deep breath. Compose myself. 'What time?'

'Two o'clock,' he replies.

'OK. I'll see you then,' I sigh and hang up. A rage of injustice surges through my body as I do up the clasp on my bra.

Nick is sitting on the bench outside the nursery. He is hunched over, tapping on his phone. As I approach I resist the compulsion to suggest he sits up as he'll get a bad back. He can, of course, sit however he wants.

'Hi,' he stands when he sees me, and then kisses me on both cheeks, taking us both a bit by surprise. 'Sorry,' he mutters. 'I'm not sure why I did that,' and hastily sits back down again, shaking his head in embarrassment.

'Forget it,' I brush it off. 'Now. What are we going to say to Betsy?' I sit down next to him on the bench.

'Well, let's hear what she's got to say, but ultimately, we think it's absolutely ridiculous?' he suggests firmly.

'Good. Glad we finally agree on something.' I hazard a smile, to which he reciprocates.

'OK, let's do this.' He stands and offers me his hand, which I accept, and don't let go of until we have been buzzed into the nursery.

'Take a seat.' Betsy gestures to the child-size bright red plastic stools and I watch as Nick concertinas his six-foot-four body into it.

Betsy has been working at the nursery since childcare began in Western civilisation, and is the first of three generations of family members who are employed here. She is the Helen Daniels from *Neighbours* of nurseries, committed to her profession until the bitter end, and will certainly stay here until it shuts down or she dies, whichever comes first.

Everything about Betsy screams 'old school', from the polyester sky-blue tabard that she wears by choice, to the crocodile clip that aggressively scrapes her wiry grey hair back, to the standard black pleather orthopaedic shoes. She was born to tell people off and is completely in her element here.

'Right then,' she smooths her tabard down over her knees and takes an *X Factor*-length pause to really unsettle us, before continuing, 'I appreciate the sensitivity of the situation, but it is our policy to speak directly to parents if an issue is brought to our attention which we deem to be dangerous and slash or inappropriate.' Good use of 'slash' I think. 'In this particular case, as I explained to Mr Jones—'

'Please call me Nick.' He's using his professional phone voice. Nice.

'As I explained to Nick, Sophie has been exposing herself to one or several of the other children during outdoor free play.'

'Well, how many is it?' I ask.

'Pardon?' Betsy asks, knocked slightly off guard.

'How many people has she been showing her bits to?' I see Nick cringe and wish I'd said vagina. 'Is it one, or several?'

'We have been made aware of one situation so far, but—'

'When you say, made aware. By whom?' Nick enquires.

'By the child,' Betsy states.

'And who is this child?' Nick follows up. He is keeping his cool, interlocked fingers resting in his lap, head tilted to one side unthreateningly.

'I, of course, can't say due to child protection, but we have it on good authority that Sophie has been pulling down her underwear and exposing herself to one, potentially more than one, child during outdoor activities. It is my duty of care to inform parents, as this kind of inappropriate behaviour may be indicative of other issues that may need addressing.' A bead of sweat runs down Betsy's otherwise stoic face.

'Hang on, what other issues? What are you implying,

Betsy?' I ask. I look over to Nick for back up, but he is open-mouthed in shock.

'I'm not implying anything. It is just our policy to—'

'Can I ask if any adults have been witness to this behaviour or was it one of the other boys or girls who told you about it?' Nick asks.

'It was reported to us by one of the children earlier to—'

'I bet it was Josh Carter,' I interrupt. Betsy flinches, only slightly but enough to confirm my suspicions. 'I knew it! You know he's been helping himself to Sophie's lunch, don't you? I mentioned it to Cassie last week. *And* he hid her bunny in the toy cupboard so she couldn't bring it home for two days until it was discovered, which was, quite frankly, a bloody nightmare for me as she refuses to sleep without it. Did you know that? I don't mean to speak badly of a three-year-old, but he can be a bit of a bugger sometimes, Betsy. I wouldn't be surprised if he made this whole thing up when he'd got into trouble for the other stuff.' I'm quite worked up now and am balancing on the edge of my plastic chair, in danger of flipping straight off it, but I know I'm onto something. This must be how Columbo feels as he says, cigar in mouth, 'Just one more thing . . .'

Betsy clears her throat and takes a sip of water from a yellow children's beaker. 'No, no I wasn't aware of that situation,' Betsy nods nervously. 'That incident had not been recorded in the book, as is procedure. I will flag this with Cassie.' Her daughter is going to get the mother of all bollockings from Betsy after this meeting, which is unfortunate as I like Cassie, but rather her than Sophie being branded a perv by some little shit with a grudge.

'So is that it?' Nick looks from Betsy to me, and back again. 'Can we go. Or is there anything else we need to discuss?'

'Well,' Betsy pulls at a loose thread on her tabard. 'I think, in light of what Mrs Jones has just brought to my attention, I will speak with Cassie to get the fuller picture and then see if we can get to the bottom of this.' She stands and offers her hand, which we both briefly shake. 'I'm sorry to have wasted your time. I will, of course let you know the outcome of any further conversations.'

'And will you be inviting Josh's mum in for a similar chat?' I ask.

'Again, I can't talk about that due to our child protection policy, but I will, of course, further investigate the allegations, and will make sure that staff are fully briefed.'

'Well, we can't ask any more than that,' I respond.

Betsy looks exhausted and even older than usual. I don't want to draw this out any longer. She does have an impossible job: I wouldn't want to look after a building full of other people's kids. Not for all the gin in the world.

'We do understand you are only looking out for the children, Betsy. We know you're just trying to keep our children safe,' I say.

'Thank you for your understanding,' she replies in a small voice, as she presses the door-release button and Nick and I step back out into the bracing wind and grey skies.

He unselfconsciously puts his arm around me and as we walk up the path away from the nursery, I naturally wrap my arm around his waist. We walk in step with each other as Nick says, 'Poor woman.'

'I know. I couldn't do it, could you?'

'Nope. No. I think our two are more than enough, thank you.' He grips my shoulder before adding, 'Great work, Miss Marple.'

For a moment we are a team, we are on the same page.

As we reach the split in the road that leads one way to my house, the other to Simon's flat, we stop for a moment

53

and hesitate, an unspoken resistance to returning to the real world of split weeks with the girls and shared online calendars.

'You were great,' Nick whispers.

'Why couldn't it be like this before?' I say, more to myself that anything else.

Nick sighs heavily and shrugs. It's a stupid, complicated question with an answer so big and messy that I wouldn't even know where to start.

As he walks off I watch him for a few seconds, willing him to turn around. He doesn't.

'LUCY. SOPHIE. FOR THE SEVENTEENTH TIME, CAN YOU COME DOWNSTAIRS FOR DINNER?' I bawl up the stairs. I sometimes think I should just make recordings of all my stock phrases and demands, and play them on the stereo at varying volumes, depending on how many times I've had to ask.

'Fuck's sake,' I say under my breath, as I jump up the stairs, two at a time.

'Girls,' I announce as I push open their shared bedroom door. 'I have asked you a million—' I stop in my tracks. 'What are you doing?' I ask them both.

'Sophie was just showing me her bits, Mummy, and I'm drawing them.' Lucy tells me plainly.

Oh fuck.

'It's just my bits,' Sophie says by way of an explanation. She has taken off her tights and pants and is standing with her dress over her head. Lucy is sitting cross-legged in front of her with her pad nestled in her lap and pencil in hand.

'Right,' I reply slowly and calmly. 'Well, how's about we keep our clothes on in the future, and go downstairs?

It's beans and nuggets for tea, and they're going cold on the table.'

'OK, Mummy,' they chime as they scurry past me.

I don't think there's any need for Betsy to know about this. Or Nick, for that matter. Definitely not Nick. Today we worked as a team. Today felt like progress. No need to undo that with the truth.

Chapter Eight

'Hello, darling,' Tania's mother says much too loudly in the tone only the privileged adopt. 'You look like you need a facial and a good night's sleep.' She strokes the side of Tania's face pityingly with a well-manicured hand. 'Why don't you and Falcon come and stay overnight? I could rustle you up something for dinner? What do you say?'

Tania's mum is sitting opposite her in The Ivy in Brighton, the only restaurant chain she'd consider stepping foot in. She is wearing a Chanel two-piece and pearls with a silk Liberty print scarf draped around her shoulders like an old, not-so attractive, Jackie O.

'You know why not, Mum. And anyway, when have you ever cooked anything?' Tania asks.

'Well, the chef, obviously, but you know what I mean. And how is my angel boy? Put that thing down and come and give Grandma a cuddle.' Francesca takes the iPad from Falcon, which he surprisingly gives up without protest, and draws him into a hug.

'You smell like apple crumble, Grandma,' Falcon says, his face pressed into her silk scarf.

'It's called Creed, darling. The same scent that Grace Kelly wore when she married Prince Rainier of Monaco, no less. But I'll take apple crumble from you.' Tania watches as her mother tenderly kisses the top of his head, before Falcon squirms out of her grip and wriggles into his own seat where he pushes the earphones into his ears and continues to watch *Paw Patrol* again.

'Isn't it bad for his brain, watching so much television, Arabella?' Francesca asks.

'No, Mum. And without it we wouldn't get any peace.' She scans the menu as her mother waves over the waiter authoritatively, much to Tania's huge embarrassment.

'We'll have two steaks, please, medium rare. And a small carbonara for my grandson. Oh and a bottle of Malbec.' She shuts the menus and passes them back.

'Mum,' Tania hisses. 'We're vegetarian.'

The waiter loiters, unsure whether an order change is imminent.

'She's not,' Francesca brushes him away with a hand. 'You're not!' she repeats.

'You're unbelievable,' Tania mutters. In actual fact, there's nothing she'd like more than a gorgeous juicy steak, but that's not the point. Her mum has never respected any of her life choices, and whether she chose to see them through or not is another matter.

'Oh come on, Arabella. Enjoy yourself a little and have a half-decent meal before you two return home.'

'Don't say *home* like that, Mum. We have a lovely flat with a garden. And can you please stop calling me Arabella. It's Tania now, it has been since I left home,' Tania is increasingly regretting coming for lunch. She could be at home filling in her tax return instead, which would be infinitely more agreeable.

'Yes, fine. I've tasted better but fill her up,' Francesca instructs the waiter as she samples the drop of wine. 'Well, you'll always be Arabella to me. That is the name I gave my sweet baby at birth.' She tries to touch Tania's face again but she moves a fraction back to dodge her hand so

57

Francesca ruffles Falcon's hair instead and he looks up from the screen, grinning at her in return. 'If I'd wanted to call you something pedestrian like Tania, I would have done. Now drink up.'

Tania goes to protest but Francesca interjects with a raised finger. 'I apologise. These are your choices. I apologise,' she says with a nod. 'Now. I had something I wanted to talk to you about.' She spreads her napkin on her lap and Tania notices how wrinkled and bony her ring-encrusted fingers look. Her mother's ageing always takes her by surprise. She just assumes she will outlive all of them out of pure determination and sense of entitlement.

Francesca takes a long sip of her drink. 'Yes, this is quite a sub-standard Malbec,' she says, mainly to herself. 'So. Christmas!' she announces, as if it's the answer to a pub quiz question.

'What about it?' Tania asks.

'Excuse me.' The waiter places her plate in front of her before circling the table to Francesca and then Falcon, who immediately starts shovelling pasta into his mouth without taking his eyes off the screen for a moment.

'Gosh. He's got a healthy appetite. He gets it from his grandfather,' Francesca glows before focusing on Tania again. 'So. As I was saying. Christmas. Your father and I have been discussing plans for the festive period and we thought this year you may like to have a *proper* Christmas with all the trimmings. It's only a few weeks away, and these things take planning. Caterers don't book themselves, darling.'

Tania's eyes widen, a sliver of steak suspended on her fork mid-air, which Francesca mistakes for excitement, so continues. 'We appreciate how important it has been for you to do it "independently".' Francesca makes inverted commas with her fingers. 'We also appreciate you are a strong woman, as you have repeatedly reminded us, but you have made your point, Arabella. We think this has gone on for long enough. We think Falcon deserves a big Christmas this year. Wouldn't you like that, Falcon? Wouldn't you like Father Christmas to come to Grandma and Gramps' house this year with all your presents?' She smiles at him. The naming of the grandparents was entirely Tania's choice, selecting titles she knew both her mum and dad would hate.

'Hold up,' Tania puts down her cutlery with an unexpectedly loud clatter. 'Do we have a say in this, this Christmas . . . sabotage?' she splutters.

'Of course, darling. Of course. We just thought you could all get out of your poky flat and be spoilt over the Christmas period. You realise that Falcon hasn't been over since he was a little boy? He probably wouldn't even recognise the place.'

'And whose fault is that?' Tania splutters, incredulously.

'Oh, you're so melodramatic, sometimes. You just need to lighten up, Arabella, or you'll end up with deep worry lines scarring your forehead. I just wanted to spoil my daughter and grandson. There's no harm in that, is there?' she asks.

'And Spiral?' Tania challenges Francesca. 'Is he included in these plans?'

Francesca takes a large gulp of wine and says, 'Of course.' She refuses to make eye contact with Tania. 'If he'd like to come that is,' she adds quietly.

'I thought as much, Mum. Why would we want to come to you for Christmas when all you'll do is make Spiral feel uncomfortable and out of place?' Tania is trying to maintain a calm, measured voice, but her temper is starting to seep through. She quickly breathes in through her nose and out through her mouth in an attempt to regain control.

'Oh, poppycock. He's always welcome at The Stables,'

Francesca disregards Tania's question with a flick of the wrist.

Tania groans and shakes her head at the mention of the name. In Tania's opinion, it is the epitome of nouveau riche to build a seven-bedroom mock-Tudor house and give it a pretentious name, like Chris Eubank buying his title of Lord.

'Can I have pudding?' Falcon says loudly, earphones still in, face covered in creamy sauce.

'Of course you can. What would you like? I bet they do a fantastic knickerbocker glory here,' Francesca replies without consulting with Tania.

'No, I think we're going Falcon,' she pulls the earphones from his ears and starts to wind them around the iPad.

'Darling, the world doesn't have to be a constant battle. Sit down and finish your steak. And let me get my lovely boy whatever he would like for afters.'

'Pleeeeeeeeeeease, Mummy.' Falcon grips Tania's arm desperately. She feels torn, as always. Why does her mother always put her in these impossible situations? It's been the same for as long as she can remember, trivialising what she believes in, mocking her life choices. This is the very reason she left The Stables all those years ago.

'Pleeeeeeeeeeease, Mummy, please.'

'Look at that little face. How can you say no to that?' Francesca coos and Tania has to use all her willpower to not pour the rest of her mediocre Malbec down her twin set.

'We'll have pudding and then we'll go,' she says through gritted teeth.

'Good girl. You look like you could do with a dessert as well, Arabella. There's nothing to you these days,' she signals the waiter again. 'And Christmas, shall we just keep that suggestion on the table? Shall I tell your father you're considering it?' Francesca asks as she delicately slices through the steak.

'No. No, Mum. No I'm not considering it. No. No, thanks,' Tania replies, exhausted.

Francesca pops the slice of steak into her mouth as Tania starts to angrily saw through her own. No need to waste the rest of a perfectly good meal. She momentarily closes her eyes as she lets the mushroom-cream-covered meat melt in her mouth.

'I'll tell your father you're still thinking about it,' her mum replies. 'Two knickerbocker glories please,' she tells the loitering waiter, shutting down the conversation before Tania has a chance to respond.

'Why is this house such a shit-tip?' Tania mutters to herself, as she steps over the pile of shoes in the entrance to the house, noticing how seconds before Falcon slung his wellies into the discarded pile just like his father does.

Her house might not be a seven-bedroom mansion, but that doesn't mean they have to live like tramps.

'RIGHT, FALCON,' she shouts after her son. 'This afternoon's activity is maths. We are going to subtract all the mess in the house and put it in the right place. OK?'

Falcon emerges from his room, iPad in hand and rubbing his eyes, yawning.

'Can't I just watch this, Mummy?'

'Nope.' She swipes it from his hand. 'We are going to make our house sparkle. OK?'

Spiral always knows when Tania has been to see her mum, as he returns to a spotless house. Although Tania ignores Francesca's throwaway comments on the lifestyle she has chosen, some of them penetrate through. The assumption that she lives in some shitty old hovel cuts deep. And it isn't helped by the fact that the flat does, in fact, currently resemble a shitty old hovel.

'Do I have to?' Falcon groans, sounding like Kevin the teenager with his unusually deep voice.

'Yep. And if you put away all your toys so I can see the floor in your room, we can watch a film before Daddy comes home. Deal?' Falcon high-fives her raised hand and retreats to his room.

Tania is on her hands and knees, scrubbing at a particularly stubborn blueberry stain on the kitchen lino, when Falcon walks back in carrying an old shoe box.

'What's this, Mummy?' he asks, walking straight over the just washed section of floor.

'Wow. Where did you find that?' she takes the Dolcis shoebox from Falcon. It is inches thick in dust.

'It was under my bed at the back, Mummy. Is it treasure?' He humphs down next to her, small sticky hands trying to clumsily wedge it open.

'Yes, it is a kind of treasure I guess. Be careful.' She rolls the dust into a cloudy sheet, and then removes the lid. A puff of dust escapes.

She sits with her back resting against the cupboard, Falcon leaning against her and the box on her knee. Inside she sees a letter to herself, a pressed flower, a dreadlock, a tape with 'songs for a rainy day' written in permanent marker pen on it, and a stack of photos.

It's a time capsule she'd made for her future self on her seventeenth birthday when she was full of optimism and energy for the future. She had completely forgotten it was here.

When she made it, she had only just met Spiral and was carefree and in love with the idea of being anti-establishment, in a way that only a girl who grew up in wealth and had never really wanted for anything could be. The box predated the acrimonious rows she was to have with her parents about her relationship with Spiral, and the subsequent nail in the coffin when her dad suggested she was just seeing him to embarrass them, which resulted in her packing a bag and moving out of her childhood home and into Spiral's squat, where she changed her name to Tania. The ultimate act of defiance, shedding herself of the last remaining thing they could take credit for – her name. She had always liked the name Tania and had adopted it during every game of 'grown-ups' as a child, so it had been the most natural leap of faith to then change it by deed poll as a permanent fixture. Once she started introducing herself like that, Arabella started to fade away, like the memory of someone you once knew.

Her hand hovers over the stack of photographs, but something holds her back.

'What does that do?' Falcon reaches into the box for the cassette, but Tania swiftly puts the lid back on again. She clutches it to her chest, catching herself off guard with the unexplained wave of sadness that washes over her.

She pulls Falcon in close, buries her nose in his thick hair and breathes deeply.

'Too tight, Mummy,' he wriggles free. 'Shall I put it back?'

'Yes. Good idea, clever boy.' She passes the box to him, and rests her head in her hands, pressing firmly on her temples.

Tania knows she made the right choice when she left her parents' house, but that doesn't mean she needs to look at a reminder of what she left behind.

Chapter Nine

'Knock, knock,' I push open the door that's been left on the latch and retrieve the door key that is still hanging in the lock.

'Come in!' a voice calls from the heart of the house.

'Go on then.' I push Sophie and Lucy through the door. Walking into Helen's house is like stepping into a vision of my future dream home. The honey-coloured wooden floors. The gleaming white walls that remain white, no tide of grubby handprints at waist height. A bespoke large lampshade illuminates the corridor. I once made the mistake of asking if it was from IKEA. Helen had mumbled something about it being a local artist, whose name I memorised and later googled. Her work doesn't come cheaper than two grand per piece. That's how much it cost to furnish our whole front room including paint and the carpet.

'Just go inside,' I command Sophie, as she tries to wedge herself in the doorway.

'I want to go home,' she grumbles, chewing on the ear of her bunny and repeatedly kicking the wall of the house.

'You go first then Lucy, and Sophie will follow,' I plead.

'OK.' Lucy strides in, takes her shoes off and scurries up the stairs of a house she knows so well, to find her friend Polly.

I pick up Sophie like a large human-shaped rugby ball and walk through to the kitchen.

'You left your keys in the door.' I place them on the island worktop.

'God, I keep doing that. I'm getting as bad as Mum for forgetting shit. Thank you,' Helen leans in and kisses my cheek, then kisses the top of Sophie's head. 'Tea or coffee?' she asks, before scoffing, 'Joke!' And opens the fridge to retrieve a bottle of Sauvignon Blanc.

'Why don't you go upstairs with the other girls?' I ask Sophie, as I put her down.

'Urghhh, OK,' she huffs through gritted baby teeth and stomps out of the room.

'I have no idea why she's so angry all the time.' I pull out one of the dining-room chairs, sit down and accept the large glass Helen is offering me. I look around at the sparkling kitchen. 'Has Chris come home yet?'

'Nope. That's why it's so clean. Cheers!' We chink glasses as the doorbell chimes.

Helen makes her way to the front of the house and I hear Tania's voice. 'Why do you live so bloody far away?' she puffs.

'Can I take anything?' Helen asks.

'No. Apart from him. Get in, Falcon. Just use your legs, that's what they're there for!' she barks at her son.

There is a patter of loud footsteps on wooden floor, followed by muffled carpet stomps as Falcon runs upstairs to join the other children.

'God, I'm knackered,' Tania announces as she throws down armfuls of tote bags full of roll mats on the kitchen floor.

'What's all that?' I ask.

'Yoga mats. I'd forgotten the community hall is being painted tomorrow and so we need to take everything out otherwise they "can't be responsible for it",' she says, making inverted commas with her fingers. 'They're yoga mats, not flipping Banksys, I told them. Can't they just put them in a cupboard somewhere? Cheers.' She takes the glass from Helen and takes a large gulp. 'Happy Friday!'

'Happy Friday!' Helen and I chorus.

We have been meeting for wine club on and off on Fridays since the children were about a year old, and it has become a lifeline for the three of us. It doesn't happen every week since life has become more complicated as we juggle work and parenting, but whenever possible, we all get together after the children have finished at their different schools, or home-schooling in Tania's case. (Although Tania has suggested she is normally free from about 1 p.m. onwards if we wanted to push back wine club to an early afternoon slot.)

'For you.' Helen ceremoniously presents a plate heaving with artisan sausage rolls.

'You could have just got Greggs,' Tania thanks her with delight. She takes a large bite of one, closing her eyes with enjoyment as she sprinkles pastry flakes all over the table and her chest.

'Enjoy,' Helen responds as she refills our glasses with a satisfying glug, glug, glug.

Every wine club, Tania and I bring a bottle of whatever is on offer in Tesco, and every time we end up taking it home again, as Helen plies us with the most delicious wine that gives you a warm glow instead of an acid hangover. We had tried in the early days to rotate who hosted, but it soon became clear that neither my nor Tania's house was anywhere near as relaxing as Helen's.

'So, how's everyone been?' Helen asks as she decants some handcrafted crisps into a large bowl and places them down with a ramekin of locally made hummus.

'My mum's trying to railroad us into going to her house

66

for Christmas, and Falcon learnt "fuck" from the green-grocer, but other than that everything's fine.' Tania brushes the crumbs off her chest onto the floor and grabs a handful of posh crisps.

'How's the homeschooling going?' Helen asks, lowering herself into the chair next to her.

'Yep,' Tania responds as she takes another huge bite of the sausage roll. 'It's going. I think that's about as much as I can say for the time being.'

'I think you're incredible,' Helen sighs. 'You must have such, I don't know—'

'Patience?' I suggest. 'I don't think I'd keep my cool all day with the girls, and then be nice to them in the evening. I think we'd drive each other fucking mental.'

'Patience of an absolute saint, this one,' Tania points to herself, smiling weakly. 'And what about you two? What have you been doing?'

'Nick saw my tits, and then we were called into the nursery because Soph had been showing her fanny to other kids,' I reply glumly.

'What?' Tania scoffs.

'I know, right? They're kids. It's ridiculous,' I take another gulp, deciding not to tell them that it was almost definitely true and I may have got a member of the nursery staff disciplined and a little boy in big trouble as a consequence.

'And your tits? When did you show them to Nick?' Tania asks casually, spraying more crumbs all over the table.

'He FaceTimed me when I was doing some "positive reinforcement" in front of the mirror,' I crunch loudly on a hummus-covered crisp.

'Positive what?' Helen asks, refilling our glasses.

'Positive reinforcement. Re-establishing a better relationship with your mind and body. Good work, Em, I do it every morning. I look at myself naked and say, "You are beautiful. You are strong. You are capable of anything." You should try it, Hels, it's a great start to the day. Mind if I finish the last one?' she points to the sausage roll.

'Help yourself. They're for you,' Helen answers.

'I just didn't think I'd be thirty-seven and the most action I'm getting is flashing my tits at my ex-husband by accident. And to add insult to injury, he looked mortified.'

'He's a fool, Em. I'd happily look at your tits all day,' Helen reassures me. 'Talking of exposing yourself, what do you think of *this*!' She places a parcel down on the kitchen table.

Tania wipes her hands on her fisherman trousers and asks, 'What is it?'

'Open it,' Helen urges, gathering sausage roll crumbs from the table into her hand and shaking them off in the butler sink.

Tania thrusts her hand into the package and draws out a bright pink ball of lace. She shakes it out to reveal what can only be described as a skimpy see-through swimsuit with no bum.

'What the bloody hell is that?' I ask.

'Chris's present for me. Nice, isn't it?' she jokes.

'Wow,' Tania and I reply in unison.

'It's way too small and gives me thrush just thinking about it. I can't return it either, as the sanitation strip has fallen off and Agent Provocateur don't want to sell products that have had someone else's vagina all over them. Is it any use to either of you?'

'Well, it's not going to be any use to me, is it?' I take a large swig of wine. 'I haven't had sex for over a year now, and it's unlikely that's going to change anytime soon. Also, what size is it? It looks titchy.'

'You need to get back out there,' Tania tells me. 'Spiral has a single friend. I could set you up with him?'

'I'm not ready for any of that, not even close,' I reply.

'Well, when you are, I'd be happy to set you up.' Tania squeezes my arm.

'What's he called then, out of curiosity?' I enquire. Spiral has very few friends who go by a conventional name.

'His real name, or the name he's known by?' She is looking at the label as she speaks. 'Fuck me, Hels. This cost one hundred and eighty quid.'

'I know. It's ridiculous, isn't it?' she sighs.

'I'll have it if you really don't want it?' Tania says.

'It's all yours,' Helen responds.

'He's called Stefan,' Tania tells me.

'As in Dennis?' I ask.

'Yep. The original Paul Robinson,' she replies.

'Stefan. That's not *too* bad,' I nod.

'But everyone knows him as Growler,' she adds under her breath.

'Why, dare I ask?'

'Well there are two stories. The clean version is that it's because he's really good with dogs. He's never met a dog he doesn't get on with, however wild they were,' she replies.

'And the other story?' Helen asks, sitting down between us both again.

'Is that he's really good at going down on women,' she explains, muffling her voice into her glass.

'That might be OK?' Helen looks at me encouragingly.

'Urgh,' I reply. 'Absolutely not. I am NOT having my first date after Nick with a guy whose name means cunnilingus. No way. Not a chance. Thanks though, Tania.'

'Just a suggestion,' she says, as she shoves the teddy

outfit into one of her yoga mat bags. 'Do you know if *he's* seeing anyone?'

'Who?'

'Nick, obviously,' Tania says, finishing off her third sausage roll with a huge bite.

The question knocks me off guard. 'I wouldn't have thought so,' I say defensively. 'Why would he?'

'Because he's single?' Tania suggests through a mouthful. 'In my opinion, men don't stay single for long at our age. They can't cope on their own.'

'Well, he's not exactly single, is he? He's still married. To me. We're separated, yes. But this is more of an extended cooling-off period, I guess. To see if there is any way back, so . . .' I let the sentence drift away.

'That doesn't mean *you* can't start to have a provisional look around. Just future-proofing yourself in case,' Helen says.

'I don't know,' I reply, unconvinced.

'All I'm saying is, if it turns out it's over for good, then there's no harm in thinking about moving on. I'm not saying get yourself a new boyfriend or anything. But as you said, you haven't had sex in over a year. That's a basic human right, Em,' Helen replies.

'But how do you know it's *actually* over? Officially? How does anyone know that for sure?' I ask, not sure I want either of them to answer.

Helen's mobile shrills from the charger plugged into the wall, she looks at the screen and says, 'Sorry, I've got to take this,' and strolls out the room.

Chapter Ten

'Hello, Helen speaking,' she answers politely, in case it might be a potential client. She has had some flyers printed off, advertising her mobile hairdressing business, which have gone out in book bags at Polly's school, a good way to connect with some of the mothers, she thought. But, as yet, there has been no response to them. Most of the mothers have time and money to burn, so she imagines that they already have long-standing relationships with eye-wateringly expensive stylists, but she thought it was worth a try none-the-less.

'Where are you?' a voice barks.

'Sorry, who is this?' Helen looks at the screen. Number withheld.

'It's Janet, who do you think it is?' her mum replies irritably.

'Why have you withheld your number?' Helen asks her.

'What? I don't understand the question. Why have I what?' she snaps.

'I didn't realise it was you. Your number didn't come up,' Helen replies.

'Oh, Liam did something to the phone so that it works abroad. I don't know what he did, probably ripping me off, no doubt.'

'Where are you?' Helen asks. She can hear noise in the background, a low-level bustle and muffled Tannoy announcements.

'I asked *you* that, Helen. This isn't a great start, to be honest. I would like to say I'm surprised but I'm not. This is quite typical of you. No, I'm *still* waiting for someone, thank you very much,' she snaps at someone at her end.

'Sorry, Mum. I'm completely lost, where are you right this moment?'

'Right this moment,' she imitates, 'I am stood in front of Caffè Nero getting in everyone's way, by the sounds of things. I have already had two coffees, neither of which were very nice, and a pain au chocolat which had no chocolate and the pain was stale and dry.'

'Which Caffè Nero, Mum?' Helen pushes.

'What do you mean, which Caffè Nero? How many are there here? It's the big one opposite Starbucks. Though why you'd build two coffee shops opposite each other is completely beyond me. The right hand doesn't talk to the left when it comes to retail planning in my opinion, not that anyone listens to me,' Janet sighs crossly. 'Next to the M&S Foodhall. There can surely only be one of those. Is that enough information for you, Helen? It's exhausting having a conversation with you sometimes. Now, how long will you be? I would very much like to have a glass of wine and a sit down on something other than a hard plastic chair that's screwed to the floor, and I refuse to part with any more money here if it can be at all helped.'

'Where though, Mum,' Helen persists. 'Where in the world actually are you right this minute? Where are you *right* now? *Right* this moment? Because you don't sound like you're at home. You don't sound like you're in Spain. And if you're not in Spain, where are you?' Helen wipes the beads of perspiration from her forehead on the sleeve of her cashmere jumper, leaving it itchy as the soft fluff sticks to her.

'GATWICK, HELEN.' She's raising her voice now, and

Helen has to hold the handset away from her ear. She hears her mum wheeze, her breath rattling in her chest, before continuing. 'I'm in Gatwick airport. Where else? I'm waiting for you, silly girl. And am, frankly, getting increasingly frustrated by these questions.'

'Why are you in Gatwick airport, Mum?' Her throat tightens and her eyes dart around the front room, fruitlessly searching for a glass of water. She tries to swallow but can't get past the huge ball of dread that's starting to grip her oesophagus.

'Is this some kind of joke, Helen? Is Jeremy Beadle going to leap out in a minute? Why am I in Gatwick airport?' she mutters angrily to herself. 'To see you, of course,' she announces, self-satisfied. 'Like we agreed. Although, I'm starting to strongly question why I agreed to it at all now, as it seems, you have completely forgotten about me. DO YOU HEAR THAT?' Her mum shouts again, this time away from the phone. 'MY DAUGHTER HAS FORGOTTEN ABOUT ME!'

'MUM,' Helen meets her voice in volume to attract her attention, 'Mum,' she repeats. 'It's fantastic that you've come to see us, but when did you think this arrangement was made?'

'We spoke about it a couple of days ago, remember? You were very insistent. I thought something must have been wrong the way you were talking. I was most worried and had Liam help me to book the flight. But, as it transpires, I shouldn't have bothered. Let down by my daughter, again. AGAIN,' she shouts. 'I might as well just jump back on a flight to Costa Del Sol. Would *that* make you happy?'

Helen's head spins as she tries to make sense of everything her mum is saying. 'Look. Stay put, Mum. I'll jump in the car and can be with you in about an hour. Just sit tight, OK?'

'Well, it looks like I'll have to, doesn't it? Looks like I'll have to spend a fortune on a glass of sub-standard chardonnay, Helen.' And with that, Janet ends the call.

Helen runs her hands through her hair and slowly breathes in through her nose and out through her mouth, but it catches and quivers with anxiety.

There wasn't a prearrangement. This wasn't a misunderstanding or crossed wires. Something is very wrong.

Chapter Eleven

'I see you haven't put your name down to volunteer for the trip to the toy museum, Mrs Jones?' Mrs Elwood corners me as she counts Lucy, who is late again, into the classroom with a firm pat on the head. She stares, unblinking, as I search for a convincing reason as to why I can't go.

The truth is, Nick is having the girls overnight and the trip clashes with the only slot Helen could book me in for a colour and cut. I haven't had a haircut since we split up and I look like a cross between Anita Dobson and Michael Bolton. I know this is selfish, but right now I need to look a little less like I've just separated from my husband and a little more like I'm in control. I think that would make me a far better person and mother, all round.

'We're several volunteers short and, as you know, the school relies on the support of parents and carers . . .'

'Yes, yes. You're absolutely right, Mrs Elwood. I'm not sure of my work schedule that week but I'll—'

Mrs Elwood raises one eyebrow, challenging me to finish the sentence.

'I'll see what I can do.' I finish.

'Great. Well I'll put you down as a strong maybe. Hello, Angela! And hello little Evie. In you pop,' she says encouragingly, her tone warm and friendly as she guides the child gently into the classroom with the flat of her hand.

'Mrs Elwood,' Angela says breathlessly, as though she's

been running, 'I've been meaning to send my apologies for the museum trip. I had really hoped to volunteer but I have a clash with a lunch for Simon's work. I'm so sorry—'

'Please don't apologise, Angela. Simon already commits so much of his time to the school, and I think we have more than enough volunteers now. Mrs Jones has only just put her name down.' Mrs Elwood gestures towards me without making eye contact.

Angela smiles at me. 'Wonderful. Thank you both.' She looks so positively healthy, with her shiny hair, bag-free eyes and dewy glow. Like someone who has spent a lot of money, time and cosmetics to look like she's just left the house make-up free. She turns to leave and Mrs Elwood focuses her attention back on me.

'They'll lock the gates if you don't get a wriggle on.' She nods to dismiss me, turns on her heels and shuts the classroom door behind her. I can hear her clapping out a rhythm to the class for their attention, and they clap the same rhythm back to her in response. I have a quick peek through the window and see Lucy sitting cross-legged in her school uniform, clapping with the rest of the pupils. She looks grown-up and tiny, all wrapped up in the same person. How is that possible?

She catches my eye and waves enthusiastically. I wave back, blowing her a kiss as Mrs Elwood marches over and pulls down the blind.

I wrap my coat around me to guard against the late autumn chill and make my way out of the playground, just as the security guard is about to bolt the main gate.

'Just made it. Another minute and you'd be on the pay-roll,' he jokes and I wonder how many times he's reeled off this gag to latecomers.

'Oh, that would be a disaster. What would I be able to

teach a load of children?' I respond self-pityingly, and suddenly gulp back a tidal wave of tears.

Seeing that I'm on the verge of a breakdown, the security guard ushers me through and locks the gate with a mumbled, 'Thanks for your cooperation,' before quickly shuffling off.

I lean on the railings outside, and let the tears spill down my cheeks, hot against my cold face. I feel like I'm in one of those dreadfully clichéd dreams, where I'm running for something that is never quite in reach. As soon as I think I'm on top of one thing, it turns out there are another five things that have crept up on me that I've forgotten about. But while I'm barking orders at the girls to brush their teeth as I desperately try to locate the latest form in a book bag about whether it's dress as an alien or a historical figure day, the children are quietly growing up.

Lucy already denies anything happens at school. Her standard response to, 'What did you do today?' is 'Nothing' or 'Can't remember.' I thought I had at least another five years of her telling me everything, before she started to totally shut down. And Sophie's no different. Taking the lead from her big sister, she ignores my invitations to tell me about her day, only occasionally complaining about how bad the nursery snacks are. She's three going on five going on ten. And next year I lose her to school as well.

This just isn't how I thought parenting would be. I imagined all four of us on long car journeys. The boot so over-packed you can't see out the back window, as we drive through France to spend the long summer holidays camping in Bordeaux; Nick and I drinking local red wine out of plastic beakers outside the tent in the evening, talking in loud whispers so as not to wake the sleeping girls, curled up under canvas, feet away.

I thought Nick and I would have carved out a bit of time

for ourselves by this point. We always said, before Lucy came along, that we'd never let children change us or alter our relationship in any way. That they'd have to fit in with us, not the other way around. That our early years of travelling together would translate into family adventures – the same beautiful countries, just better planned trips and hotels with air conditioning.

Oh, how naive we were. Once Lucy, then Sophie came along, we readjusted our expectations, but we didn't give them up, not yet. We became more realistic, but still held true to the idea that we'd make time for us soon. That by the time Lucy was at school, we would be going out by ourselves at least once a fortnight. At least. That things would get easier as the girls got older.

But our deadline for when things would improve – when we'd start hanging out more, having more sex, listening to each other more, just kept getting pushed back. Nick's work became increasingly more demanding. The pressure I put on myself to make my business work became all encompassing. The plan to put each other first, to enjoy each other again, kept getting demoted further down the list of things to do.

Until one day it just dropped off the list. Entirely.

Nick hated going to the couples' counselling sessions. I know he did. But we had to try something. Anything. I wasn't prepared to be another statistic. But I now wonder whether it did more harm than good. There is something so painfully exposing about an outsider holding a massive fuck-off mirror to your life. I do sometimes think we might have been better off not knowing. Things might have eventually worked themselves out. And then Nick need never have told about me the trouble he'd got us into.

I wipe my nose on the back of my sleeve as I make my way back to the house. It's nine thirty. I've been lost in my own thoughts for nearly half an hour outside the school. I hope the angry receptionist didn't see me or I'll undoubtedly end up on some sort of 'parent to watch' list.

As I push the key in the door, my phone beeps. It's a text from the bank.

YOU ARE NOW USING AN UNARRANGED OVERDRAFT. TO AVOID INTEREST YOUR ACCOUNT MUST BE CREDITED BY 23.45 TODAY

I check the number. It's for an account we opened for our wedding years ago. I thought we'd closed it once we'd spent all the money. I'm pretty sure I cut up the card so how could it . . .

'Oh shit. No.' A pain starts to grip my chest and I rub it with the flat of my hand.

Please Nick. Not now. I can't do this again.

Chapter Twelve

FOUR WEEKS BEFORE NICK MOVED OUT

'I often find it helps if you both describe why you think you're here today. Why don't we try that? Emily. Could we start with you?'

The counsellor speaks in a calm, soothing voice. Judy can't be much older than us both, but has a far more mature presence about her. She is wearing neutral-coloured clothing, beige trousers and a cream blouse, with a splash of colour from her statement oversized red button earrings. She's saying: I'm a serious person, you can trust me, I'm a professional. But at the same time, *hello!* Yes, I like to let my hair down now and then. You can't shock me. I've smoked a spliff back in the day at a university party. I might even have had sex on a second date.

'What. Right now?' I get a rush of panic, similar to when you're in a group seminar with the assumption that you'll just be listening to someone speaking for three hours, when it's suddenly announced, 'Can we now split up into pairs for this practical activity?'

Judy relaxes back into her leather chair and interlocks her fingers. 'Yes. Now. If you could.'

I look over at Nick, pen poised. He's brought a pad to jot notes in, like it's practise for a bloody driving-theory test.

Where to start. Why *am* I here? It seems like such a

simple question but so very complicated and messy at the same time. That's probably why Judy charges sixty-five quid an hour.

'All we do is argue,' I eventually tell her.

'What is the cause of these arguments?' Judy asks with what will soon become her signature empathetic head tilt.

Nick's nervously tapping the end of his pen loudly on the closed pad. I stare at it until it slows, then stops.

'I organise everything in the home and feel like the only thing I get in response is low-level criticism,' I say weakly.

Nick tuts, and I try to block him out, focusing on Judy instead, and instinctively tilt my head to match hers until I realise what I'm doing and instead twist my wedding band around self-consciously.

'Please. Continue,' she encourages.

'Well, I guess, it was one thing when I was on maternity leave with Lucy and then Sophie, when I had a bit more time, maybe. But I'm trying to set up a business now, as well as do everything in the house. It just feels . . .' I close my eyes momentarily while seeking the right word. 'Unfair.' I massage the stress ache in the back of my neck. 'But it would be OK, well, manageable, if Nick and I could get on. But we can't. So when I'm doing everything for everyone, and we don't even have a nice word to say to each other at the end of the day, then it just seems a bit,' I glance briefly at Nick, who is shaking his head slowly, 'pointless.'

'Can I say something?' Nick butts in. He's raised his hand like in school.

'Please do,' Judy replies.

He springs to life, appalled. 'I do my bit. I help around the house. And I do all the washing-up. It's teamwork.' He shrugs conclusively.

'It's not teamwork. Nick washes up as he has an aversion

to the dishwasher. It's not helpful; it's annoying. I don't understand why he can't just load and unload the dishwasher like a normal person. I don't think he's emptied it once in the three years we've had it.'

'That's because it's a breeding ground for bacteria,' Nick announces, like it's an actual fact, instead of his misguided opinion.

'It's not a breeding ground for fucking bacteria, Nick. Why would Currys sell a breeding ground for bacteria for two hundred quid? That just doesn't make business sense.'

'I'd just read somewhere—'

'He hadn't read it somewhere, Judy. His mum will have told him, I guarantee it,' I'm pointing at him now accusatorily.

'Why do you find it so hard to believe that sometimes my mum might be right?'

'I don't. I just find it hugely irritating that you use her like Wikipedia. She might sometimes be right, but you don't have to consult her about *everything*.' I can hear my voice getting louder. How loud does it have to get for any of it to be heard by Nick?

'You can't criticise me for having a good relationship with my mum. That's contravening—' he opens his pad again and scans down his notes, '—the rule about name-calling, isn't it Judy?'

'Seriously?' I ask, then catch Nick's response and add, 'and then he does that, Judy.' I point at him. 'He rolls his eyes, completely trivialises everything I say with a look. Like I'm nagging.'

'And how does that make you feel, Emily?'

'Like I've just become noise. Background noise. I can't imagine him ever speaking to anyone the way he speaks to me. And he's meant to love me!' I throw my arms up in despair.

'Now you're just being melodramatic, Emily,' he says, using his 'calm down, kids' voice.

'I'M NOT BEING FUCKING MELODRAMATIC!' I scream as tears of frustration spill down my cheeks.

'OK,' Judy interjects. 'I think this would be a good time to have a quick comfort break. Please help yourself to water or use the facilities.' She nods towards the door and I automatically stand to use the loo like an obedient child, even though I'm not sure I need it.

As I sit down on the cold porcelain toilet seat I try to compose myself. I don't want to spend an hour absolutely furious with Nick. We can do that at home for free. Deep breath. I flush the loo, wash my hands. Consider stealing the posh Molton Brown hand moisturiser, think better of it, then return to Judy's room.

'Come in, Emily.' Judy signals to the chair. 'Nick was just telling me about his promotion. Very interesting. Thank you for sharing, Nick.'

I smile weakly at her. I've never been completely sure of what he did before, so I'm not sure at all what he's been promoted to, other than it taking up most of his waking hours. It's something to do with recruitment but what, I couldn't tell you, so I could have equally benefitted from being in on that discussion.

'OK, so shall we pick up the conversation with you, Nick? You've told me a bit about what you do day-to-day and the obvious challenges that a role like that entails.' WHAT ARE THEY? WHAT DID HE JUST TELL YOU JUDY?? 'But could you tell me what you'd like to get out of these sessions?'

Nick is stroking his patchy beard thoughtfully. He's never been particularly hirsute, which was one of the things I initially found sexy about him, but the flipside is that his attempts to grow facial hair are totally in vain.

'It's a tricky one, Judy, as coming here was Em's idea, not mine. I completely respect what you do, your profession I mean. Completely. I just have never really thought of myself as someone who needed "counselling".'

'Well, there are many reasons to pursue an external body who's impartial to your situation,' Judy offers.

'Yep. I get it.' He fills his cheeks with air and exhales slowly and loudly. 'So. Me. What do I want to get out of these sessions?' His eyes dart to the clock, ten minutes left. He's stalling. He gets out the pad again and painstakingly flicks through his notes, page by page.

'Are there perhaps challenges you may be experiencing, either independently or as a couple?' she suggests.

'Independently or as a couple,' he repeats, adopting a Paul Daniels-esque high-pitched voice.

'Come on, Nick,' I hiss. 'At least try.'

He turns to me, and a look flashes across his face that I don't recognise. It's cold. Confrontational. 'To be honest, I know why we're here, Judy. I'm not some kind of pre-historic man-child. Em and I argue. A lot. I *do* know that. I agreed to come here to see if we can find ways to not fight so much, but quite frankly,' and he flicks through his notes again before putting them in the inside pocket of his jacket, which I notice for the first time he hasn't actually taken off since we arrived, 'I can't see what good this is going to do. Other than bankrupting us,' he shrugs nonchalantly.

And just like that, he shuts down. He sits there defiantly, challenging Judy to ask again, but she doesn't. And we all remain silent for the next few minutes until Judy announces the end of the session.

*

'Well, that went as expected,' Nick comments as we push open the imposing front door.

'You were embarrassing, Nick,' I mumble irritably.

'What? Cos I called her out?' he snaps. 'You know what Em, counsellors are ninety per cent guesswork and ten per cent charlatan.'

'Who told you that? Cathleen?' I mutter.

'Oh, that's right. Bring it back to Mum. You're so predictable. Look, can't we just agree to disagree on this one? It just seems like a waste of money and half a day's leave,' he says.

'But that's the whole reason we're here.' I throw my arms in the air in desperation. 'Because we disagree. On everything. Please, Nick,' I implore. 'Please, can you just *try* to give it a go?'

'Look,' he finally replies. 'This isn't my thing.'

'Nick, it's neither of our things. Who's "thing" is relationship counselling anyway?'

The corners of Nick's mouth crease into a slight smile and I see a splinter of light. He rubs his eye sockets with the palms of his hands like a child and then says, 'OK. If it is *really* that important to you—'

'It *really* is, Nick,' I say.

He exhales slowly before nodding, 'OK. Yes. OK then. I will give it another go—'

'But properly next time,' I insist. 'No more being all know-it-ally.'

'I don't think I was but, fine,' he agrees quietly.

'Thank you.'

As we continue to walk towards the bus stop, he looks at his watch.

'Right, I'm going to catch the second half of the Albion game in The Gladstone. You OK to pick up the girls?' he asks, grinning. 'Maybe this counselling might work after all!'

'Yep,' I reply through gritted teeth.

I think it is going to take more than the odd counselling session to get us back on track.

Chapter Thirteen

'FOR THE MILLIONTH TIME, CAN YOU JUST PUT YOUR BLOODY SHOES ON, FALCON!' Tania screams down the corridor of the two-bed flat. She steps over the piles of clean washing that haven't yet made it into drawers and pushes open his bedroom door.

Falcon is sat on the floor wearing only his pants. Littered around him are open jars and several empty raisin and oat-cake packets. He freezes, oatcake mid-air as a large glob of honey drips from it and lands on the wooden floor with a satisfying splat.

'What are you doing? Seriously, Falcon, what is this?' Tania can feel the stress heat rising, her head feels hot and prickly as she concentrates on her yoga breathing to not lose her shit with him for the umpteenth consecutive day.

'I'm learning,' Falcon replies, before pushing the entire oatcake into his mouth in one go.

'About what, exactly?' She gathers up the empty packets, and uses a dirty sock to mop up the worst of the honey.

'About the body, like Debbie taught us last week,' he wipes a streak of honey from his bare chest with a finger and then licks each one individually with a smack.

It takes Tania a beat to realise that Debbie is the library storyteller. 'And what did she teach you?'

'Remember the book we read about how food goes in through your mouth and then the good bits are used for energy and the bits we don't need come out as poo? Well, I'm eating to use the good bits, then I am going to wait to go for a poo.' He nods confidently before pointing at his little pot-bellied stomach and concluding, 'See?'

'Jesus,' Tania mutters. 'Go and wash your hands and tummy in the bathroom and then come back and get changed. We're trying a new group today and I don't want you to be the scruffiest boy there. NOW!' she barks as Falcon starts to lavishly coat another oatcake with honey.

He pushes himself to standing, cascading crumbs everywhere and huffs out the room. Tania cannot work out whether she has just been played by her only son, but suspects she probably has. She hadn't realised how clever he was at getting one over on her until she started spending such extended periods of time with him.

She leans against his bed and polishes off the rest of the snacks, wondering what today might bring. They are meeting a well-established group of homeschoolers she'd contacted via Facebook. She had requested to join the private Facebook group during the summer, but has only just been accepted into it last week, almost four months later. Tania hopes this is because they are so busy with wholesome pursuits with their children that they don't get time to administer the online group, and not, as Tania suspects, that they are a tight-knit clique who don't want her to join in with their activities.

'Mummy, come in here!' Falcon shouts from down the corridor. 'I'm in the bathroom, come quickly!'

Perhaps the only good thing about living in a poorly built stud-walled new build is the acoustics are so good that you never need to be in the same room to hold a conversation, voices just penetrate straight through. Tania brushes her hands off into the wastepaper bin and heads to the bathroom.

'See!' Falcon is pointing in the toilet. As she opens the door she's hit by the overwhelming pungent smell of shit. How is it that a five-year-old can produce such rancid smells? They're like the kind of poos you produce after a weekend at a festival when you've been holding it in for seventy-two hours as you can't face queuing for the Portaloos.

Tania holds her nose. 'Falcon, can you flush the toilet and come out?'

'But look, Mummy.' He beams proudly. 'I produced the waste from the oatcakes. Just look. Pleeeease,' he whines.

Tania holds her nose and leans over the bowl. There it is, a massive turd, curling out of the water.

'Great,' Tania's eyes water as she flushes the chain. 'Good project, Falcon. Now wash your hands and get dressed. We're going to be late.'

As she flops back onto the sofa Tania allows herself a moment of reflection. She is going to be forty just after Christmas. Forty. It feels like a milestone, but not one she is prepared for in any way.

She's not sure what she'd expected she'd be doing by now, but this doesn't feel like her *This is Your Life* moment, having just observed a shit as an educational activity.

If Michael Aspel appeared with his famous red book, what would it contain?

'Ready!' Falcon announces. He's bursting out of a Spider-Man costume that's two years too young for him.

'Put your coat on, then. It's on the floor in the corridor,' Tania tells him, too tired to argue.

'You go in first,' Tania quietly instructs Falcon as she pushes him towards the entrance of the community centre main hall. He has locked his knees and is sliding towards the door, bringing with him the rag rug underfoot.

'I don't want to. Can't we just go and learn with Debbie?' he pleads loudly, as a woman opens the large double doors to the hall.

She smiles warmly and openly and asks, 'Could you possibly be Falcon?' She squats down so she is looking at him on his level. 'What a wonderful costume you have on. We have been waiting for a Spider-Man to help us solve a problem. Do you think you could help?' She offers him her hand, which he willingly accepts.

'I'm Gill,' she explains to Tania, her knees clicking as she rises to stand. Tania wonders if she should mention she could easily correct that with some gentle stretching, but thinks better of it. 'I coordinate the group, but as you will find out, it is very much led by the children.'

'Tania,' she responds, jumping slightly as Gill squeezes her shoulder affectionately. 'Thank you for having us.' Gill and Falcon walk into the hall hand-in-hand, with a self-conscious Tania bringing up the rear.

'Everyone – this is Falcon and Tania. Falcon and Tania – everyone!' she announces, gesturing with her free arm to a room of about fifteen adults and the same if not more children of varying ages.

A chorus of 'Hellos', 'His' and 'Welcomes' follow.

'Come and take a seat, we're just making a collage about what can be found in the deep blue sea. Would you like to help?' Gill asks Falcon.

'Yes, please,' he grins, shaking off her hand and flopping down in front of a massive sheet of paper next to a willowy-looking girl, who offers him a Pritt Stick.

Tania isn't sure if she's meant to help Falcon or hang around the periphery. Some of the parents are getting stuck in, assisting their child with cutting or sticking, whereas others are assembling around the tea urn in the corner of the room. She retrieves her mobile from her pocket, the instinct to fill any child-free second with looking at pictures of people she doesn't know or yoga retreats she can't afford on Instagram taking over, when the flat of a hand presses into her back and someone says, 'He looks like he's settled in straight away if you fancy a cuppa?' The voice belongs to a woman who shares Gill's warm smile, and Tania kicks herself for assuming everyone would be smug and self-righteous.

'I'm Emma. My daughter is Shona, who looks like she is playing nicely with your son.'

The two children are leaning in together, tongues curled on lips in concentration, cutting shapes out of an old cereal box with adult scissors. Tania quashes her instincts to rush over and cut the shapes safely for him.

'A cup of tea would be lovely,' Tania smiles as she is led over to the tea table.

'Is this your first time at a group?' Emma asks her, dropping tea bags in two mugs and filling them with steaming water from the urn.

'Yes, we go to a few things at the main library, but I think I need something more structured, more, I don't know, fun,' Tania shrugs, accepting the mug gratefully.

'I completely know what you mean. I got to the point where I was thinking, what is Shona actually learning from me? What the fuck can I teach her? I can't even remember how to do long division, so how am I ever going to teach Shona anything meaningful?'

Tania visibly relaxes at Emma's swearing. Perhaps this isn't going to be so bad after all.

Falcon and Shona are whispering conspiratorially, and for the first time in months, Tania feels her shoulders dropping fractionally from below her ears. She rolls them out and back with a crack and allows herself a glimmer of a smile. Falcon bounds over, clutching a piece of cardboard, and collides with her knees, spilling her tea onto the floor, but this time, she doesn't shout, she squats down, clears it up with an old tissue from up her cardigan sleeve and, meeting his eye on the same level as Gill had earlier, asks him, 'What have you made?'

He proudly presents a roughly cut out circle with a web of lines drawn all over it. 'It's a sea horse,' he beams.

'It's lovely.' Tania brushes Falcon's cheek affectionately.

'And I've made a friend. Shona,' he points at her and Tania catches eyes with Emma and smiles. 'I've told her about the digestion system and eating and pooing and she's going to do it too and let me see hers.'

'Fantastic, maybe not while we're here though,' Tania says.

'OK,' and he turns and runs back to Shona.

Half an hour later, Gill claps a rhythm with her hands to which the children and adults respond. Emily had mentioned that Lucy's infant teacher did the same, and that the effect was hypnotic on the children. Tania had been sceptical after trying repeatedly to do the same on a one-on-one basis with Falcon at home, which commanded zero respect and just made her look like a demented seal pup, but now she watches as all the children calm and then stop what they're doing, all eyes on Gill. Like magic.

'If everyone can clear everything up that would be great, as the over-sixties Tai Chi group needs to use the space after us.' Gill's voice sounds soft even at volume. Tania sounds angry even when she's not these days, which doesn't help when she's doing the guided meditation at the end of her yoga sessions.

'Will you come back again?' Emma asks her as she takes her cup from her and adds it to the tray to be washed up.

'I think we might,' Tania responds.

'We normally meet up with the group a couple of times a week, so hope to catch you again. It was really lovely to meet you. Although I have this funny feeling that we've met before,' Emma adds.

'Me too,' Tania nods in agreement. 'I'm a yoga instructor so maybe you've come to one of my drop-in classes?'

'No, I'm not much of a yoga person. And we don't live round this way, so it's not that.' Emma shakes her head. 'It will come to me, probably in the middle of the night. Right,' she asserts. 'I'm just going to run these under the tap and then head back. We live closer to Surrey but there's nothing like this nearby, so we end up doing a two-hour round trip to come here every time. Ridiculous, isn't it? I should set up a group like this nearer me, but they're such a bunch of stuck-up wankers round our way I don't think I'd want to spend an afternoon with them.'

Shona appears and slots her hand into Emma's. 'OK, until next time,' Emma smiles.

'Absolutely. Lovely to meet you,' Tania smiles back. 'Thank you, Gill!' Tania bellows across the hall. Some of the other parents look over and give her a wave.

On the walk home, Tania quizzes Falcon about the session. 'So, what did you think?'

'It was OK,' he shrugs.

'Did you have fun?' she persists.

'Yes. Look!' His face lights up as he points at the large, shiny black Toyota Land Cruiser that's driving by. 'Hi Shona!' he shouts, jumping up and down excitedly and pointing at a child peering out of the open backseat window.

The car slows to a stop next to them, the front window buzzes down. Emma leans over to the passenger side and asks, 'Can I give you guys a lift?'

'No, no, we're not far from here, but thanks for the offer,' Tania responds.

'OK, have a good weekend!' Emma says as she closes the electric window.

As the car pulls off the grass verge, Tania notices the sticker in the back windscreen. Martin Davies Motors of Surrey. Under normal circumstances Tania wouldn't register these kinds of things. Why would you care where someone bought their car from? One posh car is very much the same as the next in Tania's opinion, especially as they are carless by choice and walk to most places.

Except Tania knows this sticker. It is the same one that is on the back of all three of her parents' cars. The showroom is just around the corner from her childhood family home.

Maybe Emma was right. Maybe they *do* already know each other.

Chapter Fourteen

'Can I get you a cup of tea?' Helen asks Janet. She has been staying with them for three nights now, with no explanation as to why she's here. Helen has tentatively approached the subject several times, conscious of Chris's imminent return in less than a week.

Janet arrived on a wave of criticisms when Helen picked her up from Gatwick.

'So is this it?' she'd asked, after Helen had heaved her oversized suitcase up the flight of stairs to the spare room. The bed wasn't made up as she wasn't expecting visitors, but other than that, it's a perfectly pleasant, airy room.

'Cup of tea?' Helen repeats to Janet, who is sitting at the kitchen table looking out the window at a bird pecking at the fat ball hanging from a tree.

'A chilled glass of Chardonnay if you have it, Helen,' she replies without taking her eyes off the bird. 'And I wasn't offered any breakfast earlier, apart from those frightfully sugary cereals, so a little morsel to accompany it would be good. Nothing complicated, just an omelette with some pancetta and a few shavings of Parmesan would suffice. A sprig of parsley if you have it, but only if it's fresh. I can't stand the dried stuff.'

'OK, Mum, I'll see what I can do,' Helen sighs.

She notices Janet absent-mindedly rubbing the old scar on her forearm with her thumb, and Helen instinctively traces her matching scar on her little finger. It's now so faint with time that it's virtually invisible, unless you knew it was there.

Polly bounds in, clings to Helen's leg and whispers loudly, 'Have you asked her yet, Mummy?'

'You can ask her yourself, if you want?' Helen tries to coax her out but she has a firm grim of her thigh.

'No, you do it.'

Polly hasn't said more than two words to Janet since she turned up, a clear reminder of how little her daughter knows her.

'Mum?' Janet looks up with a vacant expression, as if she had momentarily forgotten what she was doing. 'Polly wants to know if you still feed the cat that used to come and visit you on your balcony?'

Janet thinks for a moment before replying, 'No. Not that old thing. I think she died. Got run over by one of the local buses, I suspect. They drive like bloody lunatics, so I wouldn't be surprised.'

A little sob escapes from Polly. God, why can't she just, for once, sugar-coat the truth, if only for the sake of a five-year-old? A wave of fury starts to consume Helen, beginning as a hot prickle at the back of her neck, an unwelcome firm hand gripping slightly too tightly.

What does Janet even want? She's never shown any interest in Helen's family up until now, unless you count the odd birthday cheque for Polly, usually posted months after the event. She's never shown an interest in *anyone* other than herself, come to mention it. Since Polly's arrival, Helen has repeatedly tried to dig deep and remember a time when they were 'happy' together, as if looking for a blueprint of family life to build her own upon.

She has fleeting memories of being very young, younger

than Polly, when her dad was still around. She remembers her mum laughing then, her face kinder and less harsh, as they would walk along the promenade at Portsmouth Harbour for a day out. She remembers her hands fitting like gloves inside both her mum's and her dad's, the enthusiastic shouts of 'one, two, three, SWING!' And then those memories fade away, like the end of a Super8 film, crackling until the picture disappears to nothing. The next freeze frames are of her mum becoming an unbearable drinker; her dad being forced to leave. Janet throwing his clothes on the lawn, some stuffed in Costcutter bags, some simply dumped straight onto the grass. Her dad angrily and hastily gathering them all up and shoving them in the boot of the Metro and driving off with a screech of wheels. The phone calls from him that chimed with weekly regularity on the house phone in the corridor, then monthly, to not at all.

She'd begged and begged her mum to ask him to come back, to get him to phone her again, to give her an address so she could write to him, but her mother point blank refused.

As time went on, Helen learnt to tolerate her mother. She choreographed their movements so they coexisted without having to interact too much. Her mother made sure she never wanted for anything, or at least anything material, but Helen made a vow to herself that if she ever had a child of her own, she would surround that child with so much love that she would never know anything other than affection and warmth.

And now here her mum is. Uninvited in her house. Sitting at her kitchen table, face set in judgement, demanding table service even though she can barely boil an egg herself, casting a thin blanket of negativity and spite over the world that Helen has worked so hard to create. Helen swallows back the bile of hatred. She is better than this. To hate Janet is to let her win. Indifference is far easier to manage.

'It's OK, love. The cat was very old when we met her. Why don't we go and wash your hands then I'll make you a crumpet with jam.'

As Helen gently steers Polly out of the doorway, she decides to seize the moment and turns to her mum. 'I don't know how long you are planning to stay with us, but Chris will be back home next week.'

'Who?' She asks vacantly.

'Chris, Mum. My husband. Polly's dad.'

'Oh,' Janet remarks. 'Well, it will be nice to finally meet him.'

Helen freezes. What does she mean, 'meet him'? She's met him on countless occasions and been disparaging towards him more times than Helen can remember. She mocked him at their wedding for his 'casual suit and lack of tie'. She'd call him for advice whenever she has had an electrical problem in Spain as she was too frugal to inform the service desk because they would have charged her a call-out fee.

Helen stares at the woman who is picking strands of fluff from her mohair jumper and wonders, who is this stranger in my house?

Chapter Fifteen

I am ten minutes late to join the school trip. This isn't my fault. I'm sure Mrs Elwood told me to wait in the school reception area, which I diligently do. A queue of children are greeted with a tut from the receptionist as they sign into the late book.

'Where are all the other volunteers?' I ask her at 9.15 a.m.

'For what?' She doesn't even look up from her screen.

'For the school trip?'

'You should have headed straight to your child's class-room for a debrief,' she taps aggressively on her keyboard. 'The trips are normally scheduled to leave at ten past nine, so you may well have missed it.'

'Shit,' I mutter as I grab my handbag and peg it through the school hall towards the Otters class. Looking through the small classroom window I see all the children sitting cross-legged, straight-backed. Lucy is at the front, hanging off Mrs Elwood's every word. I push the door open with a creak, and thirty small heads shoot round to look at me.

'Mummy!' Lucy exclaims and gives me a wave.

'Eyes to the front, please!' Mrs Elwood commands. 'Don't be distracted by latecomers.'

'Sorry,' I mouth but she's not looking at me any more. Five other mums are dotted around the room and I try and catch the eye of any of them, but everyone is fixated on Mrs Elwood.

The teaching assistant hands me an orange high-vis jacket with 'VOLUNTEER' written in large letters across the back.

'Can you put this on, please?' she whispers.

I take in the classroom as I put on my safety jacket, transforming me from tardy mum to responsible adult. The room is a jigsaw of hexagonal tables with child-size primary-coloured chairs tucked around them. The word 'JOURNEY' is written in large bubble writing, and children's pictures are Blu-Tacked around it. The room has a distinctive smell of fusty lunchboxes, farts and sweaty trainers. It's exactly the same smell as my primary school and I breathe it in nostalgically.

'Otters. Can we all stand up, and in a moment we will find our grown-up.' I realise I have missed a key instruction.

'What are we meant to be doing?' I whisper to another high-vis volunteer.

Her eyes dart from Mrs Elwood to me nervously. 'We're going to take our groups onto the bus.'

'And how do we know who our groups are?'

'Mrs Elwood read them out at the beginning before you got here,' she whispers.

'Right, thanks.'

'No problem,' she smiles.

'Who's your child?' I see an opportunity to bagsie myself a parent friend in Lucy's class. I have yet to meet anyone properly.

'Ned, over there in the red coat. You?'

'I DON'T REMEMBER SAYING IT WAS TIME TO CHAT!' Mrs Elwood booms, looking directly at Ned's mum, who drops her head in embarrassment. 'Can I have *every-one's* attention please, until we get to the bus?'

Bloody hell, she is terrifying.

'Sorry,' I mutter, trying not to move my lips.

100

'Right, children. Find your adult, please!' Mrs Elwood instructs with a surprisingly loud hand clap.

'Here's the list of your children.' The TA passes me a piece of paper with four names typed in comic sans.

'Thank you. Is there anything else I missed?'

'The main thing is don't lose anyone in your group.' She smiles. 'You'll be fine. Ooh, these look like your children!'

'Mummy!' Lucy throws her arms around my legs. 'These are my friends, Evie, Alfie and Paul.' I quickly check them against my list, yes this is all of them.

'Hi guys!' I enthuse. No one responds. 'OK, let's go!'

We follow the herds of children through the school to meet the bus. Every few steps I count and recount my group. I have one job. Don't lose anyone.

As the coach pulls up outside the museum, Mrs Elwood claps a rhythm. An eerie quiet falls throughout the bus and all the children look expectantly at her. She's a sorcerer. How can she hypnotise a whole bus of four- and five-year-olds into silence?

Lucy catches my eye and puts her finger to her lips before I have a chance to say anything. I give her a double thumbs-up in response. I will not embarrass her. That is absolutely key.

'EVERYONE LEAVE THE BUS IN AN ORDERLY MANNER. STAY WITH YOUR GROWN-UPS. NO PUSHING.'

As I help my group with their seatbelts, Paul leans in and in a tiny voice says, 'I've left my packed lunch at school. Please don't tell Mrs Elwood.' He looks petrified.

'Don't worry, we'll get you something,' I reassure him, and he slips his hand inside mine as we disembark. I'm totally nailing this parent–helper shit.

'OK, can we get into an orderly line. Stay where you are children. I SAID STAY WHERE YOU ARE, ALFIE JOHNSON.' I realise he's one of mine and scan the sea of two-foot tall heads to locate him. He's at the front with Mrs Elwood. She is holding his arm in the air with some force. 'Who is Alfie's grown-up?'

I raise my hand. 'Me.'

'Please don't let your children run off, Lucy's mum.'

'Sorry.'

Alfie strops back, I gently hold his shoulder and he shrugs me off. Lucy beckons me and I bend down to hear her. She cups my ear with her hands and in a breathy voice whispers, 'Alfie is always in trouble, Mummy. He tries to run out of the playground every lunchtime, you know.'

Great. I have the bolter in my group.

'Can anyone guess how old this is?' the Museum Curator is standing in front of a model railway.

Lucy's hand shoots up, she props it up with her other hand for maximum height and makes a straining noise. 'I can, I can!'

'Yes – you. How old do you think the train set is?'

'A hundred years old,' Lucy proudly states.

'You are extremely close young lady. First prize for good guessing! It is ninety years old.' Lucy glows with pride, standing a little taller.

'My dad had one of those when we were growing up. It took over the entire front room and we weren't allowed to touch anything,' Ned's mum leans in to tell me. We are both standing at the back of the group. I have counted my cohort about twenty times. Alfie and Paul are both pressing their faces against one of the display cabinets and Lucy and Evie are holding hands a couple of steps in front of me.

'Have you been here before?'

'No. Why?' Ned's mum asks.

'One of my kids has forgotten his packed lunch. I wondered if there was somewhere to buy him a sandwich.'

'There's a Co-op over the road, I think,' she suggests.

'Do you think I'll be allowed to pop out?'

Ned's mum glances over at Mrs Elwood, who is quietly scolding a child with a pointed finger. 'Probably not,' she says.

'Never mind. He can have mine.'

'Shhhh,' Lucy turns around, finger on lips. I shrug an apology.

We hear the familiar call and response clap from Mrs Elwood.

'OTTERS!' she bellows. 'Can we all give Ms Jackson a clap to thank her for her fascinating talk.' She instructs. 'That's enough, settle down now. ALFIE, GET YOUR FACE OFF THAT CABINET. WHERE IS YOUR GROWN-UP?'

Shit. I raise my hand again, and Mrs Elwood shakes her head disapprovingly.

'We are going to go back to the education room to have our packed lunches.'

I see Paul scanning the room for me, he meets my eye and I give him a thumbs-up. He visibly relaxes. 'So please join your group and let's walk in a calm, orderly line. You are not the only people here, so let's be on our best behaviour.'

There is a scurry of activity as the children regroup. I keep my eye on Alfie, who must be hungry as he compliantly walks towards me with Paul. Lucy joins us, declaring, 'I'm staaaaaaaaaaaaaaaarving.' And finally Evie. The little brown-haired girl next to Lucy turns around and – hang on. That's not Evie. Evie was wearing a unicorn jumper. This kid has an Elsa and Ana sweater.

'Who are you?' I panic.

'Gemma Williams. 57b Rugby Road, Bright—'

'Gemma!' Ned's mum calls, beckoning her over.

'Where's Evie?' I ask Lucy, bobbing down to her height and holding both her arms to get her full attention. My heart is thudding loudly in my chest.

'I don't know,' she replies.

'What do you mean, you don't know?' I try not to raise my voice. This is not her fault.

The room is thinning out now. Children follow their grown-ups out of the room. None of the remaining kids are Evie.

'When did you last see her?'

'I think she went to the toilet,' Alfie tells me. He's opened his lunch box already and is cramming Wotsits into his mouth, four at a time.

'When?'

'I dunno.' He sprays orange dust when he speaks.

'Shit. Shit. Shit,' I chant to myself, trying to think.

'Ned's mum!' I shout as she is heading out of the room with her group. Why didn't I ask her what her bloody name was back in the classroom?

'Yep?'

'Can you take my guys too? I've lost one.'

'YOU'VE WHAT?' her eyes widen.

'Evie. She's gone to the loo, apparently.' I try to keep the blind panic out of my voice.

'Yes, sure. I'll see you in the education room. Good luck,' she says as she ushers my guys out of the room.

I follow the signs towards the toilets. The corridors are crammed full of retired people peering into cabinets. ''Scuse me, 'scuse me, 'scuse me,' I squeeze my way through until I'm stood outside the ladies, pushing the door open with undue force I shout, 'Evie? Evie are you in here?' I swing open all the cubicle doors, every one empty. 'Shit! Where the fuck is she?' I am full-scale panicking now.

I retrace my footsteps back to the entrance. There is a queue snaking around the foyer from the enquiries desk, but I make my way to the front, to the loud outrage and headshakes from a sea of white-haired visitors.

'Have you seen a little girl on her own?' I plead.

The woman wearing a badge with 'Lorraine. Centre volunteer,' pinned to her chest raises a finger at me, without taking her eyes off the screen.

'She's four and called Evie. She's wearing a unicorn sweater.'

Lorraine's finger remains in the air until she dramatically hits the return key and only then looks up.

'Done!' she proclaims. 'Now, how may I help you?'

'I've lost a child,' I fluster.

'What is she called?' Lorraine asks.

'Evie.'

'Surname?'

'I don't know. She was in my group at school and now she's disappeared.'

'OK,' she replies. 'Any distinguishing features?'

'A jumper with a unicorn on it. And brown hair. She's four. Or five. She's small. God, I can't believe I've lost her,' I shake my head in disbelief.

'I suggest re-joining your class, I will put a call out to all volunteers,' she asserts. 'You're not the first person to lose a child here, and you won't be the last,' she assures me.

'OK, I'll do that.' Adrenalin pulses through me like caffeine. 'Thank you. Thank you.'

As I hurry towards the education room, I hear Lorraine's voice over the tannoy. 'We have a code amber situation,' she announces. 'Can volunteers make their way to the front desk.'

I push open the heavy double doors to the education room. All the children are sitting around tables, lunch boxes open. Paul rushes over to me, eyes wide, and asks, 'Do you have any lunch for me?'

'Sorry, Paul, yes.' I fish out my sandwich and a packet of Mini Cheddars from my handbag. 'There you go.'

'Thank you,' he grins as he gratefully takes them from me. I weave my way through the tables to Mrs Elwood. Ned's mum catches my eye, raising an eyebrow questioning, to which I shake my head in response.

'Mrs Elwood, please can I have a word?'

She folds her arms defensively and nods, inviting me to continue.

'I've lost Evie.'

'What do you mean, you've *lost* Evie?' she snaps back.

'I thought she was stood in front of me in the museum,' I explain. 'But it turned out it was another child. Alfie thought she was in the loo but I've checked and she's not. The volunteers are looking for her and told me to wait here.'

The vein on Mrs Elwood's forehead protrudes and the tendons on her neck stand to attention.

'You had four children to keep an eye on. Just four, Mrs Jones.' She shakes her head in disgust and shouts at the teaching assistant, 'Mrs Clark? Mrs Clark? You have charge of the room. We have a situation. I'll be as quick as I can.'

'Yes, Mrs Elwood,' Mrs Clark replies in her mousy voice. Silence descends on the room. Children freeze, mid-munch, staring at me with faces full of sandwiches and tangerines.

'You're coming with me,' Mrs Elwood instructs. I follow her out the room as all the children stare at me.

'Don't worry,' I tell Lucy. She looks like she's about to

burst into tears. I've lost a child *and* embarrassed Lucy. This is a disaster.

'Where did you last see her?' Mrs Elwood barks as I struggle to keep up with her fast-paced walking.

'In the toy room.'

'Which toy room? This is a bloody toy museum,' she snaps. Are teachers allowed to swear at parents? I don't think this is the time to bring it up.

'The one with the train set. She was stood in front of me with Lucy one minute, and the next, she was gone,' I reply.

We walk past the front desk, the queue has died down now and Lorraine beckons us over. 'Nothing yet,' she says, 'but our volunteers are very experienced in these situations. We know what we're doing.'

'Well, at least someone does,' Mrs Elwood glares at me, before adding, 'Thank you for your help, Lorraine.'

We walk out of the main entrance into the late October drizzle, eyes darting up and down the street.

'Well if she's not in the museum we will have to call the police,' she says to no one in particular. 'It had to be bloody Evie, didn't it?' she mutters.

'I'm sorry,' I reply. 'I really am.'

I don't know whether she's heard me but she doesn't respond.

'OK,' she claps her hands. 'Let's have another walk around the museum and if we can't find her in the next—' she looks at her watch '—four minutes, we'll call the police as we need to get the other children back on the bus in time for pick-up.'

We march back into the building. 'You go that way,' she points left, 'and I'll go in the other direction.' And she turns on her heels, shoes clicking noisily as she strides off.

I head towards the gift shop. It is a muddle of stands and

displays, cabinets crammed with toys for sale, and rows of children's books. The shop assistant is reading E.L. James, which seems a bit inappropriate for a children's museum, but whatever gets you through the day, I guess.

I wander through the aisles, and as I reach the sweets section I see, squatting down, Evie, her hand in one of the sweets depositaries, cheeks filled like a hamster. She sees me and stiffens.

'Evie, we've been looking for you! Why did you run off?' I try not to sound cross.

'Sorry,' she mumbles, her mouth stuffed with sweets.

'We've got to go and tell Mrs Elwood.'

Evie pulls her hand from the sweet jar, clutching several jelly snakes.

'And put those back,' I point.

She drops them with a huff and we make our way out of the shop, my hand resting on her back. I am not taking any chances now.

As we approach the entrance, I see Mrs Elwood talking to a police officer. Her face is stern with concern, and she emphasises every word with a pointed finger as the policeman writes in his notebook. She glances over at us and does a double take.

'There you are,' she says warmly. 'You had us all worried, Evie!'

'I just wanted to go to the shop,' Evie replies by way of explanation.

'I'm so sorry, officer,' she turns to the policeman.

He smiles at me as he says, 'No harm done.'

He's alarmingly attractive. Beautiful brown eyes with long lashes. Full lips and skin so radiant you want to touch it.

'Thank you,' I respond shyly.

This isn't the time to be flirting, but seriously, he is quite something.

'OK,' Mrs Elwood breaks the moment with her signature hand clap. 'Let's head to the bus as all the other pupils are waiting.'

The policeman puts his hat on, nods a goodbye and finishes writing his notes in his pad. God, he even looks good in a policeman's hat. No one looks good in a policeman's hat, not even male strippers.

'Stop staring at the officer and let's get going,' Mrs Elwood instructs me.

What the actual fuck? Have I just been called out by my daughter's teacher? My cheeks flush with embarrassment and fury, as the officer looks up and chuckles.

'I don't want to have to arrest you for loitering,' he grins, placing his hand on his handcuffs.

OH. MY. GOD. Did that just happen? Is that kind of flirting even legal?

As I obediently follow Mrs Elwood to the awaiting bus, I turn to catch a final quick glance of him. He looks up from his notepad again and winks at me. Actually mother-fucking winks. I think my heart has just skipped a beat in an end-of-Richard-Curtis-film way.

'Keep up,' Mrs Elwood barks at me as I jog to catch up with her.

OK, yes I lost a child today, Mrs Elwood thinks I'm completely incompetent and my daughter is beyond mortified by me.

But on the other hand, I've just had a fizzy-knickers experience with a sexy policeman, so every cloud.

Chapter Sixteen

'We're starving, aren't we, boy?' Spiral declares as he and Falcon slam open the front door with a thud to announce their arrival.

'Yes, we're starving!' Falcon echoes, as both he and his dad fling off their shoes close to, but not on, the shoe rack.

'How was your day?' Tania asks, not really listening to the response, as she is midway through reading an online article about the holistic benefits of circular breathing.

Today is the one day a week when Spiral homeschools Falcon, and after her sunrise yoga session, it's Tania's day to catch up with a week's worth of jobs. She had a list of chores as long as her arm. She was going to batch-cook a load of lentil stew, do a big shop, drop a stack of flyers advertising her yoga classes around the local shops, and had hoped to take down the seam on several pairs of Falcon's trousers, since he's had yet another growth spurt.

She had, instead, got lost down the YouTube vortex and watched six episodes of the original *Beverly Hills 90210*. So now, to reddress the balance, she thought she'd read up on some new breathing techniques for her practice, but has only really got through the first couple of paragraphs when, to her disappointment, Spiral and Falcon return.

'We've had a brilliant day, haven't we, Falcon?' Spiral says, greeting Tania with a gentle kiss on her forehead before sloping off to bury his head in the fridge.

'Yes, it's been *totally* brilliant,' Falcon sinks his teeth into an apple he's found in the fruit bowl. 'We met Shona again. I like her.'

'Oh yes?' Tania looks up; they've pricked her attention now. She pushes down the lid of her laptop. 'Did you go to the group?'

'Yes! It was good.' Spiral opens a can of lager with a fizz, gulps back a large mouthful and flops down next to Tania on the sofa, casually wrapping his arm around her. Their oversized son quickly joins him and curls up uncomfortably on his lap. Tania is always surprised by how similar their faces are, compared to their different physiques: Spiral, all slim and athletic; Falcon, barrel-shaped and strong.

'So you met Emma?' Tania untangles herself from her boys and opens the fridge to pour herself a glass of white wine, accepting that this is now the end of her 'working' day.

'Shona's mum?' he asks.

'Yes, quite posh with long dark hair.' The wine glugs noisily into her glass and she thirstily takes a long sip before putting the bottle back in the fridge.

'Yes. Yes, I liked her. And the kids seemed to get on well together. Quite an interesting bunch, aren't they? Quite a mix of people, I thought.'

'Really?'

'Yes, absolutely. Well, there's Judith, Max's mum, who used to be a nurse and decided to give it up to homeschool. And Kristie, who's building her own sustainable house with her husband and is using it as part of Martha's education. I thought that was an interesting approach.' He takes another large gulp.

How can he have gone to one session and come back mates with everyone there, Tania wonders irritably. She's taken

111

Falcon about three times now and barely knows anyone other than Gill and Emma.

'Yes, they're all very interesting,' Tania agrees non-committally.

'And then you've obviously got Emma, that's her name, right?'

'Yep.'

'Well, Emma's really gone against the grain, hasn't she?'

'Yes, I guess.' Tania replies, not sure at all what Spiral is referring to.

'She was telling me about the posh school she went to when she was younger, and how her and her husband decided they wanted something different for their daughter. I said to her, that sounds just like your old school. Or Polly's, for that matter. But I guess you've already spoken about that,' he drains the rest of his can. 'Right. Off,' he commands Falcon, who is trying to push a strand of his hair up his dad's nose. 'I'll set about getting us some scran. Are you hungry, Tan?'

But Tania doesn't hear him. She remembers Emma now. Of course she does. She didn't know her well, but she did know her.

'Falcon, can you go and get that box that was under your bed?' she asks him impatiently.

'What, the treasure box?' he asks excitedly.

'Yes. The treasure box.'

Falcon darts out the room and returns minutes later, carrying the shoebox on outstretched arms, like a glass slipper on a velvet cushion.

She takes it from him and Falcon sits at her feet like an obedient dog, watching her every move as she gathers up the photos and slowly and methodically flicks through them. Faces she used to know smile back at her, pictures of

112

her with her arms firmly locked round the waist of another, grinning with the familiarity of friendships that would last forever, of people whose names she now no longer remembers. And halfway through the stack she sees Emma's younger face smiling back at her. It's 1991 and they're on a school trip in North Yorkshire somewhere, the picture is taken in one of the dorms. Everyone has their arms raised in the air, beaming with innocent joy and dressed in their ridiculously formal school uniforms of checked dresses and boaters, just like poor Polly has to wear now. Tania closes her eyes and tries to conjure up the memory of the trip. They went away for a week, that much she remembers, as it was the longest time she'd ever been away from home. At thirteen, she felt nervous and hugely grown-up all rolled into one heady mix. She remembers how the bus journey there took hour upon hour and how every girl immediately needed the toilet the moment the coach set off, so the on-board facilities stank of piss for the majority of the journey. Halfway there someone blocked it with a massive turd so it was out of bounds, and the teacher had to gaffer-tape up the toilet door.

She remembered arriving at the grand stately home somewhere outside of Harrogate, the coaches pulling up on the huge gravel drive framed by two large lion statues. She remembers being designated a room, being marched down a corridor that was weighted down with gilt-framed paintings of nobles, and being warned that if anyone, *anyone*, broke anything then their parents would be billed and that the cost would be eye-watering. For a school that charged ten grand a term, that figure would surely reach into the hundreds of thousands, so the girls were gripped by fear and pulled their suitcases along, breathing in to make themselves narrower.

She reached her dorm and was instructed as to which

bunk was hers, and that they all needed to unpack their suitcases and then reconvene downstairs in the drawing room to be given their itinerary for the week.

And then the door was shut with a satisfying thump of three-inch thick oak. She was in a room with twelve other girls, some of whom she knew well from her tutor group, others she only recognised from break time. The squeals of excitement were suppressed with hands on mouths as the girls realised they were away from their parents for six whole nights, the room heavy with expectation and the scent of Charlie body spray. Clothes were thrown into drawers and a photo was taken of them all beaming with delight, which Tania is now looking at.

And then someone produced a small bottle of vodka. It was passed around the room under a cloak of deadly silence. As Tania put it to her mouth she gagged from the fumes but knocked it back anyway, her throat burning, her pulse racing. And then, once everyone had had a sip, someone hid it in a secret compartment of their bag.

Emma. Emma hid it in her bag. Oh my God. Her new friend at homeschool group was her first real inspiration in life and until now, neither of them had the faintest idea.

Chapter Seventeen

'Well, is he at it again?' Rachel asks.

'He says not, but how can I be sure?' I lick the chocolate crumbs from the Twirl grab bag, slightly surprised how quickly I've polished them off.

'You *can't* be sure, Emmie. But you either give him the benefit of the doubt, or not. Your choice,' I can hear her take a gulp of something at her end.

'It's just such a mess. I want to trust him again, I really do. But he's not exactly got the greatest track record.' I peer into the kids' snacks cupboard and open a packet of Pom-Bears.

'Well, what did he say?'

'That it was a genuine mistake. That he didn't realise he still had a card for the account and it looks like his normal one. That he was buying some stuff at Sainsbury's and used it without thinking at one of those tap-in checkouts.'

'Well, that sounds completely plausible, doesn't it? And you said he'd paid it back.'

'I know. I know, it's just . . .' I sigh. Not sure how to finish the sentence.

'Right. Put the kids' snacks down,' Rachel instructs.

'How did you know?' I ask, crisp hovering mid-air.

'Because you mainline shit when you're stressed. I know you, Emmie Jones.'

'You're good,' I laugh, genuinely impressed. 'Like the Oracle.'

'Thanks. Look, you know this situation better than anyone. All I'm saying is, pick your battles. Maybe this isn't one of them.'

'Good advice,' I say, and tip the rest of the crisps directly in my mouth from the packet.

'So,' she says, excitement buzzing in her voice. 'Did you get it?'

'What?'

'What do you mean, *what*? My gift?'

'I'm looking at it now.' I turn it over in my hand. 'What if the kids had opened it?' I put it down carefully and start to unload the dishwasher with the phone propped between my ear and shoulder.

'Do they normally open your post?' Rachel asks.

'No,' I reply, 'but they might.'

'Oh, stop being such a prude,' Rachel teases. 'Thank you. No, just put it in the charity box,' Rachel replied to someone at her end. 'Sorry,' she says to me. 'I'm just picking up some dinner for me and Matt in Tesco.'

'Me and Matt is it now?' I tease.

'Shut it, Emmie. It's just dinner. Tea.' She says, downgrading it. 'Anyway, don't change the subject. When have you next got the house to yourself?'

I close the dishwasher door and switch the kettle on. 'Now.' I reply. 'The kids are at school and nursery, and it's Nick's night with them.'

'Perfect,' she exclaims. 'So why don't you give it a go? I promise you, you won't look back. How do you think I kept from losing my mind over the last two years?'

'Rachel!' I exclaim.

'Stop being so uptight!' she laughs.

'I'm not uptight, I'm just—'

'Frustrated?' she suggests.

'A bit. Maybe. But I've got bigger things to worry about at the moment than having an orgasm over lunch, Rach.' The word orgasm sounds awkward when I say it. Unsexy and cellular, like something you might find lurking at the back of the fridge. 'Look, thanks for thinking of me, but next time maybe get me a bunch of flowers. Or vouchers?' I suggest.

'The day I start buying you vouchers is the day hell freezes over,' she jokes. 'Right. Got to go, Emmie. Speak soon and enjoy it. That's what it's meant for.'

I turn the package over in my hand again. The instructions explain how the sticky-up bit at the front is for clitoral massage, whereas the sticky-up bit at the back is for anal stimulation. On one hand it looks terrifying, while on the other, not too dissimilar to some of Sophie and Lucy's bath toys.

And why did they have to add this kind of veiny effect to it? Is it so it looks more like a penis? Who has a two-pronged bright pink penis? Also, there is absolutely nothing appealing about a veiny cock. They should have gone the whole hog if they were going down that route and added a scrotum and pubes. Oh, fuck it.

'Well I guess it couldn't hurt could it?' I ask myself out loud. 'And it was a gift, so . . .'

I open the utensils draw and pull out the kitchen scissors, removing the packaging and placing it in the bin, leaving the vibrator standing menacingly on the table. I can't find any AA batteries, so instead remove the ones from the large wall clock, making a mental note to replace them when I've finished. I turn *Steve Wright in the Afternoon* down on the radio and head upstairs.

Now, just to be clear, just to be *absolutely* clear, I am not uptight. I have had my moments of sexual liberation. I got off with Claire Cunningham at school, proper snogging with tongues, not just a peck on the lips. *And* I liked it. David Kelly fingered me in the cinema during a screening of *Trainspotting*. I've had sex in Nick's mum's garden when they were sleeping upstairs. I've even had a go at doing it up the bum, although it wasn't really my cup of tea.

What I'm trying to say is, this is not a ground-breaking moment for me. Masturbating in the middle of the day is not one of those 'hallelujah' moments. This isn't my sexual awakening. It is, however, a tad irresponsible, given that I have a copy deadline at 5 p.m.

I lie down on the double bed and turn the dial on the vibrator around. Jesus, it's loud. It sounds like someone has started up an old-school Land Rover in my bedroom.

I close my eyes and try to imagine Ryan Gosling, wet from swimming, tanned and muscular. I'm lying on a sun-lounger, equally tanned, and I work out. A lot. I look great. I shield my eyes from the midday sun as he stands over me, dripping.

I wish sometimes I could just get straight to the good bit. Just get my head into feeling sexy with the switch of a button. But instead, I have to create a story to accompany it, to make it feel realistic, achievable. A narrative, if you will, that carries the plot and ends up in fireworks sex. Nick used to take the piss out of me for it. Teasing me that writing was so much a part of my life, I couldn't even have sex without telling a story.

Why am I thinking about Nick? He is the last person I want to be thinking about now. Come on, brain, work with me.

So here I am. Ryan dripping over me. He silently takes my hand and pulls me to standing, leading me through the maze of loungers towards his beachside summerhouse.

I undo my jeans and push the vibrator down my trousers. It muffles the farm transportation noise slightly. I gently place one of the sticky up bits on my clitoris and, oh wow. Wow. That feels incredible.

I fast forward through the romantic dinner, the tender kiss over the washing-up, me leading Ryan seductively upstairs, and cut straight to him towering naked over me on the four-poster bed.

I turn up the resistance on the vibrator and feel the beginnings of a rumble. My breath is becoming shallow and I arch my back as I can feel the orgasm starting to bubble and burn its way through my body, I turn the resistance up to full. Oh my fucking God, I think I'm going to—

'Emily? Are you in?' A voice calls from downstairs.

What? Is that Nick? What the fuck is Nick doing here?

'Mummy!' Oh, Christ. With the girls? He's downstairs with Sophie and Lucy? I quickly zip up my jeans and breathlessly call down, 'I'm coming! Just a minute.'

Standing up, I can still feel the throb in my knickers, swollen and tender. I wide stride my way down the stairs. They are all sat at the kitchen table.

'You know that clock's not working, Em?' Nick remarks. He's unselfconsciously flicking through my copy of *Marie Claire* that's on the table. 'I thought it was just slow, but the second hand isn't going around at all. You should change the batteries or it'll just get confusing.'

'What are you doing here?' I ask, exasperated. 'You're meant to be at your house tonight?'

'Ah yes. Sorry, we didn't mean to disturb you. I was thinking of taking the girls for a dip in the pool, but needed to pick up their costumes.' He looks up from the magazine, making eye contact for the first time. 'Blimey. Are you OK, Em? You look flushed.'

119

'Yes, yes I'm fine,' I mutter. 'You can't just walk in unannounced, you know, Nick.'

'To be fair, we did try knocking but there wasn't any answer,' Nick shrugs by way of an apology. 'Are you sure you're OK, Em? You look really peaky.'

'I'm fine. Stop fussing,' I dismiss his concern with the wave of a hand and turn around so he stops looking at me.

'You are bright pink, Mummy,' Lucy announces, opening her lunch box and emptying the contents on the table.

'All right. All of you. Enough! Nick, I will get their costumes and then you should all get on your way. I've got a deadline this afternoon.'

'No probs,' Nick remarks as he saunters over to switch the kettle on.

'No, that doesn't mean make a cup of tea. It means you all need to go.' I race upstairs and by the time I am back with both swimming costumes, goggles, armbands and novelty floats, I see Nick has brewed a cup of tea for one and helped himself to a four-finger KitKat from the biscuit tin. Peanuts is curled in his lap luxuriously, and as Nick strokes her from head to tail she seems happier, more contented with him than she is with me.

'I bumped into Josh Carter's mum at nursery pick-up today,' Nick says through a mouthful.

'Oh yeah?' I respond, busying myself at the sink.

'Yes. She was very apologetic. She said that she was keeping an eye on the situation,' he continues.

'Good. Good. Well, that is good news,' I respond. I have never been a great liar. Small fibs about birthday surprises or leaving dos – fine. But I don't want Nick to see my face or I'll have to tell him that there is every possibility that Josh Carter was, indeed, telling the truth about Sophie, so instead I begin to stack the dishwasher.

'She said she'd like to talk to you too. I wasn't sure if that was necessary, but I'll leave that with you,' he drains his tea and lets out a contented burp.

'It sounds like you've handled it, Nick.'

He nods in agreement.

In fairness, there haven't been any more 'incidents' since Betsy summoned us to the nursery, and no more cases of the disappearing lunch box, so really, it is all dealt with. Really.

'Do you want to come swimming too, Mummy?' Lucy asks.

'Not this time honey, but have fun.' I usher them towards the door, kiss both girls on the tops of their heads, and hand Nick the Sainsbury's bag full of swimming stuff.

'OK then,' Nick swaps it for an empty teacup, placing it in my hand, he loiters self-consciously, clicking his knuckles before saying, 'And are we OK after the, you know, wedding account mix-up?'

'Yes,' I nod, taking heed of Rachel's advice. 'Yes, we are OK after that.'

'Good,' he whistles a sigh of relief. 'Good. Great. I'm trying, Em. I really am. And I'd hate you to think that we're back there again. Because we're not.'

'OK,' I reply. And then add, 'I believe you.'

'OK. OK then. Look, there was something else I wanted to discuss with you, but maybe now's not the time. Maybe we can go for lunch or something soon?'

'Sounds very official, Nick?'

'No. No,' he laughs nervously. 'Just sometimes it's easier to talk when the girls aren't around. Nothing important. I'll text you about meeting up. So, we'll see you tomorrow then. Why don't you get some rest, Em? You really don't look yourself,' he says as they walk down the path.

121

As I shut the door behind them, I hear a low hum coming from upstairs. Bloody hell, I hadn't even turned the vibrator off. All in all, I think it's fair to say I've had more fulfilling afternoons.

Chapter Eighteen

'DADDY'S BAAAAAAAAAAAACK,' Polly hollers from upstairs. She has been sat in the alcove near the window in her bedroom most of the morning, waiting for his taxi to pull up.

'Is she always this devoted to her father?' Janet questions, as Helen pours her a third cup of coffee, none of which she's been thanked for so far.

'They get on very well, yes,' Helen responds, resisting the temptation to move the cafetière slightly to the right and tip the rest of it all over Janet's lap.

'It just seems unnatural to be that close. A father and daughter,' Janet quietly remarks.

'Well, you would say that,' Helen snaps.

'All I'm saying is—'

'Mum. Chris is just about to walk through the door. Can we just focus on that for now?' she asks.

'Of course. Of course, Helen. But the point I'm trying to make is—'

'What, Mum? What's your point?' Helen wipes her hands on a tea towel, wringing it into a sausage shape one way and then the other to dispel the anger that is rising in her.

Janet sighs and takes a sip of her coffee before replying, 'That in my experience—'

Helen turns to look at her mum, crossing her arms in

frustration, 'Go on?' she says, as she hears Chris's keys jangling in the lock.

'That in my experience, Helen, men aren't always what they seem. And you'd do well to remember that.'

'Jesus, Mum. I'm not doing this with you now. Just because you made some seriously shit life choices, doesn't mean we all have to,' Helen rubs her forehead with the palm of her hand, her cheeks flushed with fury.

'Silly girl,' Janet mutters.

'WHAT DID YOU CALL ME?' Helen explodes, as Chris pushes open the front door with a clash.

'Hellooooooooo,' he exclaims joyfully. 'Where are you all?' he calls from the corridor, key still poised mid-air.

'We're in the kitchen, darling. Just coming,' Helen replies through gritted teeth, not taking her eyes off Janet, who returns the steely glare. Janet is the first to break eye contact. Helen takes this as an admission of defeat, tucks the tea towel she's still clutching over the back of a chair, smooths down her hair and strides out of the kitchen with as much of a spring in her step as she can muster.

Polly leaps down the stairs, two at a time and springs into Chris's awaiting arms. He showers her with kisses as she dangles from his neck, chuckling with glee. 'God I've missed you,' he beams at her.

Chris lowers Polly to the ground and puts his rucksack down, holds Helen's face in his hands, and gently presses his lips to hers, whispering in her ear, 'I've missed you *very* much.'

'Chris. Of course it's Chris. I don't know who *I* was thinking of.' Janet announces, framed by the kitchen door and pointing at Chris like he had somehow misled her into believing he was someone else.

'Janet,' he replies. 'Lovely as ever to see you. Helen said you were visiting.'

'Well, I'm never one to turn down an invitation,' she replies.

'And how long are you planning on staying with us?' Chris asks, as he picks up his rucksack again and hangs his coat on the peg.

'Well,' she wipes a non-existent crumb from her mouth before Chris curtly pecks her cheek, 'Helen has said as long as I liked, so as long as I'm needed, I should say. I do like to help out and poor Helen does need the support, with you being away so very often. Isn't that right, Helen?'

'We haven't really discussed it, have we, Mum?' Helen replies in a monotone voice. 'And I imagine you'll be wanting to get back to Spain before too long, it's only going to get colder here as we get closer to Christmas.'

'Of course, Christmas. Well, you'd like Nana Janet to be with you over Christmas, wouldn't you, Poppy?'

'Polly,' Helen says.

'Sorry?'

'Her name's Polly, Mum, not Poppy.'

'That's what I said,' Janet snaps. 'Now are we going to open something nice to celebrate Chris's return, or are we going to stand in the corridor all day empty-handed?' Her voice is soft again.

As Polly slips her hand in Helen's as they walk back towards the kitchen, Janet turns and says, 'Now, Helen. Why don't we have a drop of the Moët that's been gathering dust in the pantry, given that it's a special occasion?'

Helen catches Chris's eye.

'You OK?' he mouths.

'No,' she mouths back. 'I'm not.'

Christmas is weeks away. Janet cannot, under any circumstances, still be staying with them then.

Chapter Nineteen

Nick brings the coffees over to the table and drops the packet sandwich that he's been carrying under his chin. I wouldn't normally come to Starbucks as it's a bit of a trek into town, but it makes a refreshing change from my normal café.

Nick spots me looking at the sandwich and says, 'Shit. Sorry, Em. You've eaten, haven't you?'

'Yes. I had something at home.'

'Cool. Yeah, it's a bit of a hectic day for me today, so didn't manage to get anything for lunch. Thanks for meeting me so close to work.' He rips open the packaging and devours half of the coronation chicken sandwich in one go, opening his mouth wide like Pac-Man. A glob of mayonnaise gets caught in his beard but I don't say anything.

I sip my drink and wonder how long it will take for him to talk about his work.

'Paul, you remember Paul from the north-west office?'

That was approximately three seconds.

'No.'

'Yes you do, Em. He's our age but looks about fifteen. We all went to the pub once when he was down visiting our branch, and you made some remark about him not being old enough to get served. You thought he was on work experience.'

'Oh, yeah, I vaguely remember.' I look at the steaming coffee. If I just pour the whole mug directly into my lap, would that be enough for him to get to the point, or would he just pass me a napkin and continue regardless?

'Well, he's doing a like-for-like comparison of the recruitment processes in each of the regional offices and is currently shadowing me to see—'

'Nick. I don't mean to interrupt, but you asked *me* to meet *you*. I'm assuming it's not to give me the latest on headhunting?'

'It's not actually headhunting, it's more—'

'Whatever. Look Nick, I have a copy deadline before I get the kids, so it would be really useful if you could just tell me why I'm here.' I was actually halfway through *The Notebook* when Nick had rung requesting a 'coffee and a chat', and I'm quite keen to get to the end of it before pick-up if at all possible.

'OK, yeah. Sorry. Sorry.' He puts his sandwich down and starts cracking each knuckle. I watch him perform his nervous ritual and wonder if he realises how well I know his mannerisms. How I can read him like a book and am currently watching him build himself up to telling me something I won't like to hear.

'OK, so I don't know whether I mentioned to you that my parents are planning a visit to do some Christmas shopping?'

'No, I don't think you did.'

'It was planned ages ago, like months ago. They were going to come down and stay for the weekend in a hotel and buy some bits while they were here. For presents, you know.' He's now nervously tapping his fingers on the table. He would be terrible under interrogation. His voice might be saying, 'I don't know what you're talking about,' but his body language would be screaming, 'IT'S ME! I'M YOUR MAN! ARREST ME!'

'OK, fine. I don't remember, though, Nick. A lot has happened over the last few months, hasn't it?'

'Yes. Yes. Of course. Well, it was on the shared calendar, so I thought—'

'Seriously, Nick. Just get to the point.'

'OK. OK.' He exhales slowly. 'So I think I might have fucked up a bit.'

He momentarily shuts his eyes, composing his next sentence.

I wait.

And wait.

And wait a bit longer for him to continue.

'Nick. Just spit it out,' I eventually order.

'OK. But you need to promise me you won't get angry first.'

'I can't do that.' The irritation fizzes in my voice.

'You know when I moved out?'

'Yes. Yes Nick. I am very aware of when you moved out.'

The image of him walking down the path to the car, arms laden with carrier bags filled with his belongings, is not one I'd easily forget.

'You know how we were going to tell our parents together because we wanted them to know that it was a mutual decision, we didn't want them to think there was someone to blame and that—'

'Yes, Nick. I remember all of this very clearly. What's your point?'

'And you remember how I said it would be easier if I told my parents myself because—'

'Because Dennis and Cathleen are fucking awkward and they'd make it all about them instead of us?' I interject.

'Well that's not exactly . . . but. OK. Yes. For the sake of argument, let's say that was the reason—'

'Because it was,' I interrupt.

'Fine, Em. So what actually happened was. Well, funny

story, really. Not exactly funny but . . . what I need to tell you and the reason I wanted to meet today was . . . It was to let you know that I didn't.'

'You didn't what, Nick?' I scrape my fingers through my hair to relieve some of the stress headache that he and the strong coffee are giving me.

'I didn't tell them. I didn't do that part of the agreement. The part where I was going to tell them on my own. I didn't do that bit. So they don't, in actual fact, know we've split up.' He shrugs apologetically but his face is filled with trepidation.

I stare at him. Through him. And try to make sense of what he has just told me.

It has been months since Nick moved out of the family home. How is it even possible to keep this from them? How can they really not know?

'Why?' I simply ask him. 'Why wouldn't you tell them?' He goes to crack his knuckle again. 'Leave your fucking hands alone, Nick. Just sit on them.' My voice has risen. It's the level I normally reserve for the kids when they don't look like they're going to stop at the kerbside.

'I couldn't,' he whispers and drops his head.

'But we sat my parents down together. You and me, together. We talked them through what we were going to do, as a team. Remember that? You said, "let's show them we're still a team for the girls", remember? My mum sobbing while she hugged you, saying that they'd still think of you as their family. Dad shaking your hand, patting you on the back. We worried whether we were doing the right thing, that we should have tried harder. Remember how we had to remind ourselves of how bad it had got? How awful those conversations were? How not even a fucking counsellor could help us? Remember that, Nick? How awful that day was because we'd upset everyone we loved, but we knew, deep down, that we were doing the right thing for the girls. DO YOU REMEMBER THAT, NICK?' I'm shouting now, I don't want to be shouting but I am. 'DO YOU REMEMBER WHAT I HAD TO ASK MY PARENTS TO DO FOR US, NICK? BECAUSE OF YOU?'

'YES!' he shouts back in defence. The only other couple in the café are looking at us, making no pretence of their interest in our conversation.

'So I assume they don't know about the money, then?'

'Of course they don't know about the money. I couldn't, Em. That would break them. Can you imagine what my dad would say if he knew? I just couldn't.' He buries his face in his hands. I can't believe that once again he has avoided any responsibility and taken the easy route out.

'I don't know what to say to you, Nick. I feel so let down. Again.'

'All right, Em, You don't have to take the moral high ground,' he mutters.

'Are you actually shitting me? When you were going to tell your folks, I thought, "Poor Nick. How completely awful for him. After everything, he's going to have to tell Dennis and Cathleen and deal with their questions and their pity on his own." I felt bad for you, Nick. I felt dreadful that you had to do it on your own. But you didn't even bother.' I hit the table with frustration and my mug leaps over, spilling the remaining inch of coffee. Nick goes to mop it up with a napkin. 'Leave it!' I sound stony cold.

Silence swallows us up. Nick avoids my eye as I wring my hands like Lady Macbeth. The only noise comes from the steamer of the coffee machine and the drip, drip, drip as my coffee splashes down onto my pleather handbag on the floor.

'I meant to. Of course, I did, Em. I went up to see them for a night, and that was my plan. But when it came to it, when I went back home and saw all the photos of us on the walls and the pictures Lucy had drawn of the family that Mum's framed, it just felt so normal. I couldn't do it. I just couldn't do it.' He buries his face in his hands, shoulders hunched as he starts to silently sob, and I feel momentarily sorry for him.

For a split second I want to wrap my arms around him and stop time. To reassure him it's all going to be OK. Until I remember the look of desperation on Mum and Dad's face when we spoke to them. How it was one of the hardest things I've ever had to do. And how Nick has just chickened out of doing the same.

'So what have you been telling them?'

'Sorry?' he looks up and blows his nose on a napkin.

'What have you been telling them when you speak to them? Have they not wondered where I am?'

'When?'

'I don't know. When you're on the phone?'

'Well, it's not like you really spoke to them regularly anyway, Em. It wasn't unusual for months to go by without you seeing or speaking to them.'

'That's simply not true,' but I do a mental calculation and the last few months haven't covered a significant birthday or Christmas so I could quite feasibly have avoided contact with them. But that is absolutely not the point.

'Do *not* try to make this about me, Nick, unless you want me to walk out right now.'

'They ask about you, and I tell them you're fine. I haven't actually lied to them,' he offers quietly and drops his head again.

'And what about the girls? They must have seen them on FaceTime, or have you been hiding them away too?'

'No, no, they've said hi to them on FaceTime, I just make

sure we're not in Simon's flat when I ring so they don't ask where they are.'

'Do they not think it's weird that I'm never with you?'

'Mum just assumes you're busy at work.'

'Jesus, Nick.' I shake my head in absolute disbelief. 'You know you're going to have to tell them, right?'

'Yes. I know. I'm sorry and I will.'

'OK. Well, that's a start, I guess.'

'But first I have a huge favour to ask you.' He inhales slowly, looks at me through glassy eyes and starts cracking his knuckles double time now. Click. Click. Click. Click. Click. One hand and then the other and then back to the first again.

'What?'

Click. Click. Click. Click. Click.

'I just want them to have a good weekend with us all first. They rarely come down here and they're so excited about visiting. They've booked themselves into the Premier Inn on the seafront. Mum has been phoning loads with suggestions of where she'd like to eat and things they'd like to do with the girls and have even suggested they'd babysit for a night so that we could—'

'Nick. What are you asking me to do?' I ask flatly.

'I'm asking . . . I'm begging, for you to let my parents think we're together. That we're still a family. Just for the weekend. We wouldn't have to invite them to the house. We wouldn't even have to see them together that much. Just lunch. Or dinner. And maybe a walk on the beach on the Sunday. What do you think? I know it's a lot to ask, Em. Stop staring at me and say something. Please.'

A beat. Two. And then I pick up my handbag. Shake the coffee from it and loop it over my arm. The fury burns in my throat as I try to contain it enough to say, 'You are a piece of work, Nick.' And I walk out.

Chapter Twenty

'I can't believe it's you, Arabella!' Emma throws her hand over her mouth in dramatic shock as she looks at the old photograph again. 'Why did you change your name? Are you a spy or something?'

'God, no,' Tania replies, pouring hot water into both mugs and passing one to her. 'Nothing as exciting as that. When I moved out of Mum and Dad's house, I just wanted a fresh start, I guess. I didn't want to be Arabella with the posh parents. I just wanted to be, well, normal.'

'Arabella—'

'Tania,' she says as Emma passes the photograph back to her, and Tania looks at the thirteen-year-old versions of themselves grinning back at her.

'Sorry, of course. Well, you sort of became an urban legend after you left, do you know that? There were all kinds of rumours about what had happened to you.'

'Like what?' Tania asks, intrigued.

'Well, one was that you'd died of a heroin overdose.'

'Total cliché,' she rolls her eyes.

'Yeah, I know right? And another one was that you'd run off with some guy three times your age, who just used you for sex.'

'That would have been more interesting,' she considers.

'Oh there are more, loads more. My favourite was that

you'd moved to Bali and were working as a honeybee for a top-class private detective.'

'A what?' Tania asks, taking a slurp of her camomile tea.

'You know. Women who set traps for rich men with a wandering eye, so the wives have evidence that they were, as suspected, a total shit. Want a biscuit?'

'Yes please,' Tania accepts a bourbon from the paper plate. 'It was pretty straightforward really. I met Spiral at a squat party when I was seventeen, we fell in love. My parents wouldn't accept it was serious, so I moved out. The end.'

'Well, don't you miss it all?'

'Not really. I sometimes wish we had a bit more money, of course I do. But I wouldn't swap it for the life I had before. All the pomp and the pretence. And it's not like I don't see my folks.'

'Oh?' Emma asks.

'Yes, I meet up with them from time to time. Well, my mum mainly, and never at the house. I can't bear it there. I don't see much of Dad. He's still a workaholic. It's not like I want Falcon to grow up without his grandparents. They are annoying, yes, but I don't want them to miss out on him.'

'Well, I think that's very humble of you,' Emma concludes, nodding her head to emphasise her point.

'I wouldn't say it was humble, as such.'

'I would. I still totally sponge off my parents *and* I think they're dicks. At least you've got morals,' Emma shrugs.

'Thanks,' Tania smiles. She'd never really seen it like that.

'I just can't believe it's you,' Emma shakes her head. 'Seriously. For you, you must have left without giving anyone at Cuthbert's School for Girls another thought, but you were a hero to everyone who was still stuck there. I can't believe you left before finishing your A levels. Your parents must have been livid. All that money they spent on school. No wonder they hate Spiral.' She shakes her head in admiration.

'It was my choice, that's the thing they never accepted. They wanted someone to blame and so it was obviously Spiral. But if I hadn't met him, I would have left anyway. I just found the whole lifestyle,' she raises her hand to her throat as she struggles for the word, 'suffocating. All those high society parties with their judgemental friends dripping in Gucci. I don't think any of them actually liked each other in the first place. It was so fake. Anyway, I did do my A levels, just later on and funded by myself, thank you very much Cuthbert's.'

'Good for you. You're still my hero.' Emma nudges her playfully. 'Now let's have another look at that photo.'

Tania passes it over.

'God, this is like a cocaine-and-champagne line-up. Remember her? Candice Windsor? Well, she owns a string of pretentious dog-grooming salons called Puppy Love, thanks to the bank of Mum and Dad. I don't think she's ever been inside any of them. And her? Octavia McMillan? Remember there was that "unnamed woman" who was caught up in a sex scandal with a high court judge recently? Well . . . let's just say that cost more than a year's school fees to keep her name out of the press. You really did do the right thing, Tania.'

'Thank you,' Tania replies. 'And you.'

'Oh, not me. I'm a complete charlatan. I've got the best of both worlds. I had no idea what I wanted to do, but having Shona gave me focus, so having time with her this way is a perfect balance. Don't get me wrong, I couldn't do this if my parents didn't help out, and she does have a tutor who comes to the house four times a week. I don't think she's going to become head of NASA with me imparting my infinite knowledge alone,' she laughs unselfconsciously. 'I'm a selfish person. I know that. I want to have it all. Hello, darling, What's that?' Emma squats down as Shona bounds over clutching what looks like the contents of a recycling box masking-taped together.

Tania watches Falcon lying on his stomach curled over his drawing, head down in concentration. She takes a moment to consider the legacy she left at home, the speculation around her sudden departure from school. She thinks about what Emma just said. Emma wants to have it all.

Tania tries to shake off the desire that has been creeping in ever since she gave birth to Falcon. If she had her time again, would she have done things differently? If she's completely honest with herself, deep down, does she want to have it all too?

Chapter Twenty-One

'Stop making excuses,' Rachel says down the phone.

'I'm not, it's just . . . It's all changed now. I don't understand how it all works.' I'm staring at the computer, cursor flashing menacingly on a blank document.

'It hasn't changed. It's exactly the same as it used to be. Just easier,' she explains.

'But it's not though, is it? I mean, I used to get pissed and then get off with someone. If we liked each other we'd probably have sex and then it may or may not, lead to a relationship. Now I have to upload photos and write something about myself. It's like boyfriend homework. I don't think I can be bothered.'

'Come on,' Rachel says encouragingly, 'that's not the right attitude. Think of it as interview prep for a job you really want.'

'But I read this article in *Marie Claire* about the best dating sites, and it talks about algorithms and analysing personality traits. Could that sound less sexy? Oh thanks, put it down there please.'

I am sat in my usual spot at Mummies Rest and the waitress has just brought me over a coffee. If I write the next Harry Potter here, I wonder if they'll sell commemorative mugs and mouse mats of me like they do for J.K. Rowling in The Elephant House?

'Up to you of course, Emmie. But you said you were fed

up with Nick's shit. Perhaps now is the time to have some fun?' she suggests.

'Maybe you do have a point. There's no harm in looking, I guess.'

'Have you decided what you're going to do about meeting his folks?' Rachel asks.

'I don't know.' I sigh. 'It would have been a hard no but I feel bad for Cathleen and Dennis. I never thought I'd hear myself saying that. But it isn't their fault that their son is a prize prick.'

'Well, you've got a bit of time to think it through.'

'Exactly. I'll just mull it over, and in the meantime, have a look to see if a single, baggage-free, Ryan Gosling lookalike might be living around the corner, eh?' I try to muster up some enthusiasm.

'That's the spirit.' I can hear the smile in her voice. 'OK, good luck with it and speak later.' She hangs up.

I scroll through the article again. It highlights the top eleven dating sites. Eleven. How are you meant to make a choice out of eleven? Why can't there just be one mega website, like the Tesco Extra of dating?

I turn to WhatsApp.

Me: Know any good dating websites?
Tania: AT LAST!!!! And no. You're asking the wrong girl. I met Spiral before they'd invented internet dating.
Helen: I do, although I think it's all changed since I used them, so don't ask me.
Me: Well, this is all tremendously helpful. Thank you.
Tania: No problem. Just don't go on about recently splitting up with your husband.
Helen: Absolutely. And don't wear that mustard-coloured top you bought the other day in your picture. It's not very flattering.

Tania: Yep. And it makes you look like you have jaundice. Wear black. You can't go wrong with black.

Me: You both said you liked me in it.

Helen: For round the house.

Me: Right. Thanks. How's your mum doing, Hels?

Helen: Don't ask. Driving me fucking mental. Chris can't hide his dislike. Understandably. He just wants to watch telly without her asking who's who and what's happening every two minutes.

Tania: Mine doesn't even call me by my name.

Me: Well, you did change it by deed poll.

Tania: Whatever. You're lucky. Your mum's lovely.

Helen: She is.

Me: Yep. I know. Now are you sure about the top?

Helen: Definitely.

Tania: Don't wear it, unless you want sympathy dates cos people think you're ill.

Me: Namastay away from the yellow top. Got it.

I don't know why I'm even considering online dating anyway. Part of me feels like a complete traitor to Nick for even considering it. Yet the other part says, fuck it. We haven't been in a proper relationship now for ages, so what's wrong with wanting to feel desired? To feel empowered? To have an orgasm that isn't instigated by a plastic penis that your best mate ordered on Amazon for you?

Maybe I'm looking at this all wrong. Maybe I should approach it like a piece of copywriting. I am currently at the 'researching the product' stage, and need to consider quality, demand, value for money and marketability. See myself as a fabulous commodity.

Easy.

I look at the cursor again and try and think what it is I want. Actually want. It's not complicated, really. Honesty.

And companionship. And the odd date that isn't self-initiated. Someone who listens to me, is interested in me and doesn't want to talk about themselves all the time. I want to sit next to someone on the sofa and not feel completely alone.

What am I doing? I'm not ready for this. Not a bit.

With a heavy sigh, I close the laptop down and finish my coffee.

Chapter Twenty-Two

TWO WEEKS BEFORE NICK MOVED OUT

'I just wish now and then you'd see how hard I work, and it would be nice if occasionally you showed an interest in my job.' His body language is stiff and uncommunicative. Arms crossed, hands wedged under his armpits.

'I do!' I protest. This is our third session and we seem to be getting progressively worse, not better, at communicating.

'No you don't. What about last night when I tried to talk to you about the presentation I'd given to the whole department? You just glazed over and turned *Corrie* on before I'd even got to the end of the story.'

'It was a presentation about data protection, Nick! It was boring. It was a boring story.'

'See?' he looks at Judy who nods at me to respond.

'Come on, Nick. Surely you see that too, don't you?' I plead.

He turns to face me again, this time interlocking his fingers like Judy. 'I don't think you realise how stressful my job can be. I don't think you understand sometimes the pressure I'm under, especially now I've taken on so much more responsibility. I'm up against it. Most of the time,' he adds.

'How *can* I understand when you don't talk about it? You don't ever talk about how you feel about anything, not really, Nick. Coming here is about the only actual time you open up, and even then it feels like it's for Judy's benefit,' I'm trying to keep a lid on my vexation but it's spilling over by the bucket load.

'Emily, would you like to elaborate?' Judy suggests.

'Yes. Everything just goes back to the way it was the moment we walk out of this room. Nick clams up, he's really bad-tempered eighty per cent of the time, and the other twenty per cent he's either playing with the kids or is out himself. He didn't used to be so fucking grumpy all the time.'

'Tell Nick,' she insists.

'You didn't, Nick. You just didn't. You used to be fun. Now I feel like I'm walking on eggshells with you.' The sadness engulfs me so quickly I am unprepared for it. I try to swallow back the tears but it is too late. As I blink they stream down my cheeks and an involuntary sob escapes. Judy passes me the box of expensive four-ply tissues and I take one for now and one for my pocket. She stands and pours two glasses of water and passes them to us both and I gulp mine down in one go, handing her back the empty glass. Judy makes some notes, her pencil scratching away efficiently on her pad, and then looks directly at me.

'Emily, would you like to continue?' she asks.

Nick can't even look at me. I just want him to hold my hand, or give me a smile, anything. Instead he has plunged his hands in his pockets and is staring at the framed print of a waterfall on Judy's wall with a stoic intensity.

'Yes, OK,' I reply, and give my nose a loud blow.

Judy scans down her pad again, tapping it with the eraser end of her pencil before looking up and saying, 'Please. Go ahead.'

I take a deep breath as I try to organise my thoughts into something resembling a sentence. Then I begin. 'You

142

say I don't take your job seriously, but you seem to forget I have one too. I am trying to run my own business, while also looking after two small children, which is virtually impossible. I just seem to spend the whole time cleaning up after everyone. Do you know how much I hate pairing socks together? It literally makes my piss boil.'

Judy is nodding at me in agreement. 'What would you like Nick to do, Emily? Are there any practical things he can do?'

'I would just like him to—'

'Tell Nick, Emily.'

'I would just like you to pick up some of the slack without me having to ask you. To cook dinner once in a while without being asked. Or run the Hoover around. Not big things, just things that would make my life easier.'

'I give them their baths when I'm home, and do bedtime and read them a story.'

'I know. I know you do.' I'm exhausted. I don't think a single word has made an impact. How do you make someone change when they don't realise they're doing anything wrong in the first place?

'Are these things you think you could start to plan into your day, Nick?'

'Yes, I guess,' but there's no conviction in his voice. 'I am the main earner though, Em, so—'

'What? What do you actually mean by that, Nick? That because you go out to work every day while I'm with the children, you don't have to do anything, like it's the 1950s? Is he fucking joking?' I ask Judy, who momentarily lets her neutral mask slip and looks fleetingly unimpressed.

'No,' he shakes his head emphatically. 'Of course that's not what I mean. But your priorities are different now. You have more flexibility in your days, whereas I, I have to be at work at a certain time. I have to be in the office, because if I'm not, they won't pay me, Em. And as I am the only one bringing in any kind of proper income at the moment, I don't think we're really in a position to jeopardise that, are we?' I don't recognise his voice. He's functional, like when he's making a complaint to Southern Rail about a late service. This voice is reserved for people he doesn't know and has no time for. Not me. Never me. A shiver slides down my spine and I shuffle in the chair.

'OK. Please take away from this that you are both opening up and starting to listen, even if it might not necessarily be things you want to hear. This is all part of the process. I look forward to seeing you both next time.' Palms pressed. Session over.

Nick nods sombrely, then cricks his neck one side and then the other. These sessions were meant to help us find coping mechanisms so that we could be kinder to each other, parent better together, and generally have a bit of an easier life. But all they seem to be doing is shining a massive floodlight on all our differences. We don't seem to agree on anything, apart from our love for Lucy and Sophie. But I can't remember the last time we said 'I love you' to each other.

Maybe Nick was right. Maybe this is all a huge waste of time and money.

Chapter Twenty-Three

'Only me!' Mum shouts through the letterbox. 'I don't think your doorbell is working.'

'You *can* just knock, Mum.' I reply loudly as I prise open the door, which has swelled under the relentless heavy rain. She's squatting on the doorstep, clutching two Morrisons bags. Her Regatta all-weather coat has fallen off her shoulders as the rain beats down. I don't know whether it's because her hair looks thinner, plastered to her head in soggy clumps, or that she's slumping down to reach the letterbox, but Mum looks older. Old. A blanket of guilt wraps around me as I think of her and Dad travelling three hundred miles to visit us.

'Your dad's resting at the Travelodge,' she puffs as she unsteadily pulls herself to standing, batting away my hand as I reach to help her. 'The drive has really taken it out of him. He wouldn't normally drive non-stop to Brighton, you know. We normally take a break at Cambridge services so we can have a wee and a filter coffee at Harry Ramsden's, but not this time, he just kept on driving. Stubborn old fool. I think it's because he missed the right exit off the motorway, but he assures me it's just because he wanted to make good time. "For what?" I said to him. "It's not like Emily will be cooking a meal for us or anything is it?"' Mum hands me the carrier bags and removes her soggy jacket. 'Where shall I put this?' she asks.

'Just hang it over the bannister,' I point. 'You know you can stay here, Mum? The girls can just bunk in with me and you can both have their room. You don't have to stay in the Travelodge every time.'

'I know, I know,' she dismisses. 'But we like it there. And it means we're not getting under your feet. Now, enough of that and come here.'

I put down the bags as Mum wraps her arms around me, pulling me in tight, but as I squeeze her back, she lets out an involuntary yelp.

I hold her at arm's length. 'Sorry, Mum, was that too hard?'

'A bear hug can never be too hard, Emily. Things just ache a bit more these days. Right, shall we unpack these?' She picks up the bags with a huff and heads into the kitchen, going on autopilot and putting away pasta, tins and cleaning products in all the wrong cupboards.

'And you didn't need to bring all this, Mum, we do have shops down here,' I tease.

'I know you do, Emily. But the Morrisons in Grimsby has always been very competitive compared to your southern supermarkets. And they had some fantastic offers on, I just couldn't resist.'

I flick the kettle on and sit at the kitchen table, watching as Mum opens and slams doors.

'So how are my favourite girls?' she asks over her shoulder.

As an only child I had forever been her favourite girl. I should be delighted that Mum adores Lucy and Sophie so much, but occasionally I have an unexpected itch for her to just adore me, followed by a giant dollop of guilt for even thinking it.

'They're good. Lucy's enjoying school and Sophie's

146

causing mischief at nursery. But they're both happy, so that's the main thing.'

'And are they . . .' Mum pauses, gathering her thoughts, clutching a tin of beans mid-air. 'Are they *coping* with you and Nick being, you know?'

'You can say it, Mum. Separated. And yes. They're fine. They seem to like that they've got two places to play, two parents to spoil them separately. They don't seem to really notice all that much, to be honest, as long as we keep to a routine. It's all fine. Everything's fine,' I reassure her, realising I may have said 'fine' at least one too many times.

'So, everything's settling down, is it?' she probes.

'Yes, Mum. And before you ask, no, it hasn't happened again. All that business has stopped. I think he's really getting it together now,' I say with undue conviction, and put the teabags in the cups, filling them up with the boiled water. 'And soon we'll be able to pay you back. I've just got a couple of new clients who are bringing in some more regular work, so I'm able to put some aside. And Nick assures me he's doing the same,' I add.

'Now listen here, Emily,' she faces me, hands on hips. 'We don't want you to worry about that, there is no hurry. None at all. Dad and I don't need it at the moment, we're perfectly comfortable. The main thing is that you are all safe and stable. Understood?'

'Yes, it's just—'

'It's just nothing,' she interrupts. Mum locks eyes with me. A beat, and then she simply states, 'Emily. I'm your mum. It's my job to keep you safe.'

There's something in her tone, the assurance, being looked after instead of looking after, that starts to unravel me. I have been all right, better than all right, on the whole.

147

But I am also exhausted. I blink back the tears but it's too late and they spill down my cheeks.

'I don't even know why I'm crying,' I sob, and wipe my runny nose on the sleeve of my cardigan.

'Don't do that,' Mum soothes, handing me a tissue from her pocket as she lowers herself into the seat next to me and gently places her arm around me, pulling me into her. She has definitely got smaller, I think as I curl down to rest my head on her shoulder. She strokes my hair, and I start to feel myself relax, suddenly feeling extremely tired, my body heavy as stone. The thought of even getting up to go to the toilet seems incomprehensible, let alone going out for the night with Tania and Helen later on.

'It can't be easy,' she whispers. 'I'm so proud of you.'

'For what?' I snuffle, going to wipe my nose again on my sleeve before remembering the tissue. 'For splitting up with my husband? That's nothing to be proud of, is it? You and Dad have managed to stay together forever.'

'Things aren't always straightforward, Emily.' She kisses the top of my head, as I remember I haven't washed my hair in days and will need to dry shampoo it before the evening. 'I don't think anyone has a happy marriage every day of their life. It's impossible. Sometimes things improve and you can move past problems, and that's great. Sometimes you can't. And when you can't, there's a choice to be made. Stay in an unhappy marriage, or look to make changes.' She sighs heavily and then continues to stroke my hair. 'All I'm saying is, it was a brave decision you made. You and Nick. You could have stayed together and torn strips off each other for the rest of your lives. But you didn't. And for that, my darling girl, I am proud of you. Both of you. Right, let's drink these teas before they get cold, hey?'

Mum pats her hair, bouffing the thinning grey nest into

shape. I remember Nanny used to do the same thing, so it must be a reflex that comes with age. I instinctively run my hands through my greasy shoulder-length dark hair.

Mum arranges a packet of chocolate Hobnobs on a plate. 'Your dad will be livid if he knows we've made a start on these without him, but that's his own fault for having an afternoon nap, isn't it?'

I start to nibble the chocolate off the top while trying to keep the biscuit in one piece and ask, 'But you and Dad have always been OK, haven't you?'

'Eat that properly, Emily, you're getting crumbs every-where,' she gently scolds.

I wonder if she heard my question or is simply choosing to ignore it, so I help myself to another Hobnob and am two large mouthfuls into it when she takes a deep breath, exhales and then begins, 'I had second thoughts before we got married.'

'What kind of second thoughts?' I press.

'That I wasn't ready for marriage. That your dad wasn't ready either.' She shrugs, and starts working at a bit of dried egg stuck to the plastic-coated tablecloth with her nail.

'When was this?' I try to hide my shock. Mum and Dad are the most solid couple I know. When I was at school, they were the model parents who would never get divorced, when everyone else's families were falling apart around us.

'Six weeks before the wedding. The church was booked, the flowers ordered. We were going to have the reception in the room above the Red Lion on the high street and your Auntie Jean was making us a wedding cake.'

'But Auntie Jean can't cook, can she?'

'I know! But she offered, and we didn't have much money, so we'd said yes.' She stares into the middle distance. Lost in her memories.

149

'And then?' I encourage.

'And then, I had a handful of wedding invitations ready to take to the post office, and your nanny simply said, "Are you sure you're ready?" I thought she'd meant to head out to post them. But she asked again, "Are you sure you're ready?" And I realised she was giving me a choice. That everything didn't have to happen now, if I didn't want it to.'

'What did you say?' I am sitting on the edge of my seat, balancing precariously in anticipation.

'Well,' Mum folds and unfolds the spare tissue she has plucked from her cardigan sleeve. 'Me and your nanny sat and talked for a long time. I told her how I loved Richard.' Mum hardly ever refers to Dad as "Richard" to me and it takes me a beat to realise who she's talking about. 'But that I couldn't imagine being his wife, being *anyone's* wife at that moment.'

'And what did Nanny say?'

'She took the wedding invitations from my hand, put them in a drawer and said that everything was going to be OK. She rang the church, rang the florist, told Auntie Jean to stop stockpiling bloody marzipan. She gave me space to decide what I wanted to do,' Mum smiles and nods to herself.

'And Dad?' I venture.

'Well, your dad wasn't so understanding to start with, naturally. He thought I meant never, when what I really meant was, not right then. We carried on courting, it was difficult at times as he felt insecure, that I didn't want to marry him, that I didn't want to be with him, which simply wasn't the case. It exposed friendships that weren't meant to be, as some of the chaps from his university teased and mocked him. Some of the girls from my work whispered behind my back. But a year on, while on holiday in Whitley Bay, I got down on one knee on the beach and I proposed to your dad.'

'No you didn't!' I shriek, throwing my hands to my mouth in surprise.

'Yes I did, Emily Jones. And your father said yes. Two months later we were married, and not long after that, I fell pregnant with you.' She clutches my face with both hands and plants a loud kiss on my forehead.

'Fucking hell, Mum! How do I not know this?'

Mum raises a disapproving eyebrow at the language, but lets it go. 'Your dad's still sensitive about it, as you can understand, so don't go bringing it up with him, love.'

'Of course,' I nod firmly.

'But the point I'm trying to make,' she continues, 'is that things don't always go according to the masterplan. But you have to follow your instincts, because that's all we can truly rely on.' She stands up with a quiet groan and says, 'Right then, shall we put that kettle on again?' Her tone different, assertive, that line of conversation closed.

'Can I have a herbal one this time?' I ask.

'Of course.' She opens the cupboard next to the sink. 'Have you moved them?' she asks.

'Ah yes, I had a big spring clean in here and moved things around a bit, made them a bit more logical. They're there now,' I point to the shelf near the kettle.

'That makes much more sense,' Mum agrees.

I check the large kitchen wall clock, which is now working again, batteries replaced.

'We have about forty minutes before we need to pick the girls up.'

'Great. I can't wait!' She pours the boiling water into the cups. 'Did I tell you that we met Rachel's new man the other day? She brought him to the pub quiz a week or so ago. I hate those things to be honest, but it was a fundraiser for the new roof on the Methodist Hall, so me and your dad went along for moral support. Anyway, we hadn't really thought about teams, but when we got to the pub Rachel and Mark—'

'Matt,' I correct.

'Yes, that's right, Matt, were there and they asked if we'd like to join them to make a team of four. We had a hoot. Here you go,' she passes me the cup. 'I liked him.'

'He went to school with us—'

'He said.'

'He was two years above us—'

'He said that too. Well, they looked very comfortable together to me,' Mum remarks before adding, 'but all young people are much more affectionate with each other than we were back in the early days.'

She stands, clears my once-sipped cup away absent-mindedly and tips it in the sink before I have time to protest, adding, 'I'll just give your dad a quick ring so he can get over here before we head out to the school. What time are we babysitting from tonight?'

'I told Helen and Tania I'd meet them at seven thirty, if that's OK with you?'

'Perfect. Now how's about you wash your face before your dad arrives? You look like you've been crying. He wants to have a chat with you about your Christmas plans when he gets here as well.'

Her back is to me at the sink, this is intentional, so I don't see her expression and how this is a 100 per cent lie. She, like me, has the most appalling poker face. Dad doesn't want to talk about Christmas with me. As long as there's a turkey and enough Baileys to put him into an overindulgence coma, Dad gives absolutely no shits about Christmas plans; these things happen *to* him not *with* him. This is Mum. She is trying to help. She is trying to get me mobilised to plan ahead, to think about the future. And I will. I really will for the girls' sake, but right now the thought of Christmas makes me want to curl up into a teeny-tiny ball, cover myself in a duvet, then a blanket, a rug and several oversized scatter cushions, and just hide underneath them until January.

Chapter Twenty-Four

'She did what?' Tania splutters, almost spitting out her Sauvignon Blanc.

'She just invited herself around to the next-door neighbours. I'd been looking for her for what felt like hours, and then I spotted Mum through their window, sitting on their sofa like they were old mates.'

'And you say she doesn't know them?' Emily asks.

'No. I barely know them!' Helen explains. 'I thought they were called Rebecca and Brian, but turns out they're Ruth and Derek, which is embarrassing as I've been sending Rebecca and Brian Christmas cards for the last four years. Anyway, when I went round to get her, it turned out she was plastered, as were they, but with her encouragement, I imagine.'

'Oh fuck,' Tania replies sympathetically.

'And that's not even the worst bit! As she tried to get off the sofa she lost her balance and somehow got herself wedged between the sofa and the table. She lost a high heel as Brian, sorry, Derek tried to help her up, and we ended up leaving it there by mistake. I haven't seen them since, but I left some flowers and a card apologising for Mum's behaviour on their door-step. And they, in turn, left Mum's shoe on our doormat.' She chuckles to herself, but the laugh quickly turns into a sob as she wipes her eyes. 'And then this happens,' Helen points to her face. 'I start to cry. It's completely ridiculous, I feel like I am walking an emotional tightrope, one minute laughing, the next falling to pieces.'

Emily wraps her arms around Helen and Tania starts to massage the pressure points on her hand.

'The thing is,' Helen continues, 'she was never meant to move in with us. That was never the plan. I'm not even sure how this has happened. I've had virtually nothing to do with her for years and now here she is, every single fucking day. Making her demands and judging the way that I do stuff.' Helen pauses, taking an uncharacteristically noisy gulp of her wine. 'I know she's my mum, but sometimes I hate her. She is just so . . .' Helen balls her hands into fists as she tries to find the word, 'selfish. She always has been. She got rid of Dad because he wasn't convenient, and then fucks off to live in Spain because it's warmer. It's not fair. None of this is fair.'

Tania and Emily pass a look between each other, before Emily asks, 'How is Chris about all of this?'

'Burying his head in the sand, as usual. Pretending nothing's happening. It's like looking after three kids at the moment.' Helen flops her head into her arms on the table and groans loudly. 'Fuuuuuuuuck. So sorry. I wanted to come out to get away from my bloody mother. I'm so fed up thinking about her every day, I don't want to spend tonight talking about her too. Everyone want the same again?' They nod as Helen scrapes back her chair and heads to the bar. She rubs her forehead with the palm of her hand as she waits to be served. How is it that Janet ruins everything, even when she's not there? Helen takes a deep breath and vows to not talk about her for the rest of the evening. Tonight is meant to be fun. She's not going to let Janet sabotage it.

*

'Here you go,' Helen places a bottle of wine on the table, quickly ducks back to the bar and returns with three tequila shots.

'Oh no, Hels, I've got a deadline tomorrow. I can't,' Emily protests.

'You can,' she replies, knocking back her shot in one well-practised move. 'I've been having such a shitty time recently. I need to get drunk with my friends.'

Emily and Tania grimace as they both down their tequila, not needing much encouragement after all.

'You're very lucky, you know, that you get on with your mum so well,' Helen says as she pours three generous glasses of wine from the bottle.

'I know,' Emily nods. Listening to Helen talk about her mum terrifies her. She has tried to imagine what it would be like for her mum to start to lose her memory like Janet, to start to behave out of character, to not be the mum she knows and loves and has grown up with, relied on, fought and cried with, but the thought is too much for her heart to cope with.

'I can't believe she came all the way down here to babysit!' Tania adds.

'Well, they're here for a couple of days, and I will take her and Dad out tomorrow. She's not *just* babysitting,' Emily adds guiltily.

'Still. She's another species to my mum, who just tries to paper over the cracks with cheques and over-the-top presents,' Tania tells them.

'Like what?' Emily ask.

'Well . . .' She takes a sip of her drink. 'Remember when Falcon was a baby and she bought us a car?'

'Oh God, yes,' Helen replies. 'It was a Jag, wasn't it?'

'Yep. Proper swanky. I must have told her a thousand

times how we don't want to drive, how we try to walk everywhere or get the bus. So, it was like a really expensive way of saying she doesn't listen to anything I say or respect our life choices.'

'I wish my mum would disrespect my life choices with a fifty-grand car,' Helen replies thoughtfully.

'Yeah, well. We had to give it back in the end. Spiral was forever getting stopped by the police because they thought he'd nicked it.'

'So what about you?' Tania squeezes Emily's shoulder.

'What about me?'

'Well, are you going to give the performance of a lifetime to Nick's parents and pretend you're still happily married?' she asks.

'Oh *that*,' Emily groans as she pulls apart the beer mat in thin strips, leaving the curls on the table. 'Yes, they're coming down this weekend after my folks leave, so I've got to make a decision. It all seems so dishonest. I can't bear to add to the lies. But on the other hand, it's just lunch really; I only have to get through lunch. I would happily put my head in a cement mixer before doing Nick a favour at the moment. But none of this is his parents' fault.'

'It's not just you going though, is it? There's the girls . . .' Tania adds.

'Yes, the girls. That's the bit that really doesn't sit well with me. I don't want them to have to lie.'

'Then don't do it,' Helen replies. 'Don't do it if it makes you feel uncomfortable.'

'God. I don't know. What would you do?' Emily asks.

'I don't know,' Helen says. 'He's not exactly got good form with telling the truth recently. Isn't this just validating it?' Helen tries to imagine if that was Chris what she would do, but it's impossible to compare. Chris is solid. Reliable.

157

He is the polar opposite of her mum. Sometimes Helen wonders if that's what she found so appealing about him in the first place.

'This is different.' Emily starts shredding another beer mat before Helen takes it from her hand.

'Is it though?'

Emily starts to pick at her nail varnish instead. 'I'll think about it. Right, should I get some more shots?' Emily asks, completely forgetting her earlier protests.

'I'm with Falcon tomorrow and Spiral says they've got to do all the snagging for the site they're fixing up, so I can't rely on him to be back at a decent time to help.'

'Is he doing flexible hours now?' Emily asks.

'Nope. I don't think so, not that he's mentioned. Why?'

'Oh nothing, really. I've just seen him outside The Gladstone a few times recently, so I just thought—'

'What kind of time?' Tania snaps.

'About two o'clock,' Emily replies breezily, unaware of the shit-storm brewing.

'And how often?'

'Err, a few times, maybe? Not too sure,' Emily says.

Helen watches the scene play out, beat by beat: Tania's tightly pursed lips; Emily's realisation that she was dropping Spiral right in it. Helen, normally the peacekeeper, cannot think of one positive alternative for Spiral's actions, so takes another large gulp of her wine instead and checks her phone to see if Chris has texted. He hasn't. There would be a time when she would feel disappointed to not hear from him but now she's just relieved, as it means her mum's behaving.

'But definitely more than once?' Tania interrogates.

'Yeah, I think?' Emily adds weakly. 'I had a few meetings last week with clients in that part of town, so drove past the pub on my way back for pick-up. He might have just been having his lunch?' Emily suggests, but Tania is not having any of it.

'Outside the pub? His favourite pub that's nowhere near the site they've been working on? I doubt it. That total shit. Has he been relaxing in the pub while I've been running around like a fucking idiot trying to squeeze in my practice around bloody homeschooling? And why would you sit at the front of the pub where you're more likely to be seen? Why wouldn't you sit in the beer garden around that back? He really is *that* stupid, isn't he?'

'So sorry, Tania, I didn't mean to get him in trouble,' Emily apologises quietly.

'Trouble? He doesn't know the meaning of the word trouble. When I finish with him—'

'There might be an explanation,' Helen finally pipes up.

'There is.' Tania knocks back the rest of her wine. 'He's a work-shy, lazy bastard. But I have his number now. He thought a ten-day silent meditation was hard. That's nothing compared to what I have planned for him,' Tania growls, as she stands to go to the bar.

'Fuck,' Emily mouths to Helen.

'Poor Spiral,' she mouths back. He has absolutely no idea the shit he's in, she thinks.

Chapter Twenty-Five

'When's Daddy home?' Falcon whines.

Today's homeschooling has been mainly watching back-to-back episodes of *Teenage Mutant Ninja Turtles*, as Tania nursed the mother of all hangovers. They did pop out to the newsagent's for Monster Munches and Coke, but other than that they have barely opened the curtains.

'Soon,' Tania croaks. She was in the shower when Spiral left this morning, so she hasn't had the chance to confront him yet.

'He's here!' Falcon beams as the door slams open with a bang. He leaps off the sofa and sprints towards the door.

Give him a chance. Maybe Helen's right. Maybe there is a totally logical explanation, she reminds herself, closing her eyes and breathing deeply.

'Hey, beautiful.' He fluffs her hair affectionately, before flopping down onto the sofa next to her.

'Come here, boy,' he calls to Falcon who is following him like a small shadow and obediently climbs up next to him on the sofa.

'My favourite is Michaelangelo, who's your favourite, Dad?' Falcon points to the TV.

'Donatello.' He kisses the top of Falcon's head noisily, before turning to Tania. How can he even remember the names of all the turtles, let alone have an opinion on them? Tania thinks. 'How was your day?' Spiral asks her as he pats her thigh affectionately.

'We've just watched telly and eaten crisps, haven't we, Mum?'

'Ha!' Spiral grins. 'I thought it might have been a late one with the girls.'

He attempts to put his arm around her, but Tania moves her head, and asks, 'Enough about our boring day. We want to hear what you've been up to, don't we, Falcon?' she says, trying to suppress the sarcastic tone.

'Tough day, love. The site is water-logged so we had to get a forklift in to start to build a dam to make it safe. It's hard work, really physical. I've spent the whole day lugging about massive planks of wood. I'm absolutely shattered. But it will be worth it. Just got the marquee to put up tomorrow, which, again, is going to be a pain as the pegs won't hold in sodden ground, so we'll have to find some inventive ways around that. Off,' he instructs Falcon, before going over to open the fridge. 'Fancy a beer? Might level you out if you're still feeling rough?'

'No thanks. So, let me get this straight. Is this the same site that you and Andy were working on before or . . .' she persists.

'No, this is different. This is for a winter wedding,' he explains, taking a noisy slurp of his beer.

'Oh right, I thought that was only going to be a small job you said,' she enquires calmly.

'Yes, it was. But these things can often be bigger than we thought. That's why we plan in some contingency. Isn't that right, Falcon?' he adds, lifting him up and holding him upside down, much to Falcon's delighted protests.

'It's funny that,' Tania continues, standing and speaking

to the back of his head. 'Because Emily's seen you in The Gladstone recently.'

'Oh, well,' Spiral splutters. 'Nothing wrong with popping in for a quick sociable pint to end the day,' he explains defensively.

'Oh, she must have got it wrong, because she said when she drove past it was lunchtime.'

Spiral pauses, just fractionally, but enough for him to give his lie away before muttering, 'She must have got it wrong.'

'She must have,' Tania replies, warming up to her subject, the acid hangover transmuting to fury. 'It's just she said she's seen you a few times sat outside. See, she's doing some work with a client that side of town, so passes by it quite often.' Tania notices that Spiral has stopped drinking, the bottle suspended mid-air. 'I just thought that was odd,' Tania adds innocently. 'What with you working such long shifts every day and everything.'

'OK, so—'

'I said she must have been mistaken, because if you weren't at work, you would certainly come home to help me with Falcon and the house and not just head to the pub. So yes, she must have got it wrong.'

'Can I just—'

'It seems to me like I have been working my arse off teaching sunrise yoga, before homeschooling Falcon most of the week, then running out to teach practice in the evening, making you dinner and sorting everything out in the house for when you come home, as you've been working so very, *very* hard. When in reality, you've been spending half the day in the pub. Would that be a good summary of what's happening here, Spiral? Would you say I have outlined the main bullet points of this situation effectively?' she asks, stony cold.

162

'Falcon, could you go to your room?' Spiral asks quietly.

'But I wanted to watch—'

'Now, please,' he kisses him and gives him a gentle pat on the bum as Falcon strops out the room, muttering, 'It's not fair.'

'Now, Tania,' he turns to face her, once Falcon has left, his face ashen. 'It's not what you think.'

Tania lowers herself into the kitchen chair. 'OK.' She's using her meditation voice, knowing the only way to not bludgeon Spiral to death with the Quorn hot dogs that are boiling on the stove is to keep her cool. 'Please tell me what I should think, Peter.'

Spiral physically flinches at the name. Tania has never, in the history of their relationship, called him Peter. The name represents another lifetime, it's a name that no longer fits the man, just like Arabella is no longer a name Tania identifies with. The name sounds foreign and uncomfortable, like calling an authority figure a twat. It doesn't go down well.

'So, if I can just explain,' Spiral peels off the label on the beer nervously. 'It turns out we're getting paid per job, not per hour.'

'That sounds nice, Spiral. But what has that got to do with spending all afternoon in the pub, instead of coming back here to help with the mountain of shit I have to deal with?'

'Well, so I still get paid the same, Tania, the money's still coming in, we're still good for that,' he rambles.

'Well, that *is* good news, Spiral,' Tania replies coldly. 'Please continue.'

'But, sometimes, not every day, but now and then, the gaffer has been letting us go about three-ish, if we've got done what we need to for that day. He says it doesn't make good business sense to get the jobs finished really quickly, otherwise folk will think they're overpaying us and then we'll have to reduce our quotes, so that's kind of it. In a nutshell.'

'So let me get this straight,' Tania locks eyes with Spiral, unblinking. 'You are doing the gaffer a *favour* by spending the afternoon in the pub, because the alternative is that the jobs will be finished sooner and everyone would have their pay docked. Is that what you're telling me? In a nutshell?' she asks sarcastically.

'Well, when you put it like that, I guess, yes. In a nutshell. Yes,' he replies stupidly, not picking up on her tone.

'OK, Spiral. This is what is going to happen,' she stands, hands on hips and Spiral realises too late how much he's fucked up.

'The after-work trips to the pub stop. Now. The money you spend there goes into the Christmas jar,' she indicates towards the jam jar that is half full of pennies and loose screws on top of the microwave. 'You come home when your shift finishes and help out. Help with the cleaning, help with Falcon, help with cooking and not just burnt eggy-fucking-bread. Deal?' she asks, but this is a rhetorical question.

'Deal,' he bows his head like a scorned puppy.

'And one final thing,' she adds as Spiral looks up pitifully.

'Name it,' he responds.

'We are all going to my mum and dad's for Christmas.' The final blow, her *pièce de résistance*. Her mic drop. BOOM. And she walks out of the room.

Chapter Twenty-Six

'Emily! Emily!' Dennis greets me, open-armed. He pulls me into an awkward hug and slaps my back like a fellow rugby player. 'So! How is my number-one daughter-in-law?' he asks, holding me by the shoulders at arm's length for the full inspection. I can't believe I agreed to this.

'I'm well, thanks, Dennis. And you?'

Nick shuffles uncomfortably next to me, kicking the edge of the kerb like a fourteen-year-old boy.

'Can't complain. Can't complain.' Dennis always says everything twice.

'And here they are, the main attraction!' Lucy cowers behind my legs and Sophie strains in the buggy to move away from his booming voice. 'Can I have a hug with my favourite girls?' Dennis's knees crick noisily as he attempts to squat down on the pavement.

'Lucy, do you want to say hi to Granddad?' Nick's voice is strained and an octave higher than normal. He has got to chill out or we're not going to make it through the starters, let alone the weekend.

'Do I have to, Mummy?' a muffled voice asks, buried somewhere in my jeans.

'Of course not!' Nick sing songs. 'Sophie?'

Sophie has her arms firmly folded. 'No.'

'Well, we have all weekend to become firm friends again,' Dennis assures us, as Nick holds him under the armpit and attempts to hoick him up into a standing position.

'Shall we go in then?' As Nick pushes open the door to the restaurant a gust of warm air escapes carrying a waft of spicy food.

'Shouldn't we wait for Cathleen?' I look at Dennis, who is already halfway through the double doors.

'She's just popped into Boots for some travel sickness tablets, Emily. You know how she doesn't travel well.' Dennis heads inside. They've only had a three-hour car journey from Nottingham, *and* they stopped for a coffee outside Dartford. How bad can Dennis's driving be?

'Thank you,' Nick whispers as I follow Dennis in.

I pretend I can't hear him, as I clutch Lucy's hand and push the buggy past him. The first thing that strikes me is how busy, yet calm, the restaurant is. Every table is occupied but the conversation is at a quiet, civilised buzz, like background chatter.

Which is when I notice the second thing. There are no children. Not one. And each table is beautifully set out with white tablecloths and candles. A large chandelier hangs elegantly from the middle of the room, and a pianist is playing something I recognise from an expensive car advert. Now, I know Nick has been in daily correspondence with his mum about what she'd like to do on her 'big weekend in Brighton', as it's been billed. So I have left all arrangements to them, but I wonder if Nick had mentioned we're bringing children with us when he made the booking?

I grab his arm and pull his ear close to my mouth. 'You could have told me we were going somewhere posh.'

'I *did* say where we were going,' he shrugs nonchalantly.

'No, you didn't. You said we'd meet at the Pavilion and walk there together. You didn't say where we'd walk to.'

'Shit, sorry, Em.' As he takes his coat off I see he's

dressed for the occasion. He's wearing a crisp white shirt and what look like his wedding trousers. He's even polished his shoes. In stark contrast, I look like I should be heading straight into the kitchen to put on an apron and help with peeling the spuds. I have on my trusty jeans complete with a yoghurt stain from Sophie's breakfast on one leg, which to the untrained eye looks a bit like spunk, my battered Converse and a T-shirt with 'Female Protagonist' embossed across my chest, which Rachel bought me for my last birthday. Lucy and Sophie are thankfully both wearing matching floral dresses that Dennis and Cathleen gave them last Christmas. I smooth down my hair and wonder if I can just wear my fake-fur leopard-print coat throughout the meal.

'Table for Jones,' Nick announces to the waiter.

We follow him to the corner table near the window. Nick and his dad scrape their chairs back in unison making the hair on the back of my neck stand to attention. Nick's irritating habits are even more annoying when experienced in stereo with Dennis.

'May I take your coats?' The waiter asks. There goes my armour. 'And would you like me to find somewhere to store the pram?'

'Yes, of course.' I lift Sophie out of the buggy and pull her coat off. 'Just sit here.' I plonk her on one of the chairs next to Nick. 'Can you keep an eye on her?'

'Course.' Lucy is already sitting on Nick's lap, scrolling through pictures on his phone. He scoops Sophie up as well, who sees her opportunity and nips Lucy's arm.

'SHE PINCHED ME!' Lucy yells at the top of her voice.

'She pinched *me*,' Sophie imitates.

The couple sat on the table next to us look round, the man glares furiously and shakes his head at his dinner date. Nick attempts to placate Lucy while holding the wriggling Sophie in a gentle headlock. I retrieve the bag of toys, my handbag and the Aldi bag full of snacks from the bottom of the pram and push it towards the waiter.

'Thank you, madam. And have you had a chance to have a look at the drinks menu?' he asks Dennis.

'Yes. Yes.' Dennis asserts. 'We will have a bottle of the 2010 Rioja please.' And he slams the menu shut with a satisfied thump.

'With pleasure, sir.' The waiter is smiling as he wheels off the pram.

'Dad,' Nick hisses over Lucy's head. 'That's ninety pounds a bottle!'

'Well, it is a special occasion isn't it? How often do we get to see our glorious family all together? CATHLEEN, CATHLEEN!' he waves enthusiastically as she weaves her way through the tables, clutching two large Boots bags. She is wearing a fascinator, an elaborate nest of green and yellow feathers like a parakeet.

Sophie crawls into my lap, cups my ear and whispers loudly, 'It smells funny here, Mummy.'

'It's going to be delicious,' I reassure her, planting a kiss on her soft cheek.

'You can have two bags of Mentos and watch *The Greatest Showman* later on if you sit in your seat for the rest of the meal,' I hear Nick negotiating Lucy into her own seat.

'Don't put your head up my top,' I squeal.

'It's my den,' Sophie announces. I wrestle her out of my clothes, but not before flashing Dennis my bra. He turns crimson and waves both arms at Cathleen, like a drowning swimmer signalling for help. 'Over here! Over here!'

'Gosh, sorry I'm late. The Boots here is fantastic, not like the one in Nottingham. You really are lucky,' she tells Nick as she leans in and kisses him on his cheek with a smack, leaving a coral-coloured lipstick mark.

'Yes, it's a big one, all right!' In a previous lifetime, Nick would have said that as a filthy joke for my benefit and we'd squeeze hands under the table, but not now. Now he is genuinely talking about the footprint of Brighton's Boots.

'You look tired. Don't you think he looks tired, Dennis?' Cathleen fusses, then, as if suddenly remembering I'm here too, wrestles her way round the table, holds my head in both hands and kisses me. I breathe in the familiar heavy scent of her perfume.

'Hello, Emily,' she smiles, before her eyes widen and she remarks, 'You look very casual. I wish I could carry off jeans.'

'Hello, Cathleen.'

'And hello my precious little angels. Can I have a cuddle with my lovely girls?' She passes her red coat to Dennis, who, in turn, passes it to a waiter. Underneath she is wearing a bold cerise floral dress. That coupled with the fascinator makes her look like she's attending a royal wedding.

'Hello, Lucy.' She strokes Sophie's face who's still curled up in my lap.

'That's Sophie, I'm Lucy.' Our eldest doesn't even look up from Nick's phone as she corrects her.

'Well, haven't you grown, Sophie?'

'No,' Sophie huffs.

'Don't worry, Cathleen. That's her default answer to everything at the moment,' I reassure her.

'Sit down. Sit down, Cathleen.' Dennis pats the chair next to him as Cathleen pushes her way through the gap between the tables in reverse.

'Well, isn't this place exquisite? Thank you darling for finding such a *wonderful* restaurant.' She dotes on Nick.

'Oh Mum, it was you who found it. I only made the booking.' He glows with satisfaction.

'It was online, Emily. I'm useless at computers. Thank goodness Nick is so tech-savvy. And how are you, Emily? How is the council?'

'I haven't worked there for over a year, Cathleen.' I open two packets of Pom-Bears and pass them to the girls. 'I've started my own business now. I'm copywriting.'

'Well, that *is* wonderful, Emily. I really don't know how you do it with the children, I really don't. I found it impossible to think of working when Nick was so young, didn't I, Dennis? And I only had my one precious boy. Here you are with two beautiful children, beavering away. How does she do it, Nick?' I know Cathleen means well. I know her heart is in the right place. I know she adores the children, but right now I want to crush her stupid fascinator with my bare hands. Instead I count to ten in my head.

'She's just very good at making things happen,' he replies and I smile gratefully at him.

'She must be. You must be. I really do admire working mothers. Your mum went back to work when you were just a baby, didn't she?'

'Yes. Yes she did.'

'Well there you have it. It's in the genes, isn't it, Dennis?'

'That's right, Cathleen. In the genes. It's all in the genes,' he mutters while studying the menu. 'Well, heaven really is a place on earth, everything looks splendid here. Do you think the children would like to try the veal, Nick?'

'I doubt it,' I mutter.

'And how about you, Nick? You work so very hard these days. Doesn't he work hard, Emily? Don't you think he looks tired?'

170

'Stop fussing, Mum. I'm fine,' he says, but I can tell by his voice he's loving the attention. 'Work's good. I've got a couple of big clients at the moment. I'm currently working with a law firm in Japan as they are going through a major restructure.'

'Did you hear that, Dennis? Nick's doing some work in Japan. You must be ever so proud of him, Emily.'

'You're not actually *working* in Japan though are you, Nick? It's all by email, isn't it?' I correct.

'Like I said,' Cathleen beams, 'he's tech-savvy.'

Sophie pushes her head up my top again. 'That's enough now, Sophie. Sit still or we'll go home.' I lift her off me and put her down on the chair beside me.

'I *want* to go home,' she whines.

'Me too. This is boring.' Lucy agrees.

'Who says things are boring?' Nick asks.

'Boring people.' Sophie and Lucy parrot flatly.

'That's right, girls. We don't say boring in our house, do we?' Nick replies.

'But you're not in our house any more,' Lucy remarks, glued to the screen.

I flash Nick a panicked look.

'That's not very kind, Lucy,' Cathleen, as ever, comes to her son's rescue.

'It's true, isn't it, Mummy? Daddy's house is better. It has got a big fridge with an ice machine. And there's a football net in the garden and a bird box for owls, isn't there, Daddy?' Lucy asks.

'It's true, Granny,' Sophie agrees, eating the Pom-Bears three at a time.

'Have you had a chance to look at the menu?' Nick squeaks.

'Well, I quite fancy the look of the steak. That would go nicely with the wine. Cathleen? Anything jump out at you?

171

Anything float your boat? Anything tickle your fancy?'
Dennis guffaws.

'What do the girls mean, Nick?' Cathleen asks, fixing her stare on Nick.

'Oh, they're just playing a game, Mum,' Nick says dismissively.

'No we're not, Daddy. That's fibbing. What? Why's Daddy looking at me like that, Mummy? You said we should always tell the truth,' Lucy insists.

'Daddy's a fibber,' Sophie echoes.

I knew this was a dreadful idea. It was totally unfair to expect the girls to stay quiet about one of the biggest changes that has happened in their life to date. I should have listened to Mum and followed my instincts.

'I think the risotto looks good, Dad.' Nick talks directly to Dennis, as if he can make the other conversation completely disappear by ignoring it.

'Nick. Can you give me a straight answer, please?' Cathleen demands.

'Who would like to try the wine?' the waiter asks. Where did he come from?

'Nick?' his dad asks.

'No you do it, Dad,' says Nick, picking nervously at a hangnail.

'Well then, that would be me.' Dennis opens his arms wide, as if about to bow.

The waiter pops the cork and glugs a drop into the glass. Dennis makes a huge production of swirling it around. He sticks his nose directly in the glass and breathes deeply.

'Ooh, that's quite a bouquet. That really is something. It *really* is something, Cathleen. Just look at the legs on that.' He holds his glass up to the light, but Cathleen's eyes are still firmly locked on Nick.

Her impatience fizzes. 'Just drink it, Dennis,' she snaps.

He throws back the wine in one gulp. 'Now *that* is a good bottle. Fill her up, my good sir!' he enthuses at the waiter, who leans over, arm behind his back and tops up Dennis's glass. He then moves around to Cathleen, me, and finally Nick. 'Excuse me, young lady,' the waiter says to Lucy, who looks up and grins briefly, before once more locking her eyes on the screen as she flicks through Nick's pictures, one-by-one.

The waiter picks up the empty packet of Pom-Bears without comment and asks, 'Are you ready to order or would you like a couple more minutes?'

'I'm ready,' Dennis announces at the same time Cathleen says, 'A couple more minutes.'

'A couple more minutes, I think. A couple more minutes,' Dennis agrees.

As the waiter turns to leave, Cathleen pounces. 'So, Nick. I think we are waiting for an explanation. What did the girls mean about your house?'

'You live in Simon's house, don't you, Daddy?' Lucy looks up from the screen momentarily.

'Lucy,' I whisper. 'That's enough.'

'Why? Granny was just asking—'

'Nick? What's going on?' Cathleen's voice quivers.

'Son?' Dennis asks.

'Emily? Can you fill in the gaps here, please? Have you asked my son to move out?'

'Now, hang on, Cathleen,' I say, far louder than I had intended.

'Daddy, who's this?' Lucy is holding the phone up to him.

'Mum, I have wanted to talk to you both about this, I just haven't found the right time, and we've been so looking forward to—'

173

'Daddy! Who's this girl?' Lucy tries again to get his attention.

'Not now, sweetheart.' Nick attempts to quieten Lucy. 'We . . . that is, Emily and I have been having some difficulties—'

'Whose idea was this? Was this yours, Emily?' Cathleen wails. 'I always knew this would happen. I should have seen this coming earlier! We worried that it wouldn't last. That it was a flight-of-fancy holiday romance.' She throws her arms in the air melodramatically.

'Cathleen,' Dennis soothes.

'You said the same, Dennis, don't pretend you didn't,' she snaps.

'Now hang on a—' I start to say, before Lucy cuts me off.

'Mummy, do you know who this is?' Lucy passes me the phone.

On the screen is a photo of Nick. He has his arm wrapped around a blonde woman I don't recognise. They are clumsily smiling at the camera, which Nick is holding at arm's length. She's wearing Nick's Fred Perry jacket that I bought him for his thirty-fifth. I had sex with him while he was still wearing it on the night of his birthday. We'd come back from an evening in the pub, and he was sun-kissed and messy-haired. The babysitter left, the house was unusually quiet with sleeping children, and he pushed me up against the corridor wall, easing my dress up as I hastily undid his belt. He took my breath away as he thrust himself into me, all the time making eye contact as he fucked me with his jeans around his ankles and his new jacket still on.

And now I am looking at a stranger wearing it, her arm clutching his waist with a familiarity that tells me she has done that several times before.

'I don't know who she is.' My voice is icy cold. 'Nick?'

My blood thumps in my head and ears like the world's biggest bass drum.

I feel totally weightless and as heavy as a boulder all at the same time. Cathleen and Dennis stare at the screen wide-eyed, then Nick turns to look at the picture and like the stupidest man on the planet, suddenly realises his mistake. It's like watching a car crash in slow motion. How his brow knots. His mouth falls open and stays open. He runs both hands through his hair and closes his eyes.

'Come on, girls, I think it's time we left.' I try to keep my voice steady and calm.

'Finally,' Lucy groans.

I look around frantically for the waiter to retrieve the buggy. I need to get out of the restaurant. I need to create as much distance between Nick and me as possible. I need Cathleen to stop staring at me and for Dennis to close his mouth.

'Can I have some more Pom-Bears?' Sophie sees an opportunity.

'You can have whatever you want. Let's just go.'

'Yesssssssssss,' the girls chorus.

'Emily, please?' Nick pleads. He extends his hand and then thinks better of it and puts it back on the table.

'Don't, Nick. We had one rule. Just one. Let's give it four months and see what happens.'

'Four months? It's been four months, Nick?' Cathleen is hysterical now. Tears begin to spill down her cheeks, and she blows her nose on the crisp white napkin.

'Not yet, Cathleen. You'll be delighted to hear that we started seeing a counsellor five months ago, for all the good that did. Nick moved out just over three months ago. And now he's seeing someone else.'

'Emily, it's not like that.' The desperation in Nick's voice only makes him look more pathetic. 'It's only been a couple of dates, nothing serious.'

'You know what? I don't actually care. Enjoy your dinner. I think you have a lot to discuss with your parents, don't you? Ask him about the money, Cathleen. Now that's a good after-dinner story. Come on, Lucy and Sophie.'

Small, warm hands grab mine as we leave.

The cold air hits like a smack in the face. I'm clutching Lucy's hand too tightly and pushing the pram at breakneck speed along the damp pavement. In the twenty minutes that we've been inside, it has become overcast and the drizzle immediately begins to soak through my T-shirt.

I feel like I'm under water. I can't get my thoughts together, they flicker through my mind like an old-fashioned slide show. Nick with a woman. Another woman. Him kissing her. Them laughing. His hands on her body. Her running her fingers through his hair. My stomach flips but I force myself to go to the place I most dread. Nick happy. Nick happy with someone else, like he's never been with me. An overpowering tidal wave of absolute deflation washes over me. I want the ground to swallow me up. See, I knew this might happen, of course I did. I just wasn't prepared for the reality of it. Of Nick moving on and so quickly. The door of possibility of us ever reconciling slamming shut. I just can't imagine him touching anyone other than me. I can't imagine a picture of his life together with anyone else.

It was either me or no one. That's not too much to ask for, is it? She looked beautiful. And younger than him. God, he's such a fucking cliché. What next? Buy a Porsche and learn an extreme sport?

'Mummy, stop pulling me. You're hurting,' Lucy shouts.

'Sorry, sorry.' I slow down. 'You OK too, Soph?'

'That's not your coat, Mummy,' Sophie giggles, pointing at the jacket I have wedged under my arm. In my haste to leave the restaurant I had unthinkingly grabbed the wrong one from the cloakroom. I now have Cathleen's signature red Principles coat, which is almost the identical colour to the lining of my fake-fur one.

'You've got Granny's coat,' Sophie chimes gleefully.

'She'll have to wear yours!' Lucy adds enthusiastically.

I look at the faces of my girls. Wide-eyed, innocent faces staring back at me, waiting expectantly for my reaction.

I can't fall apart now, not in front of Lucy and Sophie. I hate Nick for making me feel like this. But I have to lock that somewhere, because right now, there are two small people in front of me who need me to love them far more than I need to hate him.

'Won't she?' Lucy repeats, slightly more unsure this time.

I hold both of their hands in mine, kiss them loudly and force my most convincing smile, 'Well, I'm sure Granny will look absolutely fabulous in my leopard-print coat.' The girls guffaw with laughter at the implausible image. 'Now, who's for hot chocolate?' I ask them.

'ME!' the girls chorus, and just like that, life has moved on.

Chapter Twenty-Seven

'Is it not a bit weird with your mum in the next room?' Chris has the duvet covered up to his chin, his disembodied head peeping out the top.

'Yes! Of course it's weird. But what's the alternative? Have zero sex life while she's staying? I'm not waiting until you're next back home again. Now, come on, shape up, Chris!' she instructs as she tugs at the corner of the sheet. Chris is clutching tightly to the other end, as they enter into an unintentional tug of war.

'I just can't keep my mind on the job if I think Janet can hear,' he protests.

'Well, stop talking about her in the first place. That might be a start.' With one final tug, she pulls the sheet from his grasp. 'There!' she declares, satisfied, as she hops in next to him. He takes a bit of warming up, as he pecks her on the lips like he's off out for the morning instead of lying next to his naked wife.

'Come on, Chris. At least try a bit,' she pleads.

'I *am*,' he retorts sulkily. This is not the passion-filled night she had imagined. They haven't had sex once since Chris has been home. With it looking likely that he might be off again soon, Helen is keen to make sure they get at least one under their belt, so to speak, before he heads off-shore again. As she climbs on top of him, he wraps his arms around her and groans contentedly as she feels him harden underneath her. 'But you *do* have to keep it down, Chris. If you're going to groan, do it quietly,' she whispers in his ear as seductively as she can.

'That's exactly what I mean,' his hips stop moving and he runs his fingers through his hair in frustration.

'Look,' she climbs off him and rests her head on his shoulder, 'I know it's difficult having her here, but we have to at least try to keep a sense of normality. We have to at least continue with the fun stuff. We haven't had sex at all since you've been back, and that's not normal for us, is it?' she asks, tracing a line from his chest to his belly button with her index finger. 'We managed to get back on track after having Polly, didn't we? So, in the same way we had to block out the thought of her in the house when we had sex then, we now just have to do the same now with Janet. OK?' she asks, moving her hand slightly lower, 'OK?'

'OK . . .' A smile begins to creep across his face. 'God, I do fancy you.' He presses the palm of his hand into the small of her back and in one well-practised move, pulls her on top of him, burying his face into her neck, inhaling the smell of her perfume, then pulling her hair back slightly as Helen gasps, mouth silently open as she guides him inside her. Chris holds her hips as she leans forward, pushing him deeper and deeper inside her as she gently rocks. As Helen's movements start to quicken, her breath becoming short and shallow, Chris looks up at his beautiful wife, riding him with her eyes closed in pleasure. As he feels an orgasm start to pulse and throb in his balls, a noise distracts him. A squeak. A creak. His eyes dart over Helen's shoulders, and there, framed in the doorway and illuminated by the corridor light, is Janet, sleepy-eyed in a floor-length nightgown.

Helen follows Chris's wide eyes. 'MUM!' she shrieks. 'What are you doing in here?'

She quickly dismounts Chris to his quiet yelps of discomfort and pulls on an oversized T-shirt that's lying in a heap on the floor.

'I was going to ask Liam if he could show me where the heating control was. It's so cold in my flat.' Janet is sobbing, wringing her hands. 'But I think I'm lost.'

Helen leaps out of bed. 'Let me get you back to your room. Come on.' She takes her mum firmly by the elbow and turns her around. Janet is shivering. Her whole is body shaking. Helen looks to Chris, searching for answers. What is wrong with her? Her feet shuffle in the direction of her room with Helen's encouragement.

'Thank you for your help. This doesn't normally happen. I don't normally get lost.' Janet tells her in a small voice, her shaking hand firmly grasping Helen's.

'I'm sure. Let's just get you into bed again, shall we?' Helen replies softly.

'Yes. Yes. Do you know where I live?' she asks.

'Yes,' Helen says. 'Yes I know where you live.' Her voice cracking as she pushes open the bedroom door. She presses the light switch, but nothing happens.

'I'll change that tomorrow,' she whispers, to herself more than anything, but as she steps forward, pain surges through her foot. 'What the—' She reaches down and feels the hot sticky flow of blood as she pulls out a shard of glass from her foot.

'Careful, Mum, I think there's broken glass on the floor.' She guides Janet away from the door and sits her down on her bed. Helen gently lowers Janet's head onto the pillow and covers her up with the duvet, adding another blanket for warmth. She is leaning over her, halfway to kissing her on the forehead, before she catches herself. This is how she comforts Polly, she realises.

Helen carefully brushes her hand across the carpet, picking up bits of glass and putting them in the bin.

'I'll hoover it up in the morning,' she tells Janet, who rolls over in bed, pulling the duvet up under her chin. Helen pulls the door to and creeps along the corridor, past Polly's room, walking on the ball of her right foot before retrieving the first-aid kid from the bathroom to plaster over the cut.

By the time she's back in her bedroom, Chris is tucked up under the covers again, breathing deeply in sleep. She slips in next to him and lies facing the opposite direction, her mind a whirr.

Janet is invincible. She's like a dung beetle. A nuclear holocaust couldn't kill off Janet. She doesn't do vulnerable. She doesn't cry. She doesn't get ill. She's a drunk, yes. She gets confused when she's pissed, but who doesn't? Once, when she was hammered at university, Helen had gone to sleep in the reception area of her halls of residence, thinking it was her bedroom.

But tonight was different. Janet wasn't confused because she was drunk. She was scared. And now Helen feels scared too.

181

Chapter Twenty-Eight

I open my laptop. The screen lights up illuminating the screensaver of Lucy and Sophie sitting on an oversized deckchair on Margate beach last summer. They are both clutching ice creams, which drip down their grinning chins.

'OK,' I say aloud, and rub my hands together decisively. 'Let's do it.'

Firstly, a quick check of Facebook to make sure I am 100 per cent up-to-date with all activity from anyone I might vaguely know from the last three decades. On auto-pilot, I click on Nick's account, just to double-triple-check he hasn't posted any pictures of him and the girl from the phone. He hasn't. Of course he hasn't. I'd like to put it down to heightened emotional intelligence and empathy for other people, but his last post is from over eight months ago, and was a repost of a video montage of people mistakenly saying Jeremy Cunt live on air.

Back to my feed and I see one of the mums from school is starting to make artisan cakes. Her photo displays a marzipan Shaun the Sheep. It really is very good, she's very talented. 'It's very good, you're really talented!' I comment, wondering if this is a good substitute for saying hello to someone in the playground.

'Come on, Emily,' I reprimand myself, before shutting down the window and typing, 'free dating sites.'

There are 557 million results. Fuck. This is going to be more of a mission than I thought.

OK, so which ones did Rachel suggest? I go back through her texts until I find the one with several links and type one of them into the search bar.

'It's not all dick pics on this one,' she writes, followed by five thumbs up and an aubergine emoji.

Why would anyone send you a picture of their knob anyway? What goes on in a man's mind to think, she's interested, we like the same music, we've both read *Crime and Punishment* and, more to the point, enjoyed it. Right, hang on: if I can just get the right angle for this one, that's it. Boxers down, flash on – there you go, waddya think? Here's my scrotum and semi-erect penis. Now, did you say you went to Thailand in your gap year?

No. I don't think so, mate.

OK, I have to register before I can see anyone. I don't know what I'd expected, to be honest, that I'd be able to just pick someone and put them in my basket, a bit like doing the Sainsbury's online shop.

Right, so what do they need to know? I click on the button and a long and involved form pops up. Fuckarama. They want to know EVERYTHING.

The photo of Nick and the Margot Robbie lookalike flashes across my mind. If he can move on, so can I, I tell myself firmly. This is just a process. A bit of fun. I'm just shopping around to see what's out there these days. Like going through the display section in IKEA without any intention of buying anything.

I focus back on the form and type in all the basics – name, age, location, qualifications. It's like applying for a job but without any idea what the role or salary is. A bit about me – hobbies. Who has hobbies these days? Does stacking the dishwasher expertly count? Reading. I like reading. Well, I used to before the children. Keep it vague, I think. More headline information. What do / did I like to do? Swimming. Yep, add that. Walking? Everyone likes walking, otherwise how would you get anywhere? Anything else? Cooking. No. Eating. I like eating, not necessarily out, or for that matter, anything sophisticated or fussy. But I do like an oven-baked potato with real butter and extra mature cheddar.

Now, to upload a picture. Rachel had been very clear that it had to be up-to-date. By that, she said the last five years and within two stone of your current weight. She said she'd once been on a date with a guy who had used a picture of his identical twin brother. Genetically identical, at least. It turned out her date hadn't followed in his brother's footsteps of semi-professional diver, as the image of the sea-soaked naked torso had led her to believe. Instead, he was a computer game enthusiast and had sat on his arse eating Dominos for the last decade, was twice his size, with half as much hair and couldn't walk more than five metres without having to stop to catch his breath. 'He was nice,' she had assured me, 'just absolutely not what I'd expected.'

I find a picture of me on the same trip to Margate as the one of Lucy and Sophie. I've got a bit of a tan and am wearing something other than my signature Breton top. That'll do. I crop Nick out of the picture and upload it.

Now. What am I looking for? Ryan Gosling, ideally. Or the hot one from *Suits*.

This is tricky. I'm definitely *not* looking for a long-term relationship, but does 'dating' actually just mean shagging?

I WhatsApp Rachel.

Me: Does dating mean shagging?
Rach: Yes. And no.

Me: That's not helpful.

Rach: Say yes to dating, and then look at the profile pic. If he's wearing mirrored shades, a bomber jacket or has taken the picture in the bathroom mirror, yes it means shagging. If he's on a walk in the countryside or at a wedding, it's dinner or a drink.

Me: OK. That's clear.

Rach: Welcome to the twenty-first century, Emmie.

Education. Do I want someone with a degree? I don't know. I guess I'd like to have intellectual conversations, but does that discount the possibility of discussing the ethics of *Love Island*? I tick the box for high-school educated. Completing GCSEs will do for now. Height? Taller than me. Hair? Some please. Hobbies? I cut and paste my CV-worthy list. And done. The cursor hovers menacingly over submit. 'Just do it!' I instruct myself aloud.

Click.

It's that simple. I am now on the dating circuit. All I need to do now is wait . . .

Chapter Twenty-Nine

'Darling, how wonderful to hear your voice. How are you?' Tania's mum purrs down the phone.

'Fine. All good, thanks, Mum,' Tania paces up and down the kitchen, picking up individual screws from the work top where Spiral has emptied his pockets, and placing them in the jam jar on top of the fridge, that now also has £6.23 in it towards the Christmas fund.

'Well, what can I do for you? You don't normally ring in the middle of the day. I hope everything's OK?' she asks.

'Everything's just fine!' Even as she says it, doubt starts to creep into her mind. Is this a good idea? She's spent the last few days swinging between thinking it definitely is to it being her worst idea ever. She'd finally talked herself into it before dialling the number, but now Tania's actually speaking to Francesca, she's not convinced. Also, she knows that once she says it she can't unsay it.

But Tania prides herself on being a woman of her word. If she doesn't follow through with this, Spiral will just think he can continue to take the piss, and that is certainly not how Tania rolls.

'I was just thinking about what you said when we went for lunch a while ago.'

'About you looking tired, darling? Because my nutritionist recommended a fabulous collagen-based face cream. It's like filler but without the needles. Would you like me to pop a jar in the post for you?'

'Thanks but, no. No, that wasn't why I was ringing,' Tania catches sight of her reflection in the metal cooker hood. She does look a bit on the weary side and a two-hundred-pound face cream is probably exactly what she needs right now.

'Oh, but that *was* a pleasant afternoon, wasn't it?' her mum interrupts. 'We need to book in another lunch, Arabella. Somewhere a bit more upmarket next time, I'd suggest. I'm desperate to get my hands on that little boy.'

'Yes. OK, but the reason I was calling' – deep breath – 'was about Christmas,' she says, hesitantly.

'Now, Arabella, you made your point. And I have listened to you. I know you think I don't, but I heard what you said. I've spoken to your father about it, and although we're disappointed, we agreed that it's your life, of course. Not the life we would have chosen for you, but there you go. So instead, we would like to make a contribution to your festivities. I cannot bear to think of you in your cold little flat over Christmas without the money to get a proper dinner. It reminds me of one of those adverts for the Samaritans.'

Tania casts her eye around her flat. OK, it isn't a seven-bedroom mansion, but it is her home. It's cosy, yes, a bit grubby, maybe, but she loves it because it's theirs and they bought it without any help from anyone. It certainly isn't an advert for people living in sub-standard accommodation.

Tania rolls her shoulders back and clicks her neck one side and then the other. She is not going to rise to this. 'That's very generous, Mum, but—'

'I will not take no for an answer, Arabella. Don't look a gift horse in the mouth,' she replies sternly.

'It's not that, Mum,' Tania replies. This is your last chance to back out, she tells herself. 'We were thinking of coming to you after all, if the offer still stands?' Tania holds her breath.

Francesca pauses, then gushes, 'Oh, Arabella. Of course it does. We'd love to have you. Oh, Falcon will have an absolute ball. Your father will be delighted.' A slight hesitation, and then she asks, 'And Peter, will he be coming with you?' her tone changing subtly.

'Yes, Spiral will be with us of course,' Tania confirms. 'It will be the whole family.' Regret is already starting to take hold.

'Well, then. What a wonderful time we shall all have,' she says, using the voice she saves for public speaking and prize givings. All faux warmth and fake smiles.

'Great, well, let me know what we can bring nearer the time,' Tania says.

'Just yourselves, darling,' Francesca replies. 'Just bring yourselves.'

As Tania rings off, she looks around her flat again. It suddenly looks a little more tired. She notices the chips on the skirting board where Falcon's toy cars have enthusiastically crashed into it. The tide marks on the walls where the door handle has caught it when open. The cheap IKEA curtains she bought from a charity shop as a stop-gap when they first moved in, and haven't got round to replacing.

Francesca hasn't even seen the flat, but somehow her judgement lies heavy on every surface, like dank fog. Tania puts the jar of screws back on the fridge, pours herself a glass of water and takes a long cool drink. She closes her eyes and practises mindfulness. Being in the moment, holding the water in her mouth, and then swallowing slowly and with purpose.

Everything has a cause and effect. Spiral lied to her, so she threatened Christmas with her parents. She has now executed that threat, which, in turn, becomes an action.

But, however she tries to rationalise it, Tania feels she has made a very big mistake.

Chapter Thirty

'I'm making dinner for us all,' Janet declares enthusiastically. 'You go out.' She playfully pushes Helen and Polly towards the door. 'You'll only both get under my feet here. Go to the park and be back in half an hour and it'll be on the table.'

'Come on, Mummy.' Polly tugs on Helen's arm. 'Let's go!'

'Are you sure, Mum?' Helen asks nervously as Janet thrusts their coats at her. Helen has been watching her mum like a hawk in the days since she came into their bedroom. As Chris left to go back on the rig, his parting words to Helen were, 'Please don't leave your mum with Polly. I don't trust her.'

Helen has reassured him that she won't, but in the days that followed it was like the incident had never happened. Janet was her cutting, stubborn old self. So the offer of cooking is a welcome and long-overdue contribution to her stay.

'Yes. Yes. Now go, before I change my mind!' She gives Helen a final nudge before firmly shutting the front door behind them.

'Well, we better make the most of this, hey Polly?' she says, as Polly grips her hand and pulls her along the pavement.

'Come on, Mummy. Get your fast legs on!' she demands, as Helen picks up her pace.

The thing is, Janet has never, to Helen's knowledge, been

much of a cook. Her childhood memories are peppered with takeaways, microwave meals and the occasional trip to McDonald's, but really, how hard is it to boil some pasta and heat up a jar of Dolmio?

The two of them race each other down the road to the playground, enjoying the last stretch of winter sunshine before the sun sets behind the trees. For a moment, it feels a bit like how things used to be, before Janet came to stay. As Helen pushes Polly on the roundabout, she indulges in the possibility that things could maybe just slot into place. Her mum, although forgetful, can be helpful, maybe she even wants to be after all those years of neglect. Perhaps Janet has turned a corner too. What if dinner is just the start? Perhaps she might even stretch to the odd night of babysitting while she was visiting, if Helen gets Polly to bed first.

After a gym-style workout, pushing Polly on the swings, Helen checks her watch. It's been twenty-five minutes since they left. Probably time to return home.

'Come on, then. Let's go and see what Nana has made for us, shall we?'

'Just five more swings, pleeeeease. Please, Mummy, please,' Polly begs.

'OK. Let me just give Nana a call to see how she's getting on first.'

She dials the house phone and let it ring once, twice, three times until it rings out. The phone is on the wall in the kitchen, feet away from the stove, so there's no way Janet can't hear it. Something doesn't feel right.

'I think we should go back now.' Helen lifts Polly out of the baby swing she insists on going on, even though she is far too old for it.

'Nana ruins everything,' Polly complains.

'That's not kind. She's doing something nice for us

tonight, for once,' Helen picks up the pace, walking as fast as Polly's legs can match.

'I bet it will taste gross,' she sulks.

As they approach home, she hears the fire alarm screeching ominously.

Helen scoops Polly up and runs towards the house, pushing the key clumsily in the lock. As she swings open the front door, a cloud of acrid-smelling black smoke billows out.

'Stay there,' Helen instructs sharply as Polly tries to follow her into the house. 'Just for a moment, stay there.'

Helen covers her mouth with her coat, wafting away the smoke as she splutters her way into the kitchen.

Janet is sat with her head in her hands at the table.

'Mum, MUM! Are you OK?'

'I don't know what happened, Helen.' She shakes her head. 'I was only trying to boil the kettle.'

Helen looks to where the kettle normally lives. The stand is there but the kettle isn't. Her eyes dart around the kitchen frantically, and there on the gas stove is the plastic kettle, melting to the hob.

Quick as a flash, Helen turns off the gas, grabs the kettle with a tea towel, opens the back door and throws it into the garden, while a chimney of thick black smoke continues to curl and loop from it.

'WHAT DID YOU DO?' Helen shouts at Janet as she presses the button on the fire alarm, throws open all the windows and puts the extractor fan on over the oven.

'I put the kettle on, Helen,' her mum snaps defensively. 'To make *you* dinner.'

'But it's an electric kettle, Mum. You must have seen me boil it a thousand times since you've been here. Why would you put it on the fucking hob?'

'You might be thirty, Helen, but you're not too old for a hiding with that kind of language,' her mum retorts.

'I'm thirty-seven, actually, Mum. Thirty-fucking-seven. Go and sit in the front room. You can't sit in here with this smoke, it's toxic.' She waits until her mum pushes herself to standing, and then walks out of the kitchen shaking her head. 'Polly, come inside but go straight upstairs. I'll ring for a pizza for dinner.'

'You might have your fancy school and your fancy house and your fancy neighbours, but don't think you're better than me, Helen,' her mum hisses at her as she pushes her way past in the hallway. 'You have no idea the things I've done for you. No idea at all!' She pokes Helen in the chest with a pointed finger, staring at her unblinkingly, threateningly.

'What? What exactly have you done? AND WHY ARE YOU EVEN HERE, MUM?' she screams at Janet, unthinkingly poking her back. Janet's hand instinctively reaches to her chest, rubbing where Helen has touched her. What have I done? What am I turning into? Helen panics.

'Go in the front room, Mum,' she says in a whisper so quiet Janet has to lean in to hear her.

'But I'm just making dinner, Helen. I'm in the middle of dinner.' All the fury in Janet's face has fallen away.

'I'll sort it.'

'If you're sure,' Janet replies, turning the knob to the sitting-room door.

Helen creeps quietly upstairs to Polly's room. She is sat on her bed cross-legged.

'Were you shouting at Nana because she burnt the kitchen down?' Polly asks innocently.

'No. No, I wasn't shouting because of that. Can I just cuddle up with you?' Helen asks her, to which Polly wriggles over and Helen fits around her like a perfect missing jigsaw piece. She notices how the smell of burnt plastic clings to her hair and school uniform. Helen shifts her weight, retrieves her mobile from her pocket and scrolls through the contacts until she finds the number for the doctor's surgery.

The receptionist answers after two rings.

'Hello, Preston Park Practice. How can I help?' she asks chirpily.

Helen swallows back the ball of emotion that has lodged in her throat and replies, 'I need to speak to the doctor about my mum. I don't think she's well at all.'

'The doctor said *what*?' Chris asks loudly down the phone.

'Alcoholic dementia,' Helen replies.

'That can't be a thing, Hels. It's called being drunk. Janet is *always* drunk. Sorry, I'm going to have to move somewhere a bit quieter, bear with me.'

Helen can hear background noise and she tries to picture where he is. Since he's been back on the rig the house feels calmer and quieter, even with her mum's erratic behaviour. He's been called back to sort out some kind of electrical emergency, so he'll only be there for a short stint. But while Helen is trying to work out what to do with Janet, she wouldn't mind if he stays offshore a while longer until she's gone. The tension between him and Janet is so palpable and every exchange fizzes with loathing. Even Polly picks up on it and had asked her why Dad puts on his mean voice for Nana and why Nana's face looks so angry when she speaks to him.

'Is this a proper doctor? Not one of Tania's recommendations?' Chris breaks Helen's train of thought, bringing her back to the here and now, a hint of sarcasm detectable in his voice.

'It's Dr Hodgson. *Our* doctor, Chris,' Helen answers,

irritated by Chris's obstinacy. 'Anyway, it's not an official diagnosis. I described her behaviour to him on the phone and he asked a lot of questions about what she forgets and how frequently. How much she drinks and what her diet is like, that kind of thing. And he suggested this might be a possibility, but said to bring her in to do some tests, which is never going to happen as she refuses to acknowledge there's a problem. So there we are.' Helen tucks the phone in the crook of her neck as she pulls out the wet washing from the machine. 'How's she going to cope in Spain, Chris? If she can't boil a fucking kettle without burning the house down, how's she going to look after herself?'

'Has she said *when* she's going home yet, Hels?' he asks softly.

'No. I've asked her a million times, but she is an expert at avoiding a direct question. Or says she's here as long as I need her. But I've told her we're fine. We're all fine, but she clearly isn't. What can I do?' she asks, exasperated.

The silence between the two of them grows to the extent that Helen momentarily forgets Chris is on the other end of the line until he says, 'Have you rung River Cottages?'

'Where?'

'Where she lives. Have you rung and spoken to the management?'

'Do you mean Lake Apartments? River Cottage is that bloody programme with Hugh Fearnley-Whittingstall!'

'Yes. Whatever it's called, have you spoken to them yet? She might have let them know when she's planning to return. It's worth a shot, isn't it, if she refuses to tell you anything?'

'I guess. Although I don't know why she'd talk to anyone there either.'

'Well, it's worth a bash. We're clearly not getting anywhere with her.'

'I suppose so. I'll give them a ring after you,' Helen replies as she folds the fitted sheets into the tumble dryer.

'OK. Good luck and let me know how you get on.'

'Will do. Bye,' Helen signs off, fills up the new kettle with water and flicks on the switch. A cup of tea and then she'll do it. She closes her eyes for a moment. All she can hear is the rumbling of the boiling water and the hum of Lorraine's voice from the living room, as her mum mainlines daytime programme after mind-numbing daytime programme.

After a short foreign dial tone, someone answers with an 'Ola!'

'Ola,' Helen responds. 'Do you speak English?'

'Yes, madam,' replies the strongly accented voice.

'My mum, Janet Cross, lives in one of your flats, number one-four-five.'

'Yes, and how may I help you, madam?' the voice asks.

'Well, I'm not entirely sure. She has come to visit us but I'm not sure how long for or, oh, this is ridiculous. Sorry, I'm not really all that sure how you can help me.' Helen gulps back a mouthful of tea.

'One moment please while I find the tenant you are referring to.' Helen can hear the tapping of the computer in the background. 'Can I ask with whom I am speaking to?'

'Helen. Helen Wise. Janet is my mother.'

'OK,' he says, and another long pause. 'OK, I am just going to get my manager. Would you mind holding the line?'

'Of course. Is everything OK?' Helen asks.

'I will just get my manager, madam. If you can just hold for one moment.' The line cuts to Spanish pop music. Helen absent-mindedly raps her fingers on the tabletop to the tinny rhythm. After three-quarters of a song about a girl who loves kisses all over her face (Helen thinks something got lost in translation), another voice comes on the line.

'Is this Ms Cross?' a woman asks.

'No. I'm Mrs Wise. I'm Janet Cross's daughter.'

'Mrs Wise. Thank you for your patience. We have been keen to talk to you, but your mother had not left an emergency contact number so I am most grateful to be conversing with you now.' Her sing-song voice masks a seriousness that Helen cannot understand.

'Is everything OK?' Helen asks again, dread starting to grip her throat.

'Yes. Yes of course. We are just keen to confirm a forwarding address for her post, and also to, of course, confirm the arrangements for her belongings. We are happy to provide storage as a short-term solution, but after six weeks, it is our policy to destroy items if they are not returned to their owner. I hope you understand, Mrs Cross.'

'Wise. Mrs Wise,' Helen says. 'Sorry. Sorry, can you just backtrack a moment? I'm a bit, well, a lot confused. Why would you destroy my mother's belongings? Why aren't they in her flat?' Helen talks slowly and calmly but the prickle of panic is already creeping up her spine, vertebrae by vertebrae.

'Because she has terminated her tenancy with us. We have most enjoyed having her as a resident over the years, but we are also aware of her need for additional . . .' she pauses while searching for the word. 'Support.'

'What do you mean by support?'

'She spoke warmly of you, Mrs Wise, and her desire to be reunited with her family. She has had many good years with us and, as we said to her, we are sad to see her leave, but can also appreciate the need to be closer to those she loves.'

'Hang on. Hang on,' Helen interjects. 'So you're telling

me that my mum left Spain with absolutely no plan of returning?' The disquieting feeling is swelling and spreading, oozing into the gaps that are normally reserved for daydreaming and planning. Trickling between the cracks as she tries to remain calm, to not let anxiety take over, to not let the fear win.

'This is a luxury apartment block. We provide an excellent service for all of our residents, from cleaning to security to a heated outdoor swimming pool.' The manager reels off a sales pitch that she must have recited hundreds of times.

'I know. I've been there. It's lovely. But what has this got to do with Mum?'

'We offer a range of services and packages,' she clarifies. 'But what we don't offer is the extra support that your mother might need.'

'Extra support? I don't understand what you mean by that. What extra support did she need?' she asks, frustrated.

'How can I explain?' The manager pauses again as if to gather her thoughts. 'Your mother gets confused sometimes.'

'I know. I know this. I'm very much aware of this. But how has this led to her leaving her home? How has this happened?' Helen raises her voice.

A silence falls between them. Helen is concerned the manager has hung up until, she hears her let out a sigh, before saying, 'One of our members of staff found your mother naked, locked out on her balcony. She was very cold. My staff member was very embarrassed.'

'Well, that could happen to any of us, couldn't it?' Helen pleads. She, of course, knows the answer. 'Couldn't it?' repeats weakly.

'She was very distressed. I don't know how long she had been there for. We have a concierge here but these are not assisted living homes, these are apartments. We cannot look after the residents. I do hope you understand.'

'I see.' Helen can hear the start of *Frasier* in the sitting room and wonders if her mum was ever planning to tell her that she had no intention of ever returning home.

'May I resume the matter of Mrs Cross's belongings? We are most happy to care take them for the short term but—'

'We'll sort it out. I'll speak with my mother and husband, and then we'll be in touch.'

'That's most appreciated. And, as I explained to your mother, the costs of the damage to the flat will be deducted from her initial deposit, which we have held fastidiously, as well as from the accrued service charges.'

'What damage?' Helen asks.

'The flat was left in disarray, Mrs Wise. I appreciate this is all new information to you, but in keeping with a consistent line of communication, I would happily send you the report, including the photographic documentation, along with the terminated contract?'

'Yes, yes, that would be useful. Yes please.' Helen recites her email address and feels her phone vibrate to alert her to a new message.

'That is now done,' the manager concludes. 'May I expect correspondence with you regarding the belongings soon?'

'Yes. I will be in touch within the week.'

'That is much appreciated. Have an enjoyable day,' she says, which feels wholly inappropriate.

Helen retrieves her laptop from the kitchen dresser, opens up her emails and clicks on the attachment from Lake Apartments. She scrolls through the report until she comes to the pictures. There, in front of her, are images of her mum's apartment. Except it doesn't look at all like the last time Helen and Polly visited. Every surface is strewn with filth, empty bottles, food-encrusted plates, discarded takeaway containers. Another photograph documents the light fittings, each one highlighting broken bulbs still in their fittings, shards of glass dusting the floor. The bathroom is filthy, with streaks of something greasy across the walls. The tub is full of soggy clothes piled high. How did she wash herself?

Helen thinks of Janet's behaviour at their house. How she had found plates under her bed, cups in odd places, towels stuffed in the bin. She had put it down to her mother being lazy and selfish, waiting for Helen to clear up after her like the hired help, but it all starts to come into focus. She thinks of the broken light bulb she cut her foot on in the spare room upstairs. It no longer feels like an accident.

Helen lets out a long exhalation, her breath catching in her throat. On shaky legs she pulls herself to standing and traces the wall with her hand for balance as she pushes the door of the front room ajar. Her mother is sat up rigid, hands clutching her knees, watching the television intensely.

'Hi, Mum,' Helen ventures.

'Sit,' she pats the seat next to her. 'This is very funny, very funny indeed. Have you watched this before, Helen? I'm sure you have. We don't have any of the good English shows in Spain. Just dubbed versions of *Colombo* and *Miss Marple*. I'm going to have to watch as many as I can before I go back,' she shrugs, not taking her eyes off the set for a moment.

Helen lowers herself into the space next to her. She takes a beat to look at her mum. Really look at her. The deep creases on her forehead. The poorly dyed hair. The sunspots covering her arms from years of toasting herself beside the pool. The ring-encrusted hands, with thin fingers and large bony knuckles. Helen gently covers her mum's hand with her own, resting it on the top, feeling her paper-thin skin below. Janet, without thinking, sandwiches Helen's hand between hers and raises it to her mouth, kissing it tenderly, before returning it softly to Helen's lap with a gentle pat.

'See,' Janet grins, 'see?' She points to the screen, laughing, as Frasier's dad's dog runs around in circles, chasing his tail.

Helen doesn't know what to do next, so instead she sits silently next to her mum through the rest of the episode. She knows she needs to ring Chris. She knows she needs to do something, anything, as it is all feeling very out of control. But right now all she can do is sink into the sofa next to her mum as the weight of fatigue bores down on her like a chain-metal blanket.

Chapter Thirty-One

'It's been a week and nothing. Not even a flirt. Rachel says everyone gets a "flirt" as an absolute minimum. What is wrong with me?' I throw my head in my hands dramatically.

'Nothing, you're gorgeous. You could do with a bit of a trim, but other than that, I'd date you. Let's have a look.' Helen puts her hand out and I pass her my phone, then let myself sink into her oversized sofa, legs tucked underneath me. I could just shut my eyes and drift off, it's so unbelievably comfortable. How are her cushions always so plump and soft? The ones on my sofa are solid and shapeless, like mashed potato that's been left out on a plate overnight.

Helen stares at the screen, brow furrowed in concentration, then silently passes the phone to Tania.

After several minutes, she looks at me, eyes wide. 'Is that it?'

'What do you mean?' I take a slurp of the coffee Helen has made me. Proper frothy coffee from a machine. It's like drinking caffeinated soft clouds.

'I don't know where to start. I mean, is this your profile picture?' Tania turns the phone towards me. She's zoomed in on the picture of me, or more specifically the hand that is tucked around my waist. Nick's hand.

'Oh, I hadn't spotted that,' I say.

'You can't just crop a husband out and use the picture, Em. And the description is awful. When do you go swimming? And eating? What does that even mean, you like eating? Everyone "likes" eating or we'd all be dead. Jesus. No wonder you haven't had any action. This has "recently split up and have no idea what I'm doing" written all over it.' She shakes her head disapprovingly.

'Well, it's true, isn't it? So, what do I do? What should I say?' I plead.

'OK,' Tania replies thoughtfully. 'Let me have a go. Have you got any of those pictures on your phone of us out in town the other week?'

'Yes. But I think I'm absolutely hammered in all of them,' I reply.

'Doesn't matter. You looked hot. And fun,' Helen smiles.

'Not like this,' Tania points the phone back to me again. This time she's zoomed in on my crotch. My shorts were slightly pinching that day if I remember, but I hadn't realised I'd got an actual camel toe.

'God,' I mutter. 'Yep, fine. Do your worst.'

'OK, here we go.' Tania grins. She taps away, passes it to Helen who adds something, passes it back until they're both satisfied. Ten long minutes later, Tania looks up, beaming.

'And now, Emily Jones, you should start to see some action. A-ha!' she exclaims, 'You have a flirt already. Bingo!'

'Let's have a look!'

She passes the phone over to me. I am looking back at a picture of me, arms raised, hair wild, shot glass in hand and tequila lemon in mouth. 'This doesn't really capture the book-loving swimmer I'd described,' I say timidly.

'Of course it doesn't!' Helen shakes her head. 'We've obviously improved on that too.'

I click through to my hobbies. Dancing. Drinking. Zumba. Eating sushi. Wine-tasting. Advanced yoga. 'I can't do half of these things.'

203

'You can, you've at least given all these things a go. And there's nothing wrong with being a bit creative, is there?' Tania replies.

'Ooh, a flirt. Look!' I show them the screen.

'Good. Great. There you go then.'

'What do you think of him?' I show them the picture.

'Nice!' she nods, before leaning over and pressing the 'flirt back' button on my phone.

'*What have you done*??' I screech, looking at the phone accusingly, trying to work out how to unclick the button.

'Chill out, Em, this is what you have to do. Otherwise you are just a passive observer. You need to be an active participant.' She squeezes my arm reassuringly.

'What about this one?' Helen is now scrolling through the pictures and turns the screen to me. 'He looks nice.'

'He's just finished a marathon, though, Hels. He's holding his medal up,' I reply.

'So? What's wrong with that? He takes care of himself, that's not the end of the world is it?' There's a clatter from the kitchen. 'Just ignore it. It's Mum faffing around. She'll be fine,' Helen smiles weakly, but sadness washes over her.

'God, look at me going on about dating these bunch of weirdos, when you've got proper stuff going on. I'm so sorry, Hels. I'm so fucking thoughtless sometimes.' I reach out for her hand, raise it to my mouth and give a quick peck.

'Don't be ridiculous. This is exactly what I need, my two favourite women and a website full of try-hard men,' she smiles.

'Sure?' I ask.

'Sure.' She squeezes my hand back, before looking back at my phone.

'Jesus, why would you put that up as your profile pic?' she turns the phone towards us to show an image of a rotund, hairy-chested man in Bermuda shorts, grinning while stroking a camel.

'He looks like he'd have a persistent fungal infection,' Tania replies, taking the phone from her. 'Have you seen his feet? And those sandals? No thanks. Oh, hang on. What about this guy?'

I'm increasingly getting the feeling that they are both enjoying this far more than me.

'Yes. He looks nice, Em. Nice teeth,' Helen agrees.

'But he looks like he's on holiday too. Why is he OK, but the camel guy isn't?' This is all so confusing.

'Because he's in Cuba or somewhere cool, look at the dirt tracks and old-fashioned cars in the background,' Tania points out.

'Is it not a bit, I don't know, disingenuous to go on dates with more than one person at a time?' I ask.

'The world has changed since you used to down a bottle of White Lightning and get off with someone in a field, Emily. The more the merrier, until you stumble across one you like,' Tania explains.

'I guess,' I reply, unconvinced.

There's another loud crash from the kitchen followed by what sounds like breaking crockery. 'Fuck,' Helen mutters. 'I'll be back in a minute.'

'Do you think she's genuinely OK?' I ask Tania once Helen has rushed out.

'Honestly? No. But all we can do is be there for her, Em. Be her friend. She'll tell us when she needs help,' Tania replies firmly. 'Right. That's done.'

'What's done?' I panic.

'I've suggested a drink with Mr Cuba. He's keen. He responded immediately and asked when. He's called Steve. You can't go wrong with a Steve. Good reliable name.' Tania passes me back the phone. 'All you need to do now is set a date!'

'You total fucker!' I squeal. 'I can't believe you did that!'

'You're welcome,' Tania grins, and bows deeply, hands in prayer pose.

Chapter Thirty-Two

I can't remember the last time I felt this nervous. The angst of going on a date for the first time in fifteen years is comparable to the end-of-year disco at primary school. A fizzing in the pit of my stomach and an overwhelming feeling of self-consciousness. Except this time I'm not heading out to a fusty-smelling school hall, dressed like a ten-year-old Madonna impersonator in a puffball skirt and florescent socks. This time I'm going to meet someone I only know from a passport-sized picture of him smiling inanely, showing off what has now been dubbed by Tania and Helen as his 'faaaaaaaabulous teeth.'

'Wipe the toothpaste off your cheek,' says Tania, who has come to my babysitting rescue. 'Now you look gorgeous. Steve won't know what's hit him!' she pushes me out of the front door with a gentle nudge, shutting it loudly behind me.

And now I'm on the 46B into town, heading towards my first date. So far I have found out that he's not long been out of a relationship, but it was 'nothing serious' so he 'doesn't have any baggage'. He's looking for fun, with the potential of something more serious if he meets the right girl. He's clean-shaven, messy mousey hair, six foot four and has a kind smile. He regularly eats out, watches Scandi-Noir films and likes going to the pub. He's into contemporary galleries and the theatre. Mainly musicals.

He's suggested we meet in an American diner. Warning bells are going off all over the place already. I don't really want to eat with someone on a first date. I have a serious aversion to loud eaters. I regularly move seats on the train when someone noisily lip-smacks their way through a Boots meal deal. I was hoping for more of a quick pint and see how we get on. Oh my God, I hope it's not a themed place. Am I meant to dress up? I'm wearing my jeans and a Breton T-shirt, as always. I did try on a couple of other outfits but Lucy told me I looked like Mrs Elwood in the frilly blouse I put on, and since she's about a hundred and potentially the most terrifying woman on the planet, I resorted to what I feel comfortable in. I do have red lipstick on though, and semi-shaved legs, so no one can accuse me of not making an effort.

The door to the diner is covered in car bumper stickers including a personal favourite: 'If the van's a rocking, don't come knocking.' I groan loudly as I push it open. It's themed. Of course it is. All the teenage staff are wearing fifties-style outfits.

'Good evening, ma'am,' says a teddy boy with acne, in a very poor American accent. 'And how can I assist you this evening?'

'I'm meeting someone here, but I'm not sure what he looks like.' Embarrassment soars through me. Do I look as desperate as I sound? Who goes on a date with someone they've never met before?

'Of course,' he replies, thankfully dropping the accent, 'Would you like to sit at the bar and wait?' He's completely unfazed by what I've said, and I realise, of course, he's grown up in the age of internet dating. He's probably had a mobile since he was twelve. This is all perfectly normal to him. This is what people do now. I am modern. Propelled on by the thought of being a modern woman, I smile to myself as I follow him to the bar, jump up on a stool and ask the waiter for a gin and tonic.

'Sorry, ma'am,' he resumes in American. 'This is an alcohol-free restaurant. But I can recommend the coke float.'

Fuck. Fuck. Fuck. Fuck. No booze? What the actual mother-of-first-dates am I meant to do now?

'OK,' I reply. 'I'll have one of those, then.' I'm wide-eyed with fear. How am I meant to do this sober?

I check my phone for the fifth time. I know I was early, but he's now late. It's 7.37 p.m. and we definitely said 7.30. I slurp loudly on the coke float. It's tricky to drink quietly through the straw, but the waiter was right, it is very good indeed.

'Is your name Emily?' The waiter startles me.

'Yes! Yes it is,' I reply.

'Your dinner date is in the booth near the window,' he points.

'Thank you,' I reply and notice a tremor in my voice. Why didn't I front load a bottle of wine at home before I got here? I take another large slurp of my drink and hop down from the stool.

As I approach the booth, I first notice the back of his head peeping over the top of the red seat. I stop for a moment. This must be the wrong booth. This guy has grey hair and a large bald patch. My guy had thick, mousey-brown hair, blowing carelessly in the Cuban wind. I look back at the waiter who nods in encouragement, so I take a step closer. Sensing someone behind him, the man turns around.

OK. So this is everything that's wrong with internet dating. It is Steve. It's definitely Steve, because as he smiles I notice 'those' teeth. The problem is, they are framed in a much older face. Like *much* older. This guy could be Steve's dad.

'Emily?' he grins, offering me a hand to shake. The large sovereign ring on his little finger digs into my palm.

'Yes, Steve? I hardly recognised you from your—'

'My picture.' He shakes his head in mild amusement. 'I know. I know. It was taken a couple of years back.' More like a couple of decades, I think. 'I really should update it. It was taken outside my mother's house and I find the cars are often a talking point. Please, sit down,' he gestures to the bench opposite. Ah. I get it now. It's not Cuba; it's England circa 1980. It's just a very old picture when those cars were probably cutting edge, around the same time that seat belts were first introduced.

I squeeze in opposite him, careful not to bump knees. He smooths down his salmon-coloured shirt with his overly tanned hands and grins again. He really is proud of those teeth. The rest of his face is a web of deep lines, too much unprotected time in the sun. He's done an all right job of combing over his hair to cover up most of the receding patches at the front. In fact, if I'd approached him from the front, I wouldn't have realised the extent of his hair loss. But the crux of the matter is, even if he'd Just for Menned the shit out of every strand of body hair, he is far older than he'd led me to believe. And to top it off, I notice a heavy gold chain around his neck. I am on a date with a cast member from *Eldorado*.

'This is my first date,' I explain to break the silence and stop him grinning inanely at me.

'Well,' he smacks the table with his palm, 'I promise I'll be gentle.'

Get me out of here. I pick up the menu and scan down the list, looking for something small and easily digestible so I can wolf it down and leave as soon as humanly possible.

'Do you recommend anything?' I ask.

He stretches his arms along the back of the bench, revealing two large spherical sweat patches under both armpits, 'I always go for the burger. Keep it classic,' he nods.

The waiter approaches and says, 'Good evening, Steve. Do you want your usual?' Great. I'm at Steve's haunt. I wonder how many other women he's attempted to seduce in this booth.

'Yes. That would be ideal. And for the lady?' he asks me.

'Yep. Burger sounds good. And are you sure you couldn't stretch to a glass of wine? Or anything alcoholic? I'll drink anything,' I shrug good-humouredly, trying to mask the undertone of desperation.

'That's my fault, Emily. I've been dry for four years now,' and at this point he crosses himself. 'But I try to keep away from temptation and remain grateful every day.'

Why didn't he write any of this on his bloody profile??

'Completely understand,' I reply. 'I'll just have another one of those Coke things, please.'

We sit in silence, other than Steve drumming on the table to the beat of the rockabilly music.

'So,' I offer up. 'You like Scandi-Noir films then. Anything in particular?'

'*The Bridge* was good. Yeah. I liked *The Bridge*. I only watched the first series though, and not to the end because by the time I got round to watching it again it wasn't on iPlayer any more. So. Yeah. The first couple of episodes were good. Can't remember the name of the detective, but she was good. I liked her,' And he lets out a long whistle before asking, 'And you? What are you into?'

'Well,' I think, 'I like walking—'

'Yes. Me too,' he nods.

'And cooking—'

'Yep. Also.'

Wow. This is irritating. Hurry up, burgers!

'And I like doing stuff with the kids, obviously, like—'

'Obviously. Obviously.' He interjects before smacking his lips.

I wonder if I can unobtrusively get my phone out of my handbag to text SOS to Rachel, who is on standby for the emergency phone call. I'll have to distract him to do it. Or just go to the loo. As I'm about to make my excuses, the burgers arrive.

'Two classics and two floats. Have a nice day!' the pseudo-American announces.

'Excellent!' Steve rubs his hands together enthusiastically.

As the waiter disappears I think, now is the time to mention it. I have nothing to lose and this may help him with future dates.

'Steve.'

'Emily,' he replies with a mouthful of burger.

'How much luck have you had with this internet dating?' I do away with the straw and gulp down the Coke float. However disastrous this evening, I have rediscovered a childhood love of cola and ice cream.

He thinks for a moment before replying, 'Moderate.'

'OK, more specifically. How many second dates have you had?'

Again, he pauses, and for a moment I think he's going to do a tally on his fingers before he says, 'None. Nil. Nada.' He takes another huge bite. Those fabulous teeth are making light work of the burger.

'OK. Well, can I give you a word of advice?'

He nods. Cheeks bulging.

'Change your photo, Steve, and put your actual age down. Don't say you like Scandi-Noir if you don't. Do you like galleries?' I ask.

He shakes his head, pouches still full.

'Then take that off too. Musicals?'

He gulps loudly, and I try to suppress my noisy-eating aversion. 'Yes. I like *Cats*. And *West Side Story*.'

'Great! Me too! Keep that then. But be honest, Steve. I have two kids and not much opportunity to go out, so I feel there is some kind of Trade Description breach here.' I take a bite of the burger. Bloody hell, this is fantastic too. I break one of my own eating rules and momentarily close my eyes in food ecstasy. I should bring the kids here, I think. I can always sneak a gin in a tin in my bag, if absolutely necessary.

'I just don't like women my age,' he explains, downbeat. 'I don't find them attractive. That's partly why me and the wife split up. The attraction was no longer there. We had stopped having sex.'

A fleeting image of Steve's sixty-something-bum pistoning into someone flashes through my mind and I push it to one side before it affects my appetite.

'Well,' I sigh, 'unfortunate as that is, it's not really on to lure women here under false pretences. Give them the facts and then it's up to them to decide whether they want to go on a date with you. Some younger women are into guys in their sixties,' I offer.

'I'm fifty-seven,' he huffs and sulkily sucks on his straw.

'Right. Fine. What did you say you do again?' I ask him, shovelling the last of my burger in.

'I work in retail, primarily. I manage quite a large team of people in Woodingdean. But I also like to keep myself in shape.'

'Well, Steve,' I swig the last of my float and attempt to stand but the benches are screwed to the ground so I have to shuffle out. 'I am going to go now. It has been nice to meet

213

you, but I don't think we'll be doing this again,' and I offer him my hand, which he firmly shakes.

'Do you want to go Dutch?' he gestures to the table.

'No, Steve, you know, I really don't. You can think of my payment as all the fabulous advice I have given you, and I hope you find what you are looking for.'

'Well, fair enough I guess,' he shrugs, polishing off the rest of his chips in one large wide-mouthed swallow and reaching across to start on my leftovers. 'Nice to meet you too.'

I push open the double doors and inhale slowly as I retrieve my phone from my handbag and scroll through to Rachel. She picks up in two rings.

'I've been on high alert all evening. Is it over already?' she probes.

'What is wrong with people these days?' I declare as I stride down the road, trying to create as much distance between me and the diner as possible. 'And also, who meets in a diner? I'm not the bloody Fonz.'

'Never go out for food, Em. Never. You'll be stuck there until you've finished.'

'Thanks, Dear Deidre. I know that now. Hang on, I'm getting a stitch,' I slow down to a gentle stroll.

'But how was he?'

'About sixty. Bald with a pink shirt and wore more jewellery than Mr T.'

'Shit. But chin up, hey? You've made a start now, and it can't get any worse?' she offers sympathetically.

'Do you really think so?' I ask, allowing a slight shaft of optimism to creep in.

'No. Not really. Sorry, Em. It's a fucking minefield.'

Oh, brilliant.

Chapter Thirty-Three

Helen billows out the fresh duvet cover and plumps up the pillows. That's all the beds changed now, including Janet's. She gathers up the pile of sheets and takes them downstairs to load up the washing machine.

Polly is out of the bath and sat in the sitting room. As Helen passes by, the theme tune to yet another episode of *Mr Bean* plays out.

Then she hears her mother's voice. 'You have such lovely hair,' she lulls. 'You always have done. Always the softest, longest hair in the school.'

Helen gently pushes against the door, opening it just a crack so as not to disturb what is going on inside.

She smiles as she sees her mum sat on the sofa, legs straddled either side of Polly, who is cross-legged on the floor. Her mum is holding Polly's long hair in one hand and brushing it tenderly with a hairbrush in the other. Long, methodical strokes, taking it from her hairline to the end. Swoosh. Swoosh. Swoosh.

'And what shall we do today? What would you like to do?' Janet asks. Swoosh. Swoosh. Swoosh.

'I don't know. We could go to the park? I like going to the park,' Polly suggests. They must be playing a game, Helen thinks, as it's gone six thirty and no one's going anywhere now.

She can't remember her mum playing imaginary games

with her when she was a child, but perhaps it is easier with grandchildren.

'Which park would you like to go to?' Janet asks as she starts to carefully plait Polly's hair.

'Preston Park. That's the best one,' Polly answers. 'It's got a massive roundabout and big swings and baby swings.'

'I don't think I know that one. Turn your head towards me.' Polly obediently turns in the direction of Janet. Her face is illuminated by the lights on the Christmas tree. Janet's fingers work swiftly and nimbly, catching strands of Polly's hair and expertly weaving them together until half of her head is in a neat, professional-looking French plait. 'OK, other way,' and Polly turns.

'What's *your* favourite park?' Polly asks. 'We could go there instead if you like?'

'Well,' Janet stops for a moment, takes a contemplative sigh and answers, 'I like the one at the end of our road.' Helen can't remember her coming with them to that park, but perhaps she's visited it when Polly's at school and Helen's been out.

'Yes,' she confirms. 'That one is my favourite. I like the tyre swing the best.'

'I haven't seen the tyre swing, is it new?'

'No. No it's always been there. Kirsten Clark fell off it and broke her wrist, remember? Her mother was furious with her as they were meant to be going on holiday to Amsterdam on the ferry, but they missed it because she was in hospital getting a cast put on her arm. Right, do you have the hair band?' Polly passes it back to her, as Janet wraps it around the ends of the plaits. 'There,' she turns Polly's head this way and that to admire her work, 'I think you're done. We should put the dinner on, shouldn't we, before your daddy returns.'

'But he's not here at the moment,' Polly replies, standing on tip-toes to admire herself in the mirror over the mantelpiece.

'But he will be soon, and we don't want to make him cross like last time now, do we?'

'Daddy never gets cross,' Polly replies. 'Apart from when he trod on my Lego when he didn't have any shoes on. Then he said the F word millions of times. But he said sorry afterwards and told me not to say it at school.'

'Well, we could get fish and chips from the shop, or lasagne from the freezer. What would you prefer?'

'We've had dinner. We had spaghetti, remember? With cheese and garlic bread. I ate your garlic bread because you said it smelt funny. Can I show Mummy my hair?' Polly asks.

'I shall just get fish and chips. It's much more straightforward and then that's that. He can't complain about fish and chips.' Janet nods to herself. 'Everyone likes fish and chips, don't they?'

'Yes, let's do that,' Polly agrees, entering back into the game again. 'With salt and vinegar and mushy peas,' she adds.

'Good idea, Helen. Can you go and get my purse from upstairs and we can quickly pop out before he gets back so everything will be ready for him. Could you do that for me, darling?'

Helen freezes. Her hand pressed against the door. Time stands still. This isn't a game. Janet thinks Polly is Helen. Janet isn't playing dinner, she's planning it. Kirsten Clark. That was a little girl from her infant school. She moved away when she was six and Helen hadn't given her a second thought, until now, that is.

Polly energetically swings the door open, 'Mummy!' she

greets her with a grin. 'Look what Nana did to my hair! Doesn't it look brilliant? Can I sleep in it so I can wear it like this for school tomorrow?'

'Of course. Of course you can.' She picks Polly up who wraps her arms and legs around her like a monkey, clinging on playfully.

'Nana and I are going to the fish and chip shop, isn't that right, Nana?'

Janet looks up at her. 'Helen, shall I nip to the shop and get us a bottle of something nice for later on, or do you have anything in? I don't want to be drinking you out of house and home, or accused of not contributing, God forbid. That really is one of the worst things you can be accused of in my opinion. Being tight with money. It's a hard reputation to shake. Always be generous, Polly my darling, as it will serve you well in the long run.'

Polly laughs in response, unsure of what's being asked of her.

'Right. Let's get you to bed,' Helen says. 'Say goodnight.'

'Night, Nana.'

'Night, Helen,' Janet responds, as she gets drawn into another *Mr Bean*.

'Why are you crying?' Polly asks as Helen carries her upstairs. The tears spill down her cheeks and soak into the shoulder of Polly's pyjamas.

'Just because,' she replies heavily.

Helen wheels her hairdresser's case down the corridor of the nursing home. She passes Mrs Tyler's room. The door is wide open and she sees a woman sat with her, dressed impeccably in a floral frock. Her daughter, Helen assumes. She holds Mrs Tyler's hand, who is laughing at something that's just been said. Mrs Tyler looks younger when she

218

smiles, you can see a glimpse of what she might have looked like as a young woman. A gentle reminder to smile more and scowl less.

She makes her way into Mr Hughes's room. It takes a beat to register that something is different. Wrong. The bed is made as usual, but his cross-stitched cushion of an anchor isn't resting against the pillow. The pictures of him and his wife aren't lining the windowsill and his barometer isn't on the wall.

She turns a full circle, looking for signs of Mr Hughes, and then spots the box in the corner of the room containing all his belongings.

'Can I help you?' Helen jumps with a start as a carer in a blue gingham tabard frames the door. She doesn't recognise her, she must be new. The turnover of staff is so high that she rarely sees a familiar member of staff, which is why she knows her visits are so important for continuity for the residents.

'So sorry,' Helen replies, 'I had come to cut Mr Hughes's hair, I usually do it every two weeks but . . .' her voice trails off.

'Oh yes. I was told you'd be in today. Sorry, I'm new. I've just come to clear out Mr Hughes's belongings. I'm really sorry no one let you know.'

'Oh how very sad. I liked Mr Hughes,' Helen replies softly.

'Yes, I only met him for the first time a couple of days ago, but he seemed like a nice man. Very gentle.' She steps into the room as she speaks, searching for something.

'He was. Did he have any family?' Helen asks.

'Sadly not. His wife died years ago and he didn't have any children or siblings so, no. Just him.' She nods thoughtfully as she scans the room and spots the box. 'Ah, there it is.'

'OK. Well, I'll leave you to it then.'

'Yes, thanks,' the carer says, picking up the box with a huff of breath.

As Helen walks out the room, she feels an overwhelming sadness. Less than two weeks ago she was doing Mr Hughes's hair, hearing about his sea-faring days and his love of Whitby, and now his entire life has been reduced to the contents of one small box. His room stripped of any memory of him as it is cleaned and dusted ready for the next resident.

Helen wonders what will happen to the contents of the box. Who will care for his things now he's gone? No one, probably. His stuff will be thrown out or given to a charity shop, most likely. Is this what we have to look forward to? Helen thinks. Are we just putting off the inevitable, that before long we shall all be living in regimented rooms, our only pleasure being a twenty-minute conversation with the mobile hairdresser every fortnight?

She unlocks her car and sits in the driver's seat, key in the engine without turning on the ignition. She sits like that for over half an hour, not quite ready to go home and face her own mum again.

Chapter Thirty-Four

Emma lowers the heaving tray down onto the table.

'I forgot to ask if Falcon wanted a ham or cheese toastie, so I got him both,' she explains as she starts offloading the array of plates onto the Debenhams' café table.

Tania gets out her purse. 'How much do I owe you?' she asks.

'Oh, don't be ridiculous. My treat. It's hardly The Grand, is it?' she smiles as she passes Shona and Falcon a juice box. Both the children have their heads together, watching a cartoon on Tania's phone.

'Thank goodness for technology,' Tania remarks as Emma passes her the soya latte.

She takes a grateful sip, the caffeine a welcome buzz after a long day already, what with her sunrise yoga and then a morning in the park with Falcon.

'Men have done worse,' Emma tells her, taking up their earlier conversation at the swing park. 'I lie all the time. Not big stuff,' she reassures Tania, 'but just stuff to make life easier. My life easier, mainly. For example, Tom wouldn't understand that I need an hour to myself to get a Swedish massage – that is how I recharge so that I can face the world. But if I say I am seeing a chiropractor, then it's a "recognised medical profession" and he's down with that. It's just about perception.'

Tania thinks on this for a moment. She herself is constantly bending the truth to accommodate others or make life more straightforward. But that's different. That's about oiling the wheels to make life easier, not nicking the whole fucking bike and cycling off home, leaving everyone else stranded.

'There's lies, and there's being selfish,' Tania states with an affirmative nod, dismissing the fact that she is yet to tell Spiral that they will be spending Christmas at her mother's mock-Tudor monstrosity.

'I get it. I just don't think Spiral's as bad as all that. Oh, this is *so* good.' The melted cheese strings from her toastie as Emma takes a satisfying bite. 'Eat yours,' she points to Shona's untouched lunch and Tania notices Falcon's two empty plates, having scoffed both sandwiches. Wow, that boy has an appetite.

'The thing is,' Tania puts her mug down and massages the stress pressure point on her wrist, 'I don't want "not as bad as all that". All this brush-it-under-the-carpet stuff. I grew up with that. Parents making a huge show of how happy and successful they were to the outside world, when they were miserable and lonely behind closed doors. It might be how other people live, but it's not how I want to. I know Spiral didn't have an affair with someone or, I don't know, get us into massive debt without us knowing, but he still lied. And it wasn't a harmless lie, because it did have an impact. On me. And that,' she raises a finger to emphasise her point, 'is not on. That's not being a team player.'

Emma pushes her half-eaten lunch away and Tania catches Falcon eyeing it up.

'I get it,' Emma replies. 'All I'm saying is, the fact that we're even having this conversation, the fact that Spiral is desperately trying to make it up to you, means that it will be OK. You guys will be OK, because you're made of strong stuff. You can mess up but then you talk about it. You *don't*

222

just brush it under the carpet. It just shows how far you've come since you left your parents. You're not like them, not at all. Not like any of us, to be honest.' She gives Tania a broad, generous smile, then dabs the corners of her mouth with the paper napkin.

'Thanks,' Tania replies, letting the warmth of her compliment wrap around her and soak into her pores. She can feel the glow radiate inside as the magnitude of the words take hold. Emma probably doesn't have a clue, but that is the most life-affirming thing that anyone has ever said to Tania.

Chapter Thirty-Five

HAVE YOU THOUGHT ANY MORE ABOUT CHRIST-MAS? Mum shouts via texts.

This must be the seventeenth time Mum has mentioned this over the last week. I'm not trying to give her the brush-off, I just have a massive mental block every time I sit down to put a plan together. Which in itself is a massive head-fuck for an over-planner, as it's only three weeks away. I've bought presents for everyone, of course I have. I've got a freezer full of 'Mum's Gone to Iceland'-style snacks. I'm not a total fucking Scrooge, but it's the practicality of what the day might be like that fills me with dread.

Mum's tone is becoming increasingly more impatient. She has now done away with referring to me by name or adding any kisses to her messages. This might also be down to the fact that Auntie Jean has told her you have to pay per character when you send a text, so Mum uses every letter sparingly. Auntie Jean never had a TV or mobile, and answers the land line with 'Lincoln 274' like a Bletchley Park code, so I don't know why Mum would rely on her for up-to-date technological information.

My finger hovers over the reply button, but instead I put it back on the coffee table and continue to watch *Love Actually*. Emma Thompson is just opening her Christmas present from under the tree. I know it's a film, of course I do, I've watched this film a hundred times, but it doesn't stop the optimist in me thinking, maybe, just maybe this time it will be the necklace and someone will get a happy bloody ending. We could all do with a bit of cheering up.

My phone chimes as I'm gearing up for a cathartic empathy cry.

'Hi, Mum,' I sigh.

'Have I caught you at a bad time?' she asks.

'No, I was just doing a bit of work,' I lie unnecessarily, as I press mute on the TV.

'Gosh, that's late, isn't it? You do work hard, Emily. Make sure you get some downtime for yourself.' She sounds concerned and I immediately feel guilty.

'Everything's fine, Mum. Are you OK?'

'Yes. Yes, all's good here. Your dad is upstairs on the computer working on the family tree. It's quite a project you know, he's trying to go all the way back to your great-great-great-great-grandfather, but is currently stuck at Great-Auntie Margaret as he suspects she may have had an affair, so that's put a bit of a spanner in the works.' She takes a sip of a drink and sighs contentedly. 'So,' she continues. 'Did you get my text message?' Mum hates to abbreviate. Wellington boots, cardigan, Jones the Bootmaker, Coca-Cola. Everything is given its full and rightful name. For the first few months of knowing Nick, she called him Nicolas until he assured her that he was actually just Nick on his birth certificate.

'Which one?' I ask.

'Well, that's a good question, Emily. I have sent quite a few, I'm sure it's cost me a fortune. I sent one a moment ago, but I'm never convinced that you receive them. You'll have to show me how to use my mobile telephone properly when I see you next.'

'Yes, I got your message, Mum. You don't have to phone

225

me right after you send them, you know. You have to give people time to respond.'

'Well that is good news. I'm pleased they're getting through to you, great. YES, SHE GOT THIS ONE, RICHARD. NO, I DON'T KNOW YET. I'M SPEAKING TO HER NOW,' Mum yells, not taking her mouth away from the receiver. 'That was just your dad.'

'Give him my love. And move the phone when you're shouting, Mum,' I try to keep the irritation out of my voice.

'SHE'S SENDING HER LOVE,' she responds. 'Dad sends his too. So. What are your thoughts then?'

'About what?' I ask.

'Christmas. What are you thinking of doing for Christmas?' Her voice has softened, but there is a sense of urgency underpinning it. She, like me, is a planner, so this last-minute organisation about something as large as Christmas is very much out of her comfort zone.

I watch Alan Rickman grinning as his wife paints on a smile for their son, and I gulp back a sob that's rising in my throat.

'I don't know, Mum,' I croak.

'Oh love. Well,' she broaches, assuming the quiver in my voice is about that, 'I know it's going to be different this year, of course. But me and your dad would love for you and the girls to come to us.' She pauses, waiting for a response, and when she doesn't get one, continues, 'I've already ordered the turkey from Waitrose and I was thinking we could take the children to see the lights in Grimsby precinct. They have a huge tree that's shipped in from Norway now. It really is quite something.'

I let my mind drift back to the first family Christmas Nick and I had spent with the girls at home a couple of years back. We had said how grown-up we'd felt, celebrating in our own

226

home. Every other year we'd spent it at one set of parents or the other, but last year we made the decision to stay at home, just the four of us. I'd spent a fortune on decorations in Wilko and plastered the house with tinsel and fairy lights. I'd even gone to a wreath-making workshop at the nursery and painstakingly wound razor-sharp holly leaves around the circular wire until I couldn't take the pricks any more, paid my fiver and nailed it to our front door.

On Christmas Eve, we walked down to the local park to listen to the choir singing carols by candlelight. We'd dressed both the children in elf hats from the market. Nick had Lucy on his shoulders and I'd pushed the pram with Sophie.

We'd returned home and left a carrot out for Rudolf and a malt whiskey for Father Christmas in front of the wood burner, then tucked the over-excited girls up in bed.

I had imagined a romantic night with Nick, eating After Eights and drinking Baileys. But what followed was an evening of bickering and sniping, as he reassured me that he'd get up early and wrap the rest of the presents, which, out of all the Christmas planning, was his only job to do. I insisted we have everything under the tree that night, as the children were inevitably going to wake up at the crack of dawn.

'Why do you always leave everything to the very last minute?' I'd asked him accusingly, feeling the Christmas cheer seeping out of the room.

'Only *you* could organise the fun out of Christmas, Em,' he'd muttered as he sulkily ripped the wrapping paper and bit the sticky tape with his teeth, ignoring the ribbons and stick-on bows that were also in the plastic bag.

'Why don't you use scissors like a normal person?' I'd retorted.

'And why don't you stop telling me what to do?' he snapped back. 'I don't know why we've bought half this stuff anyway. Why do we have to cripple ourselves financially for the sake of one day? It's madness, Emily.'

'You said we could get them some nice things with your bonus, Nick. Why are you backtracking now? You really are a cock sometimes,' I'd spat at him as I stomped out the room, grabbing the bottle of Baileys by the neck on the way out.

I'd spent the remainder of the evening in our bedroom, drinking the rest of the bottle, while slagging him off via WhatsApp to Rachel about how tight he's become. Oh, if only I'd had the whole picture then.

I woke the next morning fully dressed, lying on top of the duvet with a throbbing headache located behind my left eye socket.

Nick had rolled over when he heard me stir, kissed me gently between my shoulder blades and whispered, 'Get in your pyjamas, there's some paracetamol on the bedside table and a glass of water.'

Christmas Day was navigated by two squealing children, FaceTiming grandparents, ignoring most of the Christmas dinner in favour of eating chocolate, and watching film after children's Christmas film. Every room twinkled with fairy lights and Lucy told us it was the best day of her life.

But I couldn't quite shake the niggling feeling that Nick and I had lost our self-edit buttons. How quickly we could switch from having a good time all together to sitting next to each other in our own separate worlds, both on our phones, or watching different things on iPads in different rooms. How low-level irritation could so quickly escalate into insults, and that neither of us had the self-restraint to let the small stuff go. Even on Christmas Eve.

'I need to check with Nick before I make firm plans, Mum, and find someone to feed Peanuts,' I tell her.

I haven't spoken with Mum about the girl from the phone. I can't. I don't know if it's out of embarrassment for him, or denial from me. He's tried to talk to me about it, of course. Nick's ability to steam in because he has something on his mind, instead of thinking how his words might affect others, could be one of his superpowers. I don't know where to start, though, so instead we have started talking to each other like automated messages. Relaying times and places that we need to meet to do with the children, but keeping things very fact-focused.

I also haven't told Mum about my less than successful foray into internet dating, or that my first date was nearer her age than mine.

'Of course, of course. I wouldn't expect anything less. But if it *does* work for you all . . .' she drifts off expectantly.

'Then we would love to come, thank you,' I say. And I mean it.

'SHE SAID SHE'D LOVE TO COME,' Mum tells Dad.

'IF IT'S OK WITH NICK,' I interject.

'Goodness that was loud Emily. That went right through me!' she gently scolds. 'I don't think you realise how your voice carries sometimes.' She pauses and breathes deeply. This is Mum's pre-announcement breath. I wait. 'I have also invited Auntie Jean to Christmas. I know she doesn't normally spend it with us, but her friend Cynthia is going on a cruise this year, so I thought it would be nice if she joined us.' Another pause. There's more to come. 'And Rachel, I bumped into her yesterday in the Co-op and mentioned that you might be coming up with the girls, so I said she should pop by in the afternoon with Callum after they've had their lunch. Oh,' she adds, 'and she was with her boyfriend – Mark?'

'Matt,' I reply flatly.

'Oh dear. I don't know why his name won't stick, I think I called him Mark. Anyway, I invited him too. And Mr and Mrs Earl next door might call round for a sherry, of course. Gosh, they're getting on now, Emily, they really do look old. So, it will be quite a little party won't it?' she enthuses.

I now see what this is. It's not just Christmas; it's an intervention. She's filling the house with people to plug the Nick-shaped hole. I know her intentions are good, but I wanted this Christmas to slip by unnoticed, to be the definition of low key. Not be paraded around as the newly single daughter.

. 'Sounds lovely. Night, Mum,' I sign off, before I say something I won't be able to unsay.

'Goodnight, my girl,' she says, and hangs up.

I turn the volume up on the TV again but my heart's no longer in it.

I scroll down to Nick's number. My finger hovers over the call button. We need to start talking, I know this. I could be the bigger person here. I should extend the olive branch, get us back on track again, make life easier.

I hesitate for a moment, then put down the phone. Why should I? Why is it always me who smooths over the cracks?

No, Nick. Not this time. This is your mess. You clear it up.

Chapter Thirty-six

'Are you sure we can afford this?' Tania whispers to Spiral over the top of the Pizza Friends menu.

'It's fine. There was over twenty quid in the jar.'

'Spiral! That was meant for Christmas!' Tania scolds under her breath.

'Oh, live a little, Tan. It's good to support a local business. Anyway, there was an offer in the local paper. Buy one, get one free on the lunchtime menu, so knock yourself out,' he whispers back, giving her a wink.

'Great,' Tania replies. Of course it was a bargain, when else has Spiral taken her out for food? But she puts her mild irritation to one side. At least he's trying. Since 'pubgate', he has cooked at least three times, and not just cremated creations in a frying pan. Proper food from the Cranks cookbook. He's been home in time to do some reading with Falcon and put him to bed the last few days. He even ran Tania a bath, put on Smooth FM and gave her a glass of wine for ultimate relaxation the other night. And now this. An impromptu lunch date on a Saturday afternoon, while Falcon plays with Lucy and Sophie. All arranged, without prompting, by Spiral.

'Chai-infused salad and a margarita for me, I think,' he slams the menu down on the table with a satisfying slap. 'What about you?'

'I might have the same,' she replies, shifting uncomfortably in her seat. This is the first time she's given Helen's lace body suit an outing. It's like wearing a Mankini made of wire wool.

When Spiral has said they had a free afternoon stretching ahead of them, Tania has mistakenly assumed that was shorthand for an hour in bed together. The outfit was a bugger to get on in the first place, and she hadn't the time to change out of it when Spiral had handed her her coat and enthusiastically announced they were going to get something to eat in town.

'You OK there?' Spiral asks.

'Couldn't be better,' she smiles.

'Good. I can't remember the last time we went out, just the two of us. Cheers!' They clink pint glasses together.

'Yeah, this is nice,' Tania replies, but her mind is elsewhere. She still hasn't told Spiral that they are to spend Christmas at her parents. The penance has now royally backfired, and Tania has already received a detailed five-course menu, sent via an external catering company asking for her feedback and dietary requirements, as well as a short but firm text from her mum with a dress code.

'Smart-casual. But obviously more smart than casual, Arabella.'

It is starting to feel very reminiscent of the awful dinner parties they used to throw when she was younger. All pomp and no feeling. She remembers one such party when she couldn't have been much older than Falcon. She had been sent upstairs to 'entertain herself' while her parents were also entertaining. A posh dinner for posh people who had little time or interest in children.

She remembers creeping into her parents' bedroom, which was out of bounds, every step being an adrenalin-fuelled adventure. She remembers opening her mother's huge walk-in wardrobe, breathing in the heady smell of perfume, and widening her eyes in awe of the rich colours, of silks and lace, flowing fabrics and shiny pearls. She remembers wanting to see what it felt like to be as glamorous as her mother, as grown-up, as elegant. She remembers tugging at one of the particularly exuberant frocks, all netting and embroidered detail, and she distinctly remembers the terrifying sound of ripping fabric as it got caught on the hanger, followed by the paralysis of fear, eyes-wide and alert as she heard her mother's footsteps entering the room.

'So it's not a major problem, but I just wanted to let you know,' Spiral finishes, as Tania zones back into the conversation.

'What's not a problem?' she asks.

'Where were you?' he jokes. 'I was just saying that Jimmy reckons there might be a bit of a lull after this job in the New Year. He doesn't reckon it's anything to worry about, just might be worth me keeping my ear to the ground for any other work that might be coming up. Oh God, Tan. Don't look so worried, it's going to be OK,' he squeezes her hand, his brow knitted with concern.

'It's not that,' she replies. 'You're not going to like this, so I'm just going to blurt it out and then we can enjoy our dinner. I've spoken to my mum and we're definitely going there for Christmas. It's all confirmed. There's no getting out of it. The caterers are booked. The wine has been ordered. So, there you have it.' Tania wipes her forehead with a napkin and takes a large gulp of her pint.

'Why?' Spiral asks gently.

'You know why. Because of you going to the bloody pub, Spiral,' she snaps back.

'Yes, yes, I know I deserve it. But why put yourself through this, Tan?' his voice soft with concern.

'I don't know what you mean?' Tania asks, confused. Spiral isn't angry, he isn't disappointed. He just seems genuinely concerned. For her.

'I just think there might have been a better way to resolve this. We could have talked it through, Tan.'

'Well. Too late now!' she snaps.

'OK. That's fine. Course it is. I just think you need to remember what it's like to be there. And whether you want to put yourself through that again.'

'It's one day, Spiral. One day. And I don't know why you're playing the caring husband card now. If you hadn't buggered off to the pub in the first place, I wouldn't have had to invite ourselves there.'

'You're right. I was just thinking it didn't go particularly well the first time we visited, did it?' he says.

'That was decades ago, Spiral. They were obviously going to hate you back then. You were two years older than me and helping their teenage daughter move out of the house in the middle of her A levels to move into a fucking squat. They were hardly going to roll out the red carpet, were they?' she replies.

'I know. I don't think your mum slapping me was necessarily the answer, but yep. I can see why they were upset, obviously,' he shrugs.

'Upset doesn't come close,' Tania mutters.

'Look. We'll be there, of course. Just make sure you protect yourself, Tan. You are your own woman. You are strong, beautiful and independent. You are not a culmination of your mum's opinions and insults. And we love you. Very much. OK?' he squeezes her hand again.

This time Tania squeezes back, 'I know. I love you both too. Let's not get this out of proportion. We'll just eat ridiculously expensive food and Falcon can be spoilt rotten for a day. That doesn't sound like the worst punishment for being a knob, does it?' she jokes, but Spiral doesn't let go of her hand.

Tania drifts back to Francesca's face as she pushed open the door to the master bedroom. Her look of sheer horror. How she marched her downstairs to make an example of her in front of the guests, demanding an apology, but Arabella couldn't find the words. She couldn't find her voice. And her mother took this as a sign of disobedience and insolence, whereas in reality, she just wanted to jump back in time to ten minutes before, when her mother didn't think she was a 'troublemaker' and still believed she was wonderful, even if it was often from afar.

The seed of disappointment had been planted, and it didn't matter what Arabella did from that point on. There was always an invisible line of expectation that she could never quite live up to. So why wouldn't she continue to push boundaries, to go off the rails? It's like, if someone is convinced you're a thief, you might as well nick something, make the accusations at least work for you.

Tania looks at Spiral, who smiles back at her and says, 'It'll all be OK.'

She unexpectedly leans over the Pizza Friends table, cups his face in hers, and pushes her lips against his.

'God, I love you sometimes,' she grins.

'What did I say?' he asks, grinning back.

'You just reminded me *exactly* why we work, Spiral. Now, I'm suggesting we fuck off the pizzas and go home. I have something to show you,' Tania already has her coat on.

'But it's a co-operative café, we can't just leave,' Spiral falters.

'Just give them the jar money anyway, come on. We're wasting time.'

235

Spiral quickly roots through his satchel and places the jar with the screws on the table. He's brought the whole bloody thing.

'Thank you!' Tania chimes as she hurries out of the café holding Spiral's hand.

She's a woman in a lace mankini, and she's not afraid to use it.

Chapter Thirty-Seven

'Going anywhere nice?' Nick asks, as I kiss the girls on the top of their heads before they push past him into Simon's flat.

'Now, you should have their pyjamas here already,' I ignore his question, 'but I've put a spare set in here.' I pass him a tote bag. 'Just in case the ones you already have are not clean. Can you also make sure you wash their hair this time, and give them both a go with the nit comb. That's in there too, as there's been a note going around at school to say there's been another outbreak.'

'I know what to do, Em. They have stayed here before,' he sighs, shoulders dropping. I notice how his T-shirt is hanging off him, like he's lost weight.

'I know they have, Nick, that wasn't a criticism. I'm just saying because I don't think you get the texts from school about nits and stuff.'

'Look, Em, I think we need to talk,' he smiles weakly. 'We haven't really sorted out Christmas, and it feels like everything's gone completely tits up recently.'

I am about to tell him *exactly* why everything's gone tits up, but I look at his face for the first time in a long time, properly look at it. He looks older. The hair dye has washed out – he definitely got his money's worth out of that one as it was more like a thousand washes instead of eight – but as a consequence, the grey now looks far more prominent and his beard, if you can call it that, is also peppered with grey and the odd wiry bright white hair springing out at odd angles. He used to stand tall but now he seems shorter somehow, like he's stooping.

'Do you want to come in?' he says. 'Do you have five minutes, or do you need to get off?'

I check the time on my phone. My date is at eight o'clock, so I have some time to spare, and no one wants to be the first to turn up.

'OK,' I reply. 'I don't have long though.'

Nick holds the door open for me and as I squeeze past him, I ask, 'How did you know I was going out? I might have just been going home after this.'

'Your perfume,' he replies.

'Sorry?'

'You've got your going-out perfume on. You only wear it for special occasions. Go through,' he indicates to the front room.

During all the times I have dropped the girls off, I have rarely been inside Simon's flat. I had a look around when he first moved in to check where they'd be sleeping to make sure it wasn't some kind of opium den, but since then, I've not really stepped over the threshold.

The first thing that strikes me is how tidy it is.

'Have you got a cleaner?' I ask.

'No. Nope. Just me, I did run the hoover round before you came over. But I mainly try to just keep on top of things so that it doesn't build up, you know how it is.' He's speaking with the confidence of a man who has always 'run a hoover' around.

'I'm impressed,' I say, hoping I don't sound patronising, but I really am.

'Well, I am staying here rent-free, so don't want to take

238

the piss. Can I get you a tea or a glass of wine?' he asks.

'Wine would be nice,' I reply. I am 99 per cent sure there will be booze this evening, seeing as we are meeting in a pub, but I'm not taking any chances after the last date with Sixty-something Steve.

He comes back in with two glasses and a bottle of red, popping the cork and filling them both up, splashing a drop onto the carpet, which he immediately soaks up with the toe of his sock. Some things don't change, I notice.

'Think the girls have gone up to their room, well, their room *here*. You know what I mean. My mum bought them a load of Duplo when they were down so they're just . . .' his sentence drifts off as he passes me the glass. 'Look, Em. About when we went out with my folks—'

'Can we not talk about that tonight,' I reply briskly.

'No, no. I understand, it's just that—'

'What did you want to sort out about Christmas?' I ask, noticing for the first time that he has a small plastic Christmas tree in the corner of the room with a string of coloured lights haphazardly draped around it, intermittently flashing on and off. It looks so sad it makes me want to cry.

'Well, I didn't know what your plans are. But I'd like the girls to come to Nottingham for some of the time to be with me, Mum and Dad. Will they be with you over Christmas in Lincolnshire?'

'Yes. But only if that's OK with you?' I feel heavy. Like a huge weight has been placed on both shoulders. I never thought I'd be sitting on Nick's friend's sofa trying to work out how to split the days over what should be the most brilliant time of year with kids. I never thought being a parent would be so messy and complicated. I never thought it could be filled with such uncertainty and instability. There is no way to tart this up. This is a bit shit.

'Yes. Yes of course. So do you want me to pick them up on Boxing Day?' he asks, unnecessarily refilling both of our glasses.

'Or we could meet in the middle, if that's easier?' I suggest.

'What about the service station at the Newark round-about? They've got a Wild Bean Café there, so you can get a drink if one of us is early?' This is the first time there has been any hint of enthusiasm in his voice. Nick will obviously be there early. He loves a Wild Bean Café, specifically the steak and kidney pies that sit congealing on heated racks all day.

'Yep. That's OK with me.' I drain the last of my wine in one uncomfortably large gulp.

'OK. Good. Well, that's sorted then.' He nods decisively, then continues nodding, lips pursed, as if he's building up to say something.

I don't want to hear whatever he has to say, so, checking the time, say, 'I have to go, Nick. Thanks for the wine.'

'I just wanted to . . . Em. Please can I just explain about—'

'No, Nick. You just can't.' I cut him off. 'If you wanted to explain, then you should have done that before you started dating celebrity lookalikes. Before you lied to your parents and made me lie too, for that matter. All I ask is that the children don't meet her. Not now. I don't want their lives to be disrupted any more than they have been recently.'

'OK. OK. I understand. But I'm here if you want to talk.' He motions, palms up, like Judy used to.

'Jesus, Nick. Course I don't want to talk. And if I did, why would it be with you? In fact, you'd be the absolute last person I'd want to talk to about you shagging someone. Can you imagine how absolutely, completely awkward that would be? Actually, I'm just on my way to a date myself, so maybe I'll talk to him about it. That would be less painful than talking to you.'

'You're dating?' Nick splutters.

'Yes. Why do you find that so hard to believe?' I'm trying not to raise my voice but it's almost impossible not to. His double standards are off the scale.

'I don't, I just thought, I don't know—' he gasps.

'What? That you were the only person moving on? Well, guess what, Nick. I've moved on too. I'm going on a date tonight and with a man who is gorgeous and uncomplicated and finds me completely irresistible.' I list off the attributes of a man I am still yet to meet. 'In fact, I'm pretty sure I'm going to shag him tonight. How's that for moving on?' I slam my glass down; the last drop of wine splashes onto the floor. Fuck it. Nick can wipe it up with his sock. I leave the front room, Nick's mouth hanging open in shock as I prickle with frustration and embarrassment.

'Bye girls,' I shout up the corridor, and they both come bounding out of their room with a stampede of feet, wrapping their arms around my legs as I shower them with kisses to a chorus of 'Bye, Mummy!'s.

As I untangle them from me and head to the front door, something catches my eye. It's Nick's Fred Perry jacket, hanging with his other coats on the rack. I angrily pull it off the peg and throw it on the floor, feeling childishly satisfied.

'Mummy!' the children squeal, delighted. 'You can't do that!'

'Emily!' he waves from the corner seat in the pub. Phew. He looks roughly the same age as his picture, so that's a good start – his profile said he was forty-five. This is progress. I wave back and weave my way through the occupied chairs towards him. So this is what people with disposable income and no responsibilities do on a Thursday night, is it? The pub is packed, and a DJ wearing a Peaky Blinders cap plays records loudly next to the bar.

'Malcolm?' I ask as I approach the table.

'Call me Mal, everyone else does.' He stands and greets me by pecking both my cheeks. Very continental. I'm also quietly delighted that he's not a Malcolm, because, superficial as this is, I found the name quite off-putting, as it reminded me of Mum and Dad's elderly neighbour who used to refer to women as 'fillies'. I couldn't imagine shouting out 'Malcolm' in the throes of passion. It sounds a bit *Abigail's Party*. But Mal, on the other hand . . .

'What can I get you to drink?' Mal asks.

As he stands, I see he's not much taller than me, no bother though. He's well dressed, with a pair of dark Levi's and a Stüssy sweater. He's got a lovely face. Very kind and as he smiles I notice he's also got good teeth. What is it with me and teeth? Maybe that's my 'type'. Clean teeth. That's not much to ask for, is it?

'Oooh, a gin and tonic please,' I reply.

'Coming up,' he says as he shimmies out from behind the table. I get another whiff of him as he passes by, his aftershave smells really nice, expensive and crisp. I'm pleased I had a bikini wax.

The walk down from Nick's flat has cleared my head. The fury gave way to indifference. I don't actually care what Nick gets up to now, as long as it doesn't affect the girls, he can do whatever the fuck he likes. As can I, for that matter.

Not that I'm planning on shagging Mal, regardless of what I said to Nick. I've only known him thirty seconds, but it is good to be prepared, as Rachel informed me. 'You don't want to fancy the arse off him and then realise that you've got pubes down to your knees, do you?'

242

But I haven't had a wax for quite some time, so it's really itchy. I subtly shuffle on my seat, as I don't think I can hazard a proper scratch without being spotted and looking like I have crabs.

'Here you go,' he passes me a large fishbowl glass. 'I got you a double. I hope that's OK.'

'That is perfect,' I reply and we clink glasses.

'Have you been on the dating scene long?' he asks. He's got deep green eyes and long eyelashes, like a cow. How is it possible that this guy is single? What is wrong with him? What's the catch?

'Nope,' I reply, taking a long drink. It's not a very elegant glass and I lose half my face in it before I can get anything into my mouth. 'You are actually my second date. The first guy lied about his age and was about a hundred, so it's reassuring to see you look like your profile! How's about you?'

He smiles thoughtfully and then replies, 'A couple of months, I guess. I haven't really met that many women, though. I've never been much of a player, I find it all a bit crude, to be honest.'

'Oh, me too,' I sigh. 'And it's so difficult to tell what a person is going to actually be like when all you've got to go on is a picture of someone and a short paragraph. I mean, no one's going to say they've got psychopathic tendencies or wank over pictures of Carol Vorderman in their spare time, are they?'

Mal laughs a hearty warm laugh. 'You're funny, Amy. I like that.'

'Emily,' I say, 'It's Emily.'

'Shit. What did I say?'

'Amy, but don't worry about it. It's close enough.' I brush it off, trying to think of something else funny to say to hear that sexy laugh again, but his brow is furrowed and he's rubbing his temples. What did I say?

'Are you all right?' I ask.

'Oh, I knew this was a bad idea.' He's shaking his head.

'What was a bad idea?' I ask. Oh God, what have I done? He's now got his head in his hands. I've broken him with my hilarious jokes.

He looks up, and his gorgeous eyes are glassy. 'I'm such an idiot. Sorry.'

'It's no problem, I've been called much worse,' I say in an attempt to lighten the mood.

Christ, he looks like he's going to burst into tears. What could I have possibly said?

'It's Amy.'

'No, it's Emily.'

'No, sorry. Amy was my girlfriend. We'd been together for nearly twenty years. Until she fucked Clive.'

'Who's Clive?'

'My supposed best mate. He's such a cunt.' Mal drains his glass. Clive and Malcolm. Bloody hell, who named these poor boys?

'I'm sorry to hear that.' I reach out to touch his arm. He's a hot crier. That's a hard balance to strike. And I am a woman who gives approximately zero fucks tonight. He pats my hand platonically and gently moves my hand off his arm.

'I didn't see it coming. I'm such a dick. The thing is, we were one doctor down at my practice—'

'You run your own practice?' I ask.

'Yes. Yeah, I took it over a couple of years ago.' This is so unfair. Who is this Amy? She's a prize idiot, whoever she is. 'So I was working long hours to make sure all the patients got seen—'

'That must have been so hard for you,' I sympathise, taking another huge mouthful of my G & T while I assess

244

how much of a disaster this date is and if it's worth getting another drink in.

'Yeah, she was lonely. I get it. I wasn't there for her. But Clive is such a massive prick, he's always been jealous of us, to be honest. Even at uni, I knew he had a thing for Amy, but why wouldn't you? She's gorgeous, she's got hair your kind of colour. Your length, I'd say. How tall are you?' he asks.

'Five foot four,' I reply cautiously. Oh fuck. I see where this is going.

'I thought so from your pictures. Amy was five four as well.' He looks at his empty glass. 'Can I get you another one?' he asks.

'Look, Mal,' I put my glass down and use my serious voice. 'I get a very strong feeling that you're not over your ex yet. I suspect you have a way to go before you're ready to see anyone else.'

'That's not true,' he pleads, as he grasps my hand. God he's got nice hands and a strong grip. 'I'm not sure where that came from, but I am 100 per cent over her. I would fucking knock Clive out if I saw him, but who wouldn't? He was supposed to be my mate. But I am over Amy. Please. Let's start again. I'll get us some more drinks in and then I want to hear all about you, I want to know everything about your life.'

'I think I'm going to go, Mal. But it has been really lovely to meet you,' I slip my hand out from underneath his.

'Why does this keep happening to me?' he asks, mainly to himself.

'Because you keep dating girls who look like your ex?' I suggest. 'Frankly, it's a bit creepy. Which is a shame, as you are properly hot, Mal. I'm so disappointed because you really are, and I would have definitely got off with you if

245

you'd tried tonight. I really needed a good snog and you would have been perfect.'

Mal picks at a scratch on his wrist. 'I had no idea I was doing that. I'm so sorry, Emily. You must think I'm awful.'

'No,' I reply. 'No I don't, but I do think you need to work through some of this anger, or speak to Amy maybe?' I've adopted the conflict management voice Judy used to use on Nick and me.

'Do you think I should speak to her?' His face lights up optimistically, eyes bright. 'I've thought about it, God I've written and deleted so many texts to her.' He pulls his phone out of his jeans and shows me the screen saver. It is a picture of a woman who does look spookily like me; if I saw it from a distance I could be mistaken for thinking it was actually me.

'This was us on holiday in Greece, we were island-hopping. Amy loves the sea. She's a real-life mermaid, I used to say.' A sob escapes and he sniffs loudly.

'Maybe just give her a call?' I suggest.

'Do you really think I should? What if she tells me to fuck off? She has every right, I did completely neglect her. I *do* get it.' How has Amy managed to come out of this smelling like roses when she's bonked his best friend? Some women are charmed, I guess.

'Do what's right for you, Mal,' I pick up my handbag and stand to leave.

Mal also stands and wraps me in a tight hug, whispering, 'Thank you. I can't believe I couldn't see what was right in front of my face. Thank you.'

'No probs,' I pat his back, like Dad does to other men. Friendly yet non-committal.

As I walk out of the pub, I chance a final look at him. He's head down texting, tongue poking out the side of his mouth in concentration. I allow myself a frantic, satisfying scratch of my bikini line and groan with relief.

Well, that didn't go to plan. I have spent the evening talking about an ex shagging someone else after all.

Shame. Although realistically, I could never date a man called Malcolm, however hot he was.

Chapter Thirty-Eight

Helen opens the car door and unplugs Polly from her car seat. 'Right, do you want to ring the bell and check if Dad's in?'

Polly leaps out and runs up the path, 'DAAAAAAAAA AAAAAAD,' she shouts as she leans on the doorbell. She sticks her fingers through the letter box and again hollers, 'DAAAAAAAAAAAAAAAD!'

Helen pushes the key into the lock. The house is in complete darkness. 'That's odd. Anyone home?' she shouts with no response. She turns on the hall light and puts her house and car keys in the pot on the sideboard.

'Can I watch *The Simpsons*?' Polly's face looks up at her expectantly as she pushes past her into the hallway.

'No, of course you can't, Polly. It's meant for grown-ups. Now take your coat off and hang it on the hook.'

Polly huffs loudly, steps out of her half-undone coat and leaves it on the floor.

'Polly. Coat!'

She stomps back, picks it up and throws it in the direction of the child's height coat peg on the wall. 'Daddy let me watch it yesterday.'

'Well, I'm not Daddy. Now go for a wee and remember to wash your hands.' Thanks, Chris, she thinks. He's only been home a couple of days and is already rocking the equilibrium.

Helen catches sight of her reflection in the big mirror. She needs her roots done; the grey is starting to show. She can't have unintentional two-tone hair as a hairdresser. Some of the women at the nursing home might not be able to remember their own names, but they notice imperfections in her appearance like a Trinny and Susannah hawk.

'Chris? Are you home?' A pair of his shoes lay discarded like he's walked straight out of them. Helen puts them in the shoe rack next to hers and hangs her coat on the bannister. 'Chris?'

'Helen is that you?' a voice calls from upstairs.

'Mum? Is Chris with you?'

'No. He popped back earlier to change his clothes and then he went out again.'

'Have you eaten?'

'Don't worry about me. I don't have much of an appetite,' the disembodied voice drifts down.

'So, is that a no?'

'I'll just have a little of whatever you're having. A bit of smoked cheese if you have any? And a light salad maybe with a bit of balsamic dressing?'

'I'm making Polly beans on toast, would you like some of that instead? It might be a bit more filling?' Helen calls up from the bottom of the stairs.

'OK, if that's all you have,' she replies curtly and Helen breathes deeply so as to not react.

'Fine. Do you want to come down to eat it and you can sit with Polly?' Helen shouts.

'Could you bring it up here, Helen. I'm having a rest, so I'd prefer it in my room.'

It's not your room, actually, Helen thinks. It's the guest room. For guests. Who have been invited to stay, not turned up unannounced and settled in for the foreseeable future.

'Yep – no problem,' she replies, getting increasingly fed up with the list of demands Janet is making as standard, like she's the bloody maid.

Helen had approached the subject of Janet's living arrangements the other day over dinner. One of the carers at the nursing home had mentioned wardened accommodation when Helen was last there doing her haircutting rounds. Residents live independently, but with support if needed. Helen had looked into it and it had all seemed quite reasonable, but Janet's response wasn't.

'And why in the name of God would I want to live with a bunch of doddery old has-beens playing dominos and wetting themselves?' she'd sneered.

'It's not like that, Mum, you have your own place. It's just you have support if you need it. That's all.'

'I already *have* my own place, thank you very much, Helen, as well you know. I had only come to stay with you for a short while. I wasn't expecting to be farmed off to the nearest old people's home while I was visiting. Maybe I should just go back to Spain. I'll pack my case tomorrow and fly back. I know when I'm not wanted,' she'd snapped, angrily shovelling macaroni cheese into her mouth.

A look had passed between Helen and Chris. Does Janet even know what's real and what's not any more?

Helen floods the kitchen with light, presses the switch on the kettle and turns on Heart FM on the radio.

'Polly, what are you doing in there?'

Her daughter emerges from the downstairs loo, the front of her dress soaking wet. 'What happened?'

'I couldn't turn the tap off, Mummy.'

'Never mind. Put this on.' She grabs a nightie that's drying on the radiator.

'But that's for bed.'

250

'Put it on anyway.' She pulls the sodden dress over Polly's head and puts it straight into the washing machine. 'Now, go and put your programmes on in the front room, anything but *The Simpsons*. I'll make you and Nana something to eat.'

As Helen opens the fridge, her mobile beeps.

HELEN, I'VE POPPED OUT TO WATCH LIVERPOOL, I'LL BE BACK AT CLOSING.

And then several seconds later:

XXX

'Typical,' she mutters to no one. Maybe this is a good short-term solution for him, but he can't permanently live in the pub. He's going to have to come home at some point.

'I'm happy to help when you need me, I just find her very difficult to be around. She's *so* negative,' he'd said by way of an explanation.

It just seemed so unfair. She knows if his mum moved in, she'd be expected to help out, so why can't he extend the same courtesy to her? She could really do with him being about a bit more as an extra pair of eyes, just to ensure there weren't any more kettle incidents.

'Helen, is that you?' the voice from upstairs calls down.

'Yes, still me! I'm just making the food. I'll be up in a minute.'

The microwave pings as the toast pops up. She butters the slices and tips beans on top, crumbling some cheese over both plates. She puts Polly's plate on the table, calling, 'Dinner's ready!' and places Janet's tea on a tray. She adds a glass of water, which her mum will turn her nose up at, and walks carefully up the stairs so as to not spill anything.

251

'Knock, knock.' Helen opens the door with her bum.

The smell hits her first. She slides the tray on to the dresser top. The curtains are shut, the room is engulfed in darkness.

Helen tugs open the curtains and throws open the window. Janet is sat up in bed, the duvet tucked under her armpits. 'Oh, I forgot how much I liked beans on toast. Such a nostalgic smell. You used to love it when you were a little girl,' she comments, oblivious to the other, overpowering stench. 'Heinz are three times the price in Spain. It's criminal.'

'Mum, has there been an accident in here?'

'What kind of accident? Is that *water*, Helen?' Janet asks disappointedly. She smooths out the sheets over her legs with the palms of her hands and as she does, another wave of pungent smell escapes from under the cover.

'Mum,' Helen asks gently. 'Could I just take a quick peek under the covers?'

'Oh, Helen, you do like to fuss. There's nothing to see, I've cleared everything up. Although I could do with a carrier bag to put those in.' She points to a pile of soiled tissues by the side of the bed.

'Shall I run a shallow bath before your dinner? I can just change the sheets and make everything a bit more comfortable in here? What do you say?' Helen quietly suggests.

'That's kind of you, Helen, but there's no need.' She dismisses the suggestion with a flutter of a hand.

Helen walks quickly down the corridor to the bathroom and turns on both taps, squeezing in a drop of Radox under the faucet.

'Should I eat this in bed?' she hears her mum call.

'No, absolutely not,' Helen panics. 'Just leave everything where it is until I come back.'

Helen leans against the bathroom wall as the room begins to fill with steam. She rubs her forehead with the heel of her hand. Everything feels so out of control. She pulls her phone from her pocket and starts to compose a text to Chris, but presses delete and puts it back. How do you even begin to articulate what is happening in a limited number of characters?

She turns off the taps and splashes the water to check the temperature.

As Helen eases Janet's legs out of the bed she pulls back the cover. The entire fitted sheet is smeared with shit, as is Janet's nightdress.

'I don't know how it got like this,' Janet exclaims, disgustedly.

They walk carefully to the bathroom, Helen holding Janet tightly under her arm. She feels smaller, weaker than she looked this morning, and Helen wonders if it is her venom and sharp tongue that gives the false impression of height. Her childhood memories were of her mother being nearly the same height as her father, but an old photograph showed that he was, indeed, about a foot taller than her, at least. It's funny how the brain reformats things and makes them fact.

She carefully removes her mum's nightdress and holds her under both armpits as Janet cautiously puts one leg and then the other in the bath. She must weigh no more than eight stone. When did she get so thin? Every one of her ribs protrudes and her skin hangs down in folds, making a hollow hammock of her stomach.

'Ohh this smells lovely, is it lavender?'

'That's right,' she pours water from the jug over her back and uses a flannel glove to wipe off the worst of the mess.

'Is Chris downstairs?'

'No, it's Polly watching her programmes. Chris is watching the football in the pub,' she replies as she pours the water over her.

253

Helen looks at Janet's body and tries to imagine it strong and powerful, like it was when she was a young woman. She continued to dress youthfully all through Helen's childhood, much to her embarrassment, and right into her teenage years. To her annoyance, Helen would find her mum 'borrowing' some of her clothes when she was in the sixth form. By university, Janet had moved to Spain, and what she wore bore no relation to Helen's life any more.

Helen pours the water over her mum's shoulders, and down her arms.

Janet raises her arms in the air, first one and then the other, like a cat stretching. 'That's lovely,' she sighs. As she suspends her right arm in the air, Helen instinctively reaches out and traces the scar on Janet's forearm with her finger.

'That was from the car accident when you were a little girl. You couldn't have been older than three,' she tells Helen.

'I know.'

'Your dad was so angry. He shouldn't have been driving the car. You should never drive when angry, you know that? You can't concentrate.' Her voice is flat and emotionless, as if she's reading the shipping forecast.

'It wasn't Dad's fault. It was a deer, Mum. Remember? A deer ran out in front of the car.'

'What deer, Helen? There aren't any deer near Portsmouth,' Janet dismisses with a flick of the wrist, as if it was the most nonsensical thing to say. 'We'd driven into town, you needed some shoes, so we were going to get you measured in Clarks. Your dad said he would drive us, even though he hated shopping. But he hated the thought of me going somewhere without him more.'

'That's not what happened, Mum. Remember?' Helen prompts gently as she pours clean warm water from the sink over her mum's hair. 'He was driving us home from the zoo, and a deer ran out onto the road. He had to swerve the car and it crashed into a field.' She softly massages shampoo into Janet's hair, putting gentle pressure on the base of her neck, which is a tangle of tension knots.

'That feels lovely, Helen,' Janet closes her eyes for a moment, before continuing, 'He thought I was flirting with the shop assistant. He was only a boy, but that didn't matter to Mick. Once he's got an idea in his head, that's it. Stupid man.'

'Mum, I think you're getting confused. Do you want me to get you out?'

'He marched us back to the car. He was furious. We didn't even buy the shoes, just left them at the cash register. And then he drove off like a man possessed. It's no wonder we crashed. It's a miracle no one was hurt.'

'Mum?' Helen whispers quietly. 'We'd been to the zoo. You, me and Dad. We were on our way home and Dad swerved to avoid a deer. We'd had a lovely day. It was just an accident. We were all fine apart from the odd scratch. Remember?' Helen encourages.

'I remember. Of course I remember. I'm not crazy, although you talk to me like I am. There was no deer. There was no zoo. There isn't a bloody zoo near Portsmouth, Helen. It was him. Always him. I *had* to get him away from us. He could hurt me, but the day you were hurt, everything changed. There wasn't a deer. There was never a deer. It was Mick. It was Mick.' Janet is hitting the water with her fists. It splashes up the walls and runs down in streams.

'OK. OK Mum. Sorry. Sorry. I hear you.'

'Is that him downstairs?' she asks, eyes wide. Janet sits bolt upright, filthy water sloshes over the side of the bath. Janet is clutching the edges of the bath, white-knuckled.

She is frozen with fear. Helen tries to unpick her fingers, one by one, but her hands are locked.

'Mum, It's OK,' she says gently, trying to retain her own building sense of anxiety.

'It's him. It's him downstairs. I can hear him, Helen. Did I get something for supper? I can't remember.' Her voice trembles with distress. Helen has never seen Janet like this before. This is the woman who is scared of nothing and expects everything from the world. Has her mind completely rewritten history, or could there be any truth in this? Could her sweet dad have been a bully? Why wouldn't Janet have told her before if so? Helen's mind starts to swim with questions as her mum asks again, 'Is that him, Helen?'

'No, Mum. It's Polly. She's watching her programmes,' she soothes.

Janet looks at her hands, palms up. 'My fingers have gone wrinkly, Helen.' Her voice instantly changes and her shoulders drop, like she's been snapped out of a trance.

'OK. Let me quickly change your bedding and then I can get you back in it when it's nice and clean.'

'No need, Helen. I'm not royalty, you don't need to keep changing my sheets every five minutes, you know.' The edge has returned to her mum's voice.

'I think I do this time, Mum.'

'Well, that's up to you, but you're only making more work for yourself,' Janet replies curtly. 'This water is rancid. Why's it so disgusting, Helen? I need to get out.' She pulls herself to standing on shaking legs. 'Please pass me a towel. No, not that one, one of the white ones. I can't abide patterned towels, they could be hiding all kinds of stains.'

Helen pulls the bathroom door too, cutting off her mum's demands mid-sentence. She's not sure how much longer she can do this.

Chapter Thirty-Nine

'That one's pretty, but I think you looked nice in the pink one.' Lucy is curled up on my bed, trying to make my phone work. It vibrates every few seconds, as she repeatedly types in the wrong pass code.

'Can you put that down, love. It's not a toy.' She passes it back to me reluctantly.

'Or you could wear your pink one?' she suggests again.

'I don't know which one you mean.' I am stood in front of the full-length mirror, holding a Monsoon dress up against me. It is a shade of pastel blue that only really looks OK with a tan, which, in December, I am clearly lacking. It has lace batwings for absolutely no reason and is cut to just below the knee. I can't remember the last time I wore it, in fact, I'm not entirely convinced it's even mine. I found it in a suitcase of clothes under the bed when I was having a post-Nick clear out and it was in a pile to go to the charity shop until Lucy pulled it out. I have, since then, convinced myself that it makes me look 'vintage chic,' in a kind of Sienna Miller way. Sophie also told me I looked pretty in it, so that sealed the deal. I'm not sure when I started to take fashion advice from my three-year-old. It smells a tiny bit of mothballs, but nothing that a squirt of perfume can't mask.

The thing is, I want to make a bit of an effort tonight. I've got butterflies for the first time since embarking on online dating.

This guy seems nice. More than nice, in fact. We've been messaging each other a bit. He's funny, sexy, well travelled. The only downside is he said he's a policeman, and I'm terrified that I will say something incriminating that will result in him having no choice but to arrest me. Other than that, I can't see how it can go wrong.

Sophie wanders in sucking her bunny's ear, climbs up on the bed and flops down next to Lucy.

'You smell funny,' she remarks. 'But you look nice.'

'Thank you, Sophie.' A guy came into Mummies Rest the other day selling perfume out of a carrier bag. I knew it was a mistake to buy a bottle, but at a third of the normal retail price, I couldn't resist a bargain. Tonight is the first time I've tried it out. Turns out it smells a bit like Coco for about a minute, and then loses its edge and starts to reek of antiseptic, so she's absolutely right. That combined with the dress, makes quite a potent and not entirely pleasant aroma.

'Now, Tania is babysitting tonight so I don't want any silly business, got it?' I tell the girls.

'Again? Tania is *always* babysitting,' Lucy groans.

'That's not true.' A wave of guilt washes over me.

'Doesn't Mummy look better in her pink dress?' Lucy insists, immediately forgetting her annoyance about Tania, and looking at her little sister for affirmation.

'Yes,' Sophie agrees blindly. Oh, fickle young minds.

'Right,' I clap my hands in an attempt to take control of the room. 'Toothbrushes are on the side in the bathroom, so go and do your teeth before Tania gets here,' I chirp enthusiastically, masking the huge knot of anxiety that is growing in my stomach.

My phone chimes on the dresser as the girls slope out of the room. It's Rachel, FaceTiming.

'So?' she grins. 'What are you wearing?'

'Perv,' I joke.

'Go on, show me.' She's walking and talking, I recognise her cul-de-sac in the background. I turn the camera to face the wardrobe and Rachel lets out a snort.

'Is it too much?' I ask, switching the phone back to front camera.

'Oh,' trying to keep the surprise out of her voice. 'I thought you were joking. Emmie, under no circumstances should you wear that dress tonight. Is there anyone coming over who can look through your wardrobe?'

'Tania's babysitting, but she's anti-fashion.'

'Anti-fashion or not, she's not going to let you go out looking like you're going to an early nineties wedding. Where did you even get it from? Turn the camera around again,' she instructs.

'What am I going to wear?' I ask glumly. 'I've had a complete mental block.'

'Well, would you normally go to the pub looking like Princess Diana?'

'But it's not the pub this time. It's a wine bar. Who even meets in a wine bar? He's going to be like Peter Stringfellow, I can just tell. I'm going to cancel and catch up on *I'm a Celebrity* instead.'

'You're just nervous. I'll help you. You said you might like this guy.'

'I know. That's absolutely the reason why I shouldn't go. I'm only going to be disappointed.'

'Nope. We're not doing this, Emmie. Fuck self-pity. Come on. Now, what else have you got? What do you normally wear? Just me!' Rachel shouts as she unlocks her front door and I follow her in on the screen.

'I just normally wear my jeans and a T-shirt,' I shrug. 'Urgh, I'm better with pre-internet dating when I just get hammered and launch myself at someone in a takeaway on the way home from a club. '

'Yes, it's different. But the rules haven't changed that much, Emmie. He's still just a bloke on a date.'

'I feel like a fucking dinosaur,' I sigh.

'I heard that word, Mummy,' Lucy wanders back in, toothbrush in mouth.

'Shit,' I mutter as I see her framed in the doorway.

'And that one,' she wags her finger at me, disapprovingly.

'What if I get myself arrested?' I ask Rachel.

'Just because he's a policeman doesn't mean he's going to arrest everyone he meets. He is allowed to go on dates too.'

'Yes,' I agree. 'I know it's just—'

'Just nothing. Now find something to wear that isn't from *Pretty in Pink* and get yourself ready,' she demands.

'OK. I will. Look, I've got to go. I'm just going to get the girls ready for bed, but I'll give you a ring if I get stuck.'

'Cool. Make sure you do,' she replies and blows me a kiss.

'I found it,' Lucy announces. She and Sophie are clutching an arm each of my M&S floor-length polyester nightie, dragging it into the room. It was a present from Cathleen for Christmas a few years ago. The 'chastity nightie', Nick and I called it, as the neckline was chokingly high and the hem skirted the floor.

'Where did you find *that*?' I exclaim.

'Sophie found it in the bottom of the wash box. We think you should wear it.'

'Yes,' Sophie agrees. 'You'll look like a princess.'

The girls snuggle into me and I breathe them both in. The weight of the two of them on my lap is reassuring. I don't even know why I'm doing this, I think. I have everything I need right here.

*

I scan the wine bar, feeling like I've completely misjudged the dress code in my black skinny jeans and low-cut black top. I look a bit like Sandy after her transformation in *Grease*. Maybe I would have been better off with the chastity nightie.

I can't really remember what he looks like. He was wearing his police uniform in one picture, and swimwear on a surfboard in the rest. He's obviously not sporting either of those looks now. Also, I can't shake the paranoia that my mouth might run away with me and I'll end up telling him about all the class A drugs I took at university, or how I used to steal Pantene shampoo and conditioner when it first came out from Boots when I was at school. Oh God. This is a truly terrible idea. As I search in my handbag for my mobile and make my way back to the double doors, a hand gently touches my shoulder making me yelp and jump five feet in the air.

'Shit!' I squeal.

'Sorry, sorry. I didn't mean to startle you. I just didn't know if you'd seen me.' It's the policeman. Or Graham as he's more widely known. He's also wearing black skinny jeans and a T-shirt with a low neck, a tuft of chest hair sprouts from the top and I wonder if stood together, we'll look like an awful manufactured pop duet about to enter Eurovision.

'Got the memo about the jeans then?' I snort.

'Ha! Yes,' he smiles awkwardly and then says. 'Can I get you a drink, or are you planning on doing a runner?'

'Ah, yes. I mean no. A drink would be nice.' My face glows with embarrassment as I shift away from the door.

'OK, do you want to . . .' and he signals to a table.

'Yes. Great,' I reply.

'And do you want a . . .'

'Red wine please,' I reply.

'Small or . . .'

'Large, please,' I reply. I'm assuming the half-finished sentences are a police thing, leaving them open-ended for the other person to complete and incriminate themselves.

I perch on a high stool and take in the bar. I've never been here before. Maybe it's new? Or at least less than six years old, back when I used to have a social life. Everyone is smartly dressed. It's a brogues and Ben Sherman kind of place. Well-manicured women lean into conversations with loud bullish men. I am completely underdressed as Sandra Dee and wish I'd at least put some earrings on.

'Here you go.' Graham passes me a glass, which looks suspiciously like a small, and he slides in opposite me. Please don't let him be tight. Or worse still, judgmental.

'I don't normally come here,' he says apologetically. 'I don't know why I suggested here to be honest. It always looked a bit wanky from the outside, but we're here now,' he shrugs with a grin.

'Are you allowed to swear?' I ask, then immediately regret it.

'What, cos I'm a copper?' he chuckles. 'Fuck yeah.'

'Phew,' I relax and take a large gulp of my wine. 'I feel like we've met before. You look familiar,' I tell him, before quickly adding, 'I genuinely do. That wasn't a line!'

God, he really is handsome. He smiles broadly at me and briefly touches my arm, sending an unexpected electric pulse through my body. 'I know what you mean,' he replies. 'I'm normally pretty good with faces because of my job, but I don't know where I know you from either. You're not a member of Pure Gym are you?'

'No,' I splutter, nearly spraying my wine over him. 'It's definitely not the gym.'

262

'Never mind. It'll come back to me,' he replies coyly. 'So you said you write for a living. That sounds exciting?'

'Yes, it can be,' I lie, thinking back to the last four copywriting jobs, mainly dominated by cleaning products that no one actually needs. 'But your job sounds more exciting. What's the most dangerous thing you've had to do?' I ask.

'It's not really like that,' he smiles. Wow! That smile. 'Occasionally we get called out for domestics, which is always harrowing. But mainly, it's just teenagers nicking things from Superdrug or lost kids in supermarkets. And a lot of desk work, which I wouldn't dream of boring you with on a first date.' Another winning smile. Is he suggesting there may be another date after this one? Just then it hits me like a bolt from the blue.

'I know where I recognise you from,' I declare loudly, pointing a finger at him.

'Oh yeah? Where?'

'The toy museum. I'd lost a child I was meant to be keeping an eye on, and the teacher rang the police.' My face blushes scarlet as I suddenly remember how outrageously flirty he'd been.

Graham clicks his finger and points back at me, 'That's it! That teacher was a bit of a dragon, wasn't she?'

'Oh my God, yeah. She's terrifying,' I agree, touching my cheek with the back of my cold hand in the vain attempt to drain some of the colour.

'You have a kid at that school then?' he asks.

'Two girls, one at school, one at nursery,' I tell him, wondering if he'd be interested in looking at a photo of them, or if that's too much. 'You?'

'Nooooooo,' he replies a bit too quickly, before swiftly correcting, 'but I love kids, and I'm a great uncle to my two nephews.' He drains his glass.

'Same again?' I gesture.

'Great. A craft ale for me please.'

As I head to the bar, I can't help smiling. This seems to be going well. Better than well, in fact. He smells good, he's got a smart haircut. He may or may not have previously had his ears pierced, but that could have been circa 2000 when David Beckham made it very fashionable. I can't fault him on that; I was planning to get a tattoo of a dolphin like Mark from Take That before Mum found out. We're all influenced by our heroes.

'Shall I take them from you?' Graham takes the drinks from my hands as I approach the table so I can hop onto the stool again. His hand lingers over mine for a minute, his index rubs my palm so fleetingly that I hardly notice, but I'm pretty sure he did.

'So. Emily.' This sounds like the start of an interrogation instead of a conversation. I imagine we're sitting opposite each other in an interview room, his chief looking on through a two-way mirror.

'Graham.' I reply.

'Have you done this . . .' he drifts off.

'You are my third date,' I state.

'Right. Right . . .' he contemplates. 'And what do you think, so far?'

'Of dating?' I ask.

'Of me?' he smiles. Christ, he's confident.

'You seem . . .' I blush again, my neck feels hot and I know it's gone blotchy. 'You seem, very nice.'

'Good.' He replies with a nod. Am I meant to ask what he thinks of me? I am so far out of my comfort zone right now, I feel like I'm drowning. The DJ has put on house music and the noise just increased dramatically.

Graham leans in and shouts, 'YOU SEEM NICE TOO.'

He's so close I can feel the warmth of his breath on my cheek. I don't think it's absolutely necessary to lean in *that* far.

'THANK YOU,' I shout back, not sure what to say next. I instead cast my eye around the bar. I watch as a man in a pin-stripe suit strides purposefully over to the bar and says something to the barman, who nods apologetically. Seconds later the music turns down to a reasonable level again.

'That's better,' I remark. 'So, you said in your profile you liked travelling. Do you get much leave from the force? I got the impression that they work you until you drop. Is that true? Is it as bad as it's made out on the news?' What am I talking about? I'm not his HR advisor. I just can't work Graham out. He's off-the-scale flirty, but also seems completely uninterested in me at the same time. Come to think of it, he hasn't said how many dates *he's* been on. At least with Sixty-something Steve and Morose Mal you kind of knew what you were getting, but I just can't get the measure of Graham.

I notice he's no longer looking at me, but someone behind me. I turn around and see a woman dressed in an extraordinary gold-sequinned micro dress. She's balancing on gold heels and is waving at Graham.

He waves back and then tells me, 'I went on a date with Sheree a while back. Nice girl. Not for me. What were you saying?' He's now looking at me intensely, as he takes my hand from the table. I'm holding my phone in it, which I then accidentally drop on the floor. Unflinching, he turns my hand in his, while I try to move my phone with the heel of my shoe towards me. 'Has anyone ever told you that you have incredible hands?' he says.

Now, I like a compliment as much as the next person, but I can genuinely say my hands have never been a source of interest.

'Can I just . . .' I point towards my phone. Oh God, I've caught Graham's inability to finish a sentence.

'Sure. Sure,' he loosens his grip.

'Do you do yoga?' he asks as I bend down to retrieve my phone and sit up a bit too quickly, flushed in the face and feeling a bit faint. I should really have had some dinner before coming out, but after Lucy and Sophie had gone to bed and I'd got changed for the millionth time into my outfit, which is getting increasingly warm under the air blasters, I forgot to eat and am starting to feel a tad pissed.

'No. No, I don't do yoga. I used to do Pilates but I couldn't really make it work with childcare. The session I used to go to was on a Thursday between seven and eight and I usually have the girls that day.' I take a sip of my wine before continuing. 'This is one of the challenges of being a self-employed single parent.' I mean it in a jokey, don't take myself too seriously way, but I notice that although Graham is nodding he is looking elsewhere again. 'What about you?' I ask. 'Do you do yoga?'

'No. No.' He's back in the room. 'Tell me about you. What is it you're looking for?'

'What, from a date?' I ask.

'Yeah, I guess,' he grins.

I exhale loudly. 'God, I don't know really. I'm not long out of a long-term relationship. I'm not looking for someone to fix me, or sweep me off my feet. I'm not looking for a "boyfriend". Just, I don't know. Escapism? Is that a reason to go on a date?'

'You still married?' He points to my ring finger. I twist it uneasily. Ridiculously, it hadn't even dawned on me to take it off.

'Separated,' I reply. 'About four months ago now. It just

wasn't meant to be,' I shrug, not prepared to divulge any more details at this stage.

'Refill?' he gestures.

'Go on then,' I reply and as he stands I add, 'Can I have a large this time?'

'Er, yes,' he reddens. Caught out. As he makes his way to the bar I check my phone and text Tania.

Me: How's it going with you guys?
Tania: All quiet on the Western Front. Just catching up on Celebrity.
How's it going your end?
Me: Not sure. I'll let you know.

I look over at Graham, who flings his head back laughing flirtatiously with the woman stood next to him at the bar, before she looks in her handbag and passes him what looks suspiciously like her card.

Me: Have a sneaky feeling he might be a player.
Tania: Don't waste your money if he's not all that x

Graham strides back to the table, broad smile on his face.

'Everything OK?' I ask.

'Yes. Yeah. So you were about to tell me about your bastard of a husband.' He covers my 'incredible' hand with his again. It's quite moist from carrying his pint and wholly unpleasant.

'He's not a bastard, not at all. He's just . . .' and I truly don't know how to finish that sentence. I feel surprised by how quickly I jump to defend him, how uncomfortable it makes me feel hearing other people speak ill of Nick.

'I'm only joking,' he replies, 'I just mean any man who let *you* go must either be a bastard or have a screw loose.' He leans in again and says softly, 'You really do have the most hypnotic eyes.'

What is happening here? The initial fizzy flirty glow has been replaced with low-level irritation. He looked so hot in the museum, but now, out of uniform, in his spray-on jeans and low-cut T-shirt, with his cheesy lines and sparkling smile, he's just a bit of a towny with a chip on his shoulder.

I somehow assumed a policeman might be a bit more, I don't know, charming, and not so much of a sex pest. I don't remember Tosh from *The Bill* trying to feel women up while out for a pint with Burnside.

I genuinely don't know what I'm doing here. I thought I wanted to move on. I thought I wanted to see people. But I don't think I do. At all. This feels like a complete waste of my time. My life is full enough with Sophie and Lucy and my friends. I don't want to be here feeling a mixture of flattery and insecurity by a man who seems either to have already bonked or is soon to have bonked nearly all the women in this awful bar. And the bar? The bar. It's like stepping back into the eighties. Cocktail bars? Yes please. Wine bars? No thanks.

I want to be at home. I want to curl up on the sofa with Tania and watch the last twenty minutes of *Celebrity*. I want to sneak a peek in Sophie and Lucy's room, get close enough that I can sniff them without waking them. Plant a kiss on their soft warm cheeks.

'And you've got the most amazing—'

'Graham. That's enough.' He sits up abruptly, clearly not used to being interrupted. 'I don't think we're looking for the same thing.'

'Well, how do you know?' His disgruntled voice reminds me of Lucy when she tries to negotiate another episode of *Hey Duggee* at bathtime. 'You said yourself, you didn't know what you were looking for, how do you know that's not me?'

And he extends his arms to give me the full Graham experience.

'Because I don't think I want anyone, actually, Graham. I thought you were hot, but I'm kind of finding you a bit creepy now, which isn't great for a policeman, to be honest. Even if you are off duty.' I take another sip, leaving over half a glass, and hop off my stool.

'Yeah. Fine. Have a good one,' he replies sulkily, and I wonder how many times, in the history of sex, a man wooed a woman into bed through sheer mardiness. Not many, I suspect.

As I pass the window of the bar on my way to the bus stop, I peek through and see Graham offering the rest of my drink to the girl in the gold dress, as he casually rests his hand in the small of her back. I wonder what part of her body he's currently finding amazing or fascinating or incredible.

The sky is inky black with a full, round moon glowing overhead. Maybe that would explain Graham's odd behaviour, I think, trying to give him the benefit of the doubt. Maybe he's strongly aligned with lunar activity.

I can't work out whether I am attracting odd men or whether it is just unfortunate or bad luck that the crop so far have been so questionable. I was known for being a weirdo magnet when I was younger. Rachel thought they could smell me a mile off. We'd be walking through Grimsby shopping centre on a Saturday, minding our own business, and suddenly a toothless man three times our age, grinning inanely and wearing just one trainer, would fall in line with us, talking to me like an old friend. Maybe this magnetism has filtered through to adulthood and I am destined to only meet the old, needy or perverted.

As I board the 46B home, my phone beeps in my pocket. The bus is unusually busy for a midweek evening, and I slot in next to an elderly lady with a pull-along tartan shopping bag, who acknowledges me with a half-smile.

I retrieve my phone and look at the screen. The elderly lady peers over at it unashamedly. I very much look forward to the day when I can read over other people's shoulders or finish off half-eaten croissants that have been left at a neighbouring table in a café without a care.

Unfortunately for the old lady this time, she catches sight of the picture I have been texted as I open it up. It's a close up of Graham's hand clutching his half erect penis, a glistening purple bell end set against the tiled backdrop of what must be the urinals in the wine bar.

The accompanying message reads, 'If you ever change your mind, this is what is waiting for you. Gx.' I consider forwarding it to the police, before deleting it and deciding that I will definitely give dating a rest for a while.

Chapter Forty

'What kind of a place were you thinking?' Emma asks Tania, as they try to synchronise pushing the swings together in the park. Falcon and Shona have both leant in to hold hands while they swing, which is both heart-wrenchingly lovely and annoyingly tricky to manoeuvre in time.

'I dunno, somewhere cheap, I guess? I just fancied getting away for a couple of nights with the girls and no husbands and kids.'

'Oh, Tania, that just sounds so impossibly sad. It's your fortieth. You need to do something fabulous,' Emma tells her, as she readjusts her cashmere scarf around her neck against the bracing December wind. Since the discovery that Tania was Arabella, Emma cannot quite shake off the presumption that she could just conveniently walk back into her old life whenever her chosen way of living got a bit much, like the girl from St Martin's College in 'Common People'.

'I'd be totally happy with that, really,' Tania assures her. They slow the swings to a standstill, as Falcon and Shona hop off and run over to the roundabout, both giggling loudly.

'Well, what about an apartment in London? You could do that for a couple of nights on a budget. I went with a bunch of girls a few months ago to this place, it was gorgeous,' Emma passes over her phone.

'Wow. That looks amazing,' Tania gasps. She scrolls through the pictures; a roof-top terrace overlooking central

London, a hot tub, a huge kitchen with an island. 'This must have cost a fortune, though. I think this might be a bit out of my price range.'

'Nonsense,' Emma snaps. 'This is a landmark birthday. You do *not* want to end up in some awful youth hostel in Deptford. Let's get a hot drink.' Tania follows her to the café booth on the corner of the play park. 'Two teas please,' she asks, and then passes one to Tania, who wraps her hands around the polystyrene cup for warmth.

'Thanks,' she replies. 'What are you planning to do for yours?' They sit on a bench facing Falcon and Shona, who spin the roundabout puke-inducingly fast.

'Well,' Emma grins, 'I am going to have two huge parties. One in London – I was thinking about Ronnie Scott's, possibly, as it's quite central for everyone – and then one in a gorgeous riad just off the main square in Marrakech for ultimate relaxation. You should come! It'll be fun.'

'God, that does sound amazing,' Tania sighs, the apartment in London suddenly feeling not quite so decadent. 'Can I have a look at that flat again?'

''Course!' Emma pulls the phone from her duck-down coat pocket and passes it over.

'And how many did it sleep?' Tania asks.

'Four, but three comfortably I'd say.' She blows her tea, steam curling from the cup.

'That would be perfect,' Tania mutters. 'And you said it was quite reasonable?'

'Yes, very much so, given the location and everything. It's getting a bit chilly. Can I give you a lift home?' Emma asks.

'That, would be great. Thanks. So, how much was it if you don't mind me asking?'

'Not at all. I think it was about five hundred quid.

272

Something like that. SHONA! FALCON! WE'RE GOING!'
she shouts over to them.

'A week?' she asks timidly.

Emma hoots, 'Oh hilarious! A night, Tania.'

Tania hands her back the phone, 'Deptford it is, then.'
She reminds herself that it isn't where she goes, it's the company she keeps that's going to make it a memorable time.

That said, she could really see herself sipping champagne
in a hot tub while her best friends sang happy birthday
to her. Maybe that'll have to wait until her fiftieth. How
depressing.

Chapter Forty-One

'The ticket has got to end in a zero or a five to win a prize,' I explain to one of Lucy's classmates, who is clutching a raffle ticket with the number 219 on it.

'What do I win?' she asks me again, and again I explain, 'Nothing, sweetheart, because the ticket has to end in a zero or a five.'

The queue behind is starting to build and I begin to wish I had volunteered for the drinks table; at least you could mainline Prosecco while manning the stall over there.

The little girl's mum finds her in the nick of time as her disappointed face starts to crumple in on itself.

Another child, another unsuccessful ticket, and I explain again how he hasn't won anything. 'Let me have a go,' his dad suggests, spinning the tombola wheel and retrieving a ticket: 105. At last.

'There you go!' I pass him the prize that correlates to the ticket, a bottle of Morrisons own-brand shampoo.

'Cheers,' he says unenthusiastically, as I pass it to him.

'Sorry,' I reply. That really is a shit prize. To buy it from the shop would probably cost less than 50p. I see Nick enter the hall with the girls and try to catch their attention. Nick wanders slowly around the stalls with them completely distracted, hand protectively on each of their shoulders.

'Fifty pee each or five for two quid,' I repeat, passing

a strip of tickets while keeping one eye on the guys. The hall is filling up now, and I'm having to raise my voice over Noddy Holder, who is blasting out over the school tannoy. I spot Tania with Falcon, she sees me and bows in prayer pose. I assume the Christmas Fair is an educational trip out for Falcon but God knows what he's going to be learning today. 'Commerce,' Tania later tells me.

'Fifty pee each or five for two quid,' I say again.

Angela, Evie's mum, circulates around the hall, asking each stall holder in turn how we are doing.

'You're making a killing,' she remarks, putting a friendly hand on my arm. 'For you.' She offers me a plastic cup of Prosecco.

'Thank you, this is exactly what I need,' I reply.

'Yep, the elixir of life,' she responds jokingly. I think I might have got her completely wrong.

She is clutching a pile of Peter James books.

'Crime fiction fan, are you?' I ask her.

Angela looks down at the books. 'Oh no. No, they're for my mum. She loves this kind of thing. I got her some Ruth Rendells and she just tore through them. They were only a pound for the lot from the bric-a-brac stall.'

'How much for a go?' someone asks me.

'Fifty pee each or five for two quid,' I reply.

'I'll leave you to it, and thanks for all your help.' Angela smiles kindly as she resumes her circuit of the hall.

I look up. It's Ned's mum. 'She doesn't hold a grudge about you losing her daughter, then?' she asks, passing me a handful of coins that I put in my money belt without counting.

'No,' I reply, handing her the strip of tickets. 'Unless there's something I should know about in this drink,' I joke.

She looks at the numbers. 'Not won anything. Never

275

mind. We should go for a drink sometime over the holidays, if you're around?'

'I'd like that. Yes please,' I reply warmly.

'Great! I'll message you,' she grins, and steers Ned back into the sea of sugar-fuelled children and Prosecco-filled parents.

Tania has joined the queue. I watch Falcon scoff down a hot dog in three mouthfuls and wonder if Spiral is aware that both members of his family are now committed carnivores.

Where are Nick and the girls now? I scan the room again, and spot Lucy sitting down to have her face painted, Sophie stood obediently next to her, watching every brush stroke intently. But where's Nick? He wouldn't have just left them, would he? A little panic bubbles.

'Have you seen Nick?' I shout to Tania. Her eyes dart around the room and then stop on the glass corridor that runs parallel to the main hall.

'There!' she shouts back, pointing.

I follow her finger and there he is, talking to someone, looking serious. Creased forehead, nodding repeatedly. Who is he talking to? I wonder. He rarely does the morning drop-offs and hasn't been to any of the school social drinks, so I'd be most surprised if he's got to know many of the parents. But maybe I'm underestimating him. Maybe he's started doing play dates for Lucy when the girls stay over. I make a mental note to ask him, in a non-judgmental, constructive way.

'Fifty pee each or five for two quid,' I say, as the woman he is talking to turns around and I get a look at her face for the first time. You have to be joking. It's the girl from the phone. The woman in his Fred Perry jacket. He's brought her to the school fair.

'What the fuck?' I say aloud.

276

'Sorry, did I not give you enough?' the parent stood at the head of the queue asks apologetically.

'Oh God, not you. Sorry. Hang on a moment. The stall's closing for five minutes,' I untie my money belt and shimmy out from behind the stall as the parents in the queue grumble and complain.

'Can you keep an eye on Lucy and Sophie, they're at the face-paint stall,' I ask Tania, squeezing her arm as I pass.

'Is everything OK?' she asks, concerned.

'No, it's not actually.' I breathe deeply as I march out of the hall. Anger starts to buzz like electricity, pulsing through my veins. I don't want to cause a scene. I do, however, want Nick and his girlfriend to get out of the school before Lucy and Sophie spot the girl from the phone.

The woman sees me before Nick, who has his back to me as I approach. Her eyes are gesturing wildly to him as Nick carries on talking, characteristically oblivious to everything that's happening around him.

'Nick!' I command.

He leaps around with a start, colour draining from his face.

'Emily!' he attempts to smile, but it looks more like a constipated grimace. 'I was just talking about you.'

'I bet you were,' I hiss. 'What do you think you're doing? This is Lucy's school fair.' An awful thought dawns on me. 'You didn't come here together did you? With the girls?'

The woman steps forward, hands raised in ceasefire. She is effortlessly attractive, a wrinkle-free tanned face and long eyelashes framing almond-shaped deep-green eyes. Her skin is radiant. How does anyone look like that in winter? Or ever? She's probably late twenties at a push. Her messy blonde bob is shiny, like she's just stepped out of the salon. Her black skinny jeans wrap expensively around her slim

277

legs, a stainless white shirt loosely tucked into them, and she wears huge hoop earrings. Every item of clothing screams childfree. She hasn't had to put that silk shirt through the wash covered in Vanish because someone has pawed her with spaghetti-covered hands. Those earrings are like a red rag to a small person who would pull and tug on them until your ears bleed.

I, in contrast, am wearing an ill-fitting red smock dress and black leggings that I got from Age Concern earlier in the week. The brief that had gone out on the class WhatsApp group said, 'dress festive'. I pull the Santa hat off my head as I wait for an answer from Nick, but the phone woman steps in.

'Of course not, Emily. Can I explain?' her voice is husky, sexy. If she wasn't already completely hot, you'd fall for her because of her voice alone. Who speaks like that in real life? If I didn't hate them both in this moment, I'd have a serious crush on her myself right now.

'I've heard so much about you,' she continues, 'it's so good to finally meet you in person.'

'This is Katy,' Nick interjects weakly, 'Katy is—'

'I'm a new friend,' she smiles her white-teethed smile. Damn they are good teeth. 'This wasn't planned. We didn't come together, I assure you. Did we, Nick?' She reaches out to touch his arm, which he shakes off. There's something in the familiarity of that gesture that makes me suddenly feel overwhelmingly sad. I fight down the feeling and try and remain focused: this is about co-parenting.

This is about Nick and I being a united front. This is not about him showing up with her at the infant school fair, where it's hard enough to make any headway with any of the parents as it is. To fit in, to get into the rhythm of the play dates and the after-school clubs and the enforced

278

friendship drinks at the pub, where most people seem to already know each other and fall immediately into cliques, leaving the rest of us to laugh loudly around the periphery of the circles, trying desperately to fight our way in.

It's hard enough attempting normality and security and consistency, without Nick arranging to meet his fucking gorgeous girlfriend under the watchful eye of sixty-odd parents, who are all now fuelled with Prosecco and mulled wine. On top of that, couldn't she have dressed down a bit – seriously, that shirt really does look amazing on her.

'I didn't realise Katy would be here, Em. I just bumped into her and—'

'The last thing I want is to make anything more complicated for you both,' she reassures us, unreassuringly. She must work in PR, or fashion, or some such industry that requires bottomless confidence and a film-trailer voice. 'I appreciate how complex families can be. I just—'

'I think you should go, Katy,' Nick cuts her off.

'But—'

'I would like to talk to Nick,' my voice is stony cold. 'About our children.'

'Yes. Of course,' she nods. 'I really didn't mean to upset anyone. Nick?' she pleads with him. 'Really, you have to believe that.'

'Please go,' he repeats icily.

'OK. Merry Christmas.' She goes to touch his arm and again he flinches, so she turns on her impossibly high heels that look so elegant, and struts down the corridor, briefly stopping to wave through the window at someone who, when I look into the hall, I can't identify.

With the click of her heels echoing along the corridor, I turn to Nick, my face reddening with fury. 'WHAT WERE

YOU THINKING?' I shout, resisting the temptation to poke him directly in the chest.

'Me, Em? Hang on. It's not me who's making a scene,' he replies, coolly. 'I realise this situation doesn't look—'

'Doesn't look what, Nick?' I cut across him.

'Urgh,' he rubs his face aggressively, then starts to crack his fingers. 'I just, just—'

'What? What did you just this time? Just forgot to mention her? That she was going to be here? You're making a bit of a habit of forgetting, aren't you? I just forgot to tell you I was bringing my girlfriend to our daughter's fair. I just forgot to tell you I haven't paid the mortgage. I just forgot to tell you we're going to have our fucking house repossessed.' I try and remain in control, but it's too late. I can feel the rage pulsing through my veins. I have an acid headache developing behind my right eye socket, which feels like someone's sticking red-hot needles in it.

'That's not fair, Em. You've gone too far. That's too far.' He's shaking his head slowly. I think he may cry, he looks so sad, but I can't stop. I don't know the last time I felt so angry. It's like it's taken over, engulfed me with a burning rage.

'Have I? Have I really? I sometimes think I haven't gone far enough.' The words tumble out of my mouth before I have a chance to check what I'm saying. 'Does she know you're a liar, Nick?'

'You're out of control, Emily. You don't ever listen. To anyone,' he replies, starting to raise his own voice to match mine.

'That's bullshit!'

'Is it? Is it really? You have no idea what is going on in my life,' he shouts, arms wide in disbelief.

I gesture to the double doors that Katy has just walked

out of. 'I think it's quite obvious what's going on in your life, isn't it?'

'Well, that's what you would see, isn't it?'

'Tell me differently, then, Nick.' I am full volume shouting now. The veins in my temples throb.

'Why should I? You won't listen anyway. Give the girls my love. I think it's best if I leave, as this is just turning toxic.' He is using his 'calm down' voice on me.

'Whatever, Nick,' I sneer.

As he turns to leave, he mutters, just loudly enough for me to hear, 'God, you're such a child.'

I see red. The rage that has been taking hold for the last ten minutes finally consumes me. How dare he? How fucking dare he? That is *not* the last word in this argument. No way.

So I shout back, 'AND YOU, NICK, ARE A MASSIVE PRICK!' just as Maria Carey's 'All I want for Christmas' comes to an end over the sound system. Silence descends in the school hall. I slowly turn to look through the glass corridor to see sixty pairs of grown-up and little eyes staring at me and there, wrapped in Tania's arms, are Sophie and face-painted Lucy, staring open-mouthed. I freeze. Tania smiles weakly at me.

This is about as low as it can get. If there was any magic in the world that could teleport me and the girls anywhere else on the entire planet, wipe everyone's memories or take me back to ten minutes ago, now would be the time to present itself.

Just then Angela walks up to me, arms folded defensively, and asks coldly, 'Did you see which way my sister went?'

'Who's your sister?' I ask in barely a whisper, although I already know the answer.

'Katy. She was here a moment ago. She'd come to offer

281

her support at the fair and see her niece, Evie.' Her voice is emotionless.

And there you have it. The day just got a million times worse.

Chapter Forty-Two

The taxi crunches up the gravelled drive, lined with tasteful floodlights, unnecessarily illuminating the way, as it is only one in the afternoon.

'Is this a palace?' Falcon enquires.

'Nope, it's Grandma and Gramps' house. You haven't been here for a long time,' Spiral replies flatly.

Tania pays the driver as they hop out of the car. 'Thanks for the Christmas tip,' he mutters, before wheelspinning off. This isn't my house, Tania thinks. This isn't my wealth, and anyway, the cost of a taxi from Brighton to Surrey on Christmas Day was eye-watering enough as it is. Her parents had offered to pay. She'd refused but is now reconsidering.

She hesitates, her finger frozen over the large ornate doorbell.

'There's still time to change our minds,' Spiral whispers, optimistically.

'You'd like that wouldn't you,' she mutters. This whole arrangement was punishment for Spiral, but now, standing outside the mansion that holds nothing but unhappy memories for her, she is starting to feel like her plan has seriously backfired and the only loser in this whole awful situation is her.

Before she lets the flutter of doubt creep in, the grand oak door creaks open and there stands her father. His large pot-bellied stomach is wrapped in a checked hunting shirt and chinos, Pringles jumper loosely tied around his shoulders.

'Merry Christmas.' He kisses both of Tania's cheeks, and offers his hand to Falcon to shake. Falcon looks up at Tania confused before high-fiving it. Her father shrugs nonchalantly, and invites them in.

'Peter,' he says, nodding sincerely at Spiral.

Every cell in her body aches for her to be back at home in her little flat with her lovely family. But they're here now.

Spiral says, 'Merry Christmas Mr Cording-Richards,' and for some reason, half bows like a Shakespearean actor.

'To you too,' her father replies curtly.

They follow him into the 'snug', which is a large room with oversized armchairs and sofas and a roaring fire. The room is almost the same size as Tania's entire flat. Her mother is sitting near the fire, legs coquettishly crossed at the ankle, drinking champagne. She stands, arms open and announces grandly, 'Well, here you all are. Let me see you all. Don't you look festive, Falcon. What an unusual outfit you've chosen,' she remarks.

'Thanks, Grandma. This is called batik, isn't it, Mum? We drew on the T-shirt with candle wax and then put it in the bath with dye and then put it in the washing machine and then put it in the dryer and now I'm wearing it. That's right, isn't it, Mum?' Falcon speaks quickly, only drawing for breath at the end of the sentence.

'That's right, love. Falcon has tie-dyed a top for you for Christmas, haven't you Falcon?' Tania says, placing her hand on his head.

'Yes. I wrote GRANDMA IS COOL on it in batik,' Falcon grins, as does Tania, although she tries to mask hers, imagining Francesca wearing it to one of Marcus Wareing's Michelin-starred restaurants.

'Oh how delightful, I cannot *wait* to see it, my talented

grandson,' her mum replies. 'And you, Peter—'

'It's Spiral,' he says. He cannot go the entire day being called that by Tania's parents.

'Of course, have you just come from work? Arabella—'

'Tania. It's Tania, Mum.'

'Good heavens, it's hard to keep up with all these name changes,' her mum laughs mockingly.

'No. No, Mrs Cording-Richards, I haven't just come from work. I have just come from our home,' he replies politely.

'Oh, I'd just thought you were wearing workman's clothes but—'

'Nope,' Spiral cuts in, 'just my normal clothes.'

Tania feels overwhelmed with guilt, as her mother systematically undermines the man she adores. She watches as Spiral tries to hold himself tall in his shirt and combat trousers. His only shirt, which he ironed before putting on. She'd plain forgot they even owned an iron, so it was quite a surprise to see him using it this morning. He has made an effort, a real effort, far more than Francesca.

'And before you ask, Mum, no, I haven't come from yoga. These are my normal clothes. We are all wearing our normal clothes,' Tania snaps.

'I was actually going to tell you I thought you looked like you'd lost weight.' This is the height of a compliment from Francesca. There is nothing greater than being thin, or being told you look thin, or telling someone they look thin. It is the crème de la crème of compliments.

'I've no idea, Mum. I think weighing yourself is a product of a commercial society that encourages you to buy diet pills and hate your body,' Tania counters. 'So what time are we eating? We need to confirm a taxi back as they all get booked up really early, with it being Christmas,' she adds. She can see a tiny chink in her mother's armour. A minuscule reaction;

she has fractionally wounded her mother. Tania suppresses the reactionary pity that threatens to take over and replaces it with defiance. She is not going to let Francesca get the better of her. Not this time. She reaches for both Spiral's and Falcon's hands as they follow her sighing mother into the dining room, which her parents pretentiously call The Great Hall.

They all sit down at the elaborately set table, with a candelabra and a grand five-foot long festive centrepiece made of holly, ivy and lilies. Tania takes a quick picture on her phone to show Emily and Helen, who are hugely intrigued by her past, unable to picture her in a massive house with posh parents.

Francesca smooths a napkin over her knees, as one of the waiting staff jumps forward to fill her glass. Who has waiting staff at home on Christmas Day other than the royal family? Shouldn't these poor people be with their own families, instead of nervously jumping around Francesca every time she moves? She is unsure whether this is how her parents live all the time, or if this is a massive display of wealth for their benefit. Either way, it is clearly making them all uncomfortable, and no one more than Spiral, who, unused to being served, tries to helpfully take the bottle off the waiter to pour the wine himself. An awkward tussle ensues, with the bottle being tugged between the two of them, resulting in red wine slopping all over the white linen tablecloth. Her mum doesn't say anything, but makes a show of rolling her eyes at Tania's dad.

'It's goose for dinner,' Francesca announces as she offers Falcon the end of her cracker. 'Pull?' she suggests.

Falcon holds onto the cracker with both hands as Spiral had shown him, guaranteeing a 100 per cent win every time.

'We're all vegetarians, Mrs Cording-Richards, sorry. I

don't know whether Tania had mentioned it, but we have been for years. The vegetables look amazing though, we can just eat those,' Spiral suggests warmly.

'Oh!' her mum exclaims in a faux-shocked voice. 'I had asked the caterers to send over the menu. Is that a new thing Arabe— Tania?'

Tania's face glows crimson red as she sees what her mother is doing. Why is she being such a bitch? Tania knows her parents have never forgiven Spiral for taking their precious daughter away from them, but what they have to understand is she left their home of her own free will. He's not Joseph fucking Fritzl. Does her mum not realise that every insult she chucks at Spiral is an insult to her and Falcon as well? What is she trying to prove? Her father, as always, sits in silence, occasionally clearing his throat dramatically. Francesca tuts at him and asks him to make that noise in one of the many bathrooms instead of at the table.

'Tania?' her mum asks again. 'It's just we enjoyed a particularly good steak the other day when we met in Brighton, didn't we? I had assumed, wrongly now, I see, that you were in fact a family of meat-eaters. But please, by all means, just eat the vegetables, which will be equally delicious.'

Silence descends over the table. Her mother takes a long self-satisfied drink of her champagne.

The fury builds in Tania. It starts as a bubble, almost like indigestion. She breathes in through her nose, out through her mouth, attempting to surround herself with white light, but no amount of emergency meditation is going to fix this situation. Spiral is gnawing at his nails, biting them to the quick. The only sound comes from Falcon, who is clanking his heavy cutlery together, that and the tick, tick, tick of the grandfather clock.

'You really are a piece of work, aren't you, Mum?' Tania replies. 'What actually is your problem?'

'Now—'

'And you can shut it, Dad. What have you ever done other than agree with Mum? Yes, Francesca; no, Francesca. How much, Francesca? No problem, I'll just get out my cheque book,' Tania mimics him with, what Spiral tells her afterwards, is quite a convincing imitation.

'This is very uncouth, darling. All this shouting on Christmas Day,' her mother remarks, purposely not making eye contact.

'No,' Tania slams her hands on the table. 'What is uncouth is to invite us to Christmas dinner just to embarrass us and ignore Spiral. Take the piss out of what we're all wearing and generally make us feel like shit.' Falcon grins at the mention of 'shit' and starts mouthing the word silently to himself.

'Well, I do apologise. That wasn't our intention, you know. Please believe me.'

Tania cannot decipher whether her mum is being sincere or not, but she is beyond caring.

'The thing is, Mum and Dad, I never liked being here. Never. I was never happy. I only came here today to punish Spiral for going to the pub when he was meant to be at work.'

'Oh, Pe—'

'Seriously, shut up, Dad. Spiral makes me happy, he always has. What I get from him, from Falcon, is something I never got from you two, not really. Love. They make me feel loved.'

'We never disapproved of you, Spiral,' her dad interjects, 'We just questioned Tania's choice of companion at the time.'

'That is complete rubbish!' Tania spits. 'Even now, even

now when we come to you at Christmas, you can't even look him in the eye.'

'It's OK,' Spiral replies softly.

'It's not though. It's just not,' Tania slumps down in her chair, exhausted. She drains her glass of champagne and says, 'I'm going to call the driver who dropped us off, see if he can pick us up. Falcon, Spiral, I'm sorry I put you through this.'

She meets her mother's eye, the woman who bought her everything but gave her nothing, then pulls out her phone and walks out of the room to make the call.

When she returns, Francesca is stood, hands clasped at her front, face stern.

'He's on his way,' Tania says.

'I am sorry this has ended like this, Arabella.'

'For the millionth time, Mum, my name is Tania.'

'Well, you will always be Arabella to me,' her mum replies drily.

'And that,' Tania concludes, 'will always be the problem. Bye, Mum. Bye, Dad.'

As they make their way to the door, her father follows her out.

'Please keep in touch, she doesn't mean it,' he pleads. 'If only for Falcon's sake.'

'Of course I will, Dad. I'm not going to punish Falcon because his Grandma can't behave. Falcon, say goodbye to Gramps and go and run in to give Grandma a hug.'

Falcon wraps his arms around his legs, 'Bye, Gramps.' As he loosens his grip, Tania notices that he's left dirty handprints on the crisp cream chinos.

As the taxi honks outside, her dad outstretches his hand. 'Spiral? Please do accept my . . . that is, our, apologies for making you feel out of place.'

And right there, Tania watches the man she loves and who drives her crackers in equal measures accept the hand of the man who has forever shown him nothing but contempt.

'Ah, before I forget,' her dad reaches into the top pocket of his shirt and retrieves an envelope. 'For you, darling.'

'I don't want your money,' Tania pushes his hand away as the taxi honks again.

'It's just to cover the taxi,' her dad insists.

Tania hesitates: it was over seventy pounds each way and they really can't afford it. 'OK. Thank you,' she says as she takes it off him.

'We do love you,' he insists, as he kisses her drily on her cheek. 'Even though we don't always show it.'

As the three of them pile into the taxi, Tania catches Spiral's hand. 'I'm so sorry about that. And about the meat thing. Mainly the meat thing,' Tania feels overwhelmingly emotional.

As the taxi winds down the drive Spiral cups her hand in his. 'It's OK. Well, it's not, but it's your choice. And choice is the last remaining privilege we have in the civilised world,' he responds softly. She is unsure whether these are his words or those of a motivational quote, but either way, she will take it that she's partly forgiven.

As they start to nod off, all three of them snuggled into each other in the back seat, she suddenly remembers the envelope her dad has given her. She tries to retrieve it from her fisherman's trouser pocket without disturbing Falcon and Spiral, both of whose heads are resting heavily on her shoulders. She rips it open, hoping her dad might have given her slightly more than the £140 that the round trip will cost them so they can get an overpriced takeaway when they get home.

She holds the cheque in her hand and focuses and

refocuses on the figure to make sure she's read it correctly.

'Fuck me,' she exclaims loudly, waking both the boys up.

'What is it?' Spiral asks sleepily.

'Mummy said the F-word *again*,' Falcon announces.

'It's a cheque from Dad,' Tania whispers.

'What's he done, made it out to Peter and Arabella?' Spiral scoffs.

'No,' Tania replies, stunned. 'It's for twenty grand.' She passes the cheque to him.

'Fuck me,' Spiral utters.

'And Daddy said the F-word,' Falcon squeals with delight.

Tania stares at the cheque. It quivers in her shaking hands. For a second, she considers ripping it up, the ultimate anti-capitalist act of rebellion. Her own private KLF moment. But something stops her.

This money could change everything for them. It's not a life-changing sum, but it could change their life. She thinks back to what Emma has said to her when they first met, how she 'wants it all'. Tania doesn't want it all, but she does have an opportunity here to put her family in a stronger position.

This is nothing to her parents. They will have spent half this supplying all their hotels with fresh flowers for the month. They have never been good at telling her they love her, they've never shown her affection and praise in a conventional way, they just throw money at problems or pay someone else to sort it out. So maybe this is her dad's way of showing he cares, using the only language he is fluent in.

She folds it up carefully and slips it into her purse.

She turns to Spiral and says, 'I know what I'm going to do with it.'

He simply kisses her on the top of her head in response as she nestles into him. He doesn't ask what, this is her business, her decision. Money isn't Spiral's priority, it never has been. They are. Tania and Falcon. And that is the fundamental difference between him and her parents. That is why she loves Spiral so fiercely. She squeezes both her boys' hands and closes her eyes.

'Happy Christmas,' she whispers.

Chapter Forty-Three

'Can I take your drinks order?' the waiter asks the table.

'Shall we have a bottle of champagne? It is Christmas, after all,' Chris suggests.

'Wonderful idea, Chris. And I will have a small sherry to start with please,' Janet announces happily.

The doctor strongly suggested Janet should cut down, or stop drinking alcohol entirely, when Helen spoke to him again recently, but then he hasn't met Janet. Helen tried it the other day and Janet completely lost her shit when presented with a cup of tea over dinner. Helen and Chris have become almost teetotal around the house, but Janet still finds a way. The shop around the corner from their house is on first-name terms with her. They know her top two favourite wines and have started stocking her gin of choice. Today Helen is not going to worry about it, though. Today is Christmas Day, they will enjoy it together, as a family.

'And for you, madam?' he asks Polly.

'She will have a water,' Janet instructs. Polly's face crumbles with disappointment.

'It's OK, Mum. She can have a lemonade if she wants today.'

Janet tuts at Helen loudly, as Polly squeals with delight.

'Her teeth will rot. But if that's what you want . . .' she drifts off as the waiter hesitates, but Chris nods at him that that is fine and he leaves the table.

'Well, this was an excellent idea, Hels. Thanks for sorting this out,' Chris leans over and squeezes her hand.

'Good. I'm pleased everyone likes it.' She squeezes back. The Goose and Gander is an old, thatch-roofed gastro pub nestled in the Downs. Helen has wanted to come for ages, the food is meant to be exceptional, but the waiting list to book a table is ridiculous. She'd rung on the off-chance and thankfully they'd had a cancellation. The cost of the meal and the taxi and the champagne could sustain a small village for a year, but it'll be worth every penny, she thinks. She breathes in the peaty smell of the open fire and allows herself a moment to relax. Before Janet brings her right back down to earth.

'I was surprised you decided against cooking at home, but then I suppose this is easier than making a meal from scratch. Thank you.' Janet accepts the sherry from the waiter and takes a noisy slurp.

'Well, I just thought it would be good to do something different this year,' Helen replies.

The truth is, she didn't have the motivation to make Christmas dinner. She didn't want to make a lunch that would be heavily criticised by Janet. She didn't want to have to justify her choice of wine, of vegetables, of pudding, of everything. This way, Janet can choose whatever the fuck she wants to eat, and if she doesn't like it, she can complain to the chef.

'Can I have chocolate mousse for pudding?' Polly asks, scanning through the menu.

'Yes—'

'No—' Janet cuts across Helen.

'Mum. Seriously, can you stop trying to parent Polly,' Helen sighs heavily, as Chris squeezes her hand again in solidarity.

'Right,' he says. 'Shall we pull a cracker then, Polly?' He takes one end and Polly takes the other.

'You spoil her,' Janet sneers, as the waiter moves discreetly around the table filling the champagne flutes. 'I'm only trying to help. I'm only trying to make things easier for you. I'm only here because you asked me to be, to help you out, Helen. If you don't want me here, you only need to say.' Her voice quivers with anger.

Helen opens her mouth to speak, but Chris interjects, saying, 'Right. Has everyone had a chance to look at the menu? I, for one, am having the turkey. What about you Polly?'

'All I am saying is—'

'Not now, Janet,' Chris asserts, calmly but firmly. 'It's Christmas Day. Let's just try and have an enjoyable meal together, shall we?' It's posed as a question, but there is no room for dispute. This is what is going to happen. This is their family Christmas. Chris is not going to let Janet ruin it.

'Can I do yours too, Mummy?' Polly asks.

'Of course,' Helen clutches one end of her cracker as Polly tugs at the other. Polly leans back for maximum leverage, but as the cracker rips in two with an underwhelming bang, she loses her balance slightly and crashes into Janet's shoulder. Her sherry is knocked from her hand, the schooner smashing on the floor into a thousand cut-glass shards.

'YOU STUPID GIRL,' Janet explodes. Shakily standing to her feet, bony finger pointing at Polly accusingly, her face creases with rage.

'I'm so sorry, I'm so sorry,' Polly repeats, frozen in her seat, clutching the other end of the cracker mid-air. 'I didn't mean to. I'm so sorry, Nana.'

Helen rushes to her side and scoops Polly out of her chair. She clings to her, trembling with shock.

'Now that,' Helen hisses at her mum, 'was uncalled for.'

Helen sits back down in her chair with Polly in her lap, who sobs quietly in her ear. Her tears and snot soaking into the shoulder of Helen's Savannah Miller top.

'You've gone too far this time, Mum.' Helen is trying to keep her voice measured, quiet, as she is conscious of every other pair of eyes on her in the pub.

'Did you not see what Helen did just then?' her mum replies. 'Did you not see? She will not grow up to behave unless I teach her manners. It is my job to teach her manners. No one else will.'

The waiter is sweeping up the glass awkwardly at her feet.

'No.' Chris replies sternly. 'No, Janet. It's not. It's ours. This is Polly, not Helen. This is our daughter, and our rules. And we do not shout at her. We do not insult her. We do not call her stupid.' Chris's hands are splayed on the white tablecloth, calm and measured, but Helen can see how tightly he is gripping it.

Janet's eyes dart from Chris, to Helen to Polly in confusion.

'She needs to grow up to be independent. To look after herself. How can she do that if she doesn't have good manners? How can she do that if she's spoilt all the time?' Janet splutters.

'Listen, Mum, I've had enough of this rubbish for one day. It's Christmas. Can't we just all be nice for one day? One bloody day.'

'You're holding me too tight, Mummy,' Polly whispers in her ear.

'Sorry, love. Chris, why don't you move round next to Janet? And Polly can sit next to me here.'

'Putting me on the naughty chair, are you now?' Janet mutters.

'OK, let's order. Has everyone decided what they'd like?' Helen chirps with as much enthusiasm as she can muster.

'Just like your father. Only listening to what you want to hear,' Janet drains her champagne flute, and holds it out expectantly for Chris to refill.

At the mention of her dad, Helen stops. Decades of asking her mum to talk about him, and nothing, but over the last few weeks she has heard repeated muddled stories, which Helen has found difficult to decipher. She doesn't know what to believe any more. Janet consistently gets her and Polly mixed up, so half the time she doesn't know who she's talking to anyway. But of all her incomprehensible tales, the one of her father's blind rage is the hardest to swallow.

'Maybe we should go?' Helen asks Chris flatly. 'This doesn't seem such a good idea now.'

'No. No, Helen. We're here now. Let's order our meal and enjoy it. Janet, choose whatever you'd like to eat, this is our treat and we'd like you to choose something you're going to enjoy. OK?'

'Can I have pizza?' Polly asks.

'You can have what's on the menu,' he replies, his voice strained.

Helen looks over at her mum, who is shredding the thick paper napkin, making long ribbon-like strips.

'Just put it down, Mum,' she lowers her hand to the table, feeling the tremor under hers. 'It's all OK. Let's just order. Would you like the turkey?'

Janet makes a huffing noise, which Helen interprets as a yes.

'And you, darling? Turkey for you?' she asks Polly, who also huffs back, once she's realised that pizza is no longer an option.

In moments like these, the weight of looking after her mother and her daughter can become almost unbearable. However difficult Janet had been in the past, she was still her mum. The woman who had brought her up, the person who made the choices on her behalf about her welfare when she was a child, about her future when she was a teenager. She was fierce and strong. She made decisions Helen didn't always agree with, but the one thing she had never been was weak.

Helen didn't always like her mum, but she never worried about her. She never thought she wouldn't be OK. She never thought she wouldn't be able to look after herself. But looking at the wrinkled hand under hers now, still clutching the strips of napkin, Helen cannot see that woman any more. There are flashes, of course, but the bitterness seems to have bled into all the cracks so she is, for the most part, either angry or confused. The speed in which she loses the thread of conversation has come on so quickly that Helen doesn't know how much of what they talk about actually goes in. Janet has her conversational fall-back prompts, which mainly consist of talking about the weather, how important manners are, how shit Helen's dad was, and whether she can have a glass of wine.

The basic needs of both Janet and Polly are now so similar, it's unsettling. The care they require, the cooking, the washing, the changing of sheets when someone has been caught short in the middle of the night, even down to the tantrums because what they want to eat isn't on the menu. Slowly but surely, Helen has been losing her mum and gaining a dependant.

Helen notices the white-gloved waiter hovering near the table and wonders how long he's been standing there for.

'We'll all have the soup to start, followed by four turkeys

with all the trimmings,' Chris tells him, passing him the menus.

'Just a bit of manchego and a few olives for me please,' Janet demands with a dismissive wrist.

'Sorry, madam, we only have what's on the menu today. There is turkey, braised pork belly, slow-cooked beef or nut roast.' He nods apologetically. He must be nineteen or twenty, working on Christmas Day for triple time, but Helen suspects that he should be paid twice that if he has to deal with customers like them.

'It's just Christmas dinner, Mum. Delicious Christmas dinner. Turkey all round,' Helen says, exasperated.

'I'm going to the bathroom,' Janet stands.

'It's over there,' Helen points. 'Do you want me to come with you?'

'I'm not a child, Helen. I can use the facilities perfectly well by myself, thank you,' she snaps, but Helen notices, as she walks off, how she stops the young waiter, who points her in the direction again.

'Why's Nana always so cross?' Polly asks, pencil in mouth as she flicks through her colouring book to find a picture to work on.

'Because she's not well,' Chris replies.

'Well, I don't shout at people when I'm poorly. She's really mean.'

Helen catches eyes with Chris. 'I'm not sure how long we can go on like this for,' he tells her softly.

'I know,' she replies half-heartedly.

'And what's all this stuff about your dad? Where has that all come from?' He fills up Helen's glass.

'I don't know. Her memories seem so vivid, it just feels cruel that after all these years she's finally talking about him and all she seems to be doing is defaming his memory. That's

299

just not how I remember him. He was a kind man, not the way she described.'

'Is that Granddad?' Polly asks without looking up from her page.

'No, not Daddy's daddy, this is Mummy's daddy. You've never met him.'

'Is he the one that got angry and crashed Nana's car?' she asks flatly, never taking her eyes off her drawing for a moment.

A look of panic passes between Helen and Chris. 'Where did you hear that?' To start with, Helen had been so very careful when talking to Chris about Janet so Polly wouldn't overhear, so her feelings about her mother wouldn't shape her opinion of her, but as the incidents have become more frequent, Helen knows she has become far less conscious of Polly's presence when she complains to Chris.

'Nana told me,' she replies nonchalantly.

'When?' Helen coaxes.

'All the time. She's told me about a million times, it's such a boring story,' she shrugs. 'Can I have another lemonade?'

'This has to stop,' Chris says. 'We can't have her talking to Polly about stuff like that.'

'Soup of the day,' the waiter announces, leaning around each one of them with care to place the large rimmed bowls in front of them. He holds the fourth bowl out in front of the empty seat.

'Just put it down please,' Helen instructs. 'She'll be back in a minute.'

He goes back to the kitchen and returns with a basket of artisan bread, which he places on the table with equal attention.

As he stands back, hands clasped behind his back to do a

mental audit that they have everything they need, another waiter hurries to the table, cheeks flushed.

'Madam,' he addresses Helen. 'May I ask you to accompany me to the bathroom. Your mother appears to be having some difficulty.'

'Of course,' Helen throws her napkin on the table and hastily follows the waiter through the restaurant. As she approaches the ladies, she can hear moaning. The waiter holds the door open, blushing with embarrassment.

'Mum. Mum, what's wrong, what's happening?' she tries to remain measured, but all she can hear is low-level groaning from the inside of the locked cubicle. 'Are you hurt, Mum? Can you open the door for me?'

She presses her ear to the teal Farrow and Ball painted door. Her mum is replying, but in hushed whispers. 'Ask him to leave. Can you ask him to leave?'

'Who, Mum?' she soothes. 'There's no one here, it's just you and me.'

'He's in a foul mood. Where's Helen?'

'I'm here. I'm right here.'

'Tell him to leave. Tell him to pack his bags and leave or I'll do it.' Her voice quakes with fear.

'There is no one here, Mum. Please can you unlock the door. I just need to check you're OK, that you haven't hurt yourself.' She hears shuffling from behind the door. 'That's it,' she says, 'just pull the bolt and we can go and enjoy our lunch.'

The door slowly creaks open. Helen sees her mum's hand peep around the frame, and a stockinged foot take a step out. Helen wonders where her shoes are.

'Helen, your father is leaving,' her voice barely a whisper. 'He will not hurt us any more. That was the last time. Come here, darling.' Helen opens the door wide, but sees her mum isn't talking to her; she follows her intense stare to see Polly standing in the doorway. Janet's outstretched arms reach for Polly, who stands frozen with confusion.

Helen has no idea what happened to her mum all those years ago, whether her dad really was the monster she now professes him to be, whether he was a violent man. If her mum had forced him to leave the home to raise her on her own, to love and protect her like a mother should. Or if he was the gentle, kind man who she remembers in faded, sepia memories. She doesn't know if her mother's broken brain is recalling long-forgotten painful memories, stored away for self-protection. Or if she has rewritten her history and is reliving a terrifying fantasy that never happened. Helen doesn't think she will ever know for sure, but what she does know is that right now, this is very real for Janet. And that is all that counts.

Helen rests her hand on her mother's arm gently. 'He's gone now,' she reassures her. 'It's just us now. You're safe. We're all safe.'

Janet's ragged breathing starts to slow, her shoulders slump and a tear rolls down her creased face.

'Polly, can you just get Nana's shoes from the loo,' she asks.

Polly squeezes around Janet and retrieves the navy court shoes.

'Thanks love. There,' Helen nods. 'Now let's put these on and get back to the table, shall we?'

'Yes,' her mother agrees. 'Yes, yes, let's have Christmas lunch. Let's have our turkey.'

She's back. Helen takes her arm as Polly clutches her hand, and they weave their way through the tables to Chris.

'Is everyone OK?' he asks.

'Yes, everyone's fine.' She guides her mum into her seat

302

and places the napkin on her knee. 'Now, let's enjoy our soup before it goes cold, shall we?' she says.

Chris's eyes search for answers.

'You're right. Things do need to change,' she answers him.

'This is delicious,' her mum smiles uncharacteristically as she noisily slurps the soup from her spoon. 'Eat up, Polly, or there won't be any pudding.' She points at her bowl.

Helen is more exhausted than she's ever been in her life. She has never needed a break more than she does right now.

'Happy Christmas.' She raises her flute, and they all clink glasses.

Chapter Forty-Four

'Right then, nearly there!' I beam, trying to catch Sophie and Lucy's eyes in the rear-view mirror.

'I feel sick,' Lucy replies weakly.

'Oh, not again,' I keep one hand on the wheel while trying to forage around in the footwell of the passenger side for a plastic bag. This is another one for the long list of reasons why it is easier to have two grown-ups travelling in the car with children. I pass her the Tesco bag just in time as she starts retching.

'Here,' she passes it back to me, and I drive for several more miles with the bag on my lap, until we pass through a town where I can stop to put it in a bin, my lap still warm from vomit. While stationary, I text Mum.

Me: We're 15 minutes away. Put the kettle on.
Mum: OK.

I make a mental note to tell her about the character count on her texts.

I pull into the drive and Dad is already waiting for us, hands on hips, big grin on face. He beckons the car in, giving a running commentary of, 'just a bit to the left. That's it. Careful of the saplings. Pull in behind Mum's. Bit more. Bit more. Tad more' before slapping the bonnet loudly.

'Can you help me carry Sophie in?' She nodded off on the last five miles to Mum and Dad's, having remained stoically awake and grumpy for the preceding 250 miles.

'Of course.' He opens the back door and lifts out her floppy warm body. 'And good afternoon to you, Lucy.'

'Hello, Grandpa. I've been sick four times, haven't I, Mummy?'

'Yes you have. It's been a loooong drive.'

'Well, let's get you all in,' Dad says, as he gently positions Sophie over his shoulder.

I take our belongings upstairs to my old childhood bedroom and sink down on the single bed. I hear Lucy and Sophie giggling hysterically from downstairs and I imagine Dad tickling them relentlessly. This is one of the two activities he does with young children. The other is to carry them around upside down. I wonder how he is going to entertain them when they're in their teens.

'Knock, knock.' Mum pushes the door open with her bum, carrying a cup of tea and a plate piled high with chocolate digestives. 'I thought you could do with some refreshments after your long drive.'

I sit up. 'Is everything OK downstairs?'

'Yes. Don't worry. Let us entertain them for an hour, why don't you shut your eyes for a bit now you're up here? They're perfectly happy and we've missed them dreadfully.' She perches next to me and strokes my hair. I get a waft of her Oil of Olay face cream. 'Have you told Nick you've arrived?'

'Nope. I'll do it in a minute.' I take a slurp of the tea.

'He must be feeling a bit low I imagine, without the girls.' She kisses my forehead and brushes my hair behind my ears.

305

'We had a bit of a row last time I saw him and we haven't really spoken properly since. I'm dreading doing the hand-over on Boxing Day, to be honest,' I confess, eating half a digestive in one mouthful.

'Well, it's Christmas. A time to put our differences aside,' Mum suggests diplomatically. As she pushes herself up, she adds, 'He is trying, Em. I know no one is perfect, but he's already paid off a big chunk of what he owes us, which couldn't have been easy.'

'What?' I sit bolt upright, coughing as the digestive goes down the wrong way. 'When? I didn't know this.'

'He set up a, you know, when it comes out every month, what's it called?' she rubs her forehead in concentration.

'Direct debit?' I suggest.

'That's the job. He set up a direct debit recently. We told him it wasn't necessary, to sort yourselves out first, but he was most insistent.'

'Bloody hell,' I whisper.

'Language, Emily. Now. Have a relax and we'll see you downstairs in a bit for our traditional Christmas Eve lasagne and chips?' she instructs, as she closes the door softly.

I retrieve my phone from my pocket and scroll through to Nick's number. There would have been a time when his was the last number I'd rung, or the last text I'd sent, but not any more.

Me: We've arrived at Mum and Dad's. See you soon x

At the last moment I delete the kiss and press send. I think back to what he told me at the fair. How I never listen to anyone, how I have no idea what's going on in his life, and I wonder if maybe, possibly, there may be a grain of truth there.

The dots appear on the screen; he's responding. Then they disappear, then nothing. He's thought better of it.

It's the afternoon of Christmas Day.

'Shall I get it?' I shout over Wham's 'Last Christmas'. The front room looks like Santa's grotto. Every inch of available space is covered in tinsel or fairy lights. I'd be surprised if they can't see this house from space with all the flashing paraphernalia.

'Your dad thought the girls might like it,' Mum had explained. I know they are trying their absolute hardest to make Christmas as normal as possible for us, but everything feels a bit forced.

'Yes, if you wouldn't mind, it will probably be Mr and Mrs Earls. Or Auntie Jean. Or maybe—'

I open the front door, the easiest way to work out who's behind it, and there, grinning with a bottle in each hand, is my oldest friend, Rachel.

'Merry Christmas, mate,' she says, as she wraps her arms around me, clinking the bottles behind my back as she does. She smells of Coco – the proper stuff, not the rip-off version I have – and is dressed in a figure-hugging gold dress, a fake-fur coat draped over her shoulders. She looks mesmerisingly sexy, like a woman who is happy and regularly having it off.

'Merry Christmas, Rach. God, I'm glad you're here, I feel like I'm losing my mind a bit,' I say.

'Not just me,' Rach steps aside, 'Callum's here. Go in.' She pushes her six-foot son through the door, he's wearing a onesie, like the kind I used to dress Sophie and Lucy in when they were babies but forty times bigger.

'Hi,' he grunts as he pushes past me.

'What is he wearing?' I mouth to Rachel.

'Fuck knows,' she mouths back. 'And you remember

Matt?' She stands aside to let the last of her party through. Matt emerges from outside. Yes I do remember him. Funny how I don't think any of us look any different at all since school, yet if we wandered back into a classroom now and sat down at a desk, the police would almost certainly be called.

'Emily!' He hasn't lost the thick Lincolnshire accent that many of us tried to shake off as soon as we could. 'It's been a while.' He leans in to kiss me on the cheek and I suddenly glow with mortification as a vivid memory of a school disco comes flooding back. I'm standing behind the sports hall leaning into him and thrusting my tongue down his throat while he inexpertly gropes about trying unsuccessfully to undo my bra. The entire experience was wholly unsatisfying and we gave up after about five minutes, smoked one of his Embassy Number Ones and headed back into the school hall.

Matt walks through to the front room as Rach catches the look on my face, winks in recognition, and says, 'Told you you knew him!'

'You could have bloody warned me!' I shriek.

'Where's the fun in that? Matt told me ages ago. Your face, though. Hilarious! I think he tried it on with most of the girls in our year at some point or other, so don't think you're special. What a guy,' she mocks playfully.

I follow them through to the sitting room. Callum is on the sofa with his fun-fur hood pulled up anti-socially over his head, while Lucy and Sophie gleefully try to clamber into his lap. Both of them are sugar-high on their new favourite drink, Coke floats.

'Mummy!' Lucy shouts, 'Callum's dressed as a Christmas rabbit.'

'No, he's a Christmas rat,' Sophie says.

'That'll teach him for going out dressed like a grown-up baby,' Rachel chuckles.

The doorbell chimes again and in walks Auntie Jean, face like a wet weekend in Worksop, dressed in an ill-fitting black ankle-length dress, a set of pearls draped around her neck, her hair tightly woven into a bun. She looks like a Victorian widow. Auntie Jean makes a beeline for me, clutches my arm firmly and plants one of her signature sloppy kisses on my cheek.

'Emily,' she nods somberly. She radiates a strong floral smell. Mum told me once she uses air freshener as perfume, I discounted it as a little sister being cruel about her sibling, but now I'm not so sure.

'Auntie Jean. Merry Christmas!' I chirp, attempting to lift her mood.

'I am *so* sorry to hear about Nick,' she says sombrely.

'He's not dead, Auntie Jean,' I reply lightly.

'I know, but your mum said about you two being, you know . . .' Her cheeks flush with embarrassment. She's backed herself into a conversational cul-de-sac.

'Separated?' I help her out. 'It's fine. We're fine. The kids are happy. It's OK.'

Auntie Jean lets out a long sigh. Her breath, in contrast to her sweet air-freshener perfume, is unpleasantly sour. I hope I don't end up like Auntie Jean if I live alone. I hope my girls will give me a nudge to brush my teeth occasionally and steer me away from a wardrobe consisting exclusively of dresses from Evans.

'Well, that is a relief.' She sighs again and I move fractionally away from her as to not get caught in the bad-breath crossfire again. 'I wasn't sure if you were going to be a total mess, Emily. My neighbour's daughter in Southport tried to kill herself when she found out her husband had

309

had an affair. She put the toaster in the bath and—'

'Jean!' Dad interrupts. 'What can I get you to drink?'

'Richard,' she replies flatly. 'A sherry please, seeing as it's Christmas.' Dad steers her away from me, but not before handing me a bucket-sized glass of red wine.

Half an hour later and the elderly Mr and Mrs Earls arrive, brandishing gifts for Sophie and Lucy, which they tear open with renewed enthusiasm.

'Callum,' they bowl over to him, climbing back into his lap. 'Look! It's a Sylvanian Family. Mine's the baby hedgehog.'

'And I've got a baby rabbit, like you,' Sophie cackles, holding the boxed toy right up to poor Callum's face. He shows minimal interest in either the toys or the girls, which seems to only encourage them further.

'I'm calling mine Callum,' Lucy announces.

'No, I'm calling *mine* Callum!' Sophie counters. I'll let them fight this one out between themselves, I think.

'So how's it going, really?' Rachel asks, perching on the arm of the easy chair I'm sat in and filling my now empty glass to the brim with Merlot.

'Honestly?' I ask.

'Always.' She rests her arm around the back of my chair with the familiarity of someone who has known me her whole life.

'I don't really know. Nick and I are functional. But that's about it. He's been paying Mum back, which is good, but he didn't bother telling me.'

'Well, that's good news, isn't it?' she asks, taking a large gulp of her wine.

I turn to face her. 'Rachel?'

'Emily.'

'Am I a good listener?' I ask her.

310

Rachel takes another sip of her wine. I wait for her to answer. Her brow furrows, thinking. A beat. Two. I hadn't expected her to say 'yes' immediately, but I didn't really think there was *that* much to think about.

'Not really,' she finally replies.

'What?' My voice comes out as a squeak. 'Really?' I mutter, noticing I've sploshed red wine down the forest-green dress that I'd splashed out on in the COS sale.

'Well, you're not, Emmie,' she says. 'You are many things. A great friend. Fun. Supportive. You would, without question, be my choice of companion on a desert island. But no, you're not a great listener.'

'That's just not true,' I protest.

'OK.' She thinks for a moment before asking, 'What apprentice scheme is Callum doing at the moment?'

I look from her to Callum, hoping the answer will magically present itself.

'You don't have to know the company he's working for, but what industry?' she prompts, taking another sip.

I sigh heavily. Come on, brain. It must be in here somewhere.

'It begins with a P,' she adds. She's enjoying this, I can tell. 'And I have told you several times, before you try that one on.'

'Give me a minute,' I insist. 'I just need a minute to think.'

'P. L. That's all I'm giving you,' she teases.

P. L. P. L. I do know this. Ah ha! 'Play-scheme worker,' I announce. 'See, I do listen.'

Rach lets out a deep loud laugh, making me jump and spill my wine for a second time. 'A play-scheme worker? Seriously Emmie. Look at him with your kids!'

We look over at Callum, who has now pulled his hood down so far that you can no longer see his eyes, but still the girls persist, trying to feed him carrot sticks while cooing, 'Come on, rabbit. Eat up.'

'Ah, yes,' I reply, defeated.

'He's training to be a fucking plumber, Emmie. Seriously. Play-scheme worker,' she grins as she shakes her head in disbelief.

'OK. Well that was a bad example,' I reply weakly.

'I've told you about a hundred times. Do you want another go at something else?' she asks.

'No. No,' I take a large gulp of what's left of my wine. 'Maybe he's right,' I say to myself.

'Who?' she asks.

'Nick. He told me I never listen. That I have no idea what is going on in other people's lives as I never listen to what they say.' I look at her hopefully, for her to contradict him.

Instead she tightens her arm around my shoulders and says, 'Well, we can't all be good at everything, can we?'

As I let the weight of her words sink in, Dad hollers, 'Who's up for opening some more presents?'

Lucy and Sophie shriek with delight and hop off long-suffering Callum's knee.

I look around at the room full of friends and family. I don't know what Matt has said to Auntie Jean, but her head is thrown back, crying with laughter. Lucy and Sophie are squatting under the tree with Dad, who's helping them shred the paper off present after present. I don't know who is enjoying it more, them or him.

Mum looks like she is talking conspiratorially with Mr and Mrs Earl, heads all bent in; she later tells me it's because they had both forgotten to bring their hearing aids.

My mind drifts to Nick, and I wonder what he is doing today. If Dennis and Cathleen have made the day festive, if he's distracted enough to not spend every moment pining after the girls. We FaceTimed him this morning, but that must feel like a lifetime ago for him. Christmas Day is, without exception, the longest day in the history of days.

Rachel wraps her arm around me. 'Come on,' she says. 'I've got a ridiculously big present for both the girls that you're going to hate in the car. Help me bring it in?' She smiles and says, 'I do love you, Emmie Jones.'

I might be a bad listener, but I heard that.

It's Boxing Day. We spot Nick before he sees us; he's hunched over one of the bar stools, sipping his coffee and eating a pasty in the Wild Bean Café.

'DAAAAADDY!' the girls holler and run towards him through the sea of red plastic chairs screwed to the floor. His face immediately lights up as he hops off the stool and squats down, arms outstretched as the girls collide into him, knocking him off his feet. He regains his balance, laughing and showering them with kisses. He holds Lucy, then Sophie at arm's length and asks them both, 'Have you both been doing some serious growing at Nanny and Grandpa's?'

'I have,' Sophie replies proudly, pushing out her chest and holding herself tall, 'but Lucy hasn't.'

'I have!' Lucy protests.

'Now girls,' I interject. 'Let's not fight. Daddy's going to take you for a second Christmas at Granny and Granddad's. How exciting is that?'

The girls fall over themselves, telling Nick about all the gifts they've been given and the food they've eaten and the films they've watched.

'Sounds like they've had a brilliant time,' he looks up to me, smiling.

'It wasn't all fun,' I reassure him. 'Auntie Jean came along to suck the joy out of the party.'

Nick allows himself a quick chuckle and I wonder if he is also remembering Auntie Jean at our wedding, telling us both matter-of-factly the current statistics on divorce and how expensive it is.

'OK,' Nick stands, scooping the girls up in one well-practised move, to their delight. 'Let's get the car seats from Mummy's car and then we can get going.'

We head out to the car park and soon Lucy and Sophie are strapped in the back seat of Dennis and Cathleen's Mondeo.

'What's that?' Nick asks, pointing at the large plastic object in my boot that's obscuring the rear view.

'A Sylvanian Family house from Rachel,' I explain.

'It's huge!'

'I know. The kids love it, unfortunately.'

As Nick opens the driver's door, I catch his arm. 'Mum said you've paid off quite a lot of the money to them. I didn't know.'

He covers my hand with his. 'I did try to tell you.'

I take a deep breath before saying, 'I'm sorry for not listening.'

Nick kisses me on the cheek, his mouth hovers there for a fraction of a second and I feel his breath. 'And I'm sorry for putting us in this situation in the first place. Merry Christmas, Em.'

He folds himself into the car and I wave manically at the children, who match my enthusiasm, throwing out kisses like opera singers receiving their encores.

Nick pulls out of the parking space, and I remain standing in the empty space until the car turns around the corner. Only then do I stop waving and give in to the tears that stream down my cheeks.

Chapter Forty-Five

THE WEEK BEFORE NICK MOVED OUT

'Can you both just *sit* down,' Judy insists. I've never heard her raise her voice before now, but she is loud. In contrast, she has her hands in prayer pose, attempting to compose herself. Her kimono-style white sleeves have slipped down to her elbows and I notice for the first time how freckly her arms are, illuminated by the sunlight that streams through the floor-to-ceiling windows.

I lower myself back into the Ercol chair. We have the same ones at home, except ours are cheap imitations.

'And you, Nick,' she demands. He is still standing at the window clutching his Parka coat, picking the fluff from the hood and dropping it on the floor.

I am shaking with rage. I hold my hand out, palm down, watch it quiver as the adrenalin pulses through my body.

'This is absolutely unacceptable behaviour.' Judy has lost her calming tone, she sounds hard.

'Can I just—' I start to say, but don't know how to end the sentence.

'Nick. I will ask you once more to sit down.' She speaks slowly and firmly, as if addressing a child.

Nick turns, drapes his coat on the back of the chair and slumps into it with a huff.

'I don't know what you want me to say.' His voice is flat. I don't recognise it any more.

'An explanation would be a start?' I suggest.

'Jesus, Em. I'm trying. I'm trying to tell you, but look what happens when I do?'

I tuck my hands underneath my armpits in an attempt to calm myself. My heart beats loudly in my ears. I look down at my jeans. They are covered in stains from grubby children's hands pawing at me for attention.

I shut my eyes and breathe slowly. The darkness helps. As I open them, I take in the room as if looking at it for the first time. The off-white wallpaper. The minimalist Danish furniture. The box of tissues on the desk. I'd never noticed before how purposefully placed everything is in the room. It suddenly feels pretentious. Fake.

On the wall behind Judy's head is a large brown mark. The floor below is covered in shards of pottery, soil and what is left of the peace plant.

'Why would you keep this from me, Nick? How did you think you'd get away with it?' I'm trying to not shout again so say each word slowly and purposefully.

'I don't know.' He drops his head in his hands and runs his fingers through his hair.

Outside I hear laughter and see a gaggle of friends walking past the window, arms draped around each other, takeaway coffees in hands, and I feel a wave of jealousy for their laissez-faire attitudes. I don't think I will ever feel carefree again.

'Nick,' Judy says encouragingly, 'how would you like to proceed?'

He is tugging on a hangnail, shoulders rounded, face stern. I feel nothing other than exhaustion as the fury seeps from my body like water.

'Nick?' she repeats, and he shrugs as he continues to work the skin on his finger.

'Emily?' I look at Judy. Her eyes widen, encouraging a response.

'I don't know. I genuinely don't know what to do right now. Is it safe, Nick? Is the house safe now?' The panic is rising like bile in my throat again.

'I'm not sure,' he whispers.

'What do you mean, you're not sure? We're either going to get evicted or not. There are only two choices here, aren't there? Aren't there?' I'm now asking Judy, though why she would know anything more about property law than Nick or me is beyond me.

'I think we need to take a couple of moments here to gather our thoughts. Can I get you both a glass of water?' she suggests.

'Yes please,' I respond even though I'm not the slightest bit thirsty.

Judy carefully steps over the pieces of broken pottery, and opens a glass bottle of water from the tea caddy in the corner of the room, fills two glasses with a glug glug glug and then passes them to us both. I take a large gulp. My throat feels sore and ribbonned from swallowing back my emotions for the last half an hour.

'Are we going to lose our home, Nick?' I ask again, more calmly this time.

'If we can find three thousand pounds to pay the mortgage arrears, then no,' his voice is barely audible. 'But if we can't, then that's a real possibility.' He drops his head again. I don't think he has made eye contact with me at all throughout this entire session.

'And if I hadn't asked you repeatedly what was wrong today, would you have even bothered to tell me? Or would

317

I have had to wait until the bailiffs turned up when I was making Lucy and Sophie's tea?'

The enormity of the situation is starting to hit me like a slow-motion car crash. We could lose our home. Our children's home. Nick's callousness could have cost us everything we have worked for.

'I've tried. I've tried to tell you a thousand times but . . .' his voice trails off as he eventually catches my eye, and sees the fury rising in me.

'Are you fucking serious, Nick? You are going to try and turn this around on me?'

'That's not what I meant, I just mean—'

'It was not me whose been defaulting on the mortgage payments, Nick. It's not me who's buried my head in the sand, walking around like everything's OK. Buying expensive presents for the girls at Christmas.' A thought strikes me as I ask, 'How *did* you pay for the presents, Nick?'

A beat. Two. Then . . .

'I put them on the credit card,' he croaks.

'But we don't have—' I stop in my tracks. 'How much do we owe, Nick?'

He's shaking his head, I know he doesn't want to tell me, but how much worse can this situation get?

'About eleven grand.' That's how much worse it can get.

'OK, Emily. Nick,' Judy interjects, cutting through the toxic atmosphere that hangs in the air like dry ice. 'We are going to have to draw this session to a close shortly, so I would like you both to consider what your next step is and how we would like to pick this up in our next session. There have been some large revelations today, and a lot to digest, so I would like you to think about how things are going to be when you walk out of this room.' Her fingers are interlaced on her lap. She is nodding slowly to emphasise every other word.

318

'Hang on, Judy,' I raise a hand in protest, 'Nick. What you are telling me is that not only do we owe thousands on the house, but you also owe thousands on a credit card?'

'Yes. Yes, that's what I'm saying,' he replies, deflated.

'How could you let this happen?' the skin on my face feels tighter and prickly.

'I don't know. I know this sounds lame, but it just happened, Em. I didn't realise how bad it had got until, well, it was too late.' He's rubbing his forehead repeatedly with the heel of his palm. 'To start with it was just falling short a bit each month, so I had to make that up. And then work froze all our bonuses over Christmas, but we'd already spent mine. There was always something that needed to be paid for or things we needed to do or places we needed to go to. The car costs an absolute fortune. You know it's over sixty quid to fill the tank up? When did it get to sixty quid? It just . . . Fuck. I don't know. It was just the small things to start with, but then it started racking up until it had got way out of control.'

'But why didn't you say something, Nick? Why did it take a fucking counselling session for you to tell me that we might lose our house? How are we even paying for these sessions? You said we could afford it, but—'

Nick drops his head again.

'Right. Of course we can't.' I look to Judy who is trying to subtly check her wrist watch. 'But hang on, you said work froze your bonus. When was that? Do you mean last Christmas?' I ask, but the thing is, I'm not sure if I'm prepared for the answer. I don't know if I actually want to find out how long Nick has been lying to me for.

'No, the one before.' He bows his head. 'It all started about eighteen months ago,' he whispers.

It all starts to make sense. The moodiness at home. The

lack of affection. The late nights at the office. The slow but steady breakdown of communication with the family. With me.

I look at Nick. Our new reality starts to uncomfortably sink in.

This has been going on for over a year and a half. Since Sophie was one and Lucy was three. I think of all the things we have jointly decided to buy for ourselves or the house. The impromptu Sunday roasts at the pub that we could have easily cooked at home. The leather Chesterfield sofa we bought second hand for a 'steal' at three hundred pounds. The iCandy pram that was almost twice as expensive as the one we had for Lucy, but the reviews were great so why wouldn't we get it for Sophie? We could afford it. Nick said we could afford it.

The anxiety knot in my stomach throbs. We didn't need any of that stuff. We could have made this stop, got it under control, if Nick had only spoken to me. If he hadn't waited until it was almost too late. The deceit burns like acid. I have always been in charge of the house finances, made sure all the bills were paid out of the joint account and been careful with the food shop. There was always money in the joint account, so why would I ever assume that we were struggling elsewhere? Nick's job was to make sure the mortgage was paid. Why would I question it? It's the same amount each month. It doesn't involve any responding to bills, or hunting around for the most competitive energy supplier. He just set up a direct debit from his account when we first bought the house. He only had to make sure there was enough money in there to cover it. Or not. As it now transpires.

I think back to the conversation Nick and I had had when we jointly decided that I wouldn't return to work after maternity leave with Sophie. That the cost of childcare for two children against the take-home pay from a job at the council that I didn't enjoy just didn't add up. For the balance of a hundred pounds a month, it made more sense for me to be with the children until the free childcare kicked in. To write when time allowed, to start to focus on what I wanted to do as well. For the first time it felt like we were getting on top of things. That there was some balance in our lives. Oh, how could I have been so stupid?

'I don't think we can do this,' my voice cracks, defying my words, so I take a deep breath and repeat, 'I can't do this.'

'Are you talking about the sessions?' Judy prompts.

'No. No. I mean Nick and me. I don't think we can do this any more.' I pause, exhale slowly and then say, 'We can't do this to each other any more, Nick. We both need some space.'

Now Nick looks at me. His eyes are glassy. I know he's trying not to blink for fear of tears spilling down his cheeks.

'Em?' There is desperation in his tone. 'Em, I know I should have told you before, it was foolish of me, I just thought I could fix it. I still can.'

'How? Where's the trust? However bad things got between us, I always thought I could trust you, but now . . . we've got to put the girls first.'

'But—' he starts to say something and stops himself.

'We'll find a way to fix the money. I'll speak to my parents, see if they can help us. But I'm not sure how to fix us,' I whisper. 'Thanks, Judy for everything and so sorry about the plant pot.'

'These things happen,' she responds.

I pick up my coat and handbag and make for the door.

And just like that, our marriage is over.

321

Chapter Forty-Six

Me: What do you mean, it's all paid for already?

Tania: Just that, brains. We're going to London for a couple of nights to a luxury apartment, more champagne than you can fill a bath with, and swanky meals. It's my fortieth. You can't say no.

Helen: I don't think I can. It's all a bit full-on here at the moment.

Tania: Which is why we're not going to Barbados. It's only a short train journey away. You need a break. We all need a break. Chris can handle it.

Helen: Let me talk to him.

Tania: Already done. He says enjoy yourself.

Helen: Really??? Wow.

Tania: So?

Helen: I feel a bit uncomfortable, you paying for everything when it's your birthday.

Tania: Well, you would. But suck it up. It's my turn to treat you both. And we all deserve it.

Me: Don't you want to spend the money on something else?

Tania: I have. Don't worry. I've just put a deposit down on a studio for a year so I can start practising yoga when I want, instead of when the shitty community centre is free. I've got a bike for Falcon so he can learn to cycle instead of sitting on his fat arse watching Teenage Mutant Ninja Turtles. *And we're buying a camper van.*

Helen: Thought you didn't agree with driving?

Tania: I don't. But I also don't agree with Uber taking the piss out of me. And it's going to make work easier for Spiral, as in, he can actually go. And we can go away at the weekends together. Falcon loves it.

Me: Sounds amazing.

Tania: Anyway, I've already paid for London. Train tickets. Everything. Non-refundable. So you have to come.

Me: I'M IN.

Helen: OK, God I need a break.

Me: NAMASTAYCATION!!

Tania: Groan.

Chapter Forty-Seven

11.24 a.m.

As the train pulls out of Brighton station, Tania rummages around in her bag.

'Ta-daaah!' She presents both Helen and me with a gin in a tin.

'I won't. It's not even midday,' replies Helen. 'I think I might just start with a coffee from the buffet cart.'

'No!' Tania snaps. 'Absolutely no way. This is my birthday, my rules. And we all deserve a break, am I right or am I right?'

'You're right,' Helen and I chorus like obedient schoolchildren, and accept the cans, opening them with a hiss. I can feel the gentle warmth of the gin wrapping around my neck like an expensive scarf. I've never left the girls for two nights before like this. They've been away from me over the weekend, but only recently and only to Nick's around the corner. It feels liberating and unnerving all rolled up together. I resist the temptation to text Nick to ask for a photograph, and put my phone back in my bag. I flick through *Grazia*, scanning the suggestions of winter holidays I will never go on, and settle down in my seat.

1.46 p.m.

'OH. MY. GOD. THERE'S A FUCKING HOT TUB OUT HERE!' Helen squeals.

I rush out to join her. The balcony, which is about three times the size of my front room, houses a hot tub, a plush outdoor seating area and a Parisian-style wrought-iron table and chairs.

'How much did you say this place cost a night again?' I ask Tania, who joins us, carrying a bottle of champagne and three flutes.

'Five hundred quid. Fucking ridiculous isn't it?' She pops the cork and we all cheer, passing her glasses as the bubbles drip down the side of the bottle. 'The fridge is full of posh food – help yourself.'

'If I owned this place I would never leave,' I reply. Never. Have you seen the bathroom? It's like something out of the Sunday supplements.' She passes me a glass and I take a long sip. God that's good, it's not Co-op own-brand Cava, that's for sure.

A text alert sounds and we all check our phones.

'It's me,' I inform them. It's from Nick.

Nick: Is Sophie allowed to wear her bridesmaid dress to the park?
Me: Obviously not.

Seriously Nick, that better be the last of these kinds of messages. This was meant to be a break for me.

Ding. Ding. It sounds again.

Nick: And do you know where Lucy's trainers are? We've got one but can't find the other.
Me: Check under her bed. Otherwise no.

Come on, Nick. I see the grey dots. I dare you to write another one. But he thinks better of it and the dots disappear.

*

3.50 p.m.

'Shall I open another one or . . .' Tania drifts off.

'Of course,' Helen replies, passing her champagne flute to her as she relaxes back into the hot tub. 'I haven't felt like this in weeks. Months. It's like my brain has started to unwind. Thank you so much for this, Tania. I can't believe we've got a full weekend of this. Does anyone else feel guilty?'

'Nope. We're not having that kind of language over the next forty-eight hours. No guilt. None. OK?' Tania demands.

'Agreed.' I reply, as I stretch out on the outdoor sofa under the heated lamp.

'There are another couple of bottles of champagne in the fridge and then it's gin and tonic or wine, I'm afraid, until the other bottles chill.'

'What kind of a dive is this?' Helen teases as she presses the button to increase the bubbles in the tub. Just then her phone buzzes. 'Can you pass that over, Tan?'

Tania passes it over and Helen looks at the screen. 'Seriously, Chris, why can't you look for her bloody coat yourself?' She types back purposefully, before adding, 'It's like he thinks it's easier to send a message to me, instead of actually going to the coat stand to look.'

'Nick's the same.'

'And Spiral.'

'How do they actually cope without us?' Helen asks.

'They don't. Did he mention anything about your mum?'

'No,' Helen sighs. 'So that can only be a good thing. I do feel really guilty—'

326

'NO GUILT!' Tania interrupts.

'—really aware,' Helen says, 'of what an ask this is for Chris. But I haven't had a weekend without having to look after someone since I can't remember when.'

'Chris can handle it,' I reply. 'He's only got to look after her for a couple of days. What's the worst that can happen?' The question hangs in the air ominously, so I change the subject. 'I think it's about time I got off with someone who isn't old or mentally unstable.'

'Or a pervert,' Tania adds.

'Yes. No pervs.'

'YAY!' Helen and Tania cheer.

'Get your phone,' Tania says, 'let's have a look to see if there's anyone hot nearby.'

'Nope. No internet. If we're going out, I'm going to see if I can meet someone in real life.'

'An old-school snog,' Helen laughs.

'Watch out, London!' Tania beams, clapping her hands with enthusiasm.

6.45 p.m.

'I feel so underdressed,' Helen comments as we walk into a bar.

'You're not underdressed, you're just dressed for the weather,' I reassure her, sounding like Mum. 'Right, you guys get a seat and I'll get the drinks.'

There are no seats free. Just high bar tables and beautiful women and men leaning next to them. How can they not be cold, I think, how can you come out just wearing a spaghetti-strap dress with no coat in the middle of January? I look at Helen in her skinny jeans and heavy knit jumper, Tania in her combat trousers and 'Smash the Patriarchy' hoodie, and me in my ever-faithful jeans, Breton top and cardigan and think, yes, perhaps Helen has a point.

'Don't even think about getting a round, this weekend is courtesy of Dad.' Tania playfully pushes me out of the way and wades through the six-deep queue to the bar, elbows out like a seasoned professional.

7.37 p.m.

The door to the ladies slams open with a loud bang.

'Are you in here, Emily?' Helen hollers.

'Yes, I'm just getting myself together.' My voice sounds slightly slurred.

'Well, Tania has got some more drinks and we've found you a new boyfriend,' she announces gleefully.

'I don't want a new boyfriend. I don't think I want a snog either now. I would just settle for a kebab and a can of full-fat Coke,' I say.

'His name's George and he's a fireman.' She ignores me. 'And he's forty with no children and lives with his mum, but that's OK as he's just moved in to save up for a deposit for a house. Which he's almost done.'

I pull myself upright, collect all my belongings from the sticky toilet floor that have fallen out of my handbag, and unbolt the door. 'How have you found all of that out? I've only been gone for five minutes.'

'I am a people person. People like to tell me things.'

'Do you not feel drunk?' I ask her.

'Yes. I feel completely hammered. Now come on, dry your hands and come and meet your new boyfriend.'

'I don't want a new boyfriend,' I repeat as she threads her arm in mine and leads me out of the ladies.

'Ta-daaah!' she gives the jazz hands as Tania points

dramatically at a guy perched awkwardly next to her. Everything about his body language screams I don't want to be here. He looks nice enough with his white T-shirt and jeans. It's difficult to tell how old he is with his shaved head, but he's definitely not forty. Forty-five, perhaps, in a good light. He raises a hand meekly in greeting, and I wonder what Tania and Helen have been telling him.

'This is my friend Emily that I was telling you about.' She drags me to sit down next to him. 'And this is George.'

'Ben,' he says.

'Sorry?'

'It's Ben. Not George,' he says.

'So why did you tell us your name was George?' she prods him gently in the chest.

'I didn't,' he shrugs.

'Well, anyway, Ben is a single fireman, aren't you?' Tania pipes up, slapping him on the back.

'I'm not,' he coughs nervously.

'What aren't you, George?'

'Single. I'm married.' He raises his arm to show the ring on his forth finger of his left hand.

'Then why,' Tania demands, 'are you trying to get off with Emily?'

'I'm not. I'm just having a drink with my friends.' He gestures to a table of men sat on the far side of the pub. 'And you accosted me when I was at the bar.'

'Urgh, go then, George.' Tania dismisses him with a wave.

'Thank you,' he replies gratefully, and picks up his pint to rejoin his friends.

'What is wrong with all the men? Why can't they just tell the truth?' Tania shouts after him, as he all but runs back to his table. 'Want one of these?' she produces a packet of cigarettes.

'Where did you get those from?' I quiz.

'They must have fallen out of George's pocket. Come on, let's neck these and go to the beer garden.' She throws back her tequila, we follow suit and trail after her into the garden.

9.02 p.m.

Helen is sitting very close to an older woman, leaning in and stroking her cheek. I can't work out if the woman is enjoying it or not. I think possibly not. 'But your skin is so soft,' she is telling her, 'and you say it's just Boots' own face cream? Why have I been spending a fortune on Chanel when your face can feel like this with Boots?'

Tania is sat opposite me chain-smoking, lighting one cigarette off the last. George has come out to ask for them back. 'I think you'll find they're mine,' she protests.

'But they have my lighter in the inside of the packet, look! I must have left them when I was sat with you.'

'I think you'll find that's my lighter,' Tania responds. She would make an excellent politician. Even George is looking like he doubts his own mind now, as he continues to try unsuccessfully to persuade Tania to return his fags.

11.43 p.m.

'George says there's a rave at an old warehouse in Shoreditch.' Tania has her arm menacingly draped around George's shoulder. We've all forgotten what his real name is, and he now seems perfectly happy to be known as George, his friends having left him hours ago.

'I think we should definitely go. Definitely,' she tells us. 'And George has given us these.' She presses something into each of our hands. As I unfurl mine I see it's an ecstasy tablet.

'Tania! I haven't taken these since university!' I squeal in mock outrage.

'Well, it's about time then, isn't it?' She puts hers on her tongue, and swallows it down with the dregs of a bottle of beer that's resting on the top of the wall.

'I haven't heard from Chris for at least an hour, do you think I should ring him?' Helen asks.

'I'm sure he's fine. Check out this picture Spiral sent.' We all look at the screen, Falcon is fast asleep, bum in the air, and coo.

'And look at this one from Nick.' It's a picture of Lucy and Sophie in the bath together, both covered in suds. I feel a pang of missing them, like I want to teleport myself back home for five minutes, gather them both up in my arms and sniff deeply.

'Enough of this,' Tania demands. 'No guilt. Remember?' and Helen and I both take the bottle of warm beer from her and swallow the pills.

12.34 a.m.

We can hear the rave before we see it. The deep thud of the bass. The spill of people on the pavement smoking. Two bouncers are standing at the door as we approach, neither seem bothered about who is going in or out. As we follow George through the double doors we are immediately hit by an overpowering smell of sweat and weed. He is instantly swallowed up by people.

'WHAT IS THIS PLACE?' Helen shouts.

'JUST FOLLOW ME,' Tania grabs hold of us and pulls us into the crowd, but there are too many people, it's like pushing your way onto the Tube in rush hour. Our hands are all sweaty and slippy and we lose our grip of her as she pushes her way forwards.

The bass thuds through my body, the floor vibrating. I turn to look at Helen, her eyes wide, pupils dilated. I feel like I'm in the eye of a storm. Every hair on my body stands on end. I run my hands through my hair and the feeling remains long after I've stopped touching my head, like deep sensory rake marks. As I turn my head, my vision follows, everyone is surrounded by a haze, like looking at the world though soft focus.

'I LOVE YOU!' Helen shouts at me, and wraps her arms around me. Every sense alive, her body feeling like an extension of mine.

'I LOVE YOU TOO!' I shout back. And I do. I love these women so much, so very fucking much. I can't imagine a world without them in it.

'I CAN'T IMAGINE LIFE WITHOUT YOU,' Helen shouts back to me. I must have said that aloud.

Tania turns, sees we're not directly behind her and shouts something. I can only see her mouth move, I can't hear a word she's saying over the drum and bass, so I just give her a thumbs-up, which seems the right answer as she nods and carries on pushing through the crowds. I clumsily pull off my cardigan, getting stuck in the right arm and then attempt to tie it around my waist.

'THIS IS COMPLETELY BRILLIANT,' I shout to Helen, but turn to see she's no longer stood next to me.

A sweaty arm brushes against mine. 'YES IT IS!' he shouts back at me, unintentionally spitting on my face. I try to wipe it away, but my arms feel heavy and light at the same time, like they're dead weights but also might float away.

'PAUL, MY NAME'S PAUL.'

'EMILY,' I shout back at him, my face set in a grin that I don't seem able to move, like all-over Botox. What the fuck did George give us?

2.21 a.m.

I've been dancing next to Paul for what feels like hours. I've no idea where Tania and Helen have gone. I tried to look for them a while ago, but got as far as the most revolting toilets in London, if not the world, and gave up.

'THIS IS SOPHIE DRESSED AS THE CAT IN THE HAT FOR WORLD BOOK DAY.' I hold my phone up to his face, his large pupils looking past the picture.

'AND THIS IS LUCY, THAT'S MY DRESS SHE'S WEARING. THEY BOTH LOVE TO DRESS UP.' I show him a different one. Paul had feigned interest in the first couple of pictures I'd shown him of the girls, and with little encouragement I am flicking through their life in images. I'm not sure how long we've been doing this for but he's definitely not interested. And I definitely don't care.

'AND THIS IS AT THE SEA LIFE CENTRE IN—'

'HERE.' Paul passes me a rolly. I put it in my mouth so he can light it for me.

As I exhale, Paul leans in to clumsily kiss me. Up very close he smells like joss sticks and BO. His T-shirt is saturated with sweat as his body pushes against me, and he presses his lips to mine, they're wet, not nice wet. More reminiscent of kissing an ageing relative. I open my mouth and he pushes his tongue inside.

'What is THAT?' I exclaim, pulling away.

He opens his mouth wide, flicking his tongue in and out quickly like a snake, to reveal a large piercing.

333

He leans in to kiss me again.

'I'M GOING TO GET SOME AIR,' I say, and turn to wade through the packed crowds towards the entrance.

2.29 a.m.

I'm sitting on the wall outside the warehouse. It's cold. I must have dropped my cardigan inside somewhere, which is a bit disappointing as I've had it since sixth form. My teeth are chattering uncontrollably. My breath comes out in dragon-like puffs. I rub one arm and then the other to generate some heat. The street lamp illuminates my swinging legs. I'm completely exhausted and full of electric energy all at once.

I suddenly miss the girls. I scroll through pictures on my phone again. Of Sophie when she was hours old in the hospital, held in the crook of Nick's arm, a two-year-old Lucy gripping his other hand, a wide grin spread across her face, eyes bright with excitement. What was it he said? 'My girls.' That was it. Nick said 'my girls' to us all.

Lucy and Sophie in a plastic kids' bath in the garden a couple of summers ago, filled to the brim with lukewarm water. It's way too small for the pair of them, but they've still managed to squeeze in all their bath toys. Nick, hands on hips, looking delighted at his invention, having driven to B&Q on the hottest day of the year only to be told, predictably, that the shop had run out of paddling pools. Moments after this picture was taken I'd snapped at him for not going to B&Q the day before as I'd instructed. I'd brushed off his enthusiasm for his makeshift solution, and told him if he'd done it my way, we'd have an actual paddling pool instead of a stupid bath. I look at the picture again. He's still smiling then. When did he stop smiling?

I scroll through again. We're at Center Parcs. Sophie is strapped to Nick's back in the papoose. I have Lucy on my shoulders. Nick grins awkwardly, holding Lucy's hand. I look cross. Why am I cross? I rub my temples and try to remember. It was about dinner. That's right. Nick had suggested he cook dinner in the apartment and I'd vetoed the idea, saying we should go for pizza. He'd said we couldn't afford to go out for dinner every night, and I'd called him tight, said we were on holiday and why should I have to cook? But he hadn't suggested I cook, he was going to do it. He'd bought the ingredients for spag bol and I remember clearing out the rotting vegetables from the fridge straight into the bin as we'd packed away to leave days later, making some off-hand remark about wasting food.

I scroll forwards. We're at Cathleen and Dennis's. A picture of me and the girls sitting on a bench in the garden. Nick's captured in the background, head down, shoulders slumped. I hadn't realised he was in the frame when I'd taken a selfie of the three of us. Had we fought then? What were we arguing about? Money. That's right. We'd fought about buying Lucy some trainers. He'd said hers still fitted, but I'd insisted on getting her some new ones as she had sports day at nursery and I thought she looked tatty in her old ones.

Another picture. We're about to go out for our wedding anniversary. I'd got us tickets to see Grace Jones, it cost a fortune but it was worth it, I'd said at the time. A once in a lifetime treat. Nick said he'd be just as happy getting a takeaway and curling up on the sofa with me. I thought it was because he'd stopped being fun. Stopped wanting to do stuff together. Become curmudgeonly. Boring.

The realisation hits me like a ten-tonne truck.

We had always both wanted the same thing. What was

best for the girls, for our family, we'd just forgotten how to communicate, long before Nick didn't get his Christmas bonus. We both got so caught up in the idea of what we thought 'family' should be like that we never once stopped to see how we could make that happen together. I feel a yearning for Nick deep down in the pit of my stomach. I want to see him, to speak to him. I have an overwhelming feeling of missing him. But it dawns on me that this isn't a fierce missing, this isn't a jealous or possessive all-encompassing missing, like I would have experienced years ago. I miss Nick. I miss having him in my life in a simple, uncomplicated way. I miss my best friend.

When I was pregnant with Lucy, Nick and I vowed that children wouldn't change us. But how could they not? How could we not change once we'd had Lucy and then Sophie? Our priorities changed, our love shifted and matured. Our life became messier and more complicated and brighter and more exhausting.

But somewhere in it all, we forgot each other.

'You coming back in?' I turn to see Paul's head poking out the warehouse door. His bald head is shiny with sweat, and there's a tattoo of a dragon creeping out of the top of his T-shirt and winding around his neck that I hadn't seen when we were inside.

'No, I think I'm going to stay out here for a bit longer,' I reply.

'Suit yourself, it's fucking freezing out here though.' He shrugs, and disappears back through the door.

The thing is, maybe Nick and I weren't good at marriage. Weren't good at being married to each other, more specifically. Maybe the transition from us, to three, to four was so much of a change that we imploded under all that pressure. But there is something we do well together at, which is the

336

thing we most need to be good at together, and that is being parents. I scroll back to the first picture of us all at the hospital with newborn Sophie and think what an extraordinary dad he is. And how completely adored he is by his children.

The drugs are now starting to wear off; my skin prickles and my head feels like it's in a vice. I need a glass of water. I need a wee. I need to speak to someone who knows me better than I know myself.

I scroll through my contacts until I find Rachel. She answers after two rings. 'What do you want? It's the middle of the night,' she says sleepily.

'It's me,' I reply.

'I know it's you. Is everything OK?'

'I just wanted to tell you that I love you.'

'That's nice,' she replies vacantly. 'Now can I go back to sleep?'

'Yes,' I croak, 'and I know I don't always listen. But I do love you.'

'You said,' she yawns. 'And I love you.' She hangs up. I look at the screen and see that I've had three missed calls from Nick. They must have been while I was inside.

I call him back and he answers immediately.

'Is everything OK? Are the girls OK?' A pain behind my eyes starts to throb.

'Yes, yes. The girls are fine,' he replies calmly. 'It's Helen's mum. Chris has been trying to get in touch with Hels but it's just ringing out, so he called me and Spiral to see if we could get hold of you guys instead. She's had a nasty fall. She's been taken to hospital.'

'OK. OK, I'll let her know. Thanks,' I suddenly feel completely sober. Every sense alert. Fuck me, I'm cold. Really cold.

'No problem.'

'Thanks again,' I sign off and then without thinking, add, 'I love you.'

He pauses, before replying, 'I love you too.'

I hang up and push my way back into the warehouse. My eyes try to adjust to the strobe lights and the dry ice makes it difficult to focus. I try to stand still against the bustle of the crowds, sweaty bodies pushing against me. And then I spot them. Helen and Tania jumping up and down, hands raised in the air.

I weave my way through the bodies. ''Scuse me. 'Scuse me,' pushing and shoving until I finally grab Helen's arm.

'There you are,' she shouts happily. 'We thought we'd lost you, you've been gone for hours. What?' she asks. 'What's wrong?' Her smile drops.

I lean in and cup her ear so she can hear me and shout, 'We have to go. It's your mum.'

Chapter Forty-Eight

'No change so far. Mum is still waiting for an MRI to see if there is any damage to her brain,' Helen is looking at her phone while resting her head against the cold train window; she hasn't noticed the grease stains from previous commuter's heads smeared along the pane. The journey home has mainly been in silence, only broken by Helen's regular calls to Chris for an update.

'He said he'd gone down to get a glass of water and found her in the kitchen slumped against the wall. He hadn't heard anything. How could he not have heard anything? What was she doing there in the first place? What if Polly had found her?'

Helen has been through the range of emotions, from crying uncontrollably, to guilt that she hadn't got the message sooner, to rage that Chris hadn't watched her mum more carefully to prevent this, to guilt again that she went away for the weekend in the first place, to practicalities, what needs to be done. When and how, which is where she is at now.

None of them have slept. They went back to the apartment from the party, packed their bags and headed to Victoria station, by which time it was 4.30 a.m. and only an hour until the first train to Brighton. They'd sat bundled together on the plastic chairs underneath the large clock, willing the time to speed up, wishing WH Smiths would open so they could get a bottle of water to quench their parched mouths.

As the train pulls into its final stop in Brighton, they tumble onto the platform, helping each other shakily down the steep steps and passing wheelie bags down as they go.

'OK,' Helen states affirmatively, 'Chris says he's waiting under the departure board. I told him I'd get a taxi up to the hospital, but he was insistent. He says Mum's asleep and comfortable. The nurses are with her if she wakes.'

Tania and Emily walk as fast as they can, trying to keep pace with Helen's long strides.

'God, you're fast,' Tania mutters, her face flushed with exercise. She is also the only one of the three of them who shunned bringing a wheelie bag in favour of a large patch-work shoulder bag, which keeps slipping down. She hoicks it back up with a huff.

'Regretting the hippy sack now?' Emily teases.

'This, my friend, has been hand-sewn by Nepalese monks. Every penny spent on this goes directly into their pockets, not like the poor children who got paid five pence to make yours.' She wipes her brow, which is sweating even though it's seven o'clock on a cold January morning.

'There he is.' Relief radiates through Helen's voice. 'They're all there!' she adds, surprised.

Stood under the departures board is Chris with Polly, Spiral trying to discreetly smoke a vape while clutching Falcon's hand, and Nick, with Sophie on his hip and holding Lucy's hand.

Helen flops into Chris's arms, sobbing. He strokes her hair and kisses her forehead; she can feel her body relax and grow very heavy in his arms, like he can carry the burden with her now.

'Nana Janet is poorly, Mummy,' Polly explains. 'And there is blood on the wall in the kitchen where she hit her

340

head, but Daddy cleaned it off with the spray, didn't you, Daddy?'

'It's not as bad as it sounds,' he clarifies. 'It was just a drop of blood; I just made a bit of a mess clearing it up. The ambulance came almost immediately; they were brilliant. And we went in the back with Nana Janet, didn't we?'

'Yes, Mummy,' Polly squeals. 'It went so fast and the doctor let me listen to my heart with his seloscope.'

'Stethoscope,' Chris says. 'The car is around the back. Shall we go?'

Helen turns to Tania and Emily, arms open and envelops them both into a hug. 'Thanks for being my friends.' She inhales the heady combination of Emily's Aussie shampoo and Tania's rose oil.

'Anything we can do, just let us know. Anything, OK?' Emily tells her.

'Keep us updated,' Tania squeezes her arm firmly.

'I will,' Helen reassures her, as Polly's warm hand slots into hers. Chris's arm drapes around her as they make their way towards the car park.

Chapter Forty-Nine

'Shall we get the bus or do you want to walk?' Spiral asks as the winter sun blinds them as they head out of the station.

Tania passes Spiral her patchwork bag. 'Of course I don't want to walk.' She rolls her eyes.

Spiral strains under the weight. 'What have you got in here?' he asks, more to himself.

'Stuff, just stuff Spiral.' She attempts to lift Falcon into a hug and thinks better of it, her arms feeling like lead weights. He really is a heavy boy now, so settles for a squat and cuddle.

'Can we go to the park?' Falcon asks. Has his voice got even deeper over the last twenty-four hours? Surely that's not possible.

'I don't know, what's Daddy got planned?' she asks rhetorically. Of course Spiral won't have planned anything, he never does. In fact, Tania was shocked that they were both there to meet her at the station so early, dressed and in Falcon's case, almost clean.

Spiral stops, puts the bag down and retrieves a piece of paper from his combat trouser pocket. He unfolds it and reads aloud in a mock newsreader's voice, 'Saturday. A trip to the recycling plant to learn about different recyclable materials. Followed by a walk around the tip to see where all the waste goes. What do you think?'

'You've been homeschooling?' Tania asks, stunned.

'Well, you said to give it a go more often, so we thought we'd put together some kind of curriculum while you were away, didn't we, boy?' he shrugs.

'And?' Tania asks apprehensively.

'We had a good day yesterday, wouldn't you say, Falcon?' His son nods in agreement.

'And you?' Tania asks, holding her breath.

Spiral takes a long thoughtful drag on his vape before replying, 'Yep. I enjoyed it actually. Better than our regular Tuesdays, wasn't it, Falcon? Turns out a bit of planning goes a long way.'

Tania allows herself a long sigh of relief, the breath coming out slowly and powerfully from her solar plexus, just like she teaches in class. The tides might just be shifting for them.

'So. Recycling plant?' Spiral asks.

Falcon's eyes are wide and glassy, tears threatening to spill down his cheeks. 'Can't we just go to the park?' he asks in his smallest voice.

Spiral folds the paper back up and slots it in his pocket. 'Well, I guess it is Saturday.'

'Everyone has to have a day off!' Tania offers, holding Spiral's face in her hands and planting a kiss firmly on his lips before whispering in his ear, 'I've had zero sleep and will be sick if I have to smell a recycling plant.'

Spiral grins at her. 'Park it is, then.'

'Yessssss,' Falcon enthuses, turning to Tania for a high five. 'Maybe we can get a sausage r—' Tania smothers his mouth with her hand, kisses his cheek and whispers, 'Ssshh-hhh,' in his ear. They don't need to go down that road again just yet.

Chapter Fifty

Nick passes Sophie to me, who clings on like a koala bear as we walk towards the car.

'We had McDonald's for tea last night,' Lucy announces.

Nick shoots her a mock-shocked expression. 'That was meant to be our secret,' he teases.

'Oh yes, I forgot,' Lucy replies.

I give her a squeeze and ask Nick, 'What are you all doing here?'

'I thought you might want a friendly face and a lift home. The girls can still come back to mine if you want to catch up on some sleep?'

'Thank you,' I reply. My eyes hurt from the strip lights in the station. My brain aches and throbs repeatedly, like being hit intermittently by a boxer's reflex bag. I feel so dehydrated that swallowing is almost impossible, and I don't think I have ever been happier to see these three human beings.

Nick pulls the car up outside the house, 'OK,' he smiles. 'This is you. Shall I bring the girls back in a few hours once you've had a chance to sort yourself out?' he suggests.

'Or,' I reply, 'you could all come in and make them pancakes?'

A chorus of, 'yes', 'let's do that', 'do that Daddy', 'let's have breakfast together', 'can I have Nutella?', 'and honey?', 'and both?' comes from the backseat.

'That would be nice,' Nick grins.

As I push the front door to and follow the cacophony of squealing children running flatfooted down the corridor, I turn momentarily to watch Nick retrieving my suitcase from the boot of the car.

'You've put it back up?' He points to the Rothko poster as he dumps the case down in the hall.

'Yes,' I reply. 'You were right. It did look good there.'

'Good. Good,' he replies, then starts to whistle as he takes his coat off and puts it on the peg. Nick only whistles when he's happy, a habit I used to find beyond annoying but today, today it feels comforting. Like coming home.

Chapter Fifty-One

Two months later

'What's for dinner?' Tania asks as she hangs up her coat and places her shoes in the shoe rack. 'I'm absolutely famished.'

'You're in luck!' Spiral announces, kissing her cheek warmly. 'It was our cooking day today.'

'It was brilliant,' Falcon squeals as he jumps off the sofa and wraps his arms around his mum's waist. She kisses the top of his head and inhales his musty hair. 'We saw a bee-hive, didn't we, Dad?'

'Yep, sport, we did.' Spiral has opened the oven, a delicious smell drifts out as he removes the baking tray and places it on the wooden block.

'The beekeeper let me try some straight from the comb, didn't he, Dad?' His face is alive with excitement. 'And we bought a jar, and honey bees must gather nectar from two million flowers to make one pound of honey, so we have to enjoy it because the bees have put a lot of work into it, isn't that right, Dad?'

'Sure is,' Spiral nods as he passes Tania a glass of chilled wine. 'So we made honey-coated carrots and mushroom wellington for dinner, didn't we, boy?'

'We did it off the phone, didn't we, Dad?'

'YouTube,' Spiral mumbles, cheeks flushed. 'He's blown my cover. Yes, we did an idiot's guide to cooking this off YouTube.'

Tania suppresses a grin. She doesn't want to appear too

impressed in case this suddenly stops. But it's been eight weeks of Spiral homeschooling, and, although the meals haven't been this elaborate every day, they have been tasty and consistent. And most importantly, she's not making them. Falcon is thriving with Spiral, and he in turn loves learning with him.

Spiral gave his notice in at work, on the understanding that if they were short-staffed they could call him in, which has only happened once so far. Tania is teaching yoga most days in her new space, and her classes are, on the whole, fully booked. She felt bad about deserting the homeschooling group, even though Spiral makes a regular appearance, so offered them all discounted classes. Emma is the only one who has taken them up so far, and seems to use it more as an opportunity to hang around after practice to bitch about the girls they used to know at school, most of whom Tania has long forgotten, so Tania in turn uses it to concentrate on her meditative breathing as Emma slags off half the forty-year-olds in Surrey.

Tania has met up with her mum a couple of times with Falcon, but she now chooses the location, favouring petting zoos and soft-play areas to expensive, child-unfriendly restaurants. Tania notes how Francesca is forever cleaning her hands with sanitiser, and will bring along a luxury hamper picnic instead of slumming it with a jacket potato from the café, but on the whole, Tania is impressed that her mum is, in her own unique way, compromising.

In an unexpected turn of events, she also received a phone call from her dad asking if she'd like to go for a bite to eat. They met at a greasy spoon in Guildford, where the staff greeted her dad like an old friend; he confessed that it's his favourite café, and always makes an effort to pop in for a sausage butty whenever he has business in the area. Tania ordered the gammon and pineapple. He's asked if he could see her again soon, and wondered if Spiral and Falcon would join them next time. Tania hasn't mentioned it to Spiral yet. She will choose her moment.

'Sit down,' Spiral booms. 'Dinner is served.'

Tania pushes the old newspapers to one side on the kitchen table, making a mental note to put them in the recycling on the way to the studio tomorrow.

Falcon, dressed as Spider-Man, is now wearing an apron, and has an old tea towel draped over his arm like a sommelier.

'For you, madam,' he beams, placing her plate down in front of her.

'Thank you, sir,' she replies.

A warm glow burns in her chest, a feeling of enlightenment she is forever encouraging her students to strive towards. Now she recognises it for what it actually is. It's contentment.

Chapter Fifty-Two

'OK, then, Mrs Jacobs. Oh, hasn't it grown back nicely?'

Mrs Jacobs pats her hair proudly. 'Yes, yes. I think it's looking rather nice.'

'Do you mind if I open the window an inch? It's quite hot in here.'

Helen fans herself with her hand. It isn't hot, in actual fact, it is just extremely stuffy. There is an underlying aroma of antiseptic cream, blended with a cabbagy smell and halitosis.

'Yes, please do, Helen. Only a touch, mind, and make sure you close it before you leave.' She's pointing a bony finger at her accusingly. 'The radiator is very unpredictable,' she explains.

'Of course. Now, what can I do for you today?' She helps her arms into the gown and does up the Velcro.

'We didn't think you were coming back.' Mrs Jacobs strains around to try to see Helen. 'We thought you'd left us to it, found somewhere else to work. Mrs Tyler thought you'd absconded to the salon in the precinct but I said, you'd never go there. It's cheap and nasty, and you have style, Helen.' Her head shakes energetically as she speaks.

'Well, that's very kind of you, Mrs Jacobs, and I'm sorry to have worried you. I've just had some family business to attend to, so had to cut back on some of my work. But I'm

349

here now and ready to do whatever you'd like me to,' Helen says.

'Just a trim please, Helen. Just a little off the back to keep it neat and tidy. Steven's coming in later today; it's his birthday. He's fifty-eight. He's going to take me out for a spot of lunch, which is very generous of him especially as it's his birthday, don't you think? We are going to his favourite restaurant. It's an American diner. It's very sophisticated, everyone there speaks American. He really is a good boy. Would you mind pulling the window too now? I can feel a breeze on the back of my neck.'

''Course,' Helen lays the scissors down on the bed and closes the window with a thud.

'Yes, I've asked him who he's courting, but a grown man doesn't want to tell his mother about these things, does he? He doesn't want to keep me informed of his comings and goings. But I have said to him, Steven, your generation hasn't invented sex, you know. We were all doing it long before you were even an idea. Ooh, is that the lavender spray again?'

'Yes,' Helen replies. 'Are you happy with that?'

'Yes, yes. It's very pleasant.'

'Well, it sounds like you have a lovely afternoon planned.' She sprays the lightly scented water around her head, then leans in to snip the wiry hairs that sprout from the nape of Mrs Jacobs' neck.

'Yes, it does, doesn't it? Maybe one of these days he might even introduce me to one of his lady friends. It would be nice to see him happy with someone before I die, which could be any day now,' she remarks.

'You're fit as a fiddle, Mrs Jacobs. There. Done.' Helen takes out her mirror to show her handiwork.

'Yes. Very good. Now be a dear and pass me my purse. Seven pounds is it?'

'Ten, Mrs Jacobs. Same as last time.'

'Sarah said you'd prefer to sit by the window in here instead of in your room to have your hair done, is that right?' The new resident is sat next to the glass door leading out to the garden. Outside a sparrow has caught her attention as it drinks from the stone birdbath.

'Who's Sarah?' she eventually asks, looking blankly at Helen.

'One of the carers here. She's the one with the long dark hair, quite young. Put your arms up please, that's great. Now, I'll just do the back up so put your arms down. Fantastic.' The mid-afternoon sun streams through the windows, as dust dances in the light. 'It's a lovely day, isn't it?' Helen comments.

'Have I been sat here long?' she asks vacantly.

'I don't know. But if you're happy here, then there's no reason to move, is there? Are you settling in OK? I don't think you've been here for very long, have you?' Helen gently brushes her shoulder-length hair. It could do with a little trim but it has been well maintained. Usually, when a new resident arrives, their hair is in a dreadful state. It is often the last thing to be tended to, and families can forget when they are dealing with the stress of moving them into a home that it's the small things that can make all the difference. Helen thinks that a good haircut is like a smart coat. If you get it right it can give you an air of togetherness, regardless of what's going on underneath it.

'It's having a whale of a time, isn't it?' The lady points to the bird, which has now been joined by a companion as they both flap their wings in the water.

'Do you like nature?' Helen prompts. It's often difficult to frame conversations when someone has just arrived. With the older residents she has got used to their idiosyncrasies: the ones who want to gossip about other residents, the ones who like to reminisce about life when they were younger, those who prefer to grill her on her own life, as if it is a window onto the outside world that they no longer connect with.

'I don't know. Do I?' she asks.

Maybe they should just remain in silence, Helen thinks. That is sometimes the least distressing thing to do. For some people, normal conversations are just too stressful, too fast-paced. Finding the words to respond, trying to follow a thread of conversation that slips from their memory, sentences drifting away from them as they try to cling on to their meaning.

Helen uses two large clips to pin up the top third of her hair, and then uses a large roller brush to comb through the rest. She closes her eyes contently and sighs deeply.

'I knew you'd enjoy that!' Sarah comments as she clears up a beaker half filled with cold tea from a neighbouring table, giving the surface a quick wipe with a J cloth that she retrieves from the front pocket of her blue tabard. 'She's good isn't she?' she continues. 'I should get her to have a go at my awful hair.'

Her eyes spring open, 'Appearance is important,' she replies sternly. 'I've always maintained that. Appearance and manners,' she repeats and closes her eyes once more.

'Would you like rose or lavender spray?' Helen asks gently.

'Rose. I like rose,' she responds.

'I know you do,' Helen whispers to her.

'My daughter is a hairdresser, you know?' the woman tells her.

'Really, is she any good? Have I got some competition here?' Helen teases.

'Yes. She's the very best, I believe. Look, they've flown off now. I wonder where their nest is? I don't see her, though.'

'That's a shame,' Helen unleashes another third of her hair, and holds the scissors in her mouth as she combs it through.

'I don't blame her. I wasn't very nice to her.' Helen stops mid comb, breathes deeply and concentrates on calming her shaking hand. 'She's a wonderful mother, though. I never told her that of course, you don't want to spoil your children with compliments, do you?' she remarks to herself. 'It can make them soft. Maybe I should have done though . . .' she trails off.

'Well, I'm sure she'd like to hear it now,' Helen suddenly feels very heavy. The weight of the day pressing down on her, as she pulls up a plastic chair and sits down to continue the cut.

'Her father was a terror, not a nice man at all. Did you say your name was Sarah?' she asks.

'Yes.' Helen replies.

'Well, Sarah, if you ever marry a man who has anger in his eyes, get out. Get out I tell you, because it will never get any better. It's in their blood, you can't change people you know. You can't ever change people. Is that rose I can smell?'

'Yes,' Helen murmurs, the word a lump in her throat.

'I like rose. Are you married?' the woman asks.

'Yes. Yes I am. Can you look out the window, that's it.' Helen cups her head and gently moves it, holding it a fraction longer than needed.

'Don't confuse flattery with love, Sarah,' she mutters to herself. 'Do you have children?'

'A daughter,' Helen replies. 'She's five.'

'Lovely age,' she starts to undo the Velcro fastening around her neck.

'I'm not finished yet. Two more minutes, can you sit still for a couple more minutes?' Helen asks.

'My husband nearly killed me, you know. What a silly woman I was,' she shakes her head in disbelief and Helen waits until she is still again. She has lost count of the times she has heard this story now; it feels like it is now part of Helen's history too. Like Janet had waited until her mind had wandered and her thoughts were no longer her own to reveal her deepest secrets.

'Always tell the truth,' she says as she pats Helen's hand, which is resting on her shoulder. 'Always tell the truth, because it will catch up with you. That's my advice. That's my advice,' and she drops her hand, her gaze drifting into the garden again. 'Shall I take this off now?' she starts to tug at the apron again.

'Yes.' Helen tenderly places her hands on both of her shoulders and kisses the top of her head as she says in a voice so quiet she is barely audible, 'Yes, Mum, you can take it off now.'

Janet pulls at the gown and runs her hands through her hair. 'Lovely. It feels lovely. Did I tell you my daughter is a hairdresser?'

'Yes. Yes you did,' Helen replies softly.

'I'm very proud of her. Not that I'd tell her,' Janet catches her eye and for a moment Helen thinks she sees a flash of recognition.

Janet holds her gaze for a beat, then two, then asks, 'Could you tell Liam to bring me my post?'

And it's gone. 'Of course,' Helen replies. 'I'll do it right now.'

'Lovely.' She looks out the window once more, patting her hair. 'You should ask my daughter to cut your hair. You are very good, but she is meant to be brilliant.'

'Thank you,' Helen replies in a whisper, pride swelling in her chest as a tear spills down her cheek.

Chapter Fifty-Three

'HELP YOURSELF TO PIZZA AND CHIPS!' Nick shouts loudly over the deafening noise of thirty children and their parents. The back room in the Fox and Hound is stuffy and hot, even though it is only March, and there is a distinct smell of trumps. I'd taken Sophie for a poo before I put her party dress on, so at least I know it's not her.

'Good idea to have it in a pub.' Spiral sidles up to me, pint of ale in hand.

'Thanks. It was Nick's idea, actually,' I reply and take a sip of my gin and tonic.

'Nice one, Nick,' Spiral replies, discreetly exhaling a cloud of sweet-smelling smoke from his vape.

It wouldn't have been my choice to have Sophie's fourth birthday in a pub. I don't think it would have even been my fifth or sixth choice, but Nick said he'd like to arrange it, and given that I have just taken on a large project with a mid-scale theatre company (oh joy – to write copy about things I am passionate about instead of cleaning-fucking-products) I was pleased to have one less thing to think about.

I don't recognise half the guests here and the children, on the whole, look a lot younger than Sophie.

'Who are all these people?' I ask Nick, who has strategically positioned himself next to the buffet table and is mainlining French fries.

'I don't know,' he replies with his mouth full. 'Sophie was

a bit non-committal about who her mates were at nursery, so I just put an invitation in everyone's lunch box to see who might turn up.'

'Oh,' I reply. 'Well, I guess that's one way to do it.'

My phone buzzes in my pocket. A text from Mum.

Mum: DON'T PANIC, WE'RE ON OUR WAY. YOUR DAD HAS JUST LOST THE KEY CARD FOR THE ROOM.
Me: No hurry, just come when you're ready. Xx

'Right, time for pass the parcel, I think. Can you do the music?' Nick asks, pointing towards the stereo.

'Sure.'

'CAN EVERYONE SIT IN A CIRCLE PLEASE?' he hollers and the children start to drift into the centre of the room, as he instructs them where to go.

'Well, this is different,' says a voice and I turn to see Cathleen. She is dressed in a floral jumpsuit that is about thirty years too young for her and has a large red fake flower tucked behind her ear like a flamenco dancer.

'Oh Cathleen, don't you look lovely. Very cheerful,' I tell her.

Cathleen touches her neck, blushing from the compliment. 'Why, thank you, Emily. I wasn't sure if it was a bit much, but I thought, it is a party. Even if it is in a pub. And Dennis is very keen on me in it so . . .' She lets the sentence drift off, as I try to shake the haunting thought of Dennis seducing Cathleen.

'Hello! Hello! Now here's my favourite daughter-in-law,' Dennis bellows as he approaches, arms wide to receive a hug. As he wraps his arms around me he says, 'So good to see you two working as a team.'

'Thanks, Dennis,' I reply as I try to disentangle myself

from his watch, which has caught in my ponytail. 'This was all Nick, though. He sorted it out. Apart from blowing up a few balloons he organised the whole thing.'

'Well, isn't he clever,' Cathleen coos. 'And what a wonderful idea to have it in a pub, it feels like a real celebration.' Well, she's swiftly changed her tune, I think.

'And your parents? Will we be seeing them?' Dennis asks.

'Yes, they should be here any moment. They're just getting themselves ready in the Travelodge.'

'Excellent. Excellent.' Dennis looks around absentmindedly as Nick gestures for me to start the music.

'Duty calls,' I tell them.

'Of course. Of course,' Dennis grins. 'Cathleen, my joy, shall we wet our whistles?' He offers her his arm, which she takes, and they make their way to the bar. The pair of them drive me crackers, but I do admire the fact that after over fifty years of marriage they can still stand the sight of each other.

The children have formed a circle of sorts, with Sophie bossing everyone around, telling them where to sit and how to play the game.

'RIGHT, PRESS PLAY!' Nick yells.

The children sit, poised, Sophie with present in hand ready to pass it on. 'Smack My Bitch Up' blasts loudly from the stereo.

I look at Nick, wide-eyed, who doesn't even seem to react.

'Just skip it,' he shouts.

Only Nick would bring the Prodigy to a four-year-old's birthday party, I think. But then I decide it's not worth mentioning. I'm getting slightly better at picking my battles these days. Slightly.

I scan the room and see Helen and Chris, coaxing Polly to join the ring. Helen catches my eye and smiles broadly.

I wave back. I spot Falcon, minesweeping the buffet. Spiral is leaning nonchalantly against the wall, pint in hand. Tania has her arm casually wrapped around him, he whispers something in her ear and she laughs.

Rachel arrived moments ago and is now sat crosslegged on the floor. Lucy is in her lap, proud of the 'grownup friend' she is introducing to everyone. And here's Nick, grinning as he encourages the children to keep passing the parcel until the music stops.

I don't know what being OK will look like in the future. What an OK family looks like. OK coparenting, OK finances. OK communicating, OK listening, OK being heard. OK living together, OK living apart.

I press pause, and Sophie rips the first layer of paper off. The room erupts into cheers as she throws her head back with glee.

I don't know what our future looks like, but what I do know, with absolute certainty, is that everything *will* be OK.

Acknowledgements

I would like to express my gratitude to everyone who supported me in the creation of this novel: to my agent, Sarah Ballard; my editor, Harriet Bourton; to Rosie Chard, Sharon Duggal, Jules Grant, Kate Lee, Katy Massey, Lou Tondeur, Bridget Whelan and Laura Wilkinson, of the Write Process writing group; to Chris Cleave and Amanda Smyth, of Arvon; to my New Writing South writing mentor, Suhayla El Bushra; to National Lottery Project Grants funding from Arts Council England. I am particularly indebted to everyone who gave up their time to help me with my research about dementia, homeschooling and separation.

As ever, nothing would be possible without the love and support of my parents, Mike Jefferson and Liz Jefferson, my sister, Lucy Roche Jefferson, and her family, my husband, Ben, and our children, Nancy and Thomas.